Kill
Switch

Kill Switch

NEAL BAER
JONATHAN GREENE

KENSINGTON BOOKS
http://www.kensingtonbooks.com

KENSINGTON BOOKS are published by

Kensington Publishing Corp.
119 West 40th Street
New York, NY 10018

All Kensington titles, imprints and distributed lines are available at special quantity discounts for bulk purchases for sales promotion, premiums, fund-raising, educational or institutional use.

Special book excerpts or customized printings can also be created to fit specific needs. For details, write or phone the office of the Kensington Special Sales Manager: Kensington Publishing Corp., 119 West 40th Street, New York, NY 10018. Attn. Special Sales Department. Phone: 1-800-221-2647.

Kensington and the K logo Reg. U.S. Pat. & TM Off.

ISBN-13: 978-0-7582-7835-7
ISBN-10: 0-7582-7835-7

First Kensington Trade Paperback Printing: January 2012

10 9 8 7 6 5 4 3 2 1

Printed in the United States of America

To Gerrie and Caleb for always being there
        —N. B.

To Robin, Mara, and Joshua—the lights of my life
And to my family and friends for their support
        —J. G.

"You were a very apt pupil!"
Scottie to Madeleine in Alfred Hitchcock's *Vertigo*

PROLOGUE

***

Rochester, July 1989

You could tell a thunderstorm was close. The air was thick with humidity, the clouds approaching from Lake Ontario an angry gray. Though Upstate New York was known for its long, harsh winters, any Rochester native will tell you a summer storm can wreak more havoc in ten minutes than a foot of snow falling over ten hours. But these were the dog days of the summer of '89. The two eight-year-old girls jumping rope in the driveway of a large white colonial at 55 Burt Street in the Park Avenue district hadn't noticed what was coming.

The dark-haired girl who lived in the house saw the car first—a gleaming white BMW speeding toward them. It suddenly screeched to a stop in front of the driveway. A man in his late forties, wearing a polo shirt and shorts, jumped out, obviously agitated.

The man said his name was Mr. Winslow and he needed to talk to them. The dark-haired girl blinked, taking a step back, sensing something was wrong. Mr. Winslow turned to Amy, the dark-haired girl's friend. He said he worked with Amy's dad, and in one excited breath Mr. Winslow told Amy her father had been in a terrible accident. He was driving through the construction area to rebuild the notorious "Can of Worms" interchange when a concrete piling crashed down onto his car. He said that her father was rushed to Strong Memorial Hospital, and he'd come to take Amy there.

Amy started to cry and follow Mr. Winslow to his car. But the dark-haired girl sensed something she couldn't explain. Before she even knew she was saying it, she asked Mr. Winslow who had sent him.

The question caught Mr. Winslow off guard. He gave the dark-haired girl a look and told her his boss sent him to pick up Amy. Amy assured her friend it was okay. Mr. Winslow wasn't a stranger.

But the dark-haired girl couldn't shake the feeling in the pit of her stomach. She remembered the warnings from her mother, who said she asked too many questions, a habit that was going to get her into trouble someday. But the dark-haired girl had to know more.

So she asked Mr. Winslow why he wasn't wearing a suit like Amy's father did if he had come straight from work. Mr. Winslow answered that he'd been at the driving range when the boss called him there.

Then she asked how he knew Amy was at this house and not her own.

Mr. Winslow let out a deep breath, then said his boss had called Amy's mother. She told him about their playdate. He then quickly opened the passenger door. They had to get to the hospital.

But the dark-haired girl's questions now bothered Amy. She said she was going inside to call her mother.

The dark-haired girl turned and raced up to the house. She assumed Amy was behind her until she heard a sudden rush of footsteps.

She turned back just as Amy screamed. Mr. Winslow had picked Amy up and was shoving her into the front seat of his car.

The dark-haired girl's screams were drowned out by a succession of thunderclaps and the downpour that followed. As the rain soaked through her clothes, she was too scared to move. All she could do was stand there and watch the BMW drive away.

PART I

CHAPTER 1

Present Day

On any given day, the ten separate jails that make up New York City's Rikers Island correctional facility hold between fifteen and eighteen thousand inmates, making it the world's largest penal colony. Of those inmates, some three thousand are classified as mentally ill. That whopping number makes Rikers one of the largest mental institutions in the United States and the best place for a budding forensic psychiatrist like Claire Waters to study the criminal mind.

Claire had worked toward this day for over a decade. After breezing through four years of medical school at Harvard, she completed an internship and residency in psychiatry at Massachusetts General Hospital, considered one of the best and most selective programs in the country. She went on to a prestigious research position at the National Institutes of Health because she wanted to dissect and study the brains of criminals.

But slicing through gray matter and staining slides of neurons every day for three years didn't give her the answers she was looking for. She knew she had to see patients again. Now she was about to begin the last stage of her training, a fellowship in forensic psychiatry, where she'd treat some of the sickest and most twisted minds humanity could imagine.

Most days Claire was a master at hiding in plain sight. She wore her shoulder-length dark brown hair straight, the bangs just long enough to veil questioning green eyes. She never wore lipstick, eye shadow, or blush—anything that might call attention to her beauty.

On the subway, at Starbucks, or just walking down the street, she blended in.

But today was different. Instead of her usual soft, well-worn jeans and comfortable, familiar flats, she wore a new, olive green Diane von Furstenberg suit and black Louboutin pumps, neither of which she could afford. The heels protruding from those trademark red soles made a staccato *click-clack* on the mottled concrete floor of Rikers Island, reverberating against the muddy-brown cinder-block walls, each step reminding her that there was nowhere to hide. Claire felt miserable in her wool suit. What had she been thinking when she bought it? July in New York City was always sticky hot, and the air inside the narrow corridor leading to the cell block was thick with the stench of men who desperately needed a shower.

Claire wore this costume to impress the director of her program, Dr. Paul Curtin, who, despite the oppressive heat, looked remarkably cool in his blue pinstriped Armani suit as he walked beside her. In his midfifties, Curtin drew attention with his wavy silver hair and slate-blue eyes. Claire was taller than average at five-seven, not including the heels she wore, but Curtin towered over her with his well-built six-two frame.

He was watching her every move, which only made things worse because she almost always was nervous before the first interview with a new patient. She tried to focus on the case file he'd given her, but her hair was a liability today, swinging into her face and obstructing her view. She was a runner, trim and in great shape, but she struggled to keep up with the man who made sure to tell her that he was a triathlete who ran the New York City Marathon every year.

I'd like to see him walk in these ridiculous shoes and read at the same time, she thought.

"His name is Todd Quimby," Curtin said, his voice coming from a half foot above her head. "Ten months into a one-year sentence for forcible touching."

"What did he do?" Claire asked, thumbing through the file. She was increasingly anxious with each step but was determined not to show it. *He gave me Quimby's file only moments before our session because he wants to know right off the bat if I've got the chops,* Claire thought.

"He pulled his pants down in front of a bunch of secretaries."

"In their office?"

"At a diner. They'd just ordered a plate of mozzarella sticks when Quimby served up his own."

"That's indecent exposure, not touching," said Claire.

"Weenie waving is called 'public lewdness' in New York State, Dr. Waters. Mr. Quimby crossed the line when one of the ladies pointed out the meager size of his 'portion,' and he tried to get her to eat it."

Claire forced a little smile at his attempt at humor as a guard unlocked the security door and they entered the cell block. Claire turned her attention to the old newspaper clippings in the file. CARNY KILLER GETS LIFE read the front-page headline from the *Daily Nonpareil* of Council Bluffs, Iowa. The 1985 story had two photos. One was of Beth Quimby, an attractive woman in her late thirties leaving a courtroom in a baggy jumpsuit; the other was of Beth's handsome son Todd, age nine, being comforted by two police officers on the day of the shooting. Claire wondered whether Todd's murdering bitch of a mother gave a damn that her one grandiose act of violence had also killed any chance for her son to have a normal life.

"Whoo-hoo. Yo, baby, let me beast that."

"Bring that kitty over here and I'll give it a good workout."

Claire looked up and saw a dozen inmates leering at her from inside their cells. She wasn't sure whether to smile nonchalantly or act tough in response to their vulgar catcalls. *Rats in cages. At least that's something I'm used to.*

"Ignore it," Curtin said evenly. "Every one of them would screw their eighty-year-old great-aunt if they could."

Claire realized that he was as comfortable in this hellhole as she wasn't.

"This Mr. Quimby's first time through the system?" Curtin asked.

Claire knew this was a pop quiz; he already had the answer and was testing her again. She flipped through the file and quickly found what she needed.

"No. He has a string of prior arrests. Possession of cocaine, ecstasy, crystal meth; criminal trespass; fourth-degree stalking; third-degree sexual abuse . . ."

"Which tells us . . . ?" he asked sharply.

"Um, seemingly minor offenses moving toward the sexual indicate a rapist in the making," Claire replied.

"He's a wannabe, all right," Curtin said. "And your job is to stop him from becoming one."

They turned a corner, arriving at a secure door marked NORTH IN-FIRMARY COMMAND—PSYCHIATRIC WING. Curtin pushed the buzzer beside it.

"Doctors Curtin and Waters," he said, holding his ID badge up to an overhead security camera. A buzzer sounded. Curtin pulled the door open and stepped through, neglecting to hold it for Claire. Fortunately, she caught the door just as it was about to slam shut. One more piece of evidence in the case she was building against her new mentor. The charge: jerk in the first degree with a lesser included offense of arrogant bastard.

Deep down, though, Claire understood. She thought of the insults she'd weathered throughout her academic career, the hazing every doctor had to endure. It didn't matter that she'd graduated with honors near the top of her medical school class—she got it just as bad as everyone else. She remembered the nurses who assured her that every first-year psych resident had to bathe the delusional homeless patients. Then, as she naïvely sponged one down, hearing those same nurses laugh outside the door because she "fell for it."

Though she survived every one of those rites of passage and skated through residency, Claire felt lost when it was over. She thought she needed to know more about the dark recesses of the human mind before she took complete responsibility for patients. So at thirty, she decided to apply to one of the most prestigious research fellowships in the country—the National Institutes of Health—where she was immediately accepted and began her study of the neuronal basis of violence and how mental illness was so intimately linked to criminal behavior. She'd treated hundreds of patients with depression, mania, schizophrenia, the whole spectrum of psychiatric disorders, and was convinced that chemical and structural abnormalities in the brain caused the impulses that drove so many people to commit crimes.

Claire Waters was drawn to the patients most psychiatrists labeled as untreatable, hopeless cases with seemingly irreparable minds. Now, as she walked past the prison cells, quickly studying each man's face, she thought, *They're not hopeless. We're just not asking the right questions*. She was determined to find the right questions in her research, a groundbreaking way of seeing psychopaths not as evil automatons with no conscience, but as individuals who had never felt fear and couldn't see it in others. Even as children, many of the inmates on the psych ward had tortured animals or hurt other kids because, Claire reasoned, they had a profound attention deficit that made it hard, if not impossible, for them to respond to frightening situations. Maybe, just maybe, if Claire and her colleagues could reprogram the circuitry in their brains, they would be able to recognize fear in others, which would prevent them from committing crimes in the future—if and when they were ever released from prison.

It was this groundbreaking work that put Claire on Curtin's radar. He recruited her from NIH with the lure of his prestigious fellowship and the chance to work with, as he called them, "the lepers of the mind." And she had taken his bait.

"I want to fix them, or at least understand them," Claire told Curtin the first time they met when he came to her lab in Washington, DC. "They didn't choose to be the way they are, just like none of us choose our parents or our childhood."

"If you truly want to make a difference, then come with me," he said. "You will help more people in three years in my program than you will in a decade buried in some government lab. And if you get through it, you'll be able to write your own ticket to any job you want."

She will help more people. The words echoed in her mind. So she'd accepted Curtin's offer. And yet here, in the prison, Curtin was aggressively questioning her as if she were a first-year med student. Which she now realized was exactly how he intended to treat her.

Claire decided then that she would beat Curtin at his game. She would always be prepared for anything he tossed at her.

"What else can you tell me about Mr. Quimby that's relevant?" Curtin asked, not missing a beat. He kept his pace, even though she had fallen behind. It was on her to keep up, and she was having a hard time. She told herself to walk faster, think faster, find the answers.

"Once Quimby's mother was convicted," Claire responded, trying not to glance down at the file, "his paternal grandmother was awarded custody of him. She brought him here to New York to live with her, in the same apartment where his father was raised."

"School records?" queried Curtin.

"Straight D student. No college."

"Employment?"

"All menial jobs," answered Claire. "Dishwasher, building janitor, security guard. Drove a cab until his first arrest six years ago, after which his hack license was revoked. Since then, he's spent most of his time in and out of jail."

"Social history?"

"Lived alone in a studio in Alphabet City. Never married."

"Psych workup?"

"Jail therapy records aren't in the folder."

For the first time since Claire arrived at Rikers Island, she locked eyes with Curtin. From the look on his face, Claire thought he was going to lay into her for not having the answers. But Curtin chose another target.

"Of course you don't have his records," Curtin said. "They're still letting the inmates run the asylum."

Claire knew his cliché carried more than a kernel of truth. In fact, it came from the part of Curtin that Claire had sensed from the beginning wasn't superficial bullshit, the true believer in him Claire both identified with and admired.

Seven years earlier, New York City had contracted with the nation's largest for-profit provider of prison medical services to run the infirmary at Rikers Island. Their idea of quality patient care was to pay certain inmates thirty-nine cents an hour to make sure their cellies on suicide watch didn't off themselves. In short order, the result was six "hang-ups" in six months, the worst jail-suicide record in the country.

At the time, Curtin's star was on the rise. Already in demand as an expert witness, he'd written two books about his groundbreaking research in forensic psychiatry, both of which sold hundreds of thousands of copies. This success led to TV appearances on CNN and what used to be known as Court TV to discuss high-profile criminal trials. His natural gift at gallows humor and his ability to make people laugh about subjects as macabre as anorexia and necrophilia had secured him spots on the talk-show circuit; he'd done *Dave, Jay,* and *Oprah* numerous times. In less than a decade, Curtin had become known as "the Dr. Oz of Forensic Psychiatry" or, as his detractors in the psychiatric community preferred, "the Jerry Springer for Serial Killers."

But when pressed, even Curtin's detractors would admit his skill as a showman produced results. He'd convinced numerous juries in execution-happy states to spare the lives of capital defendants whose mental illness drove them to commit murder. And his honesty was without question. More than once, some shyster would try retaining Curtin to confirm a client's bogus insanity defense. Proving he was more than just a highly paid mercenary, Curtin would not only refuse to commit what amounted to perjury, but he also offered in each case to testify *against* the defendant.

Within his profession, however, Curtin's reputation as the real deal stemmed from something deeper. He believed he could prevent the mentally ill from committing crimes by attacking the problem at its source. And he had at his doorstep the perfect laboratory to prove it.

Curtin viewed the suicide rate among the prisoners at Rikers Island as a moral outrage, a failure of the profession he loved. He knew most of the Psychiatric Wing's inmates had never committed a violent crime and was convinced that early intervention could prevent them from ever doing so. Using his name and prestige to bombard politicians and bureaucrats, he offered the media his services with assurances that he and the students in his fellowship program could make a difference. The city, threatened with state and federal investigations and buried in a PR crisis, was hardly in a position to refuse.

Five years later, suicides at Rikers were at an all-time low, and the recidivism rate among Curtin's patients was one-tenth the jail average. Even the number of mentally ill inmates plummeted because Curtin had convinced the powers-that-be to parole many of his patients, with two conditions: They had to continue psychotherapy, and they had to stay on their meds. The plan seemed to be working, in no small part due to the quality of students Curtin chose for his fellowship.

As they stopped in front of a door marked PATIENT INTERVIEW, Claire Waters knew it was her chance to prove herself fit to reside among

Curtin's worthy. This was the moment she had dreaded and driven herself toward for almost ten years. She was both exhilarated and terrified, which she somehow successfully hid under the thinnest veneer of calm. But she knew she'd be all right because she had the gift: the natural ability to put people at ease, to draw out their darkest secrets. Even those she barely knew would sense her deep empathy and open up to her. She was determined to show Curtin her power to connect with the sickest souls.

"What you're about to do is like nothing you've ever done as a psychiatrist before," Curtin said. "Dr. Fairborn and I will be observing you."

"I know," answered Claire.

"Are you ready, Doctor?" Curtin asked.

"Yes, sir," she replied.

Curtin smiled.

"Go get him."

CHAPTER 2

Todd Quimby jerked his head up from the metal table when Claire walked into the windowless room. A fan in the corner stirred the air into a warm breeze. *Funny, he doesn't look like a scumbag*, Claire thought, wondering how the emotional trauma hadn't taken a toll on Quimby's boyish good looks. He was thin but not gaunt; he had some muscle on him. His short auburn hair crowned a freckled face with striking green eyes.

"You the shrink?" he asked halfheartedly.

His eyes locked on hers. Claire remembered the first lesson she learned in her psych residency: The patient who looks down or away doesn't give a shit. The ones who look you in the eye want help. It's like a first date, each person sizing up the other. Claire watched Quimby's eyes dart about, down to her hands, then back to her eyes. *He's checking out my body language, looking for weakness, an advantage,* Claire realized. She wasn't about to let him read between her lines.

"I'm Dr. Waters," she said, trying to convey both authority and compassion. She wasn't sure she pulled either of them off convincingly. "I'll be your therapist while you're on parole."

"Nobody said nothin' to me about parole."

Claire tapped the folder in her hand. "It says in here you're eligible now. That's why I was brought in." She sat down in the metal chair facing Quimby. The fluorescent lights above reflected off the shiny table, giving Quimby's face a ghostly glow.

"I don't need another therapist."

"You do if you want to get out of here."

"Talking to you ain't going to make me any more ready than I am right now."

"Maybe. But after we talk, I'm going to write a report we call an *exit assessment*. The parole board will use that to decide whether you're ready."

"And if you say I'm not, so what? I can do two more months in my sleep."

Now Claire stared into *his* eyes. And she saw his bravado was covering up fear. *Use it*, she told herself.

"Once you're out, you want to stay out, right?"

"Who wouldn't?"

"You tell me. How many times have you been in here?"

"Four."

"You want to come back again?"

"My last shrink tried that tough-love bullshit on me. Didn't help."

But she got a response; he shifted uncomfortably in his chair. *Slowly,* Claire cautioned herself. *Seduce him.*

"Work with me, Todd. You've got nothing to lose and two extra months of freedom to gain."

"If you like what I tell you."

Claire leaned forward and stared right at him before she spoke. "Try me," she said invitingly.

The hint of a wry smile appeared on Quimby's face. Women didn't usually talk to him this way.

"Where do we start?" Quimby asked.

"Get right to it," said Curtin. He sat in another room several yards away, watching Claire's exchange with Quimby on three monitors. Hidden cameras were trained on each of their faces; a third camera concealed in a corner of the ceiling captured the scene from above.

"She's easing him in, Paul," came a female voice from behind Curtin. "She's doing fine."

The voice belonged to Dr. Lois Fairborn, chair of the Department of Psychiatry at Manhattan City University's School of Medicine. She was Curtin's boss, and perhaps the only person who had any sway over him. In her fifties and trying to look younger, she favored Calvin Klein suits and dark red on her lips and fingernails, maybe a shade too dark, prompting Curtin to call her "the Vampire" behind her back. Though she ran her program with iron fists, Fairborn knew full well that Curtin's fellowship was the butter on her bread. So she gave him a wide berth but made it her business to observe every new student.

"She's courting him. She'll lose him if she doesn't find a way in," Curtin said to Fairborn.

They heard Claire's voice over the monitor: "You suffered quite a trauma as a child."

Fairborn looked over at Curtin, who was smiling to himself. Both she and Curtin knew that Claire was winning. And so was Curtin, who relished the moment. His instincts about Claire were correct—he'd made the right decision in bringing her into the program.

"Why do you people always have to go back to childhood?" Quimby asked Claire.

"Childhood makes us who we are."

"I don't see why I have to talk about it," Quimby said, scooting his chair back.

"You need to. Your mother murdered your father right in front of you."

"Like father, like son. Our dicks got both of us into trouble."

"You know there's more to it than that," Claire said, leaning forward. "Tell me about that day."

"I don't remember it."

"You don't? Or don't want to?"

"Would *you* want to?" Quimby said defiantly, leaning toward her.

"I'd want to get on with my life," Claire responded without missing a beat, her eyes boring into him.

"I don't have much of a life."

"Why is that?"

"Why do *you* think?"

"Because you're afraid," Claire said. Their faces were now inches apart. She could smell his hot, minty breath. *He must have brushed his teeth before he came in,* Claire thought.

"Bullshit," Quimby muttered, lowering his head.

But not before Claire noticed the sweat beading above his upper lip. *He's the one who's bullshitting,* she thought. *Time to push.*

"What was that day like, Todd?"

"Huh?" Quimby asked, his head bobbing up. "I told you, I don't remember."

"I meant the weather. What kind of day was it? Sunny? Rainy?"

"What the hell difference does it make?"

Claire sat back, giving him more space. "I'm trying to help you remember," she offered.

"It's not working."

"Close your eyes."

"Why?"

"Why not?"

Quimby hesitated. "This is ridiculous."

"Try again," Claire said gently. "What was the weather like?"

"Who gives a crap about the weather?"

"I do. Come on. Humor me." She tilted her head in a way she hoped would make it seem like she wasn't judging him. He closed his eyes. Claire knew she had to hide her excitement.

"I'm not seeing it," he replied.

"What about noises? Sounds?"

"I hear music—the hurdy-gurdy organ pumping out . . ." He didn't feel himself starting to sway. "Just the usual carnival bullshit," Quimby said, trying to cover his trembling voice.

Claire knew she was close.

"What else?" Claire asked quietly.

"Pop. Pop. Pop. Pop. Pop. Pop. Pop. Pop. Pop. Like fireworks—only it's not night."

Claire leaned in, close to his ear, almost whispering. "What do you smell?"

"Cotton candy. Hot dogs. Burnt popcorn."

At first he thought it smelled like burnt popcorn. But then he realized it was gunpowder. Singed flesh. Blood.

For an instant, Claire smelled rain.

She could see it on Quimby's face; the memories were rising up, seeping through the barrier between Quimby's subconscious and conscious. He didn't feel himself banging his fingertips together in front of him like an autistic child.

"Pop-pop-pop-pop-pop-pop-pop-pop-pop," he sputtered, louder and faster, like darts piercing all the balloons at his favorite carnival game.

He was out of his chair, moving toward the corner of the room, his back against the wall. Claire rose, not sure what he was going to do. And then she realized. *He doesn't see me. He can see only that day.*

She knew she had him.

Curtin and Fairborn were on their feet in the observation room.

"I'm calling security," said Fairborn.

"No," Curtin said. "She's okay."

"What if he becomes psychotic?"

"He has no history of psychosis."

Watching the monitors, they saw Quimby in the corner of the room, the weight of his memories pushing him to the floor as his back slid down the wall. Claire stood next to her chair, trying to figure out her next move.

"She doesn't know what to do," Fairborn worried aloud.

"Give her a chance, Lois," Curtin said to her. "She hasn't disappointed. Yet."

And then Curtin talked to the monitor.

"Go to him, Claire," he whispered. "Go to him."

Quimby was shaking, sweating. Didn't know where he was or how he'd gotten there. But Claire knew. The way someone knows when they've found their true calling. The way, Claire realized, from that horrible day Mr. Winslow pulled up at her house two decades ago, that she could read him and others. Now her instincts kicked into high gear, and she moved slowly, carefully, unthreateningly, toward Quimby, who was sitting hunched with his knees to his chest.

His mother put her hand over his mouth. The blood was on her clothes. He could see it. Smell it. He couldn't breathe.

"Who are you?" he asked shakily.

"Dr. Waters, Todd. Are you still with me?" she asked, putting her hand on his shoulder.

Her touch calmed him, her voice so soft he could barely hear her. She held out a hand. Quimby took it and let her help him up, looking at her with a trust he hadn't felt in years.

She led him back to the table, pressing his shoulder blade. It felt sharp through his regulation jumpsuit, protruding from his skinny frame. He sat down, and Claire grabbed her chair, pulling it around the table to sit next to him.

"Tell me what happened," she said, sitting down, knowing he was ready. "What you just saw."

"I didn't see it," he responded quickly. "I heard it. Pop-pop-pop-pop-pop."

"Like a gun being fired."

"Yeah, the old Thompson at the carnival shooting gallery," Quimby said, relaxing a bit. "Thing held a hundred BBs. Sounded like the real deal."

He's stalling, Claire thought. *I almost had him, and now he doesn't want to go back. But at least he's still at the carnival.*

"You liked going to the carnival," she tried.

"I liked shooting the Thompson," replied Quimby.

"Your mother would take you?"

Quimby looked at her, his eyes narrowing. "Never. That bitch cursed the day I was born."

The words were out before Quimby realized he'd said them. *I've got him now.* "You think your mother hates you," Claire pressed.

"You're just like all the other shrinks," Quimby said. "I'm not some freak who wants to screw his mother."

"I never said you were," Claire replied evenly. "I just want to know why you feel this way."

Her words calmed Quimby down. "Because of the flyswatter."

"What did she do with the flyswatter?"

"Hit me."

"Where?"

"On my penis. 'That's a nasty little fly,' she'd say."

His mother abused him. The realization made her mind wander. *Amy . . . What terrible things did Winslow do to her?*

She'd never been able to stop thinking about her best friend's last few hours. The terror she must have felt. For Claire it was the curse that came with her gift, the haunting memory that had both pushed her into becoming a therapist and pulled her back from fully engaging with her patients.

"Are you listening to me?" Quimby asked, pulling Claire out of her memories.

"Yes, your mother hit you," she said, focusing back on Quimby.

"That's nothing. One time Mom said, 'I'll snip the little bugger off. Then we'll see what kind of man you'll be.' "

"How often did this happen?"

"Every time I did something wrong."

"Did you tell anybody?"

"She said if I did, that she'd do worse, that she was a nurse and knew right where to hit me so nobody would ever know."

"And you didn't think your father would protect you."

"He was on the road eight months a year. I didn't think he could. But I was wrong about that."

"So he found out," Claire said as she moved her chair closer to him.

"When I was six. Walked in on her doing it to me. Harder than usual."

"You're smiling," Claire observed.

Quimby hadn't felt the grin forming.

"I was thinking about what Dad did to her."

"Which was?" Claire asked, her eyes widening.

"He grabbed the flyswatter and hit her with it. 'How do you like that?' he said. Then he grabbed a rolling pin. 'He's just a boy,' he said, and he beat the hell out of her. Whack, whack, whack . . ."

Claire hid her revulsion as he imitated the motion, the half-grin still on his face. *A six-year-old enjoying the sight of his father beating his mother. How pathetic is that?*

"You weren't upset?" Claire asked, breaking eye contact with Quimby.

"She deserved it," he said, tilting his head so that he could see Claire's eyes again.

He wants to tell me. Claire looked him straight in the eyes. "Was your mother hurt badly?"

"She was all black and blue. Threatened to call the cops on him. Dad said if she did, he'd tell them he beat her because she was a child molester. That the cops in Dubuque—that's where we lived— would put her in jail and throw away the key."

"And that stopped her."

"From calling the cops. Not from packing a suitcase and leaving."

"Where did she go?"

"Appleton, Wisconsin, to her parents."

"But she came back."

"The next day. My grandfather told her she made her own bed and now she had to lie in it. Same thing he said to her when she got knocked up with me."

Claire paused, considering the implication of Quimby's last comment. *She abused her son because she resented him for ruining her life.*

"Did your mother tell you this?" she finally asked.

"My mother didn't tell me shit. My father gave me the whole story." Quimby leaned toward Claire, staring into her eyes. "I suppose you want to hear that too."

"We said *everything.*"

Quimby smiled again, now enjoying Claire's attention. "One Saturday night, the carny's in Appleton. Dad's waiting for the crowd to leave so he can close the gate when this girl comes up to him. Asks what's his favorite part of the carnival. He tells her the bumper cars. She giggles and says, 'I heard that's not the best ride here.' Dad sees her two friends standing a few feet back, giggling like idiots. Realizes he laid one of them the night before. So he says, 'Yeah, and which ride did she say was the best?' She says, 'Carnival Knowledge. Like the movie with Jack Nicholson.' So Dad tells her he'll take her on that ride if she sticks around after he closes up."

"And he did."

Quimby grinned. "Three times. Once on the bumper cars and two more times in his trailer."

Claire realized his pleasure came from her facial expression of disgust. This time, she made no effort to hide it.

"Your father described to you how he had sex with your mother."

"He told me everything he did to her. But I don't wanna get into it. She was my mother, after all."

But the grin remained. *He wants me to ask him for the details. No way.*

"When did she tell your father she was pregnant?"

"She didn't. Three months later, when the carny was back in Wisconsin, my grandfather arrested him for raping his daughter."

"Your grandfather was a cop?"

"Police chief in Appleton. Said he'd drop the charges if Dad married my mother. Dad told me it was better than doing fifteen years hard time."

"How'd your mother feel about that?"

"She wanted to abort me, but my grandfather wouldn't let her. And no daughter of his was giving birth to no bastard child, either. She hated my father from the second she said 'I do.' "

"Because he got her pregnant."

"Because she knew being hitched wasn't gonna stop him from boning every gash he could sweet-talk himself into."

"Doesn't sound like your father had a lot of respect for women."

"Sure he did. And he taught me the same."

"How old were you when he started 'teaching' you?"

"Around five, I think. 'Lot lizards'll bang anybody,' he'd say, 'so if you want to do one of them, enter at your own risk 'cause you don't know what's living up there.' "

"What's a 'lot lizard'?"

"Carnival sluts. PBQs were a lot safer."

"And a PBQ is . . ."

"Carny-speak for 'possum belly queen.' Those are the girls who'll have sex with you in the compartment under a truck. Dad said they were cleaner because they were more picky about who they did. But he said the best ones to lay are townies like my mother, because once the carnival rolled out, you'd never have to see them again. Turns out he was wrong about that, huh?"

What kind of father talks to his kid this way? Claire might as well have said it aloud because Quimby read her face and flashed that evil grin.

"He didn't just teach me. He showed me."

I have no choice; I've gotta know. "Showed you what?"

"You know, like how to have a good time watching porn videos," Quimby said matter-of-factly. "Then when I was seven, we were in Decatur, Illinois, with the carny, and he had me watch him do a nineteen-year-old to show me how to get a girl off."

There it is again—that grin. I'm gonna wipe it off his face.

"Todd . . . your father never touched you, did he?"

She had barely finished the sentence when Quimby flew out of his chair.

"You calling my father some kinda homo?"

"No, but since your mother abused you, I had to make sure," Claire said calmly, though inside she was all Jell-O. "Now why don't you sit down?"

Quimby glared at her, then obeyed.

"My father didn't hurt me," he bellowed. "He told my mother if she ever laid a hand on me again, he'd kill her. He took me on the road with him whenever I didn't have school so I wouldn't have to be near her. That man saved me from that rancid bitch."

"You and your dad were pals," Claire said. "He really loved you."

"How many fathers teach their sons to be a man?" Quimby asked. Claire blinked. "Not many. Not like my dad did with me."

Keep him on track and he's mine.

"Were you with him that day?"

"Yeah, Fat Ralphie smoked too much crank the night before, and they couldn't get him outta bed, so Dad was manning the shooting gallery and putting the moves on this girl Sara."

"Did she travel with the carnival?"

"No, she was a greenie. That's what we call a townie who comes to work for us while we're there. She was just off a shift in the ticket booth and Dad's bragging how good I am with the gun."

"Your father was using you to meet women."

"He did it all the time."

"Obviously because it worked."

"Except Sara wanted to get into *my* pants."

"How do you know?"

" 'Cause she bent over to hug me and buried my head between her massive titties. Then she kissed me, except it wasn't no peck on the cheek. Girl stuck her tongue right down my throat."

"Did you enjoy it?"

Quimby flashed the grin. "You'd like me to say yes, wouldn't you? So you can tell all your buddies over a couple of beers."

"I can't tell anyone what we discuss here," she replied, "and the only thing I want is for you to tell me the truth. This isn't a game we're playing. Do you understand?"

Her stern tone was enough to make Quimby back down. The grin disappeared.

"Hell, I was only nine," he said. "I backed away and whined to Dad that she put her tongue in my mouth. He just laughs, says in a coupla years I won't be able to get enough of her tongue. Then she asks Dad if I'm too young to 'shoot' my own gun and Dad says, 'For now, yeah, but the kid likes to juggle.' Sara leans in again and says, 'Then I'll bet he's good with his hands. He should come with us.' "

"Did you?"

"Nope. Dad says he's taking Sara back to the trailer to check her receipts, meaning he's gonna bang her. Says I can't go because if I do, who's gonna run the booth?"

"He left you there alone?"

"Why not? It was a slow Thursday afternoon, and there were plenty of carnies around in case somebody wanted to make trouble. I done it before and he trusted me. So I just kept shooting the BB gun in between customers, when all of a sudden here comes Mom through the gate in her nurse's uniform."

"What did she want?"

"What she always wanted—to catch Dad in the act. The carny was in Dyersville, only half an hour from home. Usually Dad would have me wait outside the trailer if we were that close, in case she showed up. He even gave me a whistle to blow to warn him."

"Did you?"

"Should've. She didn't see me at first, so I pulled the whistle out of my pocket, put it around my neck, and tried to sneak out from behind the booth when the one guy shooting a Thompson hits a bull's-eye and starts screaming, 'Who's gonna give me my teddy bear?' Mom hears him, turns, sees me, and comes running. I would've lost her except I tripped and she caught up."

Quimby stopped. His lower lip quivered.

"What is it, Todd?" Claire asked, knowing she was getting close to a breakthrough.

"I think I'm done now."

"Did she hit you?"

Nothing. He looked down, trying to hide the tears welling up in his eyes.

"I know it still hurts," Claire said as comfortingly as she could. "It's okay. You can see it, can't you. You can see her."

He looked up after a long silence. "She choked me," he said. "My mother choked me. With the chain from the whistle. 'Daddy'll come right away if I blow this,' I told her. 'Not this time,' she says. She slaps me across the face. 'You're a liar,' she says, 'just like your father. Well, you're both done lying to me.' "

"She knew where your father was."

"She knew where the trailers were. She just looked for the one rocking back and forth like there was an earthquake, ran ahead of me, and went in. The music from the carousel was so loud. I just stood there. I couldn't move."

Claire heard thunder in the distance, but she couldn't move. *"It's okay," she heard Amy say to her. "Mr. Winslow works with my dad."*

Claire blinked away the image. *Help him. Help him along.* "And that's when you heard the gunshots."

"Pop-pop-pop-pop-pop-pop-pop-pop-pop," he uttered. "I knew it couldn't be from the shooting gallery 'cause we were too far away. So I ran up to the trailer. That's when my mother came out and I smelled the burnt popcorn."

But Claire was looking at Mr. Winslow. "How did you know Amy was at my house?" she asked him. "Her mother told me you two were having a playdate," he replied, annoyed.

Claire recovered. "It wasn't burnt popcorn, was it."

"I saw smoke coming out of her purse. And then I saw the blood. All over her. I started to scream. She puts her hand over my mouth, grabs me. And she says . . ."

"What, Todd? What did she say?"

" 'Come see what you did to your father.' "

A sudden rush of footsteps. Amy screamed. Claire turned, just in time to see Mr. Winslow carrying Amy to his car.

She saw Quimby's tears were coming faster now. *What's happening to me?*

"I beg her, 'Don't make me go in there.' I try to run but she grabs me in a choke hold and pulls me up the steps through the door. I can't breathe. . . . I close my eyes and turn away. But she grabs my head and almost twists it off. 'You're gonna see this,' she says, and then she grabs my eyelids and pulls them open and I see them."

"Your dad and Sara."

"Mommy, Mommy, come out here! Please . . ."

"She was still on top of him. And blood's pouring out of her head.

My father's head . . . is gone. She takes this huge gun out of her purse. Points the gun at me. Pulls the trigger . . ."

Claire's chest tightened. She couldn't breathe. It was hot and humid in the room. Like a storm was coming.

"Nothing happened," Quimby sobbed. "She was out of bullets. So she threw the gun down and walked out."

"Mommy! The man took Amy away. . . ."

Claire was lost. Quimby was staring at her.

"Say something! You put me through this bullshit, so why don't you tell me why I'm so screwed up?"

That brought her back. She chose her words carefully.

"Only a psychopath wouldn't be affected by what you went through, Todd."

"That's it? That's all you got for me? That's why I keep getting into trouble?"

"I think that's why you have the attitude you do toward women."

"Oh, now I have an attitude toward women?"

"Your father made you watch him masturbate and have sex. Your mother forced you to see how she shot him to death. These experiences made you into someone who likes to watch. To shock people. To look at them and make them have to look at you. Like you've been looking at me the whole time we've been together."

Quimby's eyes filled with rage.

"I swear, as I'm sitting here right now, my mother should've shot me. I wish the bitch killed me too."

Why not me? Why didn't Winslow take me? Claire thought. Her skin suddenly grew cold. Her back stiffened. Something inside her switched off. "When was the last time you saw your mother?" Claire asked.

"The day I testified against her in court. Then I came here to live with my grandmother."

"She never took you back to visit?"

"Once. But Mom wouldn't see me," he said as he stopped crying.

"Why not?"

"She said I had his face. And she hated it. She said the whole thing was my fault."

"Todd, it's not your fault that she murdered him." *Mommy said it's not my fault. What happened to Amy was not my fault.*

"Sure it is," Quimby answered.

"Why? How could you possibly think it's your fault?" Claire replied softly.

"Because I didn't blow the whistle," Quimby said. "He protected me from her. And when he really needed me the most, I wasn't there for him. I screwed up."

Thunder. Claire could see Amy, in tears, peering at her through the window of Mr. Winslow's BMW. Somehow knowing they would never see each other again.

In the observation room, Fairborn waited for Claire to make her next move. But there was only silence.

"Something's wrong," she said to Curtin. "Why isn't Claire saying anything?"

"After what she just got out of him, you're asking that?" demanded Curtin. "Are you serious?"

"Yes, I'm serious," Fairborn shot back. "Look at her. She's as stiff as a piece of steel."

Curtin looked at the monitor. Sure enough, Claire was staring into space. Then, through the speakers, they heard Claire say, "How did you feel when you saw your mother kill your father and his lover?"

Claire knew the words were wrong as they were leaving her mouth. But Quimby's story had shut her down.

"How do you think I felt? Are you blind or didn't you see what you made me go through?"

She picked up his file, reading to cover her discomfort. "I mean, was your heart racing? Were you sweating? Breathing hard?"

"I can't remember, okay? I was nine. What difference does it make?"

"Because that's a sign of an anxiety disorder. If you're anxious now, we have medication to help you with that." *Amy, what did he do to you? Stop! Stop! I don't want to think about it. . . .*

"I've been on medication. Xanax, Klonopin. That shit didn't work."

"From the looks of things, you've been self-medicating," Claire said, her face buried in his medical records. *What is happening to me?*

"You mean the dope? I was just having a good time."

"Or were you trying to forget about a bad time."

"What the hell kind of therapist are you?"

"Therapy doesn't work without the truth. Were you high when you exposed yourself to those women?" *Dammit! Focus on him*.

"No. I just had an urge. But I learned to stifle them in here."

"Then why were you taking the drugs?"

Quimby's features tightened up. Now he leaned toward her. "You ever see something so horrible, that scared you so much you knew you'd spend the rest of your life trying to forget it?"

Claire sprang out of her chair. "I'll be seeing you once a week," she said, her voice icy. "You must be on time. It's a condition of your parole that you come to all your appointments at my office in Manhattan City Hospital."

Claire scribbled the building and room number on a slip of paper, handed it to Quimby, and without another word headed for the door.

"What's your first name?" came Quimby's voice.

Claire stopped, turned back to him. He was smiling.

"It's Claire," she answered. "Why?"

"Claire Waters? *Clear* Waters?"

"So?"

"Your parents ever tell you why they named you that?"

He was still smiling. The same look as when she first came into the room. *He thinks he has me. He's right*.

"This isn't about me."

"What the hell happened to her?" Fairborn asked as she watched Claire on the monitor leave the room.

"I don't know," said Curtin. "It's like she hit a brick wall."

"In her head," replied Fairborn. "Not in his. She was doing so well until she started looking for a chemical explanation for Mr. Quimby's problems."

"I saw it, too, Lois," Curtin replied, annoyed.

"She can't handle the stress, Paul," Fairborn said. "She can't separate herself from what the patient is going through."

"She'll learn."

"You wanted her and I supported you," Fairborn said. "But we don't need someone who dodges the truth by turning to pharmacology for answers. If she can't deal with sick, twisted people, she'll never be a star."

Curtin stood up. The light from the monitor cast a metallic glint in his blue eyes. He looked down at Fairborn, still seated.

"I'll make her a star."

CHAPTER 3

The following morning, Claire and her colleagues in the fellowship gathered in the overly bright cafeteria for what Curtin called his "prerounds postmortem," a ritual that would begin with a critique of his flock's performance from the previous day.

His students, however, saw it more like a daily beheading from the king, which had prompted them to derisively dub the exercise "the Last Supper," even though it always took place over a rushed crack-of-dawn breakfast.

Today, Saturday, would be no different. Curtin demanded that his fellows see patients on weekends. "They don't choose when to get sick," he told them, "and we don't choose when to see them."

It started out benignly enough. Curtin arrived precisely at 6:15, drinking his protein smoothie. Claire's only discomfort was her attire; she wore a lab coat (having spent an hour in the lab), jeans, and sneakers in contrast to the ties and skirts worn by the others. Curtin went around the table, throwing various questions at the fellows, all of whom answered without spectacle. Claire knew her turn would come and was convinced she, too, would get through it unscathed. She was ready. Or so she thought.

"Dr. Waters, what's your diagnosis on Quimby?" Curtin asked.

"Schizoid personality disorder," she replied, barely missing a beat.

"Based on what?" he asked.

"His description of his physiological reaction to his stressors and urges, and his profuse sweating while he recounted his story," she said, deciding to go for it and continuing. "I'm prescribing Risperdal and an antidepressant."

"And based on your assessment and treatment plan, do you think Quimby's ready to be released from jail?"

"In light of his past history and treatment, he appears stable."

"I'm not asking you how he 'appears,' Doctor," Curtin responded, his eyes skewering her. "But since you brought it up, he sure as hell didn't 'appear' stable in that room yesterday. So I'll ask you again: Is he ready for release?"

Claire fumbled. "I don't have enough facts and data to form an opinion."

"Facts and data," Curtin repeated mockingly, addressing the rest of the group, who also knew what was coming. "My point is, Dr. Waters, you're focusing on his physiological reaction. Blood pressure, respirations, and the heartbeat of a patient sitting in your office are not predictors of whether he'll get into trouble once he's on the street."

"He has to see me once a week. I'll . . . I'll evaluate him through therapy," stammered Claire.

"Not if you handle him the way you did yesterday," Curtin said.

"I got him to tell his story," Claire said defensively.

"You got him to talk about his past," Curtin chided her. "But the second he said he was afraid, you put up the white flag. You jumped on the pill wagon instead of asking follow-up questions. Instead of probing deeper to find out why your patient was scared."

Curtin looked at the group, though she knew that what he was about to say was directed at her. "This isn't residency," he began. "You're not treating children with ADD or housewives who think their hubbies are cheating on them and have an anxiety disorder you can correct with Xanax. We're the gatekeepers for the Todd Quimbys of the world. *We* decide whether they belong with the rest of us. This is the big leagues, folks. And we've got to hit a home run *every* time, with *every* patient, or someone out there could get hurt or killed."

Curtin looked around the group to make sure his message sunk in. "Be upstairs in five minutes," he said. "Except you, Dr. Waters."

Claire was so wrapped up in her own head she barely saw the sympathetic glances from her colleagues.

When they were gone, Curtin looked her up and down disapprovingly. "What's that you're wearing?" he asked.

Claire wondered why that mattered, which she made clear with her tone. "I was working in the lab," she said. "I didn't want to ruin a skirt and blouse with brain matter."

Curtin sighed and looked at her with mock sympathy. "The lab," he said. Then he asked, "Why did you accept this fellowship?"

"Because I want to understand what makes the criminal mind different," she answered, looking him right in the eyes.

"I brought you here because you're brilliant," he said, backing off. "Nobody's questioning that. And I think deep down you have what it takes to do this work. But in this business, having what it takes isn't enough. You have to wear it."

"Wear it?"

"Confidence. Extroversion. Even a little narcissism," Curtin said.

"I'm not a game-show host," she replied angrily. "I'm a psychiatrist."

"Being a psychiatrist is more than waving a medical degree and a prescription pad in someone's face."

"Excuse me?" she demanded.

"You can't just prescribe drugs as a crutch to avoid confronting your patients," Curtin replied.

"A crutch?" Claire said, her voice rising. "I'm a *scientist*. I do research—which points to a neurochemical explanation for criminal behavior."

"I don't care what it points to," he said. "What I saw from you yesterday was reaction formation. A cover. Defense mechanism. And that's not going to fly here. You're excused from morning rounds." Curtin stood up and turned to walk away.

Claire had enough. "Are you telling me I'm not cut out for this?"

Curtin turned back and smiled, as if he'd expected her to stop him. "I wouldn't send you packing after the first day. I talked this over with Dr. Fairborn, and she wants to see you."

"Now? On Saturday?"

"She's waiting in her office."

Curtin walked away. Claire couldn't help but think he had passive-aggressively passed the buck on her future to his boss. She hoped only that Fairborn wouldn't suck the blood out of her.

* * *

The Vampire was dressed in charcoal-colored slacks and a gray silk blouse that morning, her dark lipstick and nails making her look almost Goth. When Claire entered the office, she immediately felt at ease, noticing the surprising homey touches like cream-colored cashmere throws and a crystal vase filled with fragrant white roses. Fairborn couldn't have been nicer, greeting Claire like a long-lost friend, telling her how glad she was to have her on board as she guided Claire to a comfortable leather chair. Claire only then saw the lacquered Chinese fans that were splayed on the walls, a decorative message that said that everything discussed in the room would remain hidden from the world.

Fairborn began with small talk, asking Claire about her family and past, which disarmed her completely. She realized this would be less of a dressing-down than a therapy session. They were talking about Claire's childhood, which by and large had been a happy one, when Fairborn popped the question Claire knew was coming but dreaded nevertheless.

"Do you remember, as a child, being afraid of anything?"

Claire looked down. She liked this woman but wasn't ready to spill her innermost secrets. She tried to brush the question off.

"Sure. You know—monsters, snakes, the usual kid stuff."

Fairborn wasn't having it, though she remained friendly when she said, "Mr. Quimby asked you if you were ever afraid. You withdrew and changed the subject. I doubt the usual kid stuff would have made you do that."

"I didn't answer him because the question wasn't relevant to his treatment," Claire said, trying to sound as professional as she could. "We weren't there to talk about me."

"But *we're* here to talk about you," said Fairborn. "Dr. Curtin was pretty hard on you this morning, wasn't he," she stated as fact.

Claire realized that Fairborn was playing the good cop. But Claire didn't want to play.

"I don't think the way I dress has any bearing on my effectiveness as a therapist," she said defiantly.

If this bothered Fairborn, she gave away nothing. "Do you think you belong here?"

"I thought I did. But maybe I made a mistake."

Fairborn tilted her head, fingering the strand of pearls around her neck, thinking about how to respond.

Thunder rumbled off in the distance, which startled Claire. She quickly covered her alarm, hoping Fairborn hadn't noticed.

"Storm's coming," Fairborn said, eyeing Claire. "But it's supposed to blow over quickly."

"I hope so," Claire said, then added, "We don't need any more rain."

Fairborn smiled. "In this program, we look at everything, Claire— the present and the past—in order to help our patients have a future. You're too focused on the present, on brain chemicals. I think you're running from the patient's history, his life story, and I want to know why."

"All due respect, Doctor, I know the patient's past matters. Who we are is partly determined by our experiences. When Mr. Quimby didn't want to talk about his childhood, I got him to open up."

Fairborn leaned in. "And then he asked you if you'd ever been afraid. And you shut down. Why?"

"I don't know," said Claire, knowing Fairborn, a pro, wouldn't be fooled for a second.

Fairborn looked at her. "Dr. Waters . . . Claire," she began. "We come from different places, have different perspectives. But we're both shrinks. That's who and what we are. I'm not saying I have all the answers. But I've been doing this a long time. And one thing I know for certain is that you can't be a good shrink if you can't be truthful with yourself."

"About what?" Claire asked, though she already knew the answer.

"Your past," Fairborn replied without a hint of condescension. "Whatever it is that you don't want to relive through these patients."

"My past has nothing to do with this," Claire responded stubbornly.

"Of course it does, dear," Fairborn said. "You need to decide whether you're ready to face your own demons. Because until you are, you may not be ready for this kind of responsibility."

The thunder was louder, closer this time. Claire couldn't help but shudder slightly. "Maybe you're right," she said. "Maybe I should talk to you about a few things that have been bothering me."

"Good," Fairborn said, standing up. "We'll make a time twice a week to talk."

Claire stood up and Fairborn led her to the door.

"We've all got storms inside us, Claire. How we handle them is what counts."

The storms inside us. The words echoed in Claire's mind. *Maybe she'll help me find my way through them.*

CHAPTER 4

Another hot, miserable Saturday night, Nick Lawler thought. At six-one, he towered over the five other cops who together were wrestling down a filthy, violent drunk in Central Booking, the hell-hole Nick had been reassigned to seven months earlier. Beads of sweat formed on his forehead under the shock of brown hair that hung over one eye. At forty-two, Nick looked ten years younger, having kept himself in good physical condition. The drunk bucked like a raging bronco, until Nick was finally able to get the cuffs on the bastard.

"Good job, Nick," said a throaty voice behind him.

Nick turned and saw his former boss, Detective Lieutenant Brian Wilkes, smiling at him with a grin that revealed a missing upper molar on each side. Nick thought he looked like a jack-o'-lantern with his round face and flaming red hair.

"We're going to Coney Island," Wilkes said. "You got your old job back. Let's go."

"You sure?" Nick asked. The last thing he ever expected was to go back to Manhattan South Homicide as a second-grade detective of the New York City Police Department.

"Believe it, my friend," Wilkes said. "We got a homicide, and the chief of detectives wants you there."

The Big Man himself, Nick thought. And without wasting a second, Nick followed Wilkes out the door.

In the car, Wilkes handed Nick back his Glock nine millimeter, the one he'd been stripped of when he was exiled to Central Booking.

The ride down the Belt Parkway was mostly silent, Nick fixating on the pulsing of the red bubble light on the dash reflected in the windshield and the rhythm of the blaring siren. As they passed under the Verrazano-Narrows Bridge, Wilkes could stand it no longer.

"Aren't you even going to ask what this is about?"

"What's this about?" Nick deadpanned.

It made Wilkes smile as he told Nick about the body on Coney Island. "Got a call from the assistant medical examiner. Says you were on a case last year that looks a helluva lot like this one."

"Why not just pull Frankie in?" Nick asked.

"Because the only thing your ex-partner can find without directions is in his pants," Wilkes said. "Idiot didn't remember anything about the church carnival job when I called him. He off with a badge bunny when you were working that one too?"

"I don't remember," Nick said. "Frankie got laid an awful lot."

He stared at the headlights of oncoming cars whizzing past them in the opposite direction as he said it. *Flash. Flash. Flash.*

He ran down the hallway. "Jenny, I'm coming!" he screamed. . . .

"Chief of d's is all in a tizzy about how this could be a repeater . . . ," Wilkes droned on as Nick stared into the oncoming lights. *Flash. Flash. Flash.*

He took the steps two at a time. Missed one. Fell flat on his face. Felt the blood pouring from his nose as he got up . . .

". . . and we can't have people afraid to go to Coney Island. He wants someone who knows last year's case. . . ."

Bang! Flash! He heard the gun go off as he staggered through the dark into the room. He ran to check her. But he knew the chest wound was fatal the second he saw it. She was gasping for her last breaths. . . .

"Where the hell are you?" he heard Wilkes ask.

"Right here, Boss," Nick said as he shook off the image.

"You listen to me," Wilkes warned him. "I went to bat for you on this. It's provisional, you being back in the Bureau. So don't screw it up."

The neon of Coney Island's Wonder Wheel cast a sickly glow on Nick as he wove through the summer night crowd and headed toward the beach. The night was hot and humid. Nick's shirt was soaked through and his hair was matted down. As he ducked under the yellow crime scene tape, the hurdy-gurdy music and raucous laughter only made him more tense about what he was about to find.

The assistant medical examiner, Ross, pulled back the white sheet covering the victim as Wilkes and Nick approached. Nick immediately saw that her eyes were white. Completely white. At first he thought he'd been blinded by the flash of the crime scene detective's camera. But as Nick knelt beside the body, his sight returned and he noticed the red splotches around both of the victim's eyes and quickly realized what had happened.

"Crazy bastard burned her irises away," he said to Ross, who stood behind him next to Wilkes. "Some kind of acid?"

"Won't know till I crack her," Ross replied dryly, in mid-yawn. Then he added, "Perp didn't do that last year, did he?"

"No, last year he duct-taped the victim's eyes shut," Nick said. "If it's the same guy."

"I had them call you because the victims sure look the same," Ross said defensively.

About that he was correct, Nick thought, studying the naked girl in front of him. She looked to be in her late teens or early twenties, short blond hair, strikingly beautiful despite the burns. Tapered, smooth legs leading up to a Brazilian wax. Above that, a slim waist and breasts that Nick could tell would be more than ample if she were standing. Atop one of them dangled a frayed end of the rope the killer used to strangle her.

Nearly a year earlier, Nick had caught the homicide of a young blond girl who looked much like this one, except for the Brazilian wax. She was discovered in similar repose just a few yards from a carnival operating in the schoolyard of St. Jude on Manhattan's Upper West Side. Ross was the cutter on that one as well. And though Nick never thought much of his skills, tonight Ross was his savior, for he had delivered Nick from cop purgatory to the Promised Land, which in this case was the ass end of Brooklyn. All because a beautiful blond girl had been found murdered with a similar signature and modus operandi within spitting distance of the legendary Cyclone roller coaster, marking what remained of Coney Island Amusement Park.

"You got a helluva memory, pal," Nick said to Ross, sounding almost complimentary. "The victims look alike. So do the details."

Ross caught the friendlier-than-usual tone of Nick's praise. "Last thing I needed, being dragged out to this dump on a Saturday night," he said.

Score another point for Ross. Nick had forgotten that last year's carnival killing also occurred on a Saturday night. As the thought registered, he jerked his head down toward the body.

"Anyone besides me smell something like bitter almonds?"

Ross and Lieutenant Wilkes looked at each other. Sniffed around.

"All I smell is burnt popcorn and cotton candy from the vendors' carts," Wilkes said.

"I got a cold. But I'll check her for cyanide on the tox screen if it'll make you happy," Ross offered.

"Why burn her eyes this time?" Lieutenant Wilkes asked.

"Plastic bottle of acid's easier to conceal than a roll of duct tape," Nick answered.

"It's also more dangerous. For the perp," Wilkes replied.

Nick pointed toward a burn mark that seemed to go straight across the victim's forehead. "He probably had it in a plastic squeeze bottle with a nozzle so he could spray it. I'm thinking he misses with the first shot . . ."

"And hits with the second," finished Wilkes. "Okay, so he blinds her. Because he doesn't want her to see him?"

"I think he blinded her so she wouldn't see she was about to die," Nick replied.

"Serial killer with a conscience is a contradiction in terms," Wilkes retorted.

But Nick didn't hear Wilkes's remark. Something was bothering him. Still kneeling, he studied the knotted rope around the victim's neck.

"Check out the knot. I've never seen one tied like this."

"You mean it's different from the one used on the girl last year?"

"That was a simple square knot," Nick replied. "This one's more complex."

"Perp's getting all fancy and throwing it in our face," Wilkes sighed. "Why I pulled you back in."

Those last words stood foremost in Nick's mind as he went

through the routine questions at the crime scene. "Any witnesses?" he asked.

Wilkes turned to a uniformed lieutenant from the Sixty-Fourth Precinct named Garber for the answer. "So far, nobody even saw the victim on the boardwalk," Garber said. "No one's called in a missing person in the area, and no ID on her. We're still looking," he added.

Nick recalled that last year's victim had been found with her purse lying a couple of feet from her corpse, the wallet missing as if she'd been robbed. "Lotta people on the boardwalk tonight?" he asked.

"Crowd was light, according to my cops," Garber replied. "Because of the earlier thunderstorm."

"Victim's probably a local out for a walk."

"If she lived alone, could be a while before we ID her," Wilkes said.

But Nick had already moved on, turning to the young crime scene detective who was putting his camera away.

"You done here?" Nick asked.

"All yours, Detective."

It had been a while since anyone had called him that, Nick mused. The kid was obviously new, formally dressed in a white shirt and blue tie on a weekend night. His blond hair was buzz cut, which made him look like a marine. Nick wondered if the kid had heard the stories about him.

"Lawler. Nick Lawler. And you're a detective now too. Call me Nick. What's your name?"

"Terry Aitken."

Nick pulled a small, rectangular video camera from his pocket and switched it on.

"Mind killing the lights for me, Terry?"

"Sure thing," Aitken replied. "Hey, Henry, cut the lights!" he shouted to his partner. A second later, the klieg lights illuminating the crime scene went dark.

But not for Nick. He peered through the viewfinder of the camera, its night-vision function illuminating the scene in an eerie white fluorescence as he panned from the body under the boardwalk to the sand on the beach. Detective Aitken watched him, wondering what he was doing.

"I took, like, six dozen photos, sir," he said tentatively to Nick.

Nick peeked at the young detective and grinned at his deference. "I'm not second-guessing you," he assured Aitken. "Video camera gives me the perp's-eye view."

But he wasn't seeing what he hoped he would. "Any of your photos show drag marks or footprints from where he grabbed her off the boardwalk?"

"No, because the perp covered his tracks. Smeared the sand somehow."

"Show me from where," Nick commanded.

Aitken walked him several yards east and pointed to a spot in the sand. "They started right about here," said Aitken, "and stopped where we found the body." He held up his digital camera. "I got it all on here."

Good thing, thought Nick as he looked down at a mass of shoeprints, no doubt left by cops after Aitken had finished. "He was barefoot, don't you think? So he wouldn't leave shoe impressions."

"Explains why the smears are smooth. Shoes would've left a harder edge," Aitken agreed.

Nick turned his attention back to the video camera. He panned slowly alongside the boardwalk where Aitken had indicated the smears began. Saw what he was almost certain would be there.

"You got a flashlight?" he asked Aitken.

"Sure," Aitken replied, handing Nick his Maglite. "What'd you find?"

Nick turned the light on and shined it on the planks of the boardwalk just under the railing, illuminating several clean spots on the otherwise filthy wood.

"This is where he got her with the acid," Nick said. "Some of it dripped off her when he squirted it, burned the wood clean." He turned to Aitken. "Can you cut those pieces out?"

"Right away," Aitken said, and headed off.

Now Nick panned from the boardwalk up to the Cyclone roller coaster and back down as Wilkes looked on.

"Night like this, even with a light crowd, there had to be dozens of people out here," he said. "This guy squirts acid in a woman's face, she's going to start screaming."

Nick panned the camera back up to the nearest precipice on the

Cyclone, where, in the crosshairs, he could see a carful of revelers just heading down.

"If he waited for the coaster to pass by, she could've screamed bloody murder and nobody would've heard her," Nick mused.

As if to prove his point, the coaster came speeding past them in a clattering of wheels and gears and passengers shouting in glee and terror.

CHAPTER 5

The phone was into its fifth ring when Claire's hand reached out and switched on the small bedside reading lamp. A swath of light cut across the sparsely furnished bedroom, barely big enough for a king-sized bed and a scratched maple bureau Claire had picked out at a thrift shop. She grabbed the receiver from its cradle and hit herself in the forehead with it before groggily moving it to her ear.

"Hello?" she said sleepily as she glanced at the clock: 2:23 a.m.

"Clear waters run deep," said the wide-awake male voice on the other end of the line.

Claire recognized the voice and sat up.

"The saying is 'still waters run deep,' Mr. Quimby, and how did you get this number?"

"You'd be surprised what you can find out about someone on the Internet," Quimby replied, the tone of his voice chilling her.

"What do you want?" she asked, a hint of anger in her own voice. It had been only three days since Quimby's release from Rikers Island, and in her middle-of-the-night fog, Claire thought he wasn't due for an appointment until the following week.

"I have to see you," Quimby said.

"Is something wrong?" asked Claire.

"I'm afraid again."

"You don't sound afraid to me," Claire retorted, "and you shouldn't be calling me at home."

"I need your help. Now. Please," he pleaded.

The urgency in his voice softened Claire, reminding her of how vulnerable he had been during their interview a week ago.

"Go to the emergency room at Manhattan City," she said. "The psych resident on call will see you."

"You can't dump him on the resident," came a groggy male voice from beside her.

The voice belonged to Ian Bigelow, Claire's thirty-year-old boyfriend, who even with bed head was handsome enough to be a recruiting poster for Dr. Curtin's psych fellowship or just about anything else. They'd had dinner that night at Tante Louise, their favorite French bistro, and shared a bottle of pinot grigio, which was still making Claire feel a bit light-headed. She covered the receiver with her hand. "Shhh, he'll hear you," she whispered. "I'll handle it. He's my patient."

"That's right—he's your patient," Ian said. "And if you let the resident handle it instead of seeing him yourself, Curtin'll be all over you. Especially after what happened yesterday."

Claire stared at the receiver, wishing she could just hang up and erase that first meeting with Quimby.

"Cat got your tongue, Dr. Waters?" Quimby taunted.

"Go to the ER," Claire said into the receiver. "I'll be there as soon as I can."

She hung up the phone as Ian sat up and gave her a kiss. He held her in his arms and smiled. "You're a terrific shrink. Don't ever forget that."

But Claire wasn't convinced. She gave Ian a squeeze, then pulled away and untangled herself from the sheets. "I better get dressed," she said.

Ian turned over and instantly began snoring. Claire looked down at him, envious of how quickly he could fall asleep, putting the day's troubles behind him. Maybe that's why she loved him so much. He was a problem-solver, always ready to help. She could tell him her troubles and he would always help her find a way through them. She told him all the details of her interview with Quimby, and he had reassured her that she did nothing wrong, reminding her that the first meetings between the patient and doctor were a kind of journey to get to know each other before the real treatment could begin.

But even Ian's support didn't take away the anxiety Claire still felt about her first case in the fellowship program. Claire had left Quimby in the interview room, knowing she screwed up. She wasn't surprised when Curtin took her aside and let her have it.

You may not be ready for this kind of responsibility.

Fairborn's words reverberated in Claire's head as she opened her small closet and stared at the sameness of her clothes: jeans, light blue cotton shirts, a few skirts and sweaters tossed in to break the monotony, along with the new olive green suit and an older dark gray one. She paused to consider what to wear, something she rarely did.

She was pausing a lot lately, unsure of herself and the decision she had made to do a fellowship under Paul Curtin. She pulled one of the pale blue blouses from the closet and put it on as she watched Ian sleep peacefully.

Yes, she thought. *I did make the right decision coming here to do a fellowship with Ian.*

She was ready. She would help Quimby face his demons even if it meant breaching her own wall of emotional security.

Quimby was already in the psych holding room in the ER when Claire entered. The room was empty except for two chairs and an exam table, to prevent psychotic or suicidal patients from harming themselves with any instruments or equipment. Quimby flashed her a big smile, which pissed her off. *He certainly doesn't look anxious or desperate.*

"Let's get something straight," she lectured him. "I am the therapist. You are the patient. I ask the questions. And anything we discuss is about you, not me. Are we clear?"

"I really do need your help," he said.

His grin was gone. Claire realized he'd smiled out of relief that she was there, not to mock her. She looked into Quimby's fearful eyes, but she couldn't shake her own thoughts. *Did I come to help him? Or me?*

Her tone softened. "Did something happen?" she asked Quimby.

"Yes."

"Tell me."

"It was bad." He hesitated; then he said, "I picked up a hooker. Near Times Square."

Claire gave him a sympathetic nod. Yes, this was a violation of probation that could send him back to jail. But she wasn't his probation officer.

"We all have needs, Todd," she said, trying to comfort him. "That doesn't make you different from anyone else."

But Quimby's mind was elsewhere. He looked right at her.

"She was about your height. Thin. Short blond hair. Huge tits. Hot green two-piece outfit."

"Just like your father's mistress," Claire said. "The one he was murdered with . . ." She couldn't remember the woman's name.

"Sara," he said quickly, avoiding her eyes.

"Is that why you chose her? Because she looked like Sara?"

"What do you think?" he retorted, still looking away.

I'll take that as a yes, Claire thought. "Todd," she began, "listen to me. That's nothing to be ashamed of—"

"It's not about her," he blurted. "It's about me. I couldn't . . . you know . . ." he stammered, then looked right at her. "I'm ashamed about what happened."

"What happened?"

"She took me into a cheap hotel room, started telling me about how Mommy's gonna make me feel good. And I couldn't get it up. And she laughed at me, gave me my money back, and left me there. And now I can't get the thoughts out of my head."

"What kind of thoughts?"

"That if I'd killed that dirty whore Sara when I was a kid, my dad would still be alive. My mom wouldn't have had to go away."

Claire saw tears appear in his eyes. Running down his cheeks. *He thinks it's all his fault,* Claire realized.

She heard herself crying. Her mother beside her, consoling her. "It wasn't your fault," her mother said. "You didn't make that man take your friend away."

Claire realized she and Todd Quimby had a lot in common.

"You didn't make your father cheat on your mother," she said to him. "And you didn't put the gun in your mother's hand or make her pull the trigger. You were just a boy. None of what happened was your fault."

Quimby eyed her. "No, it was the whore's fault. I don't know why . . ."

"You don't know why what?" she asked gently.

"Why I was attracted to that woman tonight."

"I don't know, either. But that's what we're going to find out. You and me, together. You'll get through this. I'm going to help you."

He nodded.

"I'll prescribe something to calm you down," Claire continued. "Go straight home, get some sleep, and meet me upstairs in my office at two this afternoon."

"But it's Sunday," Quimby said tentatively.

"That doesn't matter. I'm here whenever you need me. Okay?"

Quimby nodded again, grateful for her reassurance.

Claire blew into the apartment and checked the nearest clock. It was just after six a.m. She had exactly fifteen minutes to change into a skirt and get back to the hospital for this morning's Last Supper. No way she'd ever be on time. She knew Ian would already be gone, making her wonder why she smelled fresh coffee. Until she spotted two pieces of wheat toast protruding from the toaster next to a plate covered with tin foil, atop which was a note.

" 'Breakfast is served,' " Claire read. " 'I'll round on your patients.' " Punctuated by a poorly drawn but sincere heart.

Claire smiled as she uncovered the plate, revealing two perfectly cooked eggs over easy. She wished she had an ounce of Ian's nurturing instinct. She grabbed the toast, which by now was cold (the way she liked it so the butter wouldn't melt), and placed it neatly beside the eggs. Relaxed, she turned on the TV news, then grabbed a mug from the cabinet and poured a steaming cup of coffee. She was about to sip it when the television caught her attention.

". . . murder in Times Square," Claire heard the newscaster say. "A woman found dead this morning in a hotel room . . ."

She grabbed the remote and turned up the sound as she headed to where she could see the screen, which was filled with the photo of an attractive young woman with short blond hair. "Police say the victim, twenty-two-year-old Catherine Mills, had a long record of arrests for prostitution. . . ."

Claire realized that her hand was burning from holding the scalding coffee. She set the cup down, ran for her briefcase, grabbed it, and rummaged until she found what she was looking for—the photo of Sara Belz, Quimby's father's mistress, from long ago.

She reached the TV just as the photo of Catherine Mills reappeared on-screen, next to which Claire held Sara's photo.

They could have been twins.

Quimby had confessed to her only an hour ago about his encounter with a prostitute in Times Square who resembled Sara Belz. Chills ran through her as his words rang in her head: *If I'd killed that dirty whore Sara when I was a kid, my dad would still be alive. My mom wouldn't have had to go away.*

Had Quimby made his wish come true? Had he returned to Times Square, found Catherine Mills, and murdered her? Or had he already committed the murder when he came to see her, wanting to confess but stopping just short of admitting his ultimate sin?

Either way, Claire knew she had to face the unavoidable truth. She, Dr. Claire Waters, had missed the warning signs in her last interview with her very first criminal patient, Todd Quimby. And because of her, a woman was dead. Because she allowed a killer back into society.

If he is the killer, Claire thought. Unless she was a hundred percent sure, she couldn't violate patient confidentiality and call the police.

She looked at the clock. In a little more than eight hours, she'd have to face Todd Quimby again. She'd have to confront him with the question of whether he'd murdered Catherine Mills. She'd have to get the truth from him. And she knew Quimby had no good reason to tell her the truth.

And then an idea popped into her head. It was extreme, for sure. But she needed to do something dramatic to redeem herself after freezing up at her first interview with Quimby.

She hurried over to the mirror. Stared at herself in the reflection, thinking about Curtin and Fairborn questioning her ability. She'd show them how committed she was.

Quimby didn't even look up when Claire entered the dimly lit meeting room, which was used by all the fellows to see their patients.

"I didn't get any sleep," he uttered from his position, head buried in crossed arms on the table.

"Sit up. Now," Claire ordered.

Her strident tone brought Quimby's head up. He looked at her, startled. Then, just as suddenly, he turned away from her, biting his lip.

"What's your problem?" Claire demanded as she took off her white lab coat and tossed it over the empty chair across the table from Quimby.

"I don't have a problem," Quimby shot back, avoiding her eyes.

Claire moved around the table so Quimby couldn't help but see her.

"Bullshit."

"What's the matter with you?" Quimby said, starting to lose it.

"I'm the one who should be asking you that," Claire stated.

Quimby was doing everything in his power not to look at her. "I don't want to talk today."

"Then I'll have to admit you for observation," she answered.

"Why did you do that?" he blurted out, unable to hold it in any longer.

"Do what?" she asked innocently.

But Claire knew what he meant and glanced into the one-way mirror at herself.

Her new self. In the hours before coming to the hospital, she had cut her hair short and dyed it blond. She wore a black form-fitting one-piece outfit, cut to show off her ample breasts and just the right amount of cleavage.

Claire Waters had *become* Catherine Mills and Sara Belz.

And Todd Quimby couldn't stand it. Which was exactly what she wanted.

"Do what?" she asked again, more demanding.

"You know what I'm talking about."

She spoke to his reflection in the mirror, where she could see herself. "Oh, you mean this?" she asked. "I saw my boyfriend looking at blondes. I thought maybe if I became one, he'd pay more attention to me."

"Are you making fun of me?" Quimby asked, now angry.

But Claire wasn't scared. "What makes you think I'm making fun of you?"

"Go to hell," he said. "I'm leaving."

"No, you're not," Claire warned sharply.

For some reason, Quimby obeyed her, staying in his chair as if he'd been restrained.

"What's this about?" he asked, on the verge of tears.

"You wanted to talk about me. Now's your chance," Claire replied.

"I changed my mind."

"Why? I thought clear waters run deep," Claire chided, throwing his own words back at him. She walked toward him, stopping several feet away from where he was sitting.

"I want another doctor."

"Sorry, but you're stuck with me. "

"You shouldn't have done that!" Quimby exploded. "What am I gonna do now?"

"What do you want to do, Todd?" she said with her best attempt at lasciviousness. She stepped closer, leering down at him.

"I don't know," said Quimby, desperately trying to control himself.

"What did you do this morning?" asked Claire.

"I already told you."

Claire turned on him. "You didn't tell me everything, did you?" She was now standing right beside him.

"What are you talking about?

"You went back to find her, didn't you?" Claire shouted.

"What if I did?"

"Were you mad at her because she laughed at you?" Claire faked a girlish giggle, which was so convincing that it infuriated Quimby.

"What are you giggling at?" he demanded.

"Nothing, just a joke someone told me before I came in here."

"You think I can't rise to the occasion?"

"I don't know, can you?" she asked, giving him a wink.

"You come in here looking like . . . that. . . . What am I supposed to think?"

"What do you think?" she said, almost purring.

"I think you want me."

"And if I did? What would you do then?"

Quimby rose slowly, never taking his eyes off her. Claire returned his stare, defiant. Daring him. She could feel his hot breath and it made her queasy.

"I'd start right here," he said. His lips were wet with spittle.

Slowly, carefully, he slid his hand to the small of her back. And down. In a circular motion.

"I didn't invite you to do that," Claire said.

"Oh, yes, you did," Quimby said, increasing the speed of his rotating hand. "Why else would you have gone to all this trouble, prettying yourself up for me?"

Claire wasn't prepared for his brazenness. "You can't just go up to women and do what you're doing," she said, backing away.

"But I can do it to you, can't I?" he said. "You want me to do it to you, don't you?" he asked, reaching out for her breast.

"This has to stop," she said, crossing her arms and stepping back farther.

Like a predator, Quimby sensed her fear and it empowered him. "What's the matter?" he asked. "This is what you wanted. Now you're gonna get it."

And he pounced on her.

"Let go of me!" Claire screamed.

He ripped her top, exposing her lacy bra and most of her breasts.

"Why stop now?" Quimby said, an evil smile on his face.

He was trying to pin her against the wall and get his pants down. He was much stronger than she was. With all the strength she had left, she pushed him away, falling back against the wall. Quimby eyed her with lust, ready to claim his prize.

"Give it to me, whore," Quimby said, almost salivating as he approached.

Claire reached for her lab coat on the chair and grabbed the stethoscope from the pocket. She flung the metal bell in his face, hitting him squarely in the eye. He stumbled backward, clutching his face in pain.

"You bitch!" he yelled. "You think that's gonna stop me?"

Claire wasn't waiting to find out. Crying, she threw the door open and bolted from the meeting room.

She ran, weeping, down the hall, people staring at her. Rounding a corner, she ran smack into Ian, nearly knocking him over.

"What the hell happened?" he asked. Holding her at arms' length, he took in her new look. "What have you done to yourself?"

"He tried to rape me!" Claire cried.

"Who? Where?"

"Quimby. Room four," she managed to get out.

"Call security," Ian yelled to anyone who could hear. He turned his attention back to Claire, guiding her toward an empty gurney in the hallway. "I'm gonna get him," he said.

"No, he's dangerous," Claire said.

"I don't want him hurting anyone else," Ian called back as he ran.

In seconds, he was at room 4, flinging the door open. But it was empty. He hurried back to Claire.

"Did you find him?" she asked.

"No. He's gone."

Ian pulled out his cell phone, began tapping in the numbers.

"Who are you calling?" Claire asked.

But Ian spoke only into the phone. "Dr. Curtin? It's Ian Bigelow. . . ."

Claire looked up at Ian sharply, tears in her eyes. "No, please don't."

"No, sir, but we have a situation here with Dr. Waters. . . . Yes, she's here."

Ian held out the phone to her. Claire shot him daggers, took it.

"Hello . . . Mr. Quimby. He tried to attack me. . . . Yes, sir, I'll wait."

"Is Curtin on his way?" asked Ian.

She nodded, then closed the phone. "Are you trying to get me kicked out of here?"

"Claire, you're not thinking. I had to call him," Ian said. Then he pointed to her hair. "Did you do that . . . for Quimby?"

Claire started to cry. "I screwed up, Ian. I really screwed up."

Ian sat on the edge of the gurney, took her in his arms. "It's okay, Claire. It'll be okay."

CHAPTER 6

Claire, still shaking, sat on a comfortable sofa in Curtin's office as he poured vodka into a glass. Though alcohol was forbidden in the hospital, he kept a bottle locked away for incidents like this.

"Security says Mr. Quimby made it out of the hospital—they were unable to stop him," he said.

But Claire was too traumatized to respond.

"I can prescribe some Ativan," Curtin said gently as he handed the drink to her.

"No, this is fine." Claire downed it. "Thank you," she said when she was done.

"You're welcome, Doctor," Curtin said. "Now can you please tell me what the hell you were doing?"

"What you told me to do," Claire answered, not up to being interrogated. Or maybe it was the alcohol, which had gone straight to her head, that was talking.

"I didn't tell you to color your hair and dress like a tramp," Curtin replied.

"I was thinking outside the box. Playing a role."

"Of a cheap hooker?"

Claire looked Curtin straight in the eye. "Yes, just like the woman Quimby murdered this morning."

Curtin's demeanor shifted immediately from consternation to alarm. Nothing threatened the success of his fellowship program more than releasing a patient who then went on to commit a violent crime.

"You don't mean the one in Times Square, do you?" he asked. "The one I saw on the news?"

"Yes," Claire answered. "Times Square."

"And you're sure Mr. Quimby is responsible?"

Claire recounted how Quimby had called her and described the hooker he picked up in the Theatre District. How she matched the description of Catherine Mills, the prostitute who was found dead that morning. How she, Claire, had decided to confront Quimby to get him to confess and thought changing her appearance would set him off. "You know the rest," she finished.

Curtin thought back to the other day when he had publicly berated Claire. *Maybe I misjudged her,* he realized.

"You should have come to me," he said, knowing that was the last thing Claire would have done.

"I wanted to show you I was more than just a lab rat."

"You passed with flying colors," Curtin replied with a new warmth. "This work can be extremely rewarding. But it can also be extremely dangerous." He paused. "I should have made clear that I'm here for all of you to consult me in situations like this."

The backhanded apology seemed genuine, so Claire decided to let him off the hook. "No, you were right," she told Curtin. "I finally got Quimby to crack because I listened to you."

Claire looked down, not wanting to take the discussion any further. The silence between them seemed interminable. "Claire," Curtin said uncomfortably. "Listen to me. I wouldn't risk my life for any of these patients. So the last thing I would expect is for any student of mine to risk theirs."

Claire looked at him. He actually meant it. But that didn't change what had happened. "Quimby is out there somewhere. And he's dangerous. What should we do?"

"You need to tell the police," Curtin replied immediately. "If this man is going around killing people, it's our obligation to warn them he may strike again."

"What if I'm wrong? What if this is just some terrible coincidence?" Claire asked. "I can't break confidentiality unless I'm absolutely sure."

"Confidentiality doesn't protect a patient from assaulting his therapist," Curtin said. "Quimby attacked you. He committed a crime. That's more than enough reason to go to the police."

Claire was unfamiliar with the New York Police Department. "Do I just go to our local station?" she asked.

"No," Curtin said. "Manhattan South Homicide will be handling the murder in Times Square. I'll call Lieutenant Brian Wilkes and tell him you're coming over. He runs the unit and we're old friends."

It was well into Sunday afternoon by the time Wilkes returned with Nick to the ratty precinct that housed Manhattan South Homicide. Having been up all night running from the Coney Island murder to the dead body near Times Square, Wilkes was ready to drop from lack of sleep. For Nick, the entire experience had been a massive adrenaline rush. Though he kept it to himself, Nick was happy for the first time in more than a year. He was out avenging murder victims, which he believed was doing God's work. He was back in the game.

But the rush faded the moment he entered the precinct. He always felt clammy there—summer or winter. The gray-blue paint was peeling off the water-stained walls, and the old maple chairs and desks felt sticky. As he walked past the front desk, he saw the suspicious looks, the enmity from cops who just a year ago would've slapped him on the back or traded jabs and jokes with him. Now they steered clear, but Nick could still feel their burning glares. As he and Wilkes headed up the stairs, Nick realized that in their minds he was still guilty.

"Give 'em time, Nicky. They'll come around," Wilkes said to him.

Nick could muster only a nod, though he wasn't sure he believed they would ever come around.

They were on the second floor of the building now, approaching the squad room. All Nick could think about was how his colleagues would receive him. He'd cut off contact with them nearly a year ago, sacrificing his friendships so the stench from his troubles wouldn't waft onto them.

Wilkes stopped at the door to the squad room, then exhaustedly gestured to Nick to open it. "Beauty before age," he quipped.

Nick dreaded going in. The desks were inches apart, and the overhead fluorescent lights were too bright. There was no place to get away from the judgmental stares of the other detectives.

Nick breathed in as he opened the door . . . and was blinded by a brilliant flash of light. He could only hear hearty voices shout, "Surprise!"

He must have made a face, because somebody said, "Hey, don't be so glad to see us."

"I can't see a goddamned thing," Nick said.

But as the words came out, his vision returned. His colleagues, huge smiles on their faces, stood in front of him. Detective Tony Savarese, bald and wiry, wearing his usual blue blazer and red-and-blue-striped tie, held the digital Nikon the detectives used to photograph homicide scenes. A badly handwritten banner with the words WELCOME BACK, NICKY hung by paper clips and crime scene tape from the ceiling behind them. A spread of bagels, cream cheeses, and a cake amateurishly decorated with frosting handcuffs awaited on a nearby desk.

"Bagels? I'm gone seven months and that's what I get?"

Savarese gestured to Wilkes. "The Lou told us only an hour ago. I had to put the cuffs on the cake myself. What the hell you expect on short notice, caviar?"

"A little nova would've been nice, you cheapskate," Nick shot back, to which Savarese responded by throwing his arms around Nick in a bear hug.

"About time those rat bastards downtown cleared you, Nicky," he said into Nick's ear. Savarese was the senior detective among the group and had always believed in Nick's innocence.

"Now maybe we'll get some work done around here," said Detective Kieran O'Brien, next in the reception line, welcoming Nick with a vise-grip handshake.

Sidney Potts, a veteran black detective, embraced him next. "Hear you and the kids moved in with Moms," he said. "How's that working out?"

"Like I died and went to hell," replied Nick.

"Hell is bringing some babe back to your place and having to ask Mommy for permission," O'Brien said, giving Nick a pat on the back.

This one stung Nick, but he showed none of it. As he shook hands with the others, his eyes landed on a well-dressed detective who'd returned to his desk soon after the surprise was sprung. He wore a dark-blue shirt, matching tie. A three-quarter-length leather coat hung over the back of his chair. There was a sharpness to his handsome features. His dark blond hair was combed too neatly, and his tanned face looked as if the skin was stretched too tight.

"Who's the fresh meat?" Nick asked Wilkes.

Wilkes guided Nick over to the serious young man. "Our replacement for your ex-partner Frankie. Came over from Special Victims when Frankie got transferred. Nick Lawler, meet Tommy Wessel. He's gonna be working with you."

"Good to meet you finally," Wessel said with a thick Brooklyn accent as he and Nick shook hands. "I know I got big shoes to fill."

"You already filled Frankie's shoes, kid. You showed up," Savarese quipped.

But Nick's attention was on Wessel's desk and the file atop it.

"You pulled the St. Jude murder," Nick said to Wessel, referring to the case Nick investigated last year that resembled the Coney Island and Times Square murders.

"Looked at the scene, read all the reports," Wessel replied. "I'm up to speed."

Nick glanced back over to Wessel's desk, which faced his own. The crime scene photos from St. Jude's indeed sat there. He gave Wessel a nod to show he was impressed. *Maybe the kid'll actually contribute something,* he thought.

"C'mon, Nicky," Potts shouted, spreading cream cheese on a bagel. "Have some chow."

"In a minute," Nick called back.

As the other detectives helped themselves to the food, Nick picked up the crime scene photos from Wessel's desk and studied the first one. The eighteen-year-old blonde was found in a Dumpster behind one of the carnival trucks. A length of dollar-store electrical cord wrapped tightly around her neck and tied in a simple square knot was the cause of death. The duct tape Nick remembered was also in place over her eyelids.

Her name was Elizabeth Masterson. Nobody at the carnival in the St. Jude's churchyard could recall seeing the strikingly beautiful Lizzie on any rides or at any concessions. The few people who remembered seeing her said she was there alone. Because she lived two blocks away on Riverside Drive, the theory was she had cut through the churchyard on her way home that night, and the perp chose her at random.

At the time of her death, Lizzie had just graduated with honors from an exclusive private high school and was to attend Dartmouth that fall. Instead, she now rested in a private cemetery outside the city. Until her untimely death, Elizabeth never had been in any trouble. The worst thing she did that anyone could remember was smoke pot. Once.

In the mind of a homicide cop, this made Lizzie Masterson the purest, least deserving, most innocent species of murder victim— and the most interesting to the carnivorous New York City media beast that had slathered their pages for weeks with her graduation photo along with lurid, leaked shots of the crime scene.

It had been a frustrating, high-profile investigation with too much press attention, during which the chief of detectives' hot, cigar-reeking breath bore down on the back of Nick's neck. But any leads that showed even the slightest promise quickly crashed into a succession of brick walls, and after two months of eighteen-hour days and zero answers, Lizzie's file had found its way back into the file cabinet, destined for the oblivion of cold-case status. Unless something magically turned up.

Like another victim or two done in by the same dirtbag.

That was Nick's worst nightmare: catching a fresh homicide done by the stone killer he should have collared a year ago. But Nick could hardly hold himself responsible for the new murders. He had fought tooth and nail to keep the Masterson file active. His efforts were cut short when he returned from bereavement leave following the sudden, tragic death of his wife, only to be summarily stripped of his gun and shield and transferred to Central Booking where he'd expected he would be left to rot, much like Lizzie herself.

Until now.

As he examined the Masterson photos, Nick realized what bothered him was how Lizzie's case was different from the recent murders. He laid two photos side by side on his desk. One was a blowup of the square knot tied directly over Lizzie's trachea; the other was a fresh photo of the thick rope and strange knot looped around the neck of the Coney Island victim, who still remained nameless.

"It's a Dutch marine bowline," came a voice from behind him. Nick turned. Wessel was looking over his shoulder.

"Excuse me?" Nick asked.

"The knot." Wessel gestured to the photo of Jane Doe. "It's called a Dutch marine bowline. Dutch Navy uses it."

Nick was starting to like this kid but had to give him the ritual ball-breaking. "And you know this because, what, you were in the Dutch Navy?"

"No, I looked it up on the Internet," Wessel replied, not sure if Nick was being serious.

"Wonder how we lived before the Internet," Nick said, meaning it, as Lieutenant Wilkes dropped some stapled pieces of paper on Nick's desk.

"ME just faxed over the autopsy report on your Jane Doe at Coney Island," he said, walking away.

Wessel stood by as Nick picked up the report and started reading. Wessel waited a moment, then walked back to his desk.

"You thinking this is the same perp as last year and he's evolving?" Nick asked him.

Wessel wondered if this was a test. "Could be," he answered. "Could also be three unrelated crimes . . ."

"I don't think so," Nick replied. "ME says there's a bruise resembling a hickey on Jane Doe's left breast."

Wessel looked down at the autopsy photos from last year's homicide.

"Same as on the girl from last year," he said, covering his surprise. "Anything else in there?"

"No fluids, even though she was raped," Nick replied. "And no cyanide in the tox report."

"Cyanide?"

"I smelled bitter almonds at the crime scene. Guess I was wrong . . ."

"Times Square murder . . . Her name is Catherine Mills," came a female voice from across the room. "I was told to ask for Lieutenant Wilkes."

Nick's head turned toward the voice just as Savarese pointed him out to Dr. Claire Waters. "Detective Lawler's handling that case," Savarese said to her.

"That's me," Nick shouted, crossing the room quickly at the sight of a woman who looked too much like his dead victims. He held out his hand. "Nick Lawler."

"Claire Waters," she replied, shaking hands with him.

"Why don't you come back to my desk, Ms. Waters. Did you know Ms. Mills?" he asked her as they walked.

"No," replied Claire, "but I may know the person who killed her."

"Please, have a seat," Nick said, indicating the chair beside his desk as he sat down.

Claire couldn't help but notice that Nick's desk was clean in contrast with the others, which were piled with frayed files and stacks of papers. "Did someone tell you he murdered Ms. Mills?"

"Not in so many words," Claire offered, relieved to get this off her chest. "He told me he paid her to have sex with him last night. In the Theatre District."

Nick was hopeful. This was good information, if it was accurate. "Not to be rude, but why would he confess that to you?"

"I'm sorry. I should have told you," Claire said. "I'm his doctor."

Nick was thrown. "If I murdered someone, I wouldn't confess to my doctor."

"I'm really sorry, but I had a bad morning," Claire said. "I'm a psychiatrist."

The word *psychiatrist* set Nick off. "You're a shrink and he's one of your patients," he said with open hostility.

Claire didn't know what to make of this, but it came pouring out of her like a flash flood. "He called me in the middle of the night, and I met him in the emergency room at Manhattan City Hospital. He told me he'd done something bad. He described Ms. Mills perfectly. When I got home this morning, I saw a photo of her on the news. Then I made myself look like your victim and went back and confronted him, and . . ."

Claire was showing all the signs of having been victimized herself. But Nick felt only anger toward her. "And?" he asked.

"And . . . he freaked out."

"Freaked out," Nick uttered in disgust. "Is that what shrinks call it?"

Claire couldn't understand why this cop was being so nasty. "I was scared. He tried to kill me."

"Thanks. Why don't you go downstairs and see the desk sergeant. He'll have someone take a report."

Now Claire was getting angry. "Don't you believe me?"

"Sure I do, lady, but I have two dead bodies I need to investigate," Nick said.

"Look, Detective, I know when I'm being blown off. You have a madman out there, and I know a lot about him—"

"And I'm telling you to take your story downstairs," Nick interrupted.

"Do you have a problem with me?"

"And everyone like you," snapped Nick. "I don't like shrinks."

Claire glared at him. "Not to be rude, Detective, but people who don't like shrinks are often the ones who need us the most."

By now everyone in the room was looking at them.

"Nice talking to you, Doctor," Nick muttered as he pretended to bury his head in the file. Claire shot daggers at him. Finally, she stood and walked away—but stopped when she got to the door and turned back.

"His name is Todd Quimby," Claire shouted across the room. Then she walked out.

Nick looked up from the file. Wessel was staring at him.

"You got a problem too?" Nick asked him.

"Nope, no problem," Wessel answered, turning away to look at some papers.

Nick glanced over at the empty doorway. "Damned shrinks think they know everything."

CHAPTER 7

Two cops dragged a wino past Claire, who was still fuming as she sat in a cramped cubby with an officer whose nameplate identified him as Kaplan. He couldn't have been older than twenty-two, and his crisp uniform looked brand-new. Claire was growing frustrated as he muddled his way through the police report.

"And where did you say this happened, ma'am?"

"At Manhattan City Hospital."

It seemed to take the young cop minutes just to write down this simple piece of information. "Didn't Dr. Paul Curtin call and give you all this?" Claire asked impatiently.

"We need to speak to the witness, ma'am. And the man who attacked you, what's his name?"

"Todd Quimby."

"Can you spell Quimby?"

This was more than Claire could bear. "How much longer is this going to take?"

Officer Kaplan gave her a rueful look. "I'm sorry, Doctor Waters. I'm two days out of the academy, and I don't wanna screw this up."

Claire realized she was displacing her anger with Detective Lawler on this helpless kid. "No," she said, catching herself, "I'm the one who should be apologizing to you. I'm pissed off and it's not your fault."

Kaplan seemed relieved. "I promise, I'll have you outta here in the next ten minutes. Now, if you could just run me through what happened one more time . . ."

Claire sighed and began telling her story once again.

*   *   *

Upstairs in the squad room, Nick sat at his desk, still fuming. *Damn that shrink,* he thought, *coming in here and telling me my business.* And in the next moment, he was pissed at himself. He'd lost control. His words to Claire had shot out of his mouth before he could stop them. Nick started to worry. Shrink or not, it wasn't every day someone walked in the door and handed you the answer to two, possibly three, murders.

That story of hers is crazy, he thought as he stared at the morgue photos of the three victims. *Playing dress-up to lure a patient into confessing. Who the hell does that? A shrink with more than a screw loose, that's who.*

"You okay, Detective?" Wessel asked, standing across from Nick's desk.

Nick looked up, blinking away the glare from his desk lamp. "Why the hell are you just standing there?" Nick lashed out.

Wessel seemed unsure of himself as he put a printout on Nick's desk. "Pulled the priors on Todd Quimby—the guy the shrink mentioned. Thought you'd want them."

He was waiting for Nick to explode. But Nick held back, knowing the kid was only doing the job he was paid to do. The job Nick knew he should be doing himself.

"Thanks, kid," Nick said, almost cracking a smile.

Wessel nodded in return. "Hey, can you do me a favor?"

"Like what?" Nick asked, eyeing Wessel. *What the hell does he want from me?* Nick wasn't interested in breaking in a new partner— or any partner, for that matter. He liked going solo. Made things a lot easier.

"I got eight years on the job. You said first names, right?"

Translation: Wessel disliked being called "kid." Nick got it.

"Tommy, right?"

"Thanks." Wessel nodded, still looking serious. "Mind if I ask you a question?"

"We're partners," Nick said, trying to clear the air. "Shoot."

"How come you don't like shrinks?"

Now Nick was pissed again. "Look, everybody knows what happened, so if you don't, you're either ignorant or you're patronizing me."

Wessel realized his mistake. "I'm sorry. I get it. What you went through would mess anybody up."

"I'm glad you understand. You're a nice kid, Tommy, and you're starting off like a champ. Don't screw it up with your mouth, okay?"

Wessel nodded and headed back to his desk, tail between his legs. Nick picked up the printout. The first sheet held Quimby's mug shot. He studied Quimby's face. Ordinary. A face you see everywhere—manning the counter at a 7-Eleven, working construction, or driving a delivery truck. Like millions of guys you never pay a moment's attention to. *He doesn't look like a sex offender. But what does a sex offender look like?*

Nick turned the page, perusing Quimby's history of arrests. Went to the next page, where two words immediately caught his eye:

Merchant marine.

Nick read further. Quimby had washed out of the Merchant Marine Academy on Long Island in the middle of his freshman year.

Long enough to learn how to tie maritime knots. Like a Dutch marine bowline.

Nick flipped through the pages of the printout. "Where the hell is it?" he said out loud.

"What are you looking for?" Wessel asked.

"When Quimby last did time. I got only his arrests," Nick replied, feeling the old adrenaline rush.

"I can tell you that," Wessel said. "He was in Rikers from September of last year till last week—"

Which sent Nick bolting from his desk and for the door.

"What is it?" Wessel called after him, catching up at the stairs.

"This prick Quimby went to jail after the St. Jude's murder last year and got out right before the Jane Doe at Coney Island. That's why there were no similar murders in between."

Claire stood in the street across from the precinct, trying to hail a cab. She was still angry. It was late afternoon on Sunday, and the July sun was so bright she had to squint to keep the burning glare out of her eyes. Everyone seemed to have fled the city to escape the heat except for two little girls who were jumping rope across the street. Claire watched them.

How long had it been?

The heat sent a vaporous haze around the girls as they jumped over and over until the one with blond hair tripped. The other girl stopped jumping and hugged her, as if to tell her that everything would be all right.

Why hadn't she stayed with Amy?

The sound of a car approaching made Claire turn away from the little girls. It was a cab, heading toward her with its OFF DUTY light on. She waved for the cabbie to stop.

He pulled over and rolled down the window. "Where you going?" the cabbie asked.

"Eighty-Eighth and West End," Claire answered.

"On my way to the barn. I'll take you," the cabbie replied.

"Thanks," Claire said as she got in. It was the first break she'd had all day, and all she wanted to do was go home and forget. Suddenly the door jerked open.

"Police. Stop," Nick said breathlessly to the cabbie, who threw the car into park.

"What do you want? You scared me," Claire exclaimed.

"Why'd you try to bait him?" Nick asked. "This Quimby guy."

"I thought you weren't interested," Claire answered as she got out of the cab to confront Nick.

"Look, I'm sorry about what I said upstairs. I should talk to Mr. Quimby."

"Oh, now you think I'm right?" Claire smirked.

"I don't need an argument from you, Doctor. . . ."

"Waters. Claire Waters."

"Right. Dr. Waters. I just need this Quimby's address. If you have it."

Claire eyed him. Then she pulled the file from her bag and opened it on the trunk of the taxi. Started to write on a piece of scrap paper.

"I should go with you," she said to Nick.

"No, you shouldn't," he returned.

"I know how to talk to him," Claire offered.

"If that were the case, you wouldn't be here right now, would you?" Nick said.

"What does that mean?"

"It means that next time you have a patient who you think is going to hurt somebody, stop trying to be Nancy Drew and leave the police work to the people who know how to do it."

Claire glared at him. "Next time I'll make sure I go to a detective with an open mind."

She all but flung the piece of paper at Nick. "Quimby moved in with his grandmother," she said as she got back into the cab and slammed the door.

As the cab took off, she couldn't help but glance back at Nick Lawler, whose figure shrunk in the rear window until the taxi turned the corner and he vanished.

CHAPTER 8

The sun was setting by the time Claire dragged herself into the apartment, letting the heavy, prewar door slam shut with a bang. She dropped her bag on the parquet wood floor, not caring where it landed, and collapsed onto the overstuffed sofa. Claire had bought their furniture, upholstered in muted beiges and comforting sky blues, on special weekend trips with Ian to Duchess County. Every month, they would stay at a different small B and B and hunt for bargains, each item reminding Claire of a wonderful time spent together. She knew that someday she would leave her fellowship in DC and move in with Ian, and she wanted the apartment to be a respite from her patients' psychic traumas.

"You okay?" came Ian's voice from the bedroom.

She didn't answer. *He'll come out to check on me. He always does.*

Which, in the next instant, was exactly what Ian did. He wore a light blue T-shirt and black gym shorts, and planted himself on the rug next to her. Claire looked down at him and smiled. He looked so calm sitting on a pattern of azure waves. He gently took her hand in his.

"You've had a helluva day," he said, stating the obvious.

Claire just nodded and closed her eyes. There was a long silence between them, which Ian finally broke. "Everybody's asking me what happened," he said.

"I don't want to talk about it," Claire managed.

Ian nodded, understanding. "Can I get you anything?"

"I'm good, thanks," Claire replied.

But as she heard him stand, she cracked her eyelids just enough to watch him walk into the kitchen. On any other day, this view of him might have aroused her. Tonight, however, the thought of having sex made her think of Quimby and what he'd done to those women.

Though it had always been good with Ian. They met during their psych residency at Harvard's prestigious Massachusetts General. Claire was encouraged to apply there and was all but assured of a spot. Ian, a strong, but not stellar, medical student from Stanford, had no such guarantees but matched nonetheless. They circled each other for the better part of their four-year stint, their mutual attraction palpable. The only thing holding them back was Claire's desire to keep things professional between them. Until, as their time together wound down, Claire stopped fighting Ian off and gave in to his shameless advances. He had clearly fallen in love with her. And she realized she was in love with him. She was strongly attracted to him, and the sex was the best she'd ever had in her limited experience with men. He knew how to make her relax—he'd give her a crooked smile, rub her neck, or run his fingers through her hair. And the tension that was always there somewhere deep inside her would drain away, at least for a few short, peaceful moments.

They lived apart while Claire completed her fellowship at the NIH in DC, since Ian had joined the psychiatry house staff at New York's Bellevue Hospital, one of the busiest in the nation. Claire's fellowship provided her with a reasonably normal work schedule, so she was the one who traveled to Manhattan on weekends. Depending on whether Ian was on call, these trips often amounted to little more than conjugal visits. But Claire needed to connect with him physically, as if to be recharged for the nights she spent alone with dreams of Amy being swallowed up by the earth or sucked into a whirling eddy, calling out for Claire to save her.

Their simultaneous acceptance into Curtin's fellowship program was a happy accident. Ian applied after just one year of city hospital insanity and was deferred until the following year. Claire never told him that Curtin approached her to apply, wanting her decision to be a surprise. She showed up the week before the fellowship began with all her suitcases and boxes of her belongings jammed into the

SUV she rented. The pleasured shock on his face when he entered the room was worth all the pains she had taken to keep her enrollment in the program a secret. She closed her eyes now, remembering that first night when they made love almost until sunrise.

That had been only ten days ago. Claire felt as though she'd lived a year since then, the emotional trauma of the last twenty-four hours having drained her so thoroughly as to numb her. And all she wanted now was to stay that way.

What happened next shocked her. Out of nowhere, she started to cry, her eyelids unable to block the tears from escaping. She caught herself before the sobs came, but not before Ian heard her and came rushing over.

"What's wrong?" he asked, concern written on his face.

"I don't know," Claire answered back, not understanding. How could she not know why she was crying?

"I've never seen you like this before," Ian said, handing her a tissue.

Claire wiped her still-closed eyes. "What's happening to me?" she asked Ian.

"You're feeling," Ian answered instantly.

"I don't want to feel," Claire replied. "Anything."

But she could feel him. Smell him. She allowed her eyes to open, revealing Ian kneeling beside her. Looking at her strangely. And then Claire, almost horrified, realized what that look was. She brushed away a lick of her now-short hair.

"You don't like it?" she asked.

"N-no . . . of course I do . . . ," he stuttered, sounding almost ashamed.

She saw his erection through his gym shorts. What happened next shocked Claire more than her crying.

She sprang off the couch like a lioness attacking her prey, grabbed Ian's head between her hands, and kissed him as hard as she could. As if this kiss, this electrifying force between them, could somehow erase everything that had happened to her.

They kissed wildly, frantically, for only seconds before images of dark clouds moved behind her lidded eyes.

"I want you," Claire said breathlessly. "Now."

He took her hands and the clouds disappeared as he led her toward the bedroom. As they passed a mirror on the living room wall, they saw their reflection.

"You're beautiful, Claire," Ian said.

"I'm not Claire," she said, staring at the sensual blonde in the mirror.

"Yes, you are Claire, and I love you," Ian answered. "Nothing you do can ever change that."

As they reached the bedroom door, Claire stuck out her hand to prevent them from entering. She was someone else for a moment, someone without a past. Only the present with a man whose love would save her.

"No," Claire managed. "The terrace."

Ian could barely hold back as she pulled him to the sliding glass door. A blast of warm air hit them as Claire slid the door open and they stepped onto the terrace. She turned to face Ian, grabbing the safety rail to steady herself. Ian gripped her from underneath and held her against him.

Claire lifted herself up and leaned her head back over the railing, her neck stretched to the limit. Her view of the nighttime city lights upside down made her dizzy.

Is this what autoerotic asphyxiation feels like?

"Oh my God," she cried.

"Yeah, baby, come on," Ian encouraged her.

And she did, letting out a moan so intense it shattered everything inside her, releasing all the pain stored up for all these years. And for a moment, she felt completely free, focused only on Ian holding her.

Then suddenly, just as she felt his spasms, a wave of terror came over Claire. The lights of the city spun around her. She could feel herself losing control, as if she were about to fall eighteen floors to the sidewalk and certain death. She pushed him away and ran back inside.

"I thought you wanted me," said Ian, following her. Claire grabbed her robe and tossed Ian his.

"I do," Claire said. "But I'm afraid . . ."

"Nothing's going to happen to you. I promise," he said softly. He reached out for her, and she accepted his embrace, but her mind was spinning.

Claire began to analyze her reaction chemically. She was low on serotonin after her stressful day. She craved the endorphin rush of her orgasm, which shut her emotions right down and turned on her amygdala, pumping adrenaline right into her system and causing panic.

For ten minutes, animal instincts had taken over. Now she was in control. She was herself again.

CHAPTER 9

The angry clamor of construction equipment met Nick and Wessel as they exited their beat-up, unmarked Impala. It was eight the next morning, Monday, and the night had passed without news of another murder.

"I half expected you to call and say Quimby was at it again," Wessel said, trying to make conversation.

"Asshole probably didn't want to wreck your Sunday dinner," Nick answered, trying to keep things friendly between them.

"Another murder would've PO'd my wife for sure," Wessel agreed. "One thing she hates is messing up Sunday dinner. Says it's family time. Have to put family first."

"You got kids?" Nick asked.

"A boy three, a girl two, and one on the way," Wessel replied with a grin, the first one Nick had seen.

"Damn, Tommy," he said. "You've been busy."

They headed up the street. "I got two myself," Nick said, wanting to brag. But he held himself back from telling Wessel any more.

They reached the address Claire had given them, an eight-story apartment building between Amsterdam and Broadway on 78th. The construction din came from the vacant lot next door where new condos were going up.

"Always loved this part of town," Wessel said with a frown, looking around.

"Where you from?" asked Nick.

"Westchester. Grew up in Scarsdale."

"Scarsdale? And your parents let you become a cop?"

"Nope, but I thought it would be more exciting than being a lawyer," Wessel quipped as they entered the vestibule.

Nick glanced at the piece of paper Claire had given him. He saw for the first time that she'd written her cell phone number at the bottom.

"Got it. Apartment One-B," Wessel said, reading over Nick's shoulder, his hand about to push the buzzer when Nick yanked it away just in time.

"What the hell was that for?" Wessel demanded.

"If Quimby's inside, why let him know we're here?" Nick answered, gesturing to a middle-aged woman about to exit through the security door. As she passed them, Nick and Wessel stepped through into the lobby.

The woman caught the door before it closed. "Just a minute. You two don't live here."

Wessel pulled his shield. "Police," he said. The woman seemed satisfied. She nodded and left.

As they headed down the first-floor hallway, Nick took stock of the building. About sixty years old, he figured, probably built just after World War II, and had seen better days. The chipping paint and aging water stains on the ceiling were a sure sign the landlord was trying to force out his longtime tenants so he could convert their rent-controlled apartments into more profitable condos.

"This is it," Wessel said as they reached the door to apartment 1B. A small paper tag just below the ancient peephole identified the occupant of the apartment as F. Quimby in what appeared to be the scrawl of an elderly woman.

The detectives positioned themselves on either side of the opening—you never knew what was behind a door—and Nick knocked.

"Who's there?" came a female voice from inside the apartment.

"Police. Mrs. Quimby?"

"I don't see anyone," said the voice, obviously referring to the peephole. "Show me some identification."

Nick held his shield in front of the peephole.

"You could've bought that badge," said the voice. "I want something with a picture."

Nick and Wessel exchanged bemused looks. Mrs. Quimby was either on the ball or breaking theirs.

Nick held his ID up to the peephole. One unlatched safety chain and two dead bolts later, the door opened, revealing Florence Quimby. She looked to be in her late seventies. Her undone white hair, housedress, and testy attitude made it clear she didn't expect visitors and didn't want any. Especially cops.

"What is it?" she demanded.

Nick's nostrils were suddenly violated by the stench of stale tobacco, no doubt the result of decades of nicotine buildup in the apartment. "I'm Detective Lawler and this is Detective Wessel. Is your grandson Todd home?"

"What do you people want with Todd now?" Florence asked.

"We just need to talk to him, ma'am," said Wessel.

"Yeah, right," said Florence. "Last cops who said that took my Toddy away and I didn't see him for a year."

"Is he here now?" asked Wessel.

"No, and he hasn't been for a couple of days," answered Florence.

Nick and Wessel looked at each other. "Any idea where he might be?" Nick asked.

"He doesn't tell me where he disappears to," Florence replied, sounding frustrated. "Are you here to take him back to jail?"

"May we come in?" asked Wessel.

"Unless you have a warrant, the answer's no."

Nick peered into the apartment, in which time appeared to have stopped somewhere around 1972. The garish wallpaper was peeling, Formica furniture looked beaten to an inch of its life, and the rust-colored shag carpeting was so peppered with worn spots the padding underneath was exposed.

"Toddy's not a bad boy," Florence said to them. "Why don't you just leave him alone?"

Wessel looked past her into the apartment. "All right if I have a drink?" he asked.

"I got water. I can bring it to you."

"I'd rather have a beer if that's okay."

Nick shot him a look.

"I don't keep beer in the house."

"Then whose bottle of Pabst is that?" Wessel demanded.

He gestured to the coffee table in the living room. The bottle was nearly full, its outside covered with condensation as if someone had just taken it from the refrigerator. Florence turned and looked. A panicked expression appeared on her face.

"I don't know where that came from."

And then the detectives heard it—the unmistakable creaking of an old, beat-up wooden window opening.

"I'll take the back," Wessel said, running out as Nick shoved Florence aside, pulled his gun, and dashed into the apartment.

"You can't go in there!" Florence shouted after him as he ran down the hallway.

But Nick already had the bedroom door open. Across the room, a faded yellow curtain flapped in the breeze. He ran to the window just in time to see Todd Quimby sprinting through the construction site next door. As quickly as he could, Nick climbed through the window, jumped without hesitation to the dirt below, and tumbled to the ground.

He got up and dove for cover just as a steel girder hanging from a crane came within inches of snapping off his head. Nick saw the workers in hard hats yelling at him, the noise drowning out their voices but their lips clearly warning him to get the hell out of the way before he got himself killed.

And then, three sharp blasts from a whistle nearly blew Nick's eardrums out. As if an invisible hand had descended from above and switched off the power, every piece of heavy machinery went silent; every worker froze in place. The only thing moving was Todd Quimby, and Nick could see he had a huge head start.

He scrambled to his feet and ran as fast as he could. But Quimby was already running through the open chain-link gate onto the street.

It took Nick about fifteen seconds to cover the same ground and reach the sidewalk. He looked around. There was no sign of Quimby or Wessel, and no place for them to have disappeared.

Except for the subway entrance at the corner of Broadway.

He sprinted down the block and down the stairs into the abyss. Almost immediately, his vision blurred, struggling to adjust from the bright sun to the dim lights of the station. Nick flashed his shield at the token booth clerk as he jumped the turnstile onto the southbound platform. The waiting passengers were all looking south for a train that would come from the north.

"What's going on?" Nick asked the gathering crowd.

"Cop chased some guy onto the tracks," said a bystander, pointing.

Nick ran to the southernmost end of the platform and was about to descend the short flight of stairs onto the tracks when he stopped short.

What the hell am I doing? I can't see a damn thing.

He had no choice. His partner was somewhere in that darkness.

Nick plunged forward into the tunnel. The sudden blackness once again blurred his vision, as if he were looking through filtered glass. He was virtually blind, his only frame of reference being a couple of bare lightbulbs on one wall and a red signal maybe two dozen yards ahead. Or was it closer?

Nick forged on, carefully navigating the center of the tracks to avoid electrocuting himself on the third rail.

And then he saw something move. *Is that a person?*

He ran, stumbling toward the figure. He could hear the rumble of an approaching train but couldn't tell from which direction it was coming. And then he saw the beam of the train's headlight on the northbound track beside him. It boomed past, so close he could see the passengers looking through the windows at him. Just as quickly, the train was gone, but for some reason the noise wasn't fading away.

Then he saw the light bathing him. He turned to face the certain death that would roar over him in seconds.

Suddenly, something propelled him across the tunnel onto the empty northbound tracks. He fell between the northbound rails, pulling himself up just in time to see the train that would have killed him fly past.

When it was gone, he could just make out a figure slumped beside him.

Nick hurried across the tunnel. Saw the blood on what he knew was his partner's suit. And he realized.

Tommy Wessel had pushed him out of harm's way and in doing so, had been clipped by the train.

Frantically, he knelt beside Wessel, who was fighting for every breath.

"Hold on," he screamed at Wessel. "Don't you go out on me."

This kid saved my miserable life, while that scumbag Quimby's out there, looking for someone else to kill.

He heard footsteps. Saw the beam of a flashlight.

"Police!" yelled the figure. "Are you okay?"

It was a Transit Bureau cop, no doubt sent into the tunnel by the same passengers who'd directed Nick down here.

"I got a cop down," Nick screamed at him. "Call a bus! Goddamn it, call a freakin' bus!"

As Nick looked down at the young man who had been his partner for all of twenty-four hours, he knew whatever happened to Tommy Wessel was on him.

CHAPTER 10

Police vehicles clogged the street outside Manhattan City Hospital's emergency entrance as Tony Savarese, sweating from the heat in his ever-present blue blazer, squeezed the Impala into the only spot left at the curb, beside a fire hydrant. Nick, riding shotgun, barely noticed. All he could see was Tommy Wessel lying near death on the train tracks.

The troops had arrived at the subway station within minutes, the paramedics whisking Wessel off to the hospital while at least fifty cops and detectives searched the shut-down subway tunnel for any sign of Todd Quimby. But he had vanished, probably through an emergency exit. Savarese determined that Nick was in no mental shape to take part in the search and, after debriefing him on the subway platform, drove him to be with his short-time partner.

"We're here, Nicky," Savarese said, bringing Nick back to the present.

As he exited the car, the precinct numbers on the police cruisers he passed told the story: Cops, from the lowest rookie to chiefs with stars on their shoulders, from around the corner to the farthest reaches of Queens and Staten Island, were pouring into the ER to show support and give blood. Nick himself had participated in the ritual for many a fallen cop more times than he cared to remember. But never before was the downed officer his partner.

Now, as Savarese escorted him through the double doors into the waiting room, Nick saw the dozens of cops praying, talking, crying. All turned silent as they became aware of Nick's presence. The media attention he'd gotten eight months earlier ensured that every cop in the city—and most of its citizens—knew his face. As he passed through the throng of his brethren, Nick couldn't help but notice their solemn expressions. Were they looking at him with sorrow and sympathy? Or were they thinking that once again Nick Lawler screwed up?

The sound of quiet sobbing rattled Nick, which Savarese couldn't help but notice. He wiped his bald, sweaty head with a handkerchief and led Nick through another door into a treatment area. A few feet ahead, Lieutenant Wilkes was doing his best to console Debby Wessel, a pretty, obviously pregnant, twenty-five-year-old brunette. She and Wilkes were looking through a glass window into a room where a team of doctors and nurses worked on her husband. Nick's eyes returned to Debby. *She's way too young to have to face this,* he thought.

"You can't be in here," came a voice from behind them. It was a doctor, the credentials hanging from his neck identifying him as Gavin Lester, chief of emergency medicine.

"Police, Doc," said Savarese. He pointed to Nick. "He's Detective Wessel's partner."

"Are you taking care of him?" Nick asked.

"Yes, I am," Lester replied. "We're trying to stabilize him for surgery."

"Will he make it?" Nick managed, afraid to hear the answer.

"If we can get the brain swelling down, he stands a chance."

Nick let out a breath.

"But that's the good news," Lester said, as if he'd said the same words too many times before. "His right fibula and tibia are shattered."

"Which means what, Doc?" Nick asked, hoping it wasn't what he thought.

"We'll pin his leg back together, but he'll never be the same."

His days as a cop are over, Nick thought.

"Thanks, Doc," was the only reply Nick could manage.

Lieutenant Wilkes now looked in their direction. Nick could see him whisper to Wessel's wife that he needed a moment. He walked the few feet over to them, all business.

"What'd the doc say?" asked Wilkes.

"Just that they're trying to get him up to surgery," said Savarese.

"I need you back at the scene," Wilkes told Savarese, gesturing over to Debby. "She's a mess and nobody's been able to reach Tommy's parents, so I have to stay here."

"On my way, Boss," Savarese said, looking at Nick.

"I'm okay," Nick said, reading the look. "I'll get myself home."

Savarese nodded, then headed off. Wilkes glanced over toward Debby.

"You want me to introduce you?"

It was the last thing Nick wanted. "I don't think I'm up to it," he said.

"You been looked at yet?" he asked Nick.

"I'm not hurt, Lou," Nick said.

"Have the doc check you out anyway," Wilkes ordered. "Then go home, shower up, and get back to the office. I want to know every place this guy Quimby could be hiding. And we finally got hold of Catherine Mills's parents. They live somewhere in the middle of Nowhere, Ohio, and they're driving into town, should be here by to-morrow morning—"

"I'm taking tomorrow off," Nick said, cutting him off, the words out before he even realized he'd uttered them.

Wilkes cracked his crooked jack-o'-lantern smile. "Now's not the time for comedy, Nicky."

"It's not a joke. I won't be in tomorrow."

Nick's boss gave him a long look. "Really?" retorted Wilkes. "We got a nut job running around town murdering blond women and burning their eyes out—one who almost put your partner in the ground—and you're taking a day off?"

"I need a personal day," Nick said simply. "If you got a problem with that, send me back to Central Booking."

Wilkes read the expression on Nick's face. "Look, Nicky," he began, "if all this is too much for you and you're not ready—"

"I didn't say I couldn't handle it," Nick interrupted. "I just need a day. Is that too much to ask?"

Wilkes remembered what Nick had been through the past year. "If it means that much to you, I'll cover your ass myself."

"Thanks, Boss," Nick said.

"Don't 'thanks, Boss' me, Nicky. I already stuck my balls in the paper shredder getting you your job back," Wilkes chastised him. "You won't make me look like a schmuck, will you?"

"I won't, Lou. I promise."

And as he walked out, Nick hoped he could live up to that promise.

Twenty hours later on Tuesday afternoon, Nick Lawler was on the southbound platform of Boston's Back Bay railroad station, having just gotten off an Acela Express train from New York.

He was tired, more exhausted than he could remember. Yet he knew now that he was right to make this trip. Still, his sense of duty and guilt over taking the day off at such a critical time had overcome Nick long before he reached Boston.

Nick's cell phone rang. It was Lieutenant Wilkes.

"You resting up, Nicky?" Wilkes asked with a forced friendliness.

"Yeah, Lou, I'm just hanging out at home," Nick replied, trying to sound nonchalant.

"I got good news. Your partner's up and yacking a mile a minute. Blames himself for going into the subway tunnel without backup." Wilkes waited for a response from Nick, but none came. "He's going to retire on three-quarters pay. Says he got hurt because he screwed up and lost Quimby."

He saved my life. He didn't screw up. I did, Nick thought. "I got to go, Lou. Someone's at the door. See you tomorrow."

Nick clicked off. He had someplace to go and he was late.

The light from Dr. Mangone's ophthalmoscope bore into Nick's eyes, so bright that it hurt.

"Is it getting worse?" Nick asked.

"I'm afraid so," said Dr. Mangone, peering through the large machine deep into the dark pupils of Nick's gray-blue eyes.

"How much longer?"

"A year. Maybe a little more if you're lucky," said the doctor in his thick Boston accent. "You're not driving at night, are you?"

"No," Nick lied.

Dr. Mangone looked him over. "I have to ask you a question, Mr. Barton. Who are you hiding your condition from?"

Mr. Barton. He could never get used to the doctor calling him that.

Nick first noticed something was wrong five years ago when, late one night at home, he tripped down a flight of stairs. He shrugged it off as being tired, but when he hit a parked car the next week, he got scared. It was dark and the car suddenly appeared out of nowhere. Nick made an appointment with an eye specialist who worked with the NYPD, thinking maybe he needed glasses.

But before he went in for his exam, he looked his symptoms up on the Internet: night blindness and loss of peripheral vision—these were signs of retinitis pigmentosa, an incurable disease that ended in blindness. If that's what Nick had, his police career would be over the instant he was diagnosed. He couldn't take the chance, so he'd canceled his appointment with the police department doctor and sought out Dr. Mangone, an expert in treating RP. He practiced in Boston, far enough away that no one would find out. Mangone had quickly confirmed Nick's self-diagnosis.

But now, Nick couldn't even think of an appropriate way to answer the doctor's question. He was hiding his condition from his boss, his friends, from everyone, including himself. Instead of lying, he said nothing. Dr. Mangone got up and pushed the ophthalmoscope out of the way. Nick sat back, moving his chin off the chinrest.

"Look," the doctor began, "what you do with your life is none of my business until it either affects your condition or puts you or others in danger." He shook his head. "I almost want to ask you your real name."

Nick was glad Dr. Mangone cared enough to be interested in him and the effect this insidious disease would have on his life.

"You pay me in cash, no insurance," he continued. "Your address is a post office box. And I don't know a lot of accountants who carry guns."

Nick looked down at his leg. The bottom of the ankle holster was just sticking out from the cuff of his pants. *Christ.*

"It's complicated, Doc," he said.

Dr. Mangone sighed. "You're not gonna tell me, are you."

"I can't," said Nick.

"Then listen to me. Carefully. There's no way you can clearly see what you're aiming at—especially at night. If you find yourself having to shoot someone, there's a better than average chance you will hit the wrong person."

If you only knew, Doc.

*   *   *

Nick stared out the train window into the dark night as the Acela raced back to New York. The bright streetlights of the towns along the tracks whizzed by like flashbulbs bursting in Nick's eyes. He closed them, as if that might delete today—and yesterday—from having happened.

Nick could see himself running through his apartment, past the family photos lining the walls. Running through the subway tunnel. Finding Wessel. Running into his bedroom. Seeing the blinding flash from the gun muzzle as if it were right in front of his face . . .

"Police, sir. Wake up."

Nick opened his eyes. An Amtrak police officer stood in the aisle beside his row of seats, his hand on his holstered Glock.

"Yes, Officer?"

"Put your hands on the seat in front of you."

Nick now saw cops at both ends of the car and that he was the only passenger. He realized they had evacuated the train. *Like I'm some kind of terrorist.*

"I'm NYPD," Nick told the cop, "if this is about my weapon."

"Where's your ID?" asked the cop.

"Inside coat pocket," Nick replied. "Can I reach?"

The cop nodded. Nick took out his wallet and handed the cop his shield and ID card. The cop relaxed, giving him back his creds.

"Sorry, guy," the cop apologized. "Someone saw your gun and complained. We had to check it out."

"You're doing your job," Nick said. "No apology necessary."

"Thanks for understanding," the cop said, walking away.

Nick slumped in his seat as the cops began to let the passengers back into the car. Then the train started off again.

Nick stared out the window for the rest of trip, not wanting to see the passengers looking at him with disgust because he had made them late. The train was crossing over the Harlem River now; the lit Manhattan skyline filled the window.

At least I can still see that.

And though he knew the time when he wouldn't be able to see was creeping closer, Nick breathed a sigh of relief. He was home.

*   *   *

It was just after midnight when Nick walked through the door into the ancient duplex he grew up in and now shared with his mother and two daughters. His parents had snagged the place decades earlier, the beneficiaries of once-in-a-lifetime luck combined with the city's financial ruin of the mid-1970s. Nick's father, a beat cop in the Upper West Side's 24th Precinct back then, helped evict a heroin dealer from the expansive five-room apartment. In return, the owner offered the place to Nick's father for the rent-controlled sum of $250 a month, a mere pittance for what most Manhattan apartment dwellers then and now would consider an urban mansion. Now, nearly forty years later, the rent was only $1,200, more than affordable on a detective's salary.

Nick made his way into the kitchen and went straight for the refrigerator. He hadn't eaten since before his visit to Dr. Mangone, and he was famished. He opened the door and shoved a couple of slices of cold-cut turkey down his throat, wondering why his mother hadn't saved him any dinner.

And then he felt guilty. His wife Jenny's sudden death not only left him bereft of a life partner and the girls of a mother, but it also presented a huge child-care problem. It was why Nick sold his attached house in the Queens hamlet of Whitestone and moved the girls back to Manhattan with his mother. Helen Lawler was in her early seventies, still vibrant but lonely since the death of Nick's father fifteen years earlier, and she welcomed Nick and the girls with open arms. Thus far she had kept her promise to look after her granddaughters.

"How'd it go?"

Nick turned. His mother stood in the kitchen doorway in a light green terry-cloth bathrobe.

"The girls okay?" he asked her.

"Jill got an A on her math test. Katie had a sore throat, so I kept her home."

"Did you take her to the doctor?" Nick asked, concerned.

"It's only a cold, Nick. No fever. She'll be fine." Helen knew that even a minor illness of one of his girls set him off, so she tried not to worry him.

"Thanks, Ma, for taking care of them," Nick replied. "I'm going to bed."

"You didn't answer my question," his mother chided. "How was Boston?"

Nick couldn't help but think his mother should've been a cop. "It didn't go well," he confessed.

"Then what are you going to do?" she asked him, frustrated.

"Now's not the time, Ma," he said, feeling like a child. "I'm exhausted."

"You got your twenty in. Every day after that is like you're working for half pay. That's what your father always said."

"Ma, stop. Please."

"You can do a million other things."

"Guys who see can do a million other things. Not guys who're going blind."

"Nicky, you gotta face facts."

Nick sighed. The conversation had become a tiresome daily occurrence since he shared the secret of his deteriorating eyesight. And he'd long since learned the only way to win an argument with his mother was not to get into one in the first place.

"Can we drop it for tonight?" he pleaded.

"The girls already lost their mother. They can't afford to lose their father, too, and I won't be around forever."

"I got another chance, Ma," he argued. "To prove those rats on the job were wrong about me."

"You know you didn't do anything wrong. So don't be like your father," she said as she headed for the stove. "I'm scrambling you some eggs."

That was the thing about his mother. She always had an answer and she was always right. "Don't bring Dad into this," Nick said as he sat down at the kitchen table. Nothing had changed in the apartment for years, and Nick liked that. Same place mats, same bowl of plastic fruit on the table. He found comfort in his mother's predictability.

"Your dad, God rest his soul, was always trying to prove he was a good cop and look where it got him—dead of a heart attack before he could retire." She sighed as she took out three eggs.

Nick liked how she cooked them real slow so they were soft and moist.

"Dad was a good cop who got stuck with a bunch of bad apples,"

Nick now schooled her. "He never took money like the rest of them, and he never ratted them out. He had nothing to prove."

"Neither do you, son."

She looked at him a second longer and turned back to the stove.

In silence, Nick ate his eggs and three slices of white toast almost burnt, the way he liked it. He grabbed a bottle of water from the fridge and kissed his mom on the cheek good night, just like when he was a little boy. After checking on his sleeping girls and giving each a peck on the forehead, he went into his room and closed the door. As he did every night, he removed his gun and locked it in the safe that was built into the table beside the bed. His mother and daughters had no idea where he kept his guns and never asked. And he'd told only one other person the combination, which had ended in disaster.

He switched off the light, plopped down on the bed in his clothes, and shut his eyes, waiting to succumb to exhaustion. But it didn't take long for him to realize he was in that ironic state of being too tired to fall asleep.

Nick found himself reaching under the bed, pulling out a large envelope.

Why am I doing this? Why now?

He couldn't answer his own question as he opened the flap and reached in. When his hand emerged, it held a series of newspaper clippings. He turned on the lamp on his night table and began reading the headlines, written eight months ago:

The *Daily News*: MURDER COP ACCUSED OF KILLING WIFE

The *New York Times*: NYPD DETECTIVE CHARGED IN WIFE'S SHOOTING DEATH

The *Post*: HUBBY HOMICIDE COP WHACKED WIFE

All three sported the photo that would make Nick cringe for the rest of his life: There he was in handcuffs, being led away from his Queens home in the middle of the night as his daughters watched from the doorway. The *Post* was the only newspaper that bothered to print a picture of Jenny, snapped by a neighbor whose backyard barbecue they had attended the previous Labor Day. Nick stared at the photo of his deceased wife.

Why? Why? He ran up the stairs. Down the hallway, past the family pictures on the wall. Don't do it, Jenny . . . I'm coming . . . Pop! The muzzle flash cut through the blackness. He ran into the bedroom. Her eyes were wide open in instantaneous death. Blood poured from the exit wound in her back, spreading across the white sheets. . . .

Ringing. Ringing . . .

Nick sat bolt upright. He'd fallen asleep. The ringing phone on his night table wasn't part of his recurring nightmare. He picked it up without checking the caller ID.

"Yeah."

"Wake up and get dressed," came the unmistakable voice of Lieutenant Wilkes from the receiver.

"What is it, Lou?" Nick asked groggily.

"You had your day off. Quimby did another girl."

Nick was suddenly wide awake, a pen in his hand. "Where?"

"Central Park," said Wilkes. "Ninetieth Street and the lake."

"On my way, Boss."

"You better be."

Nick hung up the phone.

He killed again. While I was gone.

Nick reached for his wallet. Fumbled for the piece of paper he knew was still inside. He unfolded it, hesitating just briefly. A year ago, he never would have considered doing what he was about to do. But too much had happened since then, almost none of it good. And Nick couldn't help but think he was responsible for Quimby killing again.

Slowly, he picked up the phone and, still not wanting to, dialed Claire Waters's phone number.

CHAPTER 11

Claire stared out the windshield as Nick maneuvered the un-marked Impala through the throng of emergency vehicles cluttered beside the Central Park Reservoir. A horde of news vans was setting up nearby, their microwave masts high in the air, preparing no doubt to beam whatever gruesome story awaited them back to their stations and out to the tristate area.

A serial killer is on the loose. He's struck again. And he's my patient.

Was *my patient,* Claire corrected herself.

Curtin had told her to take the previous day off, and she'd spent it at home, not leaving the apartment, catching up on some pleasure reading, finally relaxed enough to fall into a deep sleep spooned into Ian's warm body. Then Nick Lawler's middle-of-the-night call woke her up, reminding her that she would never really be able to relax or forget until Quimby was caught.

On the phone, Nick had been polite to the point of apologetic. He thanked Claire for giving him Quimby's address and explained how Tommy Wessel was critically injured. Claire felt sorry for Nick, appreciating how uncomfortable it was for him to break the bad news while waiting for the request she knew was coming.

"There's been another homicide," Nick said. "We've gotta stop this guy Quimby and you know him better than any of us." He then asked, almost pleaded with her to accompany him to the crime scene. Despite Curtin's admonition to stay out of it—he'd told her yesterday that Quimby was a police problem now—Claire didn't hesitate for a second.

They drove the short distance from her apartment to Central Park in silence, Claire focusing on the reflection off the windshield of the red teardrop light atop the dashboard. She hadn't been in a police car since the day Amy disappeared, and the novelty of it wore off the moment she spotted two attendants removing an empty gurney from the back of the medical examiner's van.

Lieutenant Wilkes was getting out of his beat-up unmarked Crown Vic as Nick pulled up beside him. Wilkes glared at Claire sitting in the passenger seat.

"Who the hell is this?" Wilkes demanded as Nick got out of the car. Wilkes wore jeans and a sweatshirt, and his usually well-combed red hair stuck out like straw, giving Nick the impression that his boss came over right out of bed.

"Quimby's shrink," Nick replied.

"You brought a shrink to a crime scene?"

Claire was out of the car by now and heard Wilkes's comment. She decided to kill him with kindness. "Claire Waters," she said, extending her hand. "I believe you know my boss, Paul Curtin."

Wilkes shook her hand while cutting her off at the knees. "Yeah, I know him," began the lieutenant. "And when the sun comes up, I'm gonna tell him to have his own head examined, sending you here."

"He doesn't know she's here," Nick told his boss. "I called her."

"We don't need her," Wilkes said, not caring that Claire was standing right in front of him. "We got enough problems, Nicky."

"What we've got, Boss, is three dead girls in two days," Nick replied, his voice low but emphatic. He gestured to Claire. "We know it's her patient who's doing these murders. Maybe she can shed some light on what his next move might be. She can't do any worse than we have."

Wilkes looked at him. The old Nick Lawler was back, the one who wouldn't take no for an answer, the Nick who had closed more than a few murders that were stone whodunits and considered unsolvable. The lieutenant beckoned Nick and Claire to follow him.

"I hope you can help us nail this lunatic," Wilkes said, turning to Claire, "because I'm told he really went off the deep end this time. Are you squeamish, Doctor?"

"We dissected cadavers in medical school," Claire said. "I've seen death before."

"This isn't just death," Wilkes returned. "It's murder. And believe me, there's a big difference."

Claire was sure she could handle it. "I'm a forensic psychiatrist, Lieutenant," she said. "If I can't deal with violent death, I probably should find another line of work."

Wilkes didn't have a chance to respond as reporters, gathered at the edge of the crime scene tape, fanned out to surround and pepper them with questions.

"Do you have a name for the victim?"

"Is this another blond girl?"

"Are you thinking it's the same guy who murdered Catherine Mills?"

Claire knew enough to keep her mouth shut.

Wilkes looked straight into the cameras. "Hey," he said, "you see us standing out *here*." Then he pointed to the crime scene. "That means we haven't been in there yet. Give us a break, okay? You'll get your story when we know what's going on."

He gestured to the three officers standing guard, and they lifted the yellow tape, allowing them to pass through.

The reservoir was directly in front of them, though the crime scene itself was several dozen yards away, hidden from view by leafy trees and thick shrubs. Storm clouds had gathered in the sky, blotting out the stars. Nick could smell the rain coming and knew he had to work fast before it washed the crime scene of any evidence.

As they reached the jogging path along the water, Claire thought of the dozens of times she'd run this route. She could see the glow of the klieg lights illuminating the crime scene. As they got closer, she hoped the bravado she displayed to Lieutenant Wilkes was more than just talk.

They rounded a corner. A Crime Scene Unit detective was shooting photos of the ground along the water. Claire noticed the grass had been flattened, the tips of each blade pointing away from the lake.

She was in the lake. He dragged her out. Why?

Her thoughts were interrupted as Assistant Medical Examiner Ross emerged from the bushes. "It's him, all right," he said, seeing Nick and Wilkes.

"What'd he do, drown her this time?" Nick asked.

"I don't think so," Ross replied, leading them to the body. "There's no water in her airway. More like he murdered her first, took her for a romantic midnight swim, then dragged her up here. This dude's crazy."

They reached the body, covered by a white sheet, which Ross now pulled back.

Claire gasped in pure terror. Nick grabbed her so she wouldn't fall. The victim was another young blond woman. Quimby had burned her eyes with lye as he had Catherine Mills and the victim from Coney Island, and he'd left his signature rope around her neck with the same Dutch marine bowline.

But this victim was soaking wet.

And her long hair was cut short. In clumps. By an amateur.

"We find her hair?" Nick asked.

"Crime Scene did," Ross said. "About fifty yards away."

"Why cut it?" Wilkes asked.

"Because of me," Claire replied, still shaking. "He was killing me."

Wilkes shot Nick a hard glance. "What the hell's she talking about?"

"She's right, Boss," Nick said.

"Clear waters," Claire continued, her eyes never leaving the dead girl's body. "Quimby calls me *clear waters*. That's why he dragged her into the lake. That's why he hacked off her hair just like I cut mine. He wanted me to know."

"Know what?" Wilkes asked.

"That Quimby's after Dr. Waters," Nick said. "That she's next."

"Or that this murder was my fault," Claire barely uttered.

Nick turned to Wilkes. "Can you cover me here?"

"What, you taking another day off?" the lieutenant replied.

"No. I'm taking Dr. Waters to her hospital."

Wilkes looked at Claire. She was still shaking. He actually felt bad for her.

"Don't worry, Doc," he said to her. "We're not gonna let this whacko get anywhere near you, okay?"

All Claire could manage was a nod.

"You did us a solid," the lieutenant continued, meaning it. "I'm calling Paul Curtin to ask him to assign you to us. If you're up to it."

"I have to be," said Claire.

*   *   *

An unusual early morning thunderstorm crackled as Curtin perused the crime scene photos from Central Park. He flipped through them and returned them to a manila cnvelope.

"I can't allow this," he said to Nick and Claire.

They were seated in Curtin's office. Lieutenant Wilkes had wasted no time making good on his promise to call Curtin, phoning him from the crime scene just moments after Nick and Claire left. Curtin asked to see the photos, and Wilkes had dispatched a detective to print them out and bring them to Manhattan City.

"I have to do this, Doctor," Claire pleaded with Curtin. "He's after me now."

Curtin wouldn't budge. "That's exactly why you shouldn't be involved," he said flatly.

"But I have to find out—" she began.

"Not by risking your own life you don't," Curtin retorted.

"But what if this is my fault?" Claire asked.

Curtin softened. "Nothing you did made this guy go out and kill these women. He was doing that before you met him."

"I cut my hair," Claire responded. "And Quimby made this victim look like me."

"Claire. Listen to me," Curtin said, looking directly into her eyes. "There's no way that what happened this morning was in any way your fault."

Nick decided to try to break the stalemate. "Dr. Curtin," he began. "We would've banged our heads against the wall for days, if not weeks, wondering why this fruitcake dragged that girl into the water after he did her. It took Dr. Waters here about five seconds to nail it."

Curtin wasn't giving in. "Under any other circumstances, Detective, I'd be thrilled to have one of my students working with you. But I'm not going to paint a big bull's-eye on Dr. Waters's back. She's in my program, and her safety is my responsibility."

"Taking her off the case won't stop Quimby," Nick responded.

"That's right," Curtin shot back, "and that's why I'm asking you for a protective detail to guard Dr. Waters until Quimby's locked up."

Nick stood. "My boss has already approved it," he said. "She'll have a detective with her both at home and here at the hospital."

Claire was tired of listening to these two men decide how she was going to live her life. "I'm sitting right here, guys, in case you care about what I think," she said to them. "And whether you do or not, I don't need protection."

"Well, Doctor," Curtin said in that condescending tone Claire hated, "you don't have a say in this. I'm not losing a fellow on my watch."

Claire knew he wasn't changing his mind. She nodded her reluctant assent.

"C'mon," Nick said to her. "I'll take you home."

Half an hour later, Nick's police Impala pulled to the curb of a residential block on the Upper East Side. Completely across town from where Claire and Ian lived. The rain had stopped and the air was refreshed, rinsed of its city grime.

"I thought you said you were taking me home," Clare said to Nick.

"I am," Nick replied, shutting off the engine. "Your temporary home."

Through the windshield, Claire saw Ian, a duffel bag at his feet, standing on the sidewalk with an attractive woman she didn't know.

"City seized this place from a drug dealer back in the eighties," Nick said. "We use it to keep witnesses under wraps. Sammy the Bull lived here while he was testifying against Gotti."

"And the woman with my boyfriend?" Claire asked.

"Your protection," Nick replied.

Claire was about to open the door when Nick grabbed her hand. "Listen," he said. "We're not releasing any of the details of the Central Park murder to the media."

"So you're telling me to keep my mouth shut with Ian," Claire surmised.

"All he knows is that you're being protected as a potential witness," Nick said. "I need you to keep it that way."

"You have my word, Commander," Claire said facetiously.

It made Nick grin. "C'mon, let me introduce you," he said.

They got out of the car. Claire ran right into Ian's arms. "You okay?" he asked.

"I will be," Claire answered, not letting him go.

"Dr. Claire Waters," Nick said, "Detective Maggie Stolls."

Claire reached out her hand, still clutching Ian with the other. It made Detective Stolls chuckle as she shook it. "I'm your roommate for as long as this takes," she said. Maggie had an open face that Claire immediately liked. She was tall and well toned, her dark brown hair pulled back into a ponytail, which Claire thought made her look like a professional tennis player she'd seen on television.

"Maggie'll be with you around the clock," Nick said. "Including when you're at the hospital."

Claire broke her embrace with Ian and looked at him. "You're not staying?" she asked.

Ian indicated the duffel bag. "I packed up some stuff for you," he said, "but they want me to stay at our place."

"Then you better protect Ian," Claire demanded.

"We have undercover cops on your block twenty-four-seven in case Quimby shows," Nick reassured her.

"What about you?" Claire asked Nick. "Are you staying with me?"

Out of the corner of her eye, she caught a momentary look on Ian's face.

Is he jealous? Claire liked the idea that Ian loved her so much he could be jealous of another man she spent time with, even if it was only for work.

A squawk from Nick's walkie-talkie broke Claire's thoughts. "Car seven-oh-two," said the radio dispatcher, "ten-two, your command."

"Ten-four, Central," Nick replied into the walkie. "Uh, they're calling me back to the office," Nick said to Claire, indicating the radio. "It's against procedure for male officers to guard female protectees overnight. And Quimby's my case, so the quicker I collar him, the quicker we can send you home to your life."

"C'mon," Detective Stolls said to Claire, trying to break the tension. "Let me show you your temporary digs."

Claire looked after Nick as he headed for the car. "Please," she called after him, "keep me posted."

"I will," Nick said back, getting into the Impala, starting the engine, and pulling away.

CHAPTER 12

"The problem with tracking this guy is he's all over the map," Lieutenant Wilkes said from the front of the cramped squad room. It had been nearly eighteen hours since the body was found in Central Park, and the orders from One Police Plaza, the office of the police commissioner, couldn't be clearer: Stop Todd Quimby at all costs.

In front of Wilkes stood his detectives and twenty other casually dressed cops on loan for this evening's stakeout duty. Behind him were two dry-erase boards and a blackboard, all "misappropriated" from various offices in the precinct. The blackboard on the left sported a large blown-up mug shot of Todd Quimby, his pertinent information written neatly in chalk around it. The center board displayed a map of the city; blue pins indicated every location that could be tied to Quimby, and red pins showed where each of his victims was found. And the board on the right held their photos, in life and in gruesome death. Folding chairs were jammed into every free space so that the detectives on loan had a place to sit and sort through all the leads—most of them useless—that were being phoned in.

An hour earlier, Brooklyn South Homicide had finally come through with the identity of the body at Coney Island. Rose Grimaldi was twenty and had traveled to the amusement park that Saturday night from Long Branch, New Jersey, with a group of four friends. When asked later why they never reported her missing, her friends explained Rosie wasn't feeling too well when she got off the Cyclone and said she was going home in the car she had driven up from the

Jersey Shore. It wasn't until Rose failed to show up for work early Monday morning that the local cops were called, and it took another day before they linked her to the brutal murder at Coney Island.

Nick taped up the material on the Central Park victim, whose identity was only as difficult to find as it was for Assistant Medical Examiner Ross to roll her fingerprints and feed them into the Printrak. Wilkes now pointed to her photos.

"Quimby's latest kill is one Sharon Corbett, twenty-two, came to us from beautiful Flagstaff, Arizona, six months ago. Took her bite outta the Big Apple by running up an impressive string of fifteen collars—prostitution, loitering, blah blah blah. Her latest humping ground was the Eleventh Avenue stroll between Thirty-Ninth and Forty-Second streets."

"Anybody see her there last night?" asked Detective Potts.

"Yeah," said Nick. "The other whores (which Nick, like all good New York cops, pronounced "hoo-ahs") on the track. But none of them saw her with Quimby."

"I thought this guy found his victims at carnivals," said a young Anti-Crime cop, Logan, from the back of the room.

"There's the rub," Wilkes replied, "since there ain't no carnivals on Eleventh Avenue."

"Times Square at night looks like the mother of all carnivals, though," offered Savarese.

"And Quimby's last two victims have been women with short blond hair," said Nick. "If he didn't find what he was looking for on Forty-Second, makes sense he'd go hunting elsewhere."

Wilkes pointed to the board as he spoke. "Rose Grimaldi, Saturday night, Coney Island. Catherine Mills, Sunday morning, Times Square. And Sharon Corbett late last night in Central Park. This guy's on a spree. He gave us three corpses in the last four days, and there's no reason to think he'll take a break tonight."

He turned to Nick. "Detective Lawler's run lead on these cases, and he's gonna take it from here."

Nick stepped up to the front of the room. "Quimby's last two victims were hookers, so we're sitting on every pross stroll in the five boroughs, every night, till he shows up and we nab him. We've got units deploying in Queens, Brooklyn, the Bronx, and Staten Island.

We're gonna cover Manh
up with extra radio cars a

"Lieutenant Wilkes,"
sergeant, Ramircz, stoc

"Not now, Pablo," V

"It's urgent," said
Nick everything he r

"Where?" Nick s

"De Witt Clinto

"Everybody go
tied out.

Nick offered. "That scur
finds the perfect place
"Inside some club
Nearby, two Cri
scene. Nick rea
Coney Island
"Hey, Ait
Aitken
ing this
N
wh

De Witt Clinton Park is a two
between 11th Avenue and the Hudson River
of the park consist of three softball diamonds that,
weather, are lit up for night games. Tonight, though, the floodlig
illuminated only the foulest of play.

Nick could see her as soon as he stepped through the gate into the park. She was lying in the grass behind home plate on the largest of the three ball fields.

He couldn't help but think Quimby put her there on purpose, as a message to the police. Or to him personally.

I can steal home base any time I want. And you bastards can't do a goddamn thing to stop me.

As he and Wilkes ducked under the hastily strung crime scene tape, Nick switched on his video camera and put the viewfinder up to his right eye. Zooming in, he saw immediately the telltale signs of Todd Quimby's work.

"Short blond hair, rope around her neck's knotted in a Dutch marine bowline," he said to Wilkes.

"Son of a bitch," Wilkes muttered.

As they drew closer, Nick could see the woman was lying faceup, wearing a black Armani cocktail dress. No jewelry. His stomach churned. Like it always did when something didn't make sense.

"You thinking what I'm thinking?" he asked the lieutenant.

"Damn right," Wilkes replied. "She ain't no pross."

"There must be a dozen nightclubs within six blocks of here,"

bag knows we're looking for him, so he
o hunt for his next victim."

, where we'd never see him."

me Scene Unit detectives snapped photos of the
zed one of them was Terry Aitken, the kid from the
homicide.

ken," Nick called to him.

lowered his Nikon. "Nick Lawler. Thought you'd be catch-
"

ck decided to test the kid. "Anything you want to know about
at happened here?"

"For a girl who's been lying in a baseball field, why's the front of
her dress look so clean?" Aitken pondered. "And why are there
footwear impressions in the dirt and grass all around her, but no drag
marks or signs of a struggle? I think you got a dump job on your
hands."

"Quimby ain't exactly Stone Cold Steve Austin," Wilkes growled.
"How'd the wimpy bastard carry her from the street all the way
here?"

"He had wheels, Lieutenant," Aitken said, pointing to a spot behind the fence. "Four of them. Got some nice pictures." Aitken
brought the photos up on his digital Nikon and showed them to Nick
and Wilkes.

"Shopping cart," said Nick. "Rolled her up to the backstop, carried
her the rest of the way."

"Were the lights on when the body was found?" Wilkes asked.

"No, we had someone from Parks meet us here to turn them on,"
Aitken said.

"That kind of dark, he could've carried her in here naked and nobody would've seen them," Nick said. "How many more photos you
need?" he asked Aitken.

"We're done," Aitken replied. "She's all yours."

Nick knelt beside the woman's body. With a gloved hand, he
opened her left eyelid.

"Eyes are white. He burned her. It's him all right," Nick said.

He tried to move her right arm. It wouldn't budge. "Jesus," he exclaimed, "she's in full rigor. How long ago did he kill her?"

And then Nick smelled something. Sniffed several times, enough for Wilkes to notice. "What?" asked the lieutenant.

"There it is again. Bitter almonds," Nick answered.

"You're crazy," Wilkes said, kneeling down. "I don't smell a goddamn thing."

"Not everyone can smell cyanide," Nick reminded him.

"ME said he didn't find any cyanide in any of the victims," Wilkes replied.

Nick spotted the medical examiner's van pulling up just outside the fence. "ME just showed," he said.

Wilkes nodded. "We'll let him check her out before we roll her—"

"Detectives!" a voice boomed from across the park.

They looked up. The shout seemed to come from the 52nd Street side, where someone was waving a flashlight. "I got a witness!"

"Holy shit," said Nick, standing up.

"Go," said Wilkes. "I'll stay with the ME."

Nick sprinted across the park to a break in the fence where a patrol cop, D'Ambrosi, waited. "What've you got?" Nick asked him.

D'Ambrosi guided him toward a homeless woman sitting on a bench beside her shopping cart. "Her name's Sonya," he said, "and she's wearing a little too much ice for someone of her station in life. If you know what I'm saying."

He aimed his torch on Sonya, whose earlobes glittered in the light.

"Sonya, baby," D'Ambrosi said as he and Nick reached her. "Why don't you show the nice detective here your lovely earrings?"

Nick needed about a second to know exactly where the princess-cut diamond studs had come from.

Sonya smiled. "My boyfriend gave them to me," she said in a husky voice betraying years of nicotine and alcohol abuse.

"Sonya was headed out on the town with those rocks and her new Prada handbag," said D'Ambrosi, snatching the purse away from her.

"Hey, sonny, you gonna arrest yourself? That's my property you're stealing," Sonya snapped as D'Ambrosi riffled through it.

"Your property?" Nick asked her politely. "Your boyfriend give that to you too?"

"You look like a nice young man," Sonya said to Nick, coming on to him. "I found that bag in the garbage."

"Is that where you found the earrings too?" Nick asked, kneeling beside her.

She looked away, ashamed.

"Sonya, dear," Nick said, "did you see the young lady out there on the baseball field?"

She avoided his eyes as she answered. "She wasn't breathing. She wasn't gonna need this stuff."

"I need it, Sonya," Nick said. "I need it because someone hurt that girl and I have to find out who. You'd want me to do that for you, right?"

"I guess so."

"Sonya, did you wheel your cart out there?"

"Couldn't leave it here. Vultures around here'd take it before I got three steps away. I got all my stuff in there, you know."

"Detective Lawler," said Officer D'Ambrosi. "Think we got an ID on the victim."

He handed Nick a New York State driver's license he found in her purse. The smiling woman in the photo was absolutely the victim.

"Who is she?" asked Lieutenant Wilkes, joining them.

"Tamara Sorenson, twenty-eight. Address in Bedford."

"Bedford, huh? Rich girl from the suburbs comes to the big city for a good time, gets more than she bargained for," said Wilkes.

"Least we know who she is," said Nick. "Bad news is the shopping cart that made those tracks out by the body belongs to Sonya here, not Quimby. He must've carried her out there after all."

"After he stripped her," said Lieutenant Wilkes.

Nick shot him a look. "What're you talking about?"

"When the ME rolled her, there was grass and dirt on the victim's back. Under her dress."

Nick realized what that meant. "So she was naked when Quimby raped and strangled her. Then he carried her out here and threw the black dress on her after she died to try to make her look like the whore he wanted her to be."

Wilkes glanced back to where the medical examiner was working on Tamara Sorenson's body. "I told the ME to front-burner this one," he said to Nick. "Finish the scene, then get down to the morgue. If they don't have her on a table and cracked by the time you get there, light a fire under their asses. I want every piece of forensics they can tweeze or scrape off her."

Four hours later, at three in the morning, Nick walked into the autopsy suite. Assistant Medical Examiner Ross was just finishing sewing the "Y" incision he'd made in Tamara Sorenson's torso.

"You're late and I couldn't wait," Ross said, not looking up.

"She was strangled," Nick retorted. "I needed to be here for that?"

"Yeah, but she would've died anyway," Ross replied.

Nick wasn't expecting this. "Died of what?" he asked.

Ross looked up. "Lymphoma," he said.

"Cancer? You're sure?" Nick asked, staring at the young woman's face. Her features were delicate. The word that came immediately to Nick's mind was *kind*.

"I'm a pathologist," Ross retorted, "and I know cancer of the lymph nodes when I see it. Except I've never seen it like this."

"What exactly do you mean?"

"It's everywhere, like it was devouring her. Metastasized to her brain, spleen, abdomen—even her spinal fluid. And that's not all that's wrong with this picture."

Nick didn't need the drama. "You wanna tell me what the hell you're talking about?" he demanded.

Ross took off his mask. "She's in her twenties. I've never even heard of such an advanced case of Hodgkin's disease in anyone, male or female, under fifty. Chickie here wouldn't have been able to make it to the bathroom, let alone run around clubbing in a dress that ends just above her C level."

"I got there around nine last night," Nick said, "and she was already stiff as a board."

"Factor in lividity and core body temp and I'll put actual time of death soon after eleven o'clock two nights ago."

"You're saying Quimby murdered this one late Monday night or early Tuesday morning *before* Sharon Corbett in Central Park."

"Glad we're speaking the same language, Nicky," Ross said affably.

Nick wasn't satisfied. "Do me a solid," he said to Ross. "Check her for cyanide, too, like the others. And tox screen her for everything you can."

"Everything like what?" Ross asked.

"Everything like everything," Nick said impatiently.

"No need to get snippy," Ross retorted. "We aim to please."

"Sorry," Nick said. "Guess this one's just getting to me."

He wasn't lying. His stomach was churning again. Something was way out of place with Tamara Sorenson.

CHAPTER 13

"You want me to see your patients tomorrow on morning's rounds?" Eddie Sanchez asked Claire as they exited the secure double doors of Manhattan City's psych ward. It was a muggy Thursday afternoon, and the heat hadn't dissipated over the first week of Claire's fellowship.

"Thanks, Eddie," Claire answered as she signed out at the security desk, "but if I don't get back to some kind of normal routine, Curtin's gonna be all over me."

"If it's any consolation, all the fellows think you rock," Eddie said with a smile. "I don't know how any of us would've dealt with a serial killer as our first patient. If there's anything we can do . . ."

The attention made Claire feel deeply uncomfortable. After the glare of interest she received when Amy was kidnapped, she spent her whole life avoiding any kind of attention, and now she was under the spotlight Todd Quimby had cast on her.

"I appreciate everyone's concern," Claire said. "But I just want to move on."

Eddie nodded, giving her the space she obviously wanted. Claire walked away toward the hospital exit. "See you tomorrow," she said, without looking back at Eddie.

Quimby's name had barely passed through her mind when she felt a hand grab her so fast she didn't have time to scream in terror before she saw who it was.

Nick Lawler.

"What is wrong with you?" she demanded. "You scared me."

"Sorry," Nick said, meaning it. "I don't want to get you in trouble." He pulled Claire through a doorway into the staff lounge.

"Trouble's exactly what I'm going to be in if Curtin sees us talking. I thought you were out chasing Todd Quimby."

"I was," he replied, "until last night's murder."

"Oh, God," Claire muttered, feeling a mix of terror and nausea wash over her.

"You didn't know?"

"No," she answered. Claire had avoided the newspapers and television for the last twenty-four hours for exactly this reason. She didn't want to know, but now she had no choice. "Another prostitute?"

"That would be too easy," Nick began. "Her name's Tamara Sorenson, and I need your help on this one."

"If Curtin even hears we spoke, I'm out the door."

"He took her clothes," Nick said quickly, "threw a black cocktail dress on her before he dumped her body—but that was *after* he raped and killed her. Which he did a day *before* he took Sharon Corbett for her moonlight swim in the Central Park lagoon."

"Hold on," Claire said. "Quimby hasn't taken any trophies that we know of. And he would have had to stash Ms. Sorenson's body somewhere for an entire day. None of this is consistent with his MO."

"That's not even the half of it," Nick continued. "Tamara Sorenson had terminal cancer. Hodgkin's lymphoma. ME said she had tumors the size of lemons in her spleen, liver, and brain."

"This woman was how old?" Claire asked as she sifted through her mind all the symptoms and treatments for the disease.

"Twenty-eight."

Claire's mind was already racing. *Tamara Sorenson was so young to have such advanced disease. Someone must have been treating her. But who? Or was she in complete denial about it, pretending it wasn't happening?*

The saga of Todd Quimby had just become more than the hunt for a serial killer. He was now part of a bona fide medical mystery, something Claire could really sink her teeth into. But she had to be careful not to let Curtin, the five-hundred-pound gorilla, land on her head.

"What do you need me to do?" she asked Nick.

"For starters, I have to tell the victim's parents. I was hoping you'd come with me."

"To make a death notification?"

"You're a doctor. I want to know more about Tamara's condition, and you know what questions to ask."

Claire hesitated, Curtin's admonition looming large. She knew she was playing with fire, but this was worth a little heat.

"I just have some charts to sign and then I'm off shift," she said. "But we can't be seen anywhere around the hospital together, including outside, or I'm toast with Curtin."

"Maggie's in on this," Nick answered, referring to her bodyguard, Detective Stolls. "Just get in the car with her and she'll bring you to me."

The Sorenson home was a huge, stately colonial in the super-upscale Westchester County suburb of Bedford, about thirty miles from Manhattan. Claire stood uncomfortably beside Nick as he rang the doorbell.

"How are you going to explain bringing a doctor with you?" she asked.

Nick hadn't thought about that. "Just go with the flow," he said as the dead bolt turned and the door opened. A trim, toned, casually dressed woman stood before them.

"Mrs. Sorenson?" asked Nick.

"Yes, Gloria Sorenson," she answered. "Can I help you?"

Nick displayed his shield and ID card. "I'm Detective Lawler from the New York City Police Department, and this is Claire Waters," he said.

He wants her to think I'm his partner, Claire realized, even more uncomfortable about the charade.

"Police?" Gloria said. "Is something wrong?"

"May we come in?" Claire asked gently.

"Oh, of course," said Gloria, standing aside and allowing them to enter. The house was gorgeous, immaculate, beautifully furnished with large canvases of color-drenched abstract art.

"Michael!" Gloria shouted upstairs as she closed the door. "I need you, now. The police are here."

"What happened?" exclaimed Michael Sorenson as he hurried down the stairs. He was a handsome, fit fiftysomething. *They're the perfect couple,* Claire thought, *and we're about to shatter their world.*

"We're here about your daughter, Tamara," said Nick.

"What about Tammy?" Michael asked, concerned.

Nick had done this many times, and it never got any easier.

"There's no easy way to say this, so I'm just going to tell you. We found your daughter in a park on the west side of Manhattan. Unfortunately, she's deceased."

The Sorensons exchanged looks. Not of horror, but of confusion.

"There must be some mistake," Gloria said. "Tammy's on vacation in Hawaii."

Now it was Nick's and Claire's turn to be confused.

"The woman we found had a driver's license in her purse identifying her as Tamara Sorenson at this address," Nick said. He handed the license to Tammy's father, who showed it to his wife.

"That's Tammy," Michael Sorensen replied. "But she never even goes to Manhattan. And she's five thousand miles away. . . ."

His voice trailed off, fearing the worst. Nick took out a photo from his coat pocket.

"This was taken by the medical examiner. We need you to make a positive identification."

Gloria grabbed Michael's arm as Nick showed them the picture of their lifeless daughter's face.

"Yes, that's her. Oh, God. Oh, God," cried Gloria, falling into Michael's arms. Michael looked around in shock, as if someone else would walk in and tell them it was all a horrible mistake.

"We're terribly sorry for your loss," Nick said.

"How did she die?" Michael asked, tears in his eyes.

"I'm afraid she was murdered," Nick said.

"That's just too horrible!" Gloria exclaimed.

"Do you know who killed her?" Michael asked, barely getting out the words.

"We think we do. And every cop in New York is looking for him right now," Nick assured them.

Gloria turned to Michael. "Why did she tell us she was in Hawaii?"

Claire was wondering the same thing. "Was your daughter well enough to travel?" she asked them.

"Of course," Michael said. "What kind of a question is that?"

The realization hit Nick and Claire at the same time.

They didn't know.

Nick nodded to Claire. "Mr. and Mrs. Sorensen," she said carefully. "The medical examiner performed an autopsy on your daughter. He found she had terminal cancer."

"Impossible," Michael said. "We're her parents, for Christ's sake. How would we not know something like that? If that were true, why wouldn't she tell us?"

"Frankly, we'd like to know that too," replied Claire.

"When was the last time you heard from Tammy?" Nick asked.

"I spoke to her two days ago," Gloria replied. "She sounded perfectly okay to me."

"And you're sure she was calling from Hawaii," said Nick.

"She couldn't have been," Claire said, before the Sorensons could answer. "Tammy's cancer was advanced to the point where there's no way she could have made that kind of trip."

"I don't understand," Michael said. "You're saying she was so sick, but we saw her just a few weeks ago and she looked absolutely fine."

Claire said what came next as gently as she could. "Your daughter had stage-five metastatic disease. Her cancer originated in her immune system and had infiltrated every major organ. I don't mean to be crass, Mr. and Mrs. Sorenson, but it's a wonder Tammy could even talk two days ago."

Michael Sorenson eyed Claire. "You don't talk like any police officer I've ever spoken to," he observed, "but you sound exactly like every doctor I know."

Claire wasn't about to lie to these people. "I am a doctor," she said, covering for Nick. "Detective Lawler asked me to come here tonight to help make sense of all this, and none of it makes any sense at all. Tammy couldn't have been cancer-free three weeks ago when you saw her, or even mobile, with the severity of cancer the medical examiner found in her."

Michael was clearly getting irritated. "My daughter had a life-insurance physical two months ago," he said, "and she was approved for the policy last week. We both know that never would've happened if even a trace of cancer had been found. How do you explain that, Doctor?"

Claire was absolutely flummoxed by this. "Scientifically, I can't," she answered. "I've never heard of a tumor that grew so fast." Then she had a thought. "Can you tell me what your daughter did for a living?"

"Tammy had a PhD in molecular biology," Gloria said, starting to cry again. "She worked for a firm called Biopharix up in Cold Spring."

"I haven't heard of them," Claire replied, "but I'm sure Detective Lawler will be checking them out."

"First, though, I'd like to check out your daughter's bedroom if that's okay with you," Nick said.

"Oh, Tammy never changed the address on her license," said Michael. "She hasn't lived here since she left for graduate school."

"She has an apartment in White Plains," Gloria added.

"Can I have your permission to search the apartment?" asked Nick.

"I'll get you the key," Michael said. "Anything to help you find the person who killed our daughter."

He left the room. Gloria's eyes, though, were on Claire. There was something about her, Gloria thought, something more than just curiosity about Tammy's cancer. She cared.

"Please," Gloria now said to Claire, "when you find something out, you'll tell us, won't you? We have to know. She was my little girl."

She was my little girl.

How many times did Amy's mother say that?

"I promise that you'll be kept apprised of every development," Claire said to her, looking right at Nick to make sure he got the message.

"When can we get her?" Gloria asked, her voice barely a whisper.

"You can see her now," Nick said, "and we'll release her body as soon as all the toxicology labs come back."

Gloria closed her eyes. Just as Amy's mother had when she saw Claire for the first time after Amy was kidnapped.

Twenty minutes later, Nick's gloved hand turned the key in the lock of Tammy Sorenson's front door. She lived in a pleasant, newly renovated apartment complex just outside downtown White Plains, Westchester County's seat.

The conversation during the short ride had been one of stark confusion. Nick and Claire both thought that Tammy Sorenson was the piece of the Todd Quimby puzzle that didn't fit: She had a PhD, didn't live in the city, and was terminally ill. Why would Quimby have chosen her?

"Maybe somehow they knew each other," Claire suggested. "What if there's a link between them, somewhere in their past?"

Nick agreed they couldn't rule it out. "Tammy looks like Quimby's other victims," he said, hypothesizing. "He had to run somewhere after he lost us in the subway. Maybe he called his friend Tammy, came up here to hide out, and when he saw her with the short blond hair, he snapped and murdered her too."

"Like he almost did to me," said Claire.

"It would explain where he stashed her body for a day—in her own apartment," said Nick.

"But not how he got her thirty miles to that softball field in Manhattan," argued Claire. "Unless he stole a car, or used Tammy's."

Nick knew she was right. He called the Sorensons back, who told them that Tammy drove a dark blue Toyota Camry. But it was parked right outside her apartment complex when they drove up. Somehow Tammy got to the city and Quimby got to her.

Now, at the apartment, Nick removed the key from the lock. He handed Claire a pair of latex gloves. "If there's a crime scene in there," he warned, "you touch nothing unless I tell you to."

Nick opened the door and turned on the light. The old parquet floor shone as if it had just been refinished, the paint was fresh, even the couch pillows were perfectly placed.

Nick gestured for Claire to follow him in. They walked past a tiny, nearly empty galley kitchen and switched on an overhead light.

And what they saw only deepened the mystery of Tammy Sorenson.

"It's too neat," Nick said. "Like she hasn't been here in weeks."

"Never mind that," Claire replied. "This doesn't seem like a lived-in apartment."

Right again, Nick realized. It was too perfect. "Furniture looks cookie-cutter. Like it was rented."

Claire took a quick look at the numerous photos in frames adorning tables and shelves. Tammy with her parents, her friends, on boats, the beach.

"I'll check the bedroom," offered Claire.

"No, I'll do it. Remember what I said."

"Yes, touch nothing," Claire said.

She stood in place as Nick opened the doors to the bedroom and bathroom and turned on the lights in each. He pulled open the mirror over the sink to reveal the medicine cabinet.

"If she had cancer, she'd be on medication, right?"

"Enough to fill a whole pharmacy," Claire answered.

"There isn't one pill bottle in here," said Nick, stumped, as he closed the medicine cabinet.

"Unless he cleaned up after himself, Quimby didn't murder Tammy in this apartment," he said. "I'm gonna ask the White Plains cops to have their crime scene unit dust this place for prints just to find out if he was ever here."

The gloves were starting to bother Claire. "Can I take these off?" she asked.

"How're you gonna help me if you do that?"

"Help you do what?"

"We didn't come here just to look around," Nick told her. "Tammy's parents are her next of kin. They gave us permission to search the place. And that's what we're going to do. You take the bedroom and I'll look around in here."

"What exactly am I looking for?

"Anything that seems unusual or helpful to us."

"And if I find something?"

"Just shout. But leave everything the way you find it."

Claire nodded and stepped into Tammy's bedroom. But this didn't look like any woman's bedroom she'd ever seen. The night tables, dressers, and headboard of the king-sized bed were a dark cherry and cut in sleek, straight, almost masculine lines. The sheets, folded over the neatly positioned bedspread, were white, as were the towels in the bathroom.

"Place looks like a hotel," she shouted to Nick.

He stuck his head in the doorway. "Yeah, unless the previous tenant was a guy and she bought his furniture from him when she moved in here."

Good point, Claire thought as Nick went back to his search, and she gingerly opened the top drawer of the dresser. It was filled with women's panties and thongs, haphazardly thrown in instead of being neatly folded. As she opened the other drawers and the closet, Claire found them just as disorganized and totally at odds with the rest of the apartment. And then the psychiatrist in her took over.

The apartment's a metaphor for Tammy's life. All put together on the outside but inside she was a mess.

She was about to join Nick in the living room when she noticed a strange protrusion in the bedspread about halfway between the floor and the top of the mattress. Thinking maybe she had moved something she shouldn't have, she tried to smooth it out.

But it was hard. Like something was poking out.

"Detective!" she shouted. "I need you in here."

Nick was there in seconds.

"I think there's something in this bed."

He lifted the bedspread. Sure enough, the corner of a small bound book stuck out from under the mattress just enough to cause the odd lump in the fabric. Carefully, Nick had Claire hold up the bedspread as he took a photo with his cell phone. Then he grabbed the book with two gloved fingers and pulled it from its hiding place. It had no title or print of any kind on the spine or front cover. Claire knew instantly what it was.

"It's her diary," she said to Nick.

"You haven't even looked at it," Nick said.

"I'm a girl," Claire said with a knowing smile. "Under the mattress is just one of the many favorite places we hide our diaries."

"Hide them from who?"

"Any busybody who'd want to read it. It's a privacy thing."

Nick threw her a look as he opened it. Again, Claire was correct. The smooth white pages bore the curvy, neat handwriting that could only be female.

He flipped through the pages until he found where Tammy had stopped writing.

"You ready for this? Her last entry was three weeks ago."

"Right around the time her parents say they last saw her," Claire said.

"What do you make of this, Dr. Holmes?" he asked, handing the open book to Claire.

She read the odd entries aloud.

"Steve and Mark—Red . . . Five."

"Frank—Imagine . . . Three."

"Jordan—Starlight . . . Five."

"Here's the last one from three weeks ago. Some guy with the initials E. B.—Red . . . Five plus."

"Any idea what the hell that means?"

Claire had a pretty good idea. "I think it's a sex diary," she said.

Nick shook his head. "That something else you girls do?"

"Of course we do. I can understand why Tammy wrote them down."

"And why would that be?"

"Because from the looks of this, she didn't have sex with the same man twice."

This prompted Nick to look over her shoulder. "You're right," he said after a moment. "What are the numbers?" he asked.

"I think it's a rating system," Claire replied.

"I thought that was a guy thing," Nick said.

"Tammy was a scientist, so the attention to detail fits. What I don't understand are the words: 'Red, Imagine, Starlight . . .' "

But Nick knew exactly what they were. "Because you're not from here. Red, Imagine, and Starlight are all nightclubs on the West Side. Three blocks from where we found Tammy."

They looked at each other. It was starting to make sense.

"You think this was her bucket list? Like she knew she was dying and decided she was gonna go out with a bang? No pun intended."

And then it hit. Frantically, she began turning pages, speed-reading each one, looking for the name she was almost certain would be there. She had to go back only ten pages before she saw it.

"Todd—Red . . . Two."

"What's the date on that?" asked Nick.

"Eight months ago," Claire answered.

"That's right around the time Quimby was arrested," Nick said.

"Tammy met him at the club," Claire realized. "She slept with him because that's what she did. My guess is, he came back looking for her after he got out of jail and saw her with another guy."

Nick knew where she was going. "He stalks her, murders her, keeps her on ice, and dumps her in the ballpark on home plate. To be found when the sun comes up or the lights are turned on. So everyone could see her for what Quimby thought she was."

"A whore," said Claire. "She was just another whore to him."

CHAPTER 14

After Nick dropped Claire off at the safe house, she barely slept, tossing and turning, obsessed with the mystery of Tammy Sorenson. The same question flashed over and over in her mind:

How could Tammy have been cancer-free two months ago and riddled with metastatic disease now?

"As far as the murder investigation's concerned, all we need to know is how she's connected to Todd Quimby," Nick had said when she mentioned the cancer to him in the car on the way home from Tammy's apartment.

He doesn't understand. He's a cop. I'm a doctor. A scientist. And scientifically, the case of Tammy's sudden onset of lymphoma is an anomaly that must be investigated.

She considered mentioning it to Dr. Curtin, briefly deluded by the remote possibility her mentor would see the value in getting to the bottom of this medical riddle. Until she came back to reality and realized it would be more like waving a red flag in front of a bull. Curtin had expressly ordered her to steer clear of anything Quimby, an edict she had flagrantly disobeyed. If he found out what she'd been doing, he would surely expel her from the fellowship program, a risk Claire didn't want to take.

Not yet, anyway.

Instead, she decided she'd solve the puzzle herself, and only when all the evidence was in place would she present it to Curtin as a fait accompli.

First, though, she had to gather the evidence, assuming any could be found. She picked up the phone and called Tammy's mother.

"Mrs. Sorenson?" Claire said into the receiver, staring at the blank walls of her interim apartment. "It's Claire Waters. I was at your house with Detective Lawler last night. . . ."

"Yes, Doctor," came the voice of Tammy's mother, Gloria. "Do you have any information for us?"

"Not yet," Claire answered. "But there's something I'm hoping you can help me with."

"Of course. My husband and I will help in any way we can," Gloria answered.

"Mr. Sorenson mentioned last night that Tammy had just undergone an insurance physical," Claire said, "By law, the insurance company is required to send the applicant a copy of the results. Did Tammy ever mention anything about that to you?"

"She didn't have to," Gloria replied. "The results were mailed here to the house and my husband opened them by accident. We actually read them to Tammy over the phone."

"Is there any chance you could fax them to me?" Claire asked.

"Give me the number and I'll do it right now," Gloria said.

Claire could only wonder how Gloria was holding up. No doubt she and her husband were making funeral arrangements for their daughter, something no parent should ever have to do. Which is why Claire hated to push this grieving mother.

"Mrs. Sorenson, I know this is a horrible shock and I hate to impose, but if it's okay, there's one other thing I need your help with."

"Please," Gloria said, "don't feel in the least like you're imposing."

"Do you happen to know if Tammy had an internist?"

"Yes, she goes to the same . . . *went* to the same doctor my husband and I have been seeing for years—Phil Gentry at Westchester Medical Center in Valhalla."

"Would you be willing to sign a release authorizing Dr. Gentry to provide me with her medical records?"

Claire could hear the hesitation on the other end of the phone.

"Is this about the cancer?" Gloria asked.

She was not about to lie to this poor woman. "Yes, it is," Claire replied.

"And you think her being sick has something to do with her murder?"

Claire had to be careful here, because not even Nick knew what she was doing.

"We just have to cover all the bases," she said evenly. "It's routine in a case like this."

Routine in an unexplained, sudden case of rare, aggressive, metastatic Hodgkin's lymphoma, Claire thought, justifying the ruse to herself.

"I'm sure if you call Phil and explain why you need Tammy's records, he'd be glad to give them to you," said Gloria.

The last thing Claire wanted was another doctor asking questions about what the records were really for. Fortunately, she had an out.

"The federal privacy laws regarding medical records are very strict, even after a patient's death," she said to Gloria, "and if I called Dr. Gentry, he'd ask me to come to you first for permission, which is why I'm doing that now. Believe me, the last thing I want is to disturb you at a time like this."

"All right," said Gloria. "If you fax me the release, I'll take care of it."

Claire felt a twinge of guilt. A lie was a lie, no matter how little and white and necessary it seemed, and she wasn't done yet.

"I can't thank you enough, Mrs. Sorenson. Is there anything else I can do to help you and your husband? You were able to recover Tammy from the medical examiner with no problem?"

Claire had asked that question for a specific reason.

"Yes, the funeral home picked her up this morning," Gloria said, sounding empty.

"Can you tell me when the service is?" Claire asked. "Detective Lawler will want to know." *At least that wasn't a lie*, Claire thought, knowing full well homicide detectives routinely attended their victims' funerals to see who showed up in case one of the mourners turned out to be the killer. She also knew Nick would be attending for sure.

"Monday," Gloria said.

"Can you tell me the name of both the church and the cemetery?" Claire asked.

"I can e-mail them to you if you'd like," Gloria replied. "She's being buried in our family plot here in town."

Claire silently breathed a sigh of relief, for Gloria had unknowingly provided her with the information she really needed: Tammy wasn't going to be cremated. She wanted Tammy's body intact and six feet under just in case the need ever arose to exhume her remains for further study. That would be impossible if she was reduced to ashes and spread over some mountainside.

She thanked Gloria profusely before hanging up, promising to accompany Nick to the funeral if she possibly could and once again offering her condolences.

Claire checked her watch. It was 8:32 on Friday morning. *Dammit,* Claire thought. Curtin's Last Supper was at nine sharp today, and though she had no patients to present, she knew she best not be late.

Claire bolted into the hospital and ran right into Ian, nearly knocking his armful of files to the floor.

"Jesus," he cried, "you got a train to catch?"

"Sorry," Claire answered, giving him a hug. "I don't want to be late."

Ian shook off the surprise as they walked toward the meeting.

"You didn't call me last night," he said.

She gave him a kiss. "I'm sorry, I went to bed early—I was so exhausted." Claire racked up another lie. But she justified it out of her love for Ian. She knew he'd worry if he found out that she was disobeying Curtin.

"I understand. I'm just missing you so much," Ian said.

Claire couldn't stand deceiving him. "Ian"—she paused—"I didn't have a chance to tell you. Nick asked me to go with him to notify the parents of the victim from two nights ago. I didn't want you to worry."

"Curtin told you to stay away from the Quimby case," Ian replied. "And now you're calling him 'Nick'?"

"I'm sorry I didn't tell you before. I feel responsible for what's happened. That's why I went with him—to do everything I can to stop Quimby."

Ian took Claire's arm, guiding her into an alcove. "I'm not jealous," he said, rubbing her shoulder the way she loved. "It's just that you're going through all this and . . . you won't even let me help."

She looked at him. For a moment, all the insanity of the last week melted away and it was just the two of them.

"I do need your help," she said to him quietly. "And I have to get to the bottom of this, Curtin or no Curtin."

"You're not a detective, Claire."

"It's not just about the murders. The victim from two nights ago had metastatic Hodgkin's lymphoma. And she was only twenty-eight."

Ian's face registered his shock. "I'm a shrink but even I know that's out of whack," he said.

Claire told him the story and let him in on her plan. "I think you're crazy," he said when she finished, "but I love you, and whatever you need, I'm in."

"Any doctor who saw an advanced case like Tammy's would've notified the Tumor Registry," Claire said to him. "Can you check and see if it was ever reported?"

"Of course," Ian assured her. "I'll get you a printout." Then he added, "If that's what it takes for a guy to get laid around here."

"Come over to my place tomorrow night," Claire said with a lascivious smile, "and you'll get more than that."

She kissed him and walked away.

"Wait a minute," said Ian, still savoring the kiss as he caught up with her. "Why not tonight?"

"I got about an hour of sleep last night," Claire answered.

"Message received," Ian said.

"I wouldn't be much fun," Claire continued.

"I miss you," replied Ian.

"I miss you too."

And as they walked together toward the meeting, Claire was satisfied she hadn't *exactly* lied to Ian. He would only worry about her, and she couldn't take that on top of everything else. She also knew she wouldn't be going back to the safe house to sleep until the wee hours of the next morning—that is, if everything went according to plan.

Rain poured from the sky as Claire finally emerged from the front doors of the hospital at six in the evening. She cowered under an umbrella, quickly spotting Maggie Stolls's police-issue dark gray Dodge Charger. She got into the front passenger seat.

"Tough day at the office?" Maggie asked as Claire clumsily closed her umbrella.

"I wish it was over," Claire replied. "But that asshole Curtin wants me to stick around and finish up some paperwork."

"You look like toast," Maggie observed. "How the hell will you stay awake?"

"Lots of coffee," said Claire, looking at Maggie for the first time since getting in the car. She was about the same age as Claire, Brooklyn born and raised and lived there still. And like most Brooklynites, she would gladly tell you to go to hell if she thought you deserved it. Claire turned on her best shrink approach to help Maggie feel comfortable and trust her: *Get Maggie to talk about herself.*

"You know, we can talk for a bit before I have to go back inside," Claire said. "I could use a break." Claire smiled at Maggie when she noticed that Maggie's ponytail was damp and frizzy from the rain. "What made you decide to become a cop?"

"I was about to graduate with a degree in accounting when a girlfriend dared me to take the police exam. I walked in and aced it without even studying," Maggie said, shrugging her shoulders. "I realized then a life of crunching numbers wasn't for me." She paused, then asked, "What about you? When did you know you wanted to be a shrink?"

"I always knew," Claire said. "I love hearing people's stories and helping them sort them out."

"Me too," Maggie said. "I guess we're a lot alike—though I'm helping the victims and you're helping the perps."

"Not always," Claire reminded her. "Prosecutors use shrinks too."

There was a brief, uncomfortable silence between them, punctuated by the pouring rain.

"Can I bring you anything, like dinner?" Maggie asked her.

"It's bad enough you have to protect me," Claire said. "I won't make you a delivery girl too. Besides, I'm too tired to eat."

"I'm starving," Maggie said. "I'll go grab a slice at that place around the corner and be right back."

Maggie and Nick had decided Todd Quimby was way too smart to show his face again at Manhattan City Hospital, and even if he did, he'd have to come through the front doors. Claire was glad the protection wasn't overkill. Especially tonight.

"It'll be a late one," she said to Maggie.

"I'll keep the meter running," Maggie replied jokingly. "Call me on my cell when you're ready to go."

"Thanks," Claire said, getting out of the car and opening her umbrella. She ran back through the hospital doors, stopping just inside. She shook the water off her umbrella as she watched Maggie pull away and drive around the corner.

Then Claire walked back out of the hospital and ran to where a man was just exiting a taxi.

She got into the backseat before he could close the door, and the cab pulled away.

CHAPTER 15

Nick awoke with a start, his eyelids open but his eyes seeing nothing. A brief, terrifying thought overtook him before he remembered the windowless room in the precinct where he'd chosen to grab a few hours of much-needed sleep.

He fumbled for the button that lit up his watch. The numbers on the face slowly came into focus: 9:17 p.m. Shit. He sat bolt upright—and promptly hit his head on the underside of the top bunk.

Rubbing his head, Nick swung his feet to the floor. He shook off the ever-increasing soreness of middle age and cursed the city of New York for forcing the best detectives in the world to nap on decrepit bunk beds, purchased no doubt from some nameless discount warehouse at least a decade before Nick was born. He breathed in the stale air and felt a twinge of panic. The last time he was here, a year ago, he could see the outlines of the beds from the light leaking under the door. Tonight he saw only black.

He maneuvered carefully around the dark room, which was no bigger than a large closet; in fact, Nick thought, it probably *was* a closet before it was commandeered as the precinct "crib." He peeled off his gym shorts, put on his jeans, undershirt, and sweater, and laced up his black Reeboks. No need for his usual suit tonight. He was going hunting.

In the forty-eight hours since Tammy Sorenson's body had been found on home plate in De Witt Clinton Park, Todd Quimby had become the most feared criminal in New York since David Berkowitz, the notorious "Son of Sam" serial killer, murdered seven young people parked in lovers' lanes thirty-five years earlier. Quimby's body count was now four women (and one critically injured detective, Tommy Wessel), causing the police commissioner, a raging control freak on a good day, to declare war. The PC, a sergeant back in '77, remembered all too well what the Son of Sam cost the Big Apple back then. No way was he giving Quimby carte blanche to scare the masses away from his turf. Not on his watch.

His orders were clear: screw the city's budget deficit. Blanket overtime was approved, vacation days and time off revoked for every cop in the Five Boroughs. Todd Quimby would be captured at all costs; they would pursue him until he was either locked up or, as the PC was heard to say to a select few, dead. The Boss of Bosses let it be known that the cop or cops who stopped Quimby from dropping another corpse would be rewarded with promotions and plum assignments.

Damn him for saying those exact words to the press, Nick thought.

He hadn't been home since Tammy's murder, running down every possible lead, each one leading nowhere. Even worse, though, were the now-constant, always-annoying encounters with the New York news media. Cops loved tipping off their "friends" in the press, and in a high-profile case like this, the NYPD leaked like Hoover Dam had burst. Every reporter worth his salt knew Nick was the lead detective on the case, which translated into at least a dozen microphones and TV cameras being shoved up his nose every time he walked in or out of the precinct. Always polite (because you never knew when you'd need them), Nick gave a friendly "No comment" unless the reporter "went Geraldo" (the cops' term of derision for any bastard who got in their face), to which he would give a glare and walk away.

Of course, what he really wanted to tell them was to get the hell out of his face so he could do his job. And after two relentless days without sleep, Lieutenant Wilkes had ordered Nick to the crib. Nick chose not to argue with his savior, the man who literally resurrected his career, and went without protest to catch three hours of shut-eye.

Now, four hours later, Nick emerged from the bunk room, clipping his holster to his belt and adjusting his eyes to the much brighter light of the hallway just in time to see Savarese bounding toward him.

"Just coming to get you," he said to Nick.

"What's up?" Nick replied.

"Heard back from Tammy Sorenson's employer, Biopharix. Human Resources confirmed she took two weeks' vacation."

"Did she tell them where she was going?" Nick asked, hoping for even the smallest lead.

"Nope," Savarese said. "We checked her credit cards. No plane, train, or hotel reservations. For Hawaii or anywhere else."

They entered the buzzing squad room, which was too small to handle the sheer number of bodies assigned to the case. Detectives doubled up at desks, almost falling over one another as they walked in and out. Phones rang off the hook as Wilkes, in his tiny office at the far end of the room, screamed expletives into his phone and then slammed it down on the cradle.

"You think Tammy checked in somewhere secretly for treatment?" Savarese asked. "Some kind of private clinic or something?"

Nick couldn't help but think of his secret trips to the ophthalmologist in Boston.

"If she did, it's gonna be a bitch finding out where, what with the federal privacy laws," Nick replied. "When was the last time she used a credit card?"

"The night we found her," answered Savarese.

"Which was two nights after she was murdered," Nick replied, grabbing a marker and writing *credit cards* in dark blue ink on the dry-erase board. "Means Quimby used her credit cards. For what?"

"Bar tabs at every hot club in Manhattan. Guy's been busy. He hit the Iguana, Baby Face, South of SoHo, Red . . ."

Nick scribbled the club names on the board. "Hold on. That's the same club Tammy went to three weeks ago," he said, circling the name *Red*.

"And there's a charge here to Red the night she was killed," Savarese said, scanning the printout.

"What? Why didn't you tell me?" Nick challenged him.

"I only just got her financials—"

"I got it!" Nick interrupted with an excitement Savarese hadn't seen in over a year. "Tammy kept a diary of all the clubs where she picked up men. She went back to Red the night she was killed—it's only two blocks from De Witt Clinton Park."

"Which means Quimby met her there," Savarese added.

"The clubs are his hunting ground," Nick said, underlining *Red* on the board for emphasis.

"Then we'd better get detectives into every one of them, right?" growled Wilkes, now beside them. Neither detective had seen him come over.

Nick grabbed his jacket from his chair. "I'll take Red—"

"Not so fast," Wilkes interrupted. "Maggie Stolls just called in. Your shrink gave her the slip."

The news worried Nick and pissed him off. "Did Maggie say how?"

"She told Stolls she was working late and then took off," Wilkes replied.

Claire wouldn't intentionally ditch her protection after everything that happened, Nick thought. *Or would she?*

"Maggie's gotta get back to the safe house in case Dr. Waters shows up," Nick said.

"She's on her way," replied Wilkes. "And you've gotta get out there and find that crazy shrink. Before Quimby does."

"I need to find Quimby," Nick shot back, turning for the door.

"And I don't need a murdered psychiatrist," Wilkes shouted back, turning all the detectives' heads. "I got enough problems as it is. Find her, Nick. Now."

Nick stopped and turned back to face Wilkes, knowing it was useless to argue.

"Okay," he said simply, and headed out.

Total darkness. Then searing bright red lights, flashing on, off, on, off, against the pounding beat of hip-hop as Nick pushed his way into the club, struggling to see.

Then the lights came on low, allowing his eyes to finally focus on the sea of bodies gyrating against one another like bacteria in polluted waters. He was in Red, one of the clubs that appeared in Tammy Sorenson's sex diary and, posthumously, on her credit card statement.

As he flashed his detective's shield to the bouncer outside the club, Nick couldn't help but notice the thick red velvet rope that held back the waiting crowd. He knew he was crossing the line in more ways than one. He was actively disobeying Lt. Wilkes's order to find Claire. Violating a direct command from his superior, the one who'd saved his ass. An offense punishable by loss of vacation, pay, or, if they really wanted to get you, termination from the police department and forfeiting one's pension.

Or, if he found Todd Quimby inside the club, a promotion.

Until the job learned about his secret disability.

How long can I keep it from them? Nick thought as he moved through the crowd, passing patrons who looked at him like he was a freak of nature. Did they make him for a cop? In a room full of Armani and Hugo Boss, did his Men's Wearhouse Super 180 wool pinstripe pants and turtleneck peg him as a wannabe? He'd stopped at home to change, putting on the hippest outfit he owned. *What was I thinking? I'll never fit in,* he thought as he felt someone bump him in the shoulder.

"Sorry," Nick said instantly to a good-looking guy in his thirties dancing with a woman wearing a dress that barely covered her obviously enhanced breasts.

"Watch where you're going, asshole," the guy said.

Nick wasn't in the mood. "*Sorry* doesn't work for you?" he asked in a way that sounded like a dare.

The guy, who was obviously trying to pick up the woman, got in Nick's face. "You need to apologize to the lady too."

"And what if I don't?" Nick returned.

"You the cop?" came a voice from behind them.

Nick turned to face a man in his late forties, the lines in his face a testament to years of hard partying. "I'm Andros Szabo. The owner."

Nick displayed his shield. "Detective Nick Lawler," he said. He shot a look to the jerk, who made the prudent decision to step back. Nick caught the wink the woman with the fake breasts shot him as she walked away from the troublemaker. Nick then turned to Szabo. "Somewhere we can talk?" he yelled above the din.

Szabo nodded, parting the crowd and leading Nick up a flight of stairs and into a plush office with a huge one-way mirror that looked out over the gyrating bodies.

"Appreciate the time," Nick said, pulling a photo of Tammy Sorenson from his pocket and handing it to Szabo. "Have you seen this woman in here?"

Without missing a beat, Szabo nodded. "A shame. Such a beautiful girl," he replied in his Eastern European accent, looking up at Nick. "I see the news."

"You know her," Nick said.

"Tammy," Szabo replied. "Everybody knows Tammy," he said with a smile.

Nick knew exactly what he meant but wanted to hear it from him. "Can you be more specific?"

Szabo looked at him like he was a rube. "Every night, she come in. Have a drink, go on the dance floor. Pick up a guy. Leave with guy. Every night, different guy. Tried to leave with me one night," he said wistfully. "I know better."

Nick pulled out a mug shot of Quimby. "This one of the guys?" he asked.

Szabo frowned. "The killer on the TV. I have not seen him in here."

"But you'd tell me if you did, right?" Nick pressed.

The club owner looked straight at him. "I get hundreds of people in and out of here every night. The beautiful women, I notice. This man, he would be just another face in the crowd."

Nick knew he was telling the truth. Now came the sales pitch.

"Mr. Szabo, I need your help."

"Whatever I can do."

"I'm guessing you have security cameras in the club."

"Of course," said Szabo. "State-of-the-art."

"How long do you keep the video from any particular night?"

Szabo was reading his mind. "It is stored on a hard drive and recycled after two weeks. If you send your computer expert here, he can clone the hard drive for you."

Nick smiled. "Thank you, sir. You've done this before, I imagine."

"I watch the crime drama marathons on cable TV. And you are welcome. But I'm not sure you'll find what you look for."

"Why not?" Nick asked.

"The girl, Tammy. She hasn't been here in a while."

"We know," Nick said, "but her credit card's been used at your bar numerous times in the last few weeks."

Szabo's face darkened. "You are serious," he replied. "And you think it was the killer using it?"

"Mr. Szabo, can you tell me the last time you actually saw this woman in the club?"

Szabo sighed. "I told you, she wanted to leave with me. I declined; then I had remorse. I told my people at the rope to let me know the next time she came in and to send her directly to me. That was three weeks ago."

A sudden burst of light from the dance floor drew Nick's attention to the one-way mirror. The DJ had turned on the bright white lights, illuminating the crowd.

"Detective, are you okay?" Szabo asked.

But Nick didn't answer, his eyes focused on a woman with short blond hair, in a short black dress, dancing. His eyes darted to another woman, taller but with the same short hair, similar black dress. Then another. And another. And another . . .

Quimby had his pick in this place.

Nick saw another one, but she wasn't dancing. *She looks too stiff, like she doesn't belong here,* Nick thought. She turned around just as the lights came down and began to strobe, casting a red gash across her face—a familiar face.

"Can you excuse me?" Nick turned away from the one-way mirror.

"Do you see your killer?" Szabo asked, alarmed, picking up a walkie-talkie. "I'll have my people stop him."

"No, it's not him," Nick retorted, heading for the door. "Just someone I may know."

"Your eyes are better than mine, then," said Szabo. "To me the faces are all the same from up here."

"I'll be back," Nick said, going out the door and hurrying down the stairs. He knew Szabo was right. How could he trust his eyes from so far away? But he had to be sure.

He reached the floor of the club. It took a couple of seconds to adjust to the strobing lights and the pounding music as he scanned the direction where he'd seen the woman. Nothing.

There! Blond hair—as if on fire from the flashing red lights—

heading through the dancing crowd. Toward the back. She had a cell phone to her ear. He moved toward the vision, trying not to bump into anyone, hoping the woman didn't see him.

Nick grabbed the woman's arm and roughly turned her around. Claire violently shook it off, dropping her phone, which went crashing to the floor.

"Get your hands off me!" she said.

And then she saw who it was.

"What the hell do you think you're doing?" Nick yelled over the din.

"You know what I'm doing," she fired back as she bent over and picked up the shattered phone, displaying it to him. "Look what you did."

Nick yanked her toward the front door. "You're coming with me," he said, literally pulling her outside.

"Where are you taking me?"

"To the safe house. Or the precinct lockup. Your choice."

The bouncers eyed Nick as he pulled Claire along. He flashed his shield, lest they tried to intervene. She struggled to keep her balance in the black pumps she'd bought at Bloomingdale's on the way over. She got the black dress there, too, and had put it on in the changing room, asking the store to hold her other clothes until she could pick them up in the morning.

"I'm trying to help you," Claire said, trying to catch her breath as Nick pulled her along.

"You're trying to help yourself into an early grave."

They reached the car. Nick let go of her.

"That hurt," Claire said, rubbing her arm.

"Not close to how much Quimby would've hurt you if he saw you in that getup. You want to get yourself killed?"

"I have to find him."

"That's my job, not yours."

"He met Tammy here before. I thought maybe he'd come back to Red for his next victim."

Nick had to admire her logic. *If she wasn't a shrink,* he thought, *she might make a good cop.* "I thought the same thing, but something's wrong."

Claire looked at him. She could see he was disturbed, which

drained away the anger she had felt toward him for pulling her out of the club. "What is it, Nick?"

"Tammy used her credit card at Red the night she was killed. But the owner says she hasn't been there for three weeks."

This stopped Claire short. "Tammy's parents said she left three weeks ago for Hawaii, and we know she never went there."

"And Quimby murdered her two nights before her body turned up," Nick replied, opening the door for Claire.

"So Quimby met her two nights earlier," Claire said. "But I don't see how she could have gone to the club in her condition."

"According to the club owner, she didn't," Nick added, perplexed. "But he could be wrong. We'll know for sure when I get the surveillance video from the club. But Quimby's face has been all over the media. He'd be stupid to show up in public, and so far he hasn't been stupid."

Nick closed Claire's door and headed to the driver's side. He got in and stared out the windshield at the club's sign. Bright red neon dots exploded like balloons popping.

Claire looked at Nick. He was calmer now. "Tammy's cancer wasn't on the Tumor Registry," she said, watching for his reaction.

"What does that mean?" Nick asked, turning toward her. Their faces were inches apart, and Claire could see deep sorrow in his eyes.

"Anyone with an aggressive cancer like Tammy's would have been presented to a board of oncologists," Claire replied. "Her case was unusual, and her doctor would have wanted the best minds to give their opinions."

"And you know this how?" Nick asked.

"Ian found out for me," Claire answered. "That was him on the phone back at the club, saying none of it was making any sense."

"Did he say anything else?" Nick asked.

"I didn't get the chance to ask him anything," Claire said, exasperated, "because you made me drop my phone."

Nick looked at her. He handed her his cell. "Call him back," he said.

"He won't answer if he doesn't recognize the number," Claire replied.

"Then we'll ask him in person," Nick said evenly, turning the ignition. A blast of chatter from Nick's walkie-talkie squawked on the front seat between them.

"Midtown North Commander, responding from Queens."

"Car eight-oh-two, responding, Central."

Car 802 was the handle for Wilkes's unmarked Crown Vic. Nick grabbed the walkie.

"Car seven-two-three to Central," he said into the mouthpiece.

"Seven-two-three," came the response from the dispatcher. "Ten-two your commander at the West Side Rail Yards. Other units responding."

Nick looked at Claire. From the expression on his face, Claire knew what it meant.

"Oh, no," she said.

Savarese walked Claire and Nick into the crime scene. "Sector car found her. Cops said she was a regular on the stroll up in the forties, but they don't know her name. Detective from Manhattan North is coming down to ID her."

"Heads up," warned Savarese. "The boss is on fire."

Nick didn't even have time to reply when Lt. Wilkes spotted him and stormed over.

"Where the hell have you been?" he demanded.

Nick indicated Claire. "You told me to find her, right?"

Wilkes eyed Claire's outfit and decided not to ask. "Guess it's a good thing you're here, Doc, because he's escalating."

He led them over to a body covered by a white sheet. Wilkes pulled the sheet down so they could see.

The victim was again a pretty blond girl, in an outfit that screamed hooker—gold sequined top, skirt slit up the sides to the waist. Once again, a rope secured with a Dutch marine bowline knot was looped around her neck. But her face was a red, blotchy mess, making her unrecognizable.

"He burned her face off," Nick observed grimly.

"Like he threw the lye right on her. He's getting sloppy, Nick," Wilkes said.

"Or he's getting to the end of his rope," Claire added, drawing looks from the detectives at her unintended pun.

Nick scanned the surroundings. "No signs of a struggle."

"He picks her up in a car, does the deed, and dumps her here," offered Wilkes.

Nick knelt beside the body. Took a few quick sniffs. Turned to Claire. "You smell anything?"

"Bitter almonds? Again?" asked Wilkes.

"Yeah."

"You're nuts," said Wilkes. "No pun intended," he added.

"What does this lunatic have in store for us next?" asked Savarese.

"Me," said Claire, choking on the word.

CHAPTER 16

"I talked to my boss," Nick said, swallowing the last of his midnight bacon and eggs. "We're upping your protection."

Claire simply nodded, eyeing the nearly full bowl of salad greens that she hadn't wanted to order in the first place.

"You should eat something," Nick said.

"You're starting to sound like my mother," Claire answered.

They had come to the all-night diner on 11th Avenue directly from the crime scene. Other than the victim displaying Quimby's MO and signature, the Crime Scene Unit found nothing to explain how he transported the body to its final resting place. All Nick was able to determine was that nineteen-year-old Lucy Chapman, a runaway from Indianapolis, known on the hooker stroll as "Cookie," was a fresh kill, dead no more than an hour before being discovered by a guy in a late-model BMW parked just yards away. He'd spotted her body after one of Cookie's competitors listlessly gave him the "service" he had paid fifty bucks for. The john, a businessman from Teaneck, New Jersey, was assured by responding patrol cops that they were interested only in what he saw before noticing the body. He said that he had been concentrating on getting his money's worth and didn't even see the dead hooker until he'd exited his car to grab a towel out of the trunk.

"You'll have a cop with you at all times," Nick told Claire, "both in and out of the hospital."

"I can't take a cop on rounds," Claire said. "And how will I explain the extra protection to Curtin?"

"I'll explain it," Nick said calmly as his phone spewed Lady Gaga.

"Hi, sweetheart . . . I miss you too . . . I'll be home in an hour. I can't wait to see you. Bye, sweetie."

Claire stared at him as he hung up. It was the first time she'd seen this side of Nick. "Your kids," she said.

"My oldest daughter, Jill," Nick answered. "She woke up and saw I wasn't home. Wanted to know if she'll ever see me again."

"You've been working some long hours," said Claire.

"Haven't been home in three days," he said, reminding himself.

Claire noted the lack of a wedding ring on Nick's hand. "You're divorced."

"Widowed," Nick corrected.

"I'm sorry," Claire replied, embarrassed by jumping to conclusions—something as a psychiatrist she tried not to do.

"Don't be. She killed herself," Nick said flatly.

Claire looked at him. *That was an odd comment.*

"Surprised you didn't hear about it."

"Why would I?"

"It was all over the media. You want to know how she did it?"

He's not looking at me, Claire noticed.

"If you want to tell me," she answered.

Nick took a quick gulp of coffee, as if it were a scotch and he was about to confess to something awful. "She shot herself. With one of my guns. Eight months ago."

"Did you know she was suicidal?" Claire asked reflexively.

The question caught Nick off guard. He looked at her sharply. "How would I know that?"

"Sorry. None of my business," Claire said.

But in her head, she knew he'd made it her business. She could feel the guilt inside him, ready to burst. And though she wanted to help him, this was neither the time nor the place for an impromptu therapy session.

He needed to tell someone. He chose me.

"No, I'm sorry," Nick said, realizing the position he'd put her in. He glanced at her. She looked sad to him. "You've got enough problems without hearing mine."

A hint of a smile crossed Claire's face. "I'm a shrink," she said.

"Not a very good one, maybe. But I get dumped on for a living. Don't worry about it."

Nick stood. "C'mon," he said. "I'll take you home. Such that it is."

They walked into the vestibule of the brownstone that was Claire's safe house. Claire was nervous as she fumbled for the key to the security door. *My turn to confess now,* she thought.

"I like Maggie," she said to Nick. "I don't want there to be any . . . you know, bad blood."

"She's okay. She didn't get into any trouble," Nick said.

What she didn't know, and what Nick would never tell her, was that it was anything but simple. It had taken no small amount of skill on Nick's part to calm his boss down and assure him that there was no harm done because Claire was safely with him. Once calm, Wilkes promised not to give Maggie a rip, after Nick embellished how mentally fragile Claire was and that firing Maggie might push Claire over the edge.

"You sure she's not mad at me?" Claire asked Nick.

"She trusted you," Nick replied. "But her job is to protect you. She would never walk out on you. None of us would."

Claire found the key to the security door. She opened it and Nick held it for her as she walked through. He looked at her, hesitating. Claire knew what he was thinking.

"The only way out of this place is the way we came in, and I'm not going to make it down the fire escape in these heels," she assured him. "And Maggie will never let me out of her sight again."

"Okay. I guess I can trust you getting upstairs by yourself," Nick said, relenting. "Get some sleep." He opened the security door and turned to leave.

"Nick."

He turned back, a troubled look on his face, which Claire couldn't help but catch.

"Something wrong?" she asked him.

"Just tired, I guess," he replied. But it was more than that.

I'm ashamed. She said my name and I liked the sound of it.

"Thank you," Claire said, meaning it.

Nick turned away. "Try to get some rest," he said.

Claire watched him leave, then walked up the flight of stairs to the apartment door. She gingerly inserted the key in the lock and turned it, pushed the door open, and stepped through into the darkness. The apartment was dark but for a sliver of light coming through the slightly ajar bathroom door, through which Claire could hear water running. She wasn't looking forward to the confrontation but decided to make light of it nonetheless.

"Hey," she shouted toward the bathroom. "Hurry up in there— I've got to pee."

If Maggie heard her, she wasn't acknowledging. Claire walked into the living room, reached in the darkness for the lamp. She located the small knob just below the lightbulb and switched it on.

She threw her coat over a chair, wanting to collapse into it. Instead, she headed toward the bathroom door, hoping Maggie wasn't so pissed off she wouldn't talk to her.

"Look," she shouted over the running water, "I just want to say how sorry I am."

Claire stopped cold, hearing a *squish* under her pumps as if she'd stepped on a wet sponge. She looked down. The carpet was soaked. Her eyes darted toward the bottom of the bathroom door.

Water. Seeping out under the door.

She glanced toward the door to Maggie's bedroom. Closed.

Claire realized what must have happened. Maggie had run herself a bath, gone into her room, probably stretched out on her bed waiting for the tub to fill, and fallen asleep. Hoping the water hadn't yet leaked through to the apartment below, Claire hurried toward the bathroom door.

"Maggie," she yelled, "wake up. I need you out here . . ."

She pushed the door open. And for a moment she wasn't sure she was seeing right.

What she saw was Maggie, naked, hanging dead from a rope thrown over the metal shower curtain rod and tied around her neck. With a Dutch marine bowline.

Claire let out a bloodcurdling scream, which lasted only a second before a gloved hand cut off what was left of her air and a rope looped around her neck and tightened.

* * *

Nick was getting into his car across the street when he heard it. A scream.

But by the time his head spun around, it had stopped. He stood there, leaning against the open car door, wondering if he'd imagined it.

Then he thought of the telltale *click* of a gun being cocked.

My bedroom. If only I'd gotten there in time . . .

He shook his head, thinking of that horrible night as he glanced up at the window of Claire's apartment. The light was on; nothing seemed to be out of place. And Maggie was there to protect her. Nick waited one more second before he got into the car and closed the door.

Claire gasped for air as her attacker pulled her violently backward, out of the bathroom. She had one hand between the rope and her windpipe, the other trying in vain to wrench his hand from her mouth. She tried desperately to bite him, but he was too strong. And then she remembered her spike-heeled shoes.

With everything she had left, she drove one of those spikes as far into his foot as she could.

He let out a cry of pain, involuntarily loosening his hold on the rope long enough for Claire to catch her breath and yank it away from him. She tried to scream again, but he was too fast for her, grabbing her around the neck in a choke hold and, in a burst of energy and anger, lifting her off the floor.

Claire flailed, kicking frantically, knocking over everything in her reach, knowing he'd cut off the blood flow to her brain and that she had only seconds before passing out. In desperation, she lifted her legs so the spiked heels faced the murderer behind her and kicked as hard as she could.

Her third thrust connected squarely with the killer's thigh.

Instantly, she felt his arm go limp around her neck as he tried to remain standing. Claire kicked him again, connecting with his knee and driving him backward, but also throwing her off balance and sending her crashing to the ground.

For the first time, she caught a glimpse of the man. He wore dark clothes, a hood over his head. A ski mask over his face.

And work boots. Dirty ones.

Like the ones Todd Quimby wore. It's him.

She was on the other side of the living room now, near the windows that looked out onto the street. She struggled to her feet, her eyes on the apartment door. If she could just get there.

Claire tried to run. But Quimby was too fast for her, latching onto the back of her dress, ripping it as he tried to pull her down.

She clutched the one lamp that gave light to the apartment but couldn't get the leverage she needed to whack him over the head with it.

So instead, with a sudden burst of adrenaline, she heaved it forward as hard as she could.

It sailed through the plate-glass window, shattering it into a million pieces on its journey to the sidewalk below and plunging the apartment into darkness.

Even with his police radio blaring, Nick heard the *smash*.

He had turned the car around and driven past the safe house one last time. He jammed on the brakes, screeching to a stop.

He looked in his rearview mirror, just in time to see a lamp land on the sidewalk behind him.

Nick jumped from the car, his Maglite in hand. He shined the beam up toward Claire's apartment. The jagged edges of glass that had once been the picture window gleamed like so many daggers.

Pulling his Glock, he ran for the brownstone. He burst through the front door but was stopped by the interior security door, which was much too heavy to kick in.

Aiming carefully to avoid ricochet, he fired at the lock. On the third shot it literally flew off the door.

Nick barreled through, taking the stairs two at a time.

"Police!" he screamed as he reached the second floor landing, hoping to scare the hell out of whoever was in the apartment.

With no thought to his own safety, he kicked in the apartment door. Swept his light across the darkness, illuminating the wreck of an apartment.

"Police!" Nick screamed again. "Hands in the air!"

"He's gone," came Claire's weak voice from across the room.

Nick holstered his gun and ran toward the voice, stumbling over the detritus of the struggle, finally reaching Claire, who was lying on the floor by the shattered window, the rope around her neck tied in what Nick could clearly see was a Dutch marine bowline. He helped Claire to her feet. "Are you okay?"

"I will be," she replied.

"Where's Maggie?"

"In the bathroom. Dead."

This wasn't the answer Nick expected.

"Quimby?"

"He heard gunshots and ran. Through my bedroom. I heard the window open," Claire said. "He must've gone out the fire escape."

"You sure you're not hurt?" Nick asked.

"I don't think so," said Claire, still in shock.

"Call nine-one-one," Nick told her. "Tell the operator you have a ten-thirteen at this address—that's a cop in trouble. They'll be here in two minutes."

He ran toward the bedroom. "Be careful," Claire shouted after him.

Nick climbed through the open window onto the fire escape. He climbed down the ladder, landing on the ground in an alley behind the brownstone. He shined his light in both directions. Quimby was gone.

Nick ran to where the alley spilled onto the sidewalk. He looked up and down the poorly lit street. There wasn't a soul out at this hour. Not that his failing eyes could make out, anyway.

And then he heard it. The distinct *groan* of a car engine turning over.

He aimed his light in the direction of the sound. Near the end of the block, a car was pulling out of a spot beside the curb.

Nick squeezed between two parked cars out to the street. The car headed toward him. Though its headlights were off, Nick could make out its shape. A '90s-era Buick Century sedan.

Quimby's grandmother owns a Buick Century. . . .

The car picked up speed, veered to the left, and bore down on him.

He's aiming for me!

With a second to spare before the car flattened him, Nick dove across the hood of a Hyundai, landing on the sidewalk as the speeding Buick sideswiped two other cars and kept on going.

Nick could hear the approaching sirens as he picked himself up and ran for the Impala, double-parked right where he'd left it, the engine still running. He jumped behind the wheel, threw it into gear, and jammed his foot on the gas, spinning the car into a screeching U-turn.

With one hand he palmed the wheel, straightening out the car as he put the red bubble light in the window with the other. Suddenly, Claire ran out into the street, her torn dress flapping in the wind, her feet bare. Nick slammed on the brakes as Claire yanked the passenger door open and all but fell in.

"Go!" she yelled at Nick.

She pulled on her seat belt as Nick stomped the gas pedal and flipped on the siren.

"Where's the Buick?" he demanded.

"Why the hell are you asking me?"

"Just answer the question!"

Claire could see it clearly, a block ahead of them. "End of the next block."

The Impala lurched to the right, sideswiping a parked pickup truck.

"Are you trying to kill us?" Claire asked.

"I don't see the car," Nick said.

"He turned right at the corner," Claire shouted, now scared. "What the hell's wrong with you?"

"I can't see at night!"

"Then pull over!"

"We'll lose him," Nick said. "We have to switch."

"While the car's moving?"

"I'll keep my foot on the gas. You grab the wheel and come under me."

Claire looked at him like he was nuts.

"Now!" he said.

She unlatched her seat belt and slid toward him as he lifted himself up off the seat, allowing her to slide under him.

They completed the maneuver and Claire could see the Buick careening into another right turn two blocks ahead of them.

She stomped on the gas as if she was born to drive. Made the two blocks in ten seconds, effortlessly turning the car around the next corner.

"Who taught you how to drive?" Nick asked incredulously.

"My father," said Claire. "Who hires a cop who's night-blind?"

"They don't know."

"Don't know what?"

"I have retinitis pigmentosa."

Claire looked at him sharply.

"Eyes on the road," Nick said to her.

"Retinitis pigmentosa? And you're carrying a gun?"

"Shut up and drive."

Ahead of them, Claire saw the Buick swerve onto an off-ramp for the FDR Drive.

"Jesus. He's going the wrong way."

"Where?" asked Nick.

"South on the northbound lanes of the FDR."

"Don't follow him. Too dangerous."

"One step ahead of you," Claire said.

She spun the wheel, expertly maneuvering the Impala onto the on-ramp for FDR Drive. "We'll parallel him," she said.

"You should've been a cop," Nick said, grabbing his handheld radio: "Central, seven-two-three, in pursuit of a nineties-model Buick Century heading south in the northbound lanes of the FDR Drive from Twenty-Third Street. Driver is a suspect in six homicides. Get Highway to shut down the FDR!"

Nick could hear the dispatcher clearing the frequency. Putting this out over the radio was the last thing he wanted to do because this would draw the media. But he had no choice.

Fortunately, it was the middle of the night and traffic on the Drive was light. Claire could see the Buick up ahead in the opposite lanes, dodging cars right and left.

Nick screamed into the walkie-talkie. "He just passed Houston Street. Shut him down at the Brooklyn Bridge!"

They came around the curve under the Williamsburg Bridge. Claire floored it, gaining on the Buick, coming nearly abreast of it when the Buick put on a burst of speed, lurching forward and away.

Nick glanced at the Impala's speedometer. Its needle was approaching triple digits.

"Don't lose him," Nick urged.

The Buick lurched left, hugging the guardrail along the East River, sparks flying.

"What the hell is he doing?" Nick asked.

They were just about to pass under the Manhattan Bridge, Claire realized. "He's going to take the Brooklyn Bridge exit."

"He's going too fast. He'll never make the turn at the top of the ramp."

They were almost upon the exit. Inexplicably, Quimby sped up, pulled away from Claire and Nick, and shot up the exit ramp.

"Stop the car!" Nick ordered. "He's gonna crash!"

Claire slowed the Impala to a stop just as the Buick breached the concrete guardrail and sailed into the air.

Nick was already screaming into the radio for harbor rescue as Quimby's car did a perfect arc into the murky water of the East River and vanished beneath the surface.

CHAPTER 17

The sun was just peeking over the horizon as a barge with a crane on board approached three NYPD harbor launches idling near the site where Todd Quimby's car had sailed into the river. Bubbles skimmed the deep purple water as two scuba divers surfaced with a body in tow.

Claire and Nick watched the activity with Deputy Medical Examiner Ross from the pier of the South Street Seaport, just a few hundred yards away, as the cops heaved Quimby's bobbing corpse onto the nearest of the boats, which started its engines and headed toward them.

"What a cluster," Nick muttered under his breath.

It had been nothing less. The NYPD's Harbor Unit, long proud of its rapid response time, was tied up on a 911 call off Bay Ridge, Brooklyn. The first launch showed up twenty minutes after Nick radioed for help, all but ensuring that Todd Quimby would drown.

"If anyone asks—" Nick whispered to Claire.

"You were driving," Claire interrupted. "Got it."

Claire saw a look on his face she hadn't seen before but knew well. She'd seen it in the mirror herself too many times since her friend Amy had disappeared.

Fear.

But as the launch eased up beside the pier, Claire was feeling something else. Relief. Because in just a few moments, she would positively identify the serial killer who'd scared the hell out of not only her, but also all of New York City.

The launch's engines went silent. Quimby's body lay faceup on the aft deck, intact. Claire couldn't take her eyes off him as she spoke the words that would end this nightmare once and for all.

"It's him."

"For the record," Nick said, "can you tell me who you know the deceased to be and where you know him from?"

"His name is Todd Quimby," Claire replied without emotion. "He was one of my patients."

"Good enough for me," ME Ross said as his techs stuffed Quimby into a body bag, hoisted him onto a gurney, and rolled him away.

Nick turned to Claire. "It's over," he said. "Let's go."

He walked toward the Impala. Claire fell into step beside him, surreptitiously passing him the car keys.

"What now?" Claire asked him.

"Crime Scene Unit will supervise the recovery of the Buick, transport it to the garage at the lab. They'll go over it from stem to stern for evidence—if it hasn't been washed away."

A pang of regret hit Claire as she realized she'd never be able to interview Quimby and ask him why he murdered all those women. But more importantly, she'd never get to ask him if he knew how sick Tammy Sorenson was when he raped and killed her. She stopped beside the Impala as Nick remote-clicked the locks.

"Can I borrow your phone?" Claire asked.

"Sure," Nick replied, pulling it out of his pocket and handing it to her.

"I'll only be a minute," Claire said as she moved away from him for privacy.

Nick got in the car and watched Claire press the numbers. Then she turned her back to him.

Claire realized she hadn't even thought about Ian in the adrenaline rush of the chase and the aftermath of the crash. The phone rang until she heard his quiet, soothing voice come on, asking callers to leave a message. Claire hung up before the beep and checked her watch: 6:23 a.m.

I called too late, she thought, realizing that he was on rounds before Curtin's Last Supper. Frustrated, she got into the car.

"I'm going to have to write this all up," Nick said, now weary. "There are a couple things I've got to ask you."

"Go ahead," Claire said as she watched the sun break through streaks of red across the horizon.

"How'd you get into the safe house this morning?" Nick asked, taking out a small notebook.

"I unlocked the door and walked in," Claire said, confused. "Why?"

"When I got upstairs last night, I just kicked the door in. I didn't look to see if it was jimmied."

"The door wasn't forced. That means Maggie let Quimby into the apartment," Claire said. "But why would she do that?"

"Maggie was a good cop," Nick reassured her. "I'm sure she saw him through the peephole, recognized him, let him in thinking she could collar him, and he overpowered her."

They looked at each other, knowing what this meant.

"He was following me," Claire said, letting out a breath.

"It doesn't matter now," he said. "You're safe."

Safe? She'd never felt completely safe. Not after Amy. And Quimby's death still left her with a nagging question: What about Tammy? The story of her cancer didn't make sense. Then she remembered that Ian had found something last night but didn't have the chance to tell her before her phone broke.

"Can you drop me off at my apartment?" she asked Nick.

"You don't want to come up to the safe house with me?" Nick answered. He seemed to want her to go with him.

"I need to answer some questions about Tammy Sorenson," Claire said. "Ian has the information and he's gone to work. Maybe he left something at home for me."

"Quimby's dead. What difference does that make now?"

"It makes a big difference to me."

Nick shot her a look. "Keep your eyes on the road," Claire warned him.

He looked straight ahead.

"It's on the way," he said. "I'll drop you off."

For some reason Nick couldn't explain, his gut churned as the words came out of his mouth.

What's that about?

"Thank you," Claire replied.

"I'm walking you upstairs," Nick said.

Claire looked at him, perplexed. "Why?"

"Because if Ian left information about Tammy, I want it too," Nick answered.

"Okay," said Claire with a sigh of relief. *We're in this together. Nick will help me find the truth.*

Claire and Nick arrived at the door to her apartment. She was one step ahead of him and put the key in the lock.

Nick looked at her as she fumbled with the uncooperative dead bolt. She twisted the key back and forth, and it finally gave way. She pushed the door open a crack.

"I have to get over to the safe house. Boss is waiting for me."

And then he stopped. Like something slapped him in the face. His sense of smell had become more sensitive since his eyesight began to deteriorate, and the odor he now detected emanating from Claire's apartment made him wince.

"If Ian left anything, I'll bring it to your office," Claire said, about to step inside when Nick roughly pulled her back.

"What are you doing?" she demanded.

"Stay here," Nick ordered, reaching for his gun.

"There's nobody inside, Nick," Claire argued. "Ian's at work and Todd Quimby's in the morgue."

"Please," Nick said. "Just do what I say."

The look on his face frightened Claire, which Nick caught immediately.

"It's probably nothing," Nick said.

Claire nodded, now alarmed.

With his gun pointed down and at his side, Nick entered the apartment. He closed the door all but a crack. Across the room, a curtain billowed from the breeze entering through an open window.

The window to the fire escape.

Nick felt the adrenaline course through his body.

Something happened in this apartment.

With his free hand, he yanked an ever-present pair of latex gloves from his back pocket. As he put on the gloves, he noticed his hands were shaking. He reached the end of the entry hall where the living room began and switched on the light. Nothing was out of place.

Except for a blank piece of paper lying on the floor, as if someone had dropped it there.

Or slipped it through the crack under the closed door it lay in front of.

Nick now moved in that direction, the odor he smelled getting stronger. He knew whatever had happened was behind that door.

Nick turned the knob, then pushed the door, letting it swing open.

And stepped back in horror.

It was Ian, lying faceup on the bed, naked. His eyes were burned out, Quimby's signature rope tied around his neck, his wrists lashed to the headboard. The white comforter under him was a sea of sticky dark red from where he'd been slashed in the genitals.

He was murdered before Maggie, Nick realized. *Quimby wanted Claire for himself. And Ian was the only thing stopping him.*

"Oh, God," came a small voice from behind Nick.

He wheeled around. "Don't look," he said, taking her arm protectively.

She pushed his hand off her and started into the room as if she hadn't heard him.

"You can't go in there," Nick said, his voice returning. "That's a crime scene—"

"It's my home," Claire uttered in the same small voice, some unknown force propelling her toward Ian, the tears flowing as she got closer to the foot of the bed.

I killed him. Just like I killed Amy.

She felt Nick take her arm. It was as if a wave of empathy were passing from him to her like an electric current that brought her walls crumbling down.

Slowly, Claire dropped to her knees and started to sob. Nick didn't stop her as she buried her head in the part of the comforter that was unstained with Ian's blood.

CHAPTER 18

———◆———

Nick stood by as Crime Scene Detective Aitken exited Ian's bedroom with a large paper evidence bag, out of which protruded the white comforter.

"How much more?" he asked Aitken.

"This is the last of it," replied the young cop. "Anything else I can do?"

Nick checked to make sure he'd covered all the bases. Then he spotted Ian's computer monitor across the room and remembered what Claire had told him the previous night about the suspicious circumstances surrounding Tammy's medical records.

"Take the desktop. If he has a laptop or tablet, make sure you grab that too," Nick told Aitken.

"Anything in particular you want Computer Crimes to look for?" asked Aitken.

"I want to see everything from the past week," Nick replied in an urgent tone.

"You got it," Aitken said, then added as he exited the apartment, "At least the bastard won't be doing it to anyone else."

Alone at last, Nick took a look around. It was as quiet as it had been four hours earlier when he and Claire made their gruesome discovery. Claire was in such shock that Nick called an ambulance and then had to convince her to let the paramedics take her to Manhattan City Hospital.

"I'm a doctor," Claire argued. "There's nothing wrong with me."

"You're not much of a doctor if you really believe that," Nick said.

He realized how much he regretted making that statement, thinking he was too hard on Claire. And he wondered how she was doing.

Nick walked to the bedroom door and took one last look inside. The Crime Scene Unit had taken most of what was bloody, so it didn't look half as bad as it did earlier.

Don't do it, Jenny . . . I'm coming . . . Pop!

Nick shook his head, trying to dislodge the image.

Her eyes were wide open in instantaneous death. Blood poured from the exit wound in her back, spreading across the white sheets.

He blinked away the memory. He realized that Claire was going through the same horror—and guilt—he had experienced when his wife committed suicide. Then he remembered having to clean up the mess his wife left on their bed.

Nobody should have to go through that kind of pain. Ever.

He pulled his cell phone and dialed.

"Peege," he said into the phone, "it's Nicky. I need a favor. Today. And I'll pay you whatever you need."

Claire thought she was dreaming. The hushed sounds of the hospital, the exhaustion, the lousy mattress, all brought back memories of her internship when she'd sneak into an empty room in the wee hours and steal a fifteen-minute nap.

But as she opened her eyes and the blurriness dissipated, she realized that this time she was the patient.

"Hello, Claire."

Groggy, she turned her head. Dr. Curtin, wearing a sweatshirt and jeans, sat in a chair against the wall. Claire tried to sit up, thinking she had to look presentable. Curtin stood and put his hand on her shoulder.

"No," he said in the gentlest, un-Curtin-like voice she'd ever heard from him. "You need to rest."

"What happened?" Claire managed through her stupor.

"You were in shock when they brought you in," Curtain said, "so I admitted you."

"To the Psych Unit?" Claire asked.

"Medicine," Curtin replied. "Neither of us wants a psych admission on your record."

Claire nodded. "How long have I been out?"

"About six hours," Curtin said. "I gave you Ativan and a sleeper."

"Ian . . ."

Curtin nodded and took her hand. "I called his parents. We're taking care of the funeral arrangements."

For some reason, her mentor looked different. Gaunt. Drained. Clearly Ian's death was taking its toll on him too.

"Are you okay, Doctor?"

"I will be. But right now I'm much more concerned about you."

Curtin squeezed her hand tenderly.

He can be compassionate when he wants to be, she thought.

"Claire, I want you to listen to me. In all the years I've been doing this, I've never had a fellow go to the lengths you have not only to help a patient, but also to save others from him. I consider myself a pretty good judge of people, especially of my own students, but I couldn't have been more completely wrong about you."

Claire looked at him quizzically.

"You proved me wrong. And that doesn't happen often, as I'm sure you know."

A weak smile broke out on Claire's face. "At least that you admit to."

It was the first time she'd attempted any kind of humor with Curtin, and it made him grin.

"You need to take some time off. Maybe even the rest of the year."

"But . . . but I'll fall behind," Claire stammered.

"Don't worry about that," Curtin assured her. "You can come back next year, or the year after that, or whenever. As long as I'm running this program, there's a place for you here. And I couldn't be prouder to have you as a student and colleague."

Claire didn't know what to say. Curtin sensed it and got up to leave.

"I'm going to write up your discharge papers. If there's anything you need, you call me."

"Doctor?"

"Yes?"

"Thank you," Claire replied. "For everything."

Curtin nodded in a way that made Claire feel better.

"I'm so, so sorry about all this, Claire. In ways you can't even imagine." He looked down, then back at her. "Let me know if you need anything."

He turned and walked out.

"Doctor Curtin?" Claire called after him.

Curtin spun around. "Yes?"

"There is one thing."

Claire opened the door to her apartment, the fear gripping her as she stepped inside.

"The mess is in the bedroom," Claire said.

"Why don't you let me go in first and have a look, dear?" Dr. Lois Fairborn said gently.

Claire nodded. She was glad Fairborn was there. Coming home alone and having to clean up the slaughterhouse that was her bedroom was the last thing she could possibly bear. She'd asked Curtin if he could arrange for Fairborn to accompany her to the apartment. Curtin not only said he would, but also promised he'd go if Fairborn balked.

Which, of course, Fairborn hadn't. The Vampire had become quite fond of Claire as a result of their therapy sessions, seeing her as a work in progress—not to mention that Fairborn genuinely cared about her.

"Claire? Do you want me to go in first?"

Claire stood motionless in the entry hall, feeling as if she were hanging on to the edge of a cliff.

"Yes. Please."

"We'll get through this together, okay?" Fairborn said in a reassuring voice.

Claire appreciated Fairborn's encouragement but still felt scared out of her wits and didn't want to go any further.

She could hear Fairborn opening the bedroom door. But there was no gasp of shock, and it took only a moment before Fairborn returned.

"Come with me," she said.

"You want to help me face my fear?"

"I want to help you overcome it."

She held out her hand. Tentatively, Claire took it. She let Fairborn lead her to the bedroom.

"Take a look," she said.

Claire glanced at her shrink, then took a few steps forward toward the threshold. What she saw stunned her. The tableau she'd seen earlier that morning was completely gone, as though some higher power had simply erased it.

The bedroom was spotless. Her bed—*their bed*—was made neatly, covered with the same white comforter that, hours before, had been soaked in Ian's blood. But not a drop of blood, nor a trace of what had happened, remained in the room.

Then the door to the bathroom opened. A little girl, about ten years old, walked out. Claire gasped.

"Amy? Is that you?"

"Hi, Claire. Wanna play hopscotch?"

"What are you doing here?"

And then everything slowed down. Another little girl walked out of the bathroom. Claire gasped as the girl grabbed Amy's hand.

Claire was looking at her eight-year-old self.

She moved toward them. And they saw her.

"Hi," said Amy. "Are you okay?"

"What's wrong?" asked Little Claire.

Claire looked in the mirror. She saw tears rolling down her face.

"Are you lost?" asked Little Claire.

"Are you looking for someone?" Amy asked.

"I'm looking for you," Claire said, kneeling in front of Amy. "Where are you?"

"I went away," Amy said. "A man took me. He was bad."

"What did he do to you?" Claire asked Amy.

"I can't tell you," Amy said innocently. "He said I couldn't tell anyone."

Claire began to sob. "I saw him take you away. I was there. Where did he take you? Please, tell me where."

"Don't cry," Amy said in a comforting voice. "He hurt me but now I'm okay. I'm resting."

Amy turned to Little Claire. "C'mon, Claire. Let's go outside."

The two smiled at her and headed back toward the bathroom. They disappeared through the door.

"No! Don't go, please! Not yet! I have to know what happened."

She yanked open the bathroom door. Nobody was there. She pulled the curtain to the bathtub aside, as if they were playing hide-and-seek. But the bathtub was empty.

And then Claire saw it. Another door. At the far end of the bath-tub. She stepped in. She opened the door and walked through with-out hesitation.

She was in front of her old house. The home where she grew up, watching herself as an eight-year-old jumping rope with Amy in front of the driveway.

"Claire! Amy!" she called to them.

But they just kept jumping rope. As if they didn't hear her. As if she wasn't there.

Or maybe they're the ones who aren't there. How could they be there?

An unseen hand pulled her back through the door into the bath-room.

She heard this noise, like a pump.

She looked down. A woman sat on the porcelain inside the bath-tub. Pulsating, like she was about to explode. Like a million memo-ries were about to burst out and drown her.

Claire felt herself reach up and touch her head. It was open, as if someone had lifted the hood of a car.

She looked in the mirror. Her skull was gone. There was just the pulsating brain above her forehead, ready to pop.

"Are you okay, dear?" came a voice that sounded like her mother's.

Claire turned. Dr. Fairborn was standing there, looking con-cerned.

"I saw them. I saw *her*," she said.

"Who?" asked Fairborn.

"Amy," Claire said, as if Fairborn should know. "The girl I killed when I was little."

"Claire—"

"She was my best friend, and she was kidnapped right in front of me. I didn't do anything to stop it and now she's dead. I killed her. And now I've killed my boyfriend because Todd Quimby got jealous."

"You didn't kill anyone," Fairborn reassured her.

"But I did!" Claire exclaimed, tears flowing again. "I made myself look like a whore—his whore—because I wanted you and Dr. Curtin to respect me."

Claire felt herself spinning. She was weeping now. Fairborn led her into the living room and sat her down on the sofa.

"I don't know what's wrong with me," Claire sobbed.

"There's nothing wrong with you," Fairborn assured her.

"But I don't do this. I don't cry . . ."

"You've shut down your emotions for such a long time, and now they're coming to the surface. The best thing you can do is let them out."

"Please. Tell me why. Why Amy? Why Ian?"

"I wish I could tell you, Claire. But that's a question for a higher power."

Claire looked at her sharply. "Oh, come on. We're doctors. We turn to science for the answers."

Fairborn nodded gently. "Science can never tell us why your friend Amy was kidnapped or why Todd Quimby murdered—"

"But it can. Todd Quimby had schizoid personality disorder," Claire said, as if reciting from a textbook. "He should have re-sponded to the meds I prescribed." Claire put her head down and sobbed harder.

"You're looking for answers where there are none," Fairborn said.

"What am I going to do?" Claire cried.

"Forgive yourself."

"I don't know how."

Fairborn paused, considering how to respond. Then she faced Claire, taking her by both arms. "Remember when you interviewed Quimby for the first time? How you struggled and struggled, and fi-nally you got him to spill his guts? He was your first patient at Rikers and you hit a home run."

"And then I dropped the ball."

"Because you're human, Claire. We all are. We can't predict how we're going to act from minute to minute, let alone predict how oth-ers will act. We want to tell ourselves that we can explain behavior if we have enough information. But there's a human factor—our pa-tients don't tell us everything. And God only knows what they don't want to tell themselves. Or what we don't want to tell ourselves."

Claire looked at Fairborn, her face pleading for something to hang on to.

"I know you're in pain. It's not going to go away tomorrow, or the next day, or even next month. It will get better with time. But only if you stop blaming yourself for what happened to these women. And to Ian. And to your friend Amy."

The tone in Fairborn's voice made Claire believe it was possible.

"I'll try," Claire said. And she closed her eyes tight against the world and its cruelty.

Todd Quimby lay on the autopsy table, his chest precisely cut open in the Y incision, a victim of his own mother's cruelty, who then set out to turn his rage on others. ME Ross looked down at Quimby's body and examined the dead man's heart. It looked normal, like any other man's his age. Ross smiled to himself. There were no signs inside it of the evil Quimby bore. There never were in all the killers' hearts Ross had examined.

And then Ross looked at Quimby's lungs.

That's odd, he thought. *Why have the blood cells in his lungs burst?*

Ross decided to take samples of the water from Quimby's lungs and send them to the lab.

Maybe there's a good explanation for this, he thought. *Science will give me the answer. It always does.*

PART II

CHAPTER 19

Nick sat at his desk staring at eight manila case folders, seven of them holding the story of a life Todd Quimby had viciously ended. The last and thickest file belonged to Quimby himself. Nick could almost feel them all staring back at him, asking the same question he was: Why?

He'd explain to the families of the seven young victims that Quimby's killing spree was most likely borne of some deep-seated mental illness. Then he asked himself, *Is it my job to answer that question? Isn't it enough that we seek justice for the dead? Whatever God does, he does for a reason. Good people get murdered; good people commit suicide.*

Good people go blind.

And yet, buried in those files, Nick couldn't help but think that there had to be an answer. It was human nature to want a reason, an explanation for why seven innocent people had been brutally murdered.

A week after Quimby's grand finale of snuffing the life out of three people in one night, he remained a mystery. Nick knew he would remain that way forever. Because with Quimby dead, Nick would never have the chance to interrogate him, to extract a confession where he would admit what he did, maybe even proudly, as some of them were known to do, with a sick, twisted smile on his face. There would be no trial, where the victims' families would see justice done as Quimby was convicted by a jury of his peers and sentenced to spend the rest of his miserable life in prison.

Nick felt cheated. *Face it, life is never fair.*

Nobody knew that better than he did.

He lifted his head, his failing eyes still able to take in the activity in the squad room, which was quiet tonight. Like the entire city, Nick mused, now that Quimby's wretched soul was in hell.

Over the week, Nick's stock as a cop had skyrocketed from zero to hero status. He'd given dozens of interviews, the media carnivores forgetting all about their vendetta against him after the death of his wife. His valor erased their animosity, as if the suicide of Jenny Lawler had never happened. They were all a bunch of douche bags. Nick smiled as he considered the irony.

Big hero. I couldn't even drive the damn car.

His reverie was interrupted by a stapled sheaf of papers landing on his desk. Nick looked up to see Lieutenant Wilkes walking away.

"What's this?" he asked.

"I gotta teach you how to read too?" Wilkes said gruffly.

Nick picked up the papers. It was a fax from the medical examiner's office.

Todd Quimby's autopsy report.

"Any highlights?" Nick shouted to his boss.

"Big surprise. The bastard drowned. Nothing unusual pending toxicology results. Cause of death is being a lousy driver. Finish your fives and close those cases out."

The thick files on Nick's desk were lined up in the order in which the murders occurred. Nick instinctively pulled out the one on the right—Quimby's last kill.

Detective Maggie Stolls.

In the NYPD, a cop killed in the line of duty is entitled to what is called an "inspector's funeral," though the moniker had for decades been considered a joke. The rank of inspector was roughly equivalent to a colonel in the army, and only one inspector had died on the job in the police department's history.

Still, Nick had been at the church on Flatbush Avenue in Brooklyn, along with thousands of other cops, some from as far away as California, to mourn Maggie's untimely death. Privately, many questioned her judgment for letting Quimby into the safe house without calling for backup and thought she'd brought her demise upon herself. The one or two jerks with the stones to mention that within earshot of Nick quickly found themselves up against the nearest wall with Nick in their faces assuring them they would never have a fraction of the guts Maggie had.

Maybe all the guts in the world didn't matter when you're up against a madman, Nick thought. *Or maybe I'm telling myself that because I feel responsible for Maggie's death. If I'd only gotten there earlier* . . .

"Excuse me," came a voice from across the room. "Is Detective Lawler here?"

Nick looked up, alarmed. He knew that voice, and the man who owned it had no business in the city of New York, let alone in this squad room.

"I'm Detective Savarese," Tony said, rising from his chair and heading toward the doorway. "Can I help you?"

"I got it, Tony," Nick said, bolting to the door in a preemptive strike he knew was futile. The voice belonged to Dr. Frank Mangone, his ophthalmologist from Boston. Other than Claire Waters and his mother, he was the only person on the planet who could reveal Nick's secret.

Nick tried to play it down, as if he'd been expecting Mangone. "Nice to see you," he said to the doctor, shaking his hand. "Why don't we talk outside?"

A minute later, the two men emerged from the precinct onto the street.

"What the hell are you doing here?" Nick demanded.

"I should ask you the same question," Dr. Mangone replied, matching Nick's anger and not missing a beat.

"How did you find me?" Nick snapped.

"You're not much of a cop if you can't figure that one out," the doctor said. "Your picture's all over the Internet. Congratulations on catching your serial killer."

"And that gives you license to stalk me?"

"It gives me license to stop you from killing someone."

"I'm not going to kill anyone, Doc. I'm okay. "

"You're going blind and it's not going to get any better. You've got to turn in your gun."

"Sorry, Doc. Not a chance."

"Then for Christ's sake, give it to someone. You have no business walking around with that thing."

"I'm a cop."

"You can't see a damn thing at night!" Mangone exploded. "Is that how your wife died?"

"What are you talking about?" Nick roared.

"Did you shoot her by accident? Because you didn't see her?"

Nick knew he had to bring it down a notch.

"My wife got her hands on my gun and shot herself with it. Her death has nothing to do with my problem."

"It's not just your problem anymore. It's mine too."

"I don't understand," Nick said as he led the doctor away from the building and down the street, as if they were old friends—in case anyone saw them.

"I took an oath," Dr. Mangone began, "to do no harm. By allowing you to continue as a police officer and carry a gun, I'm putting countless people at risk."

"Are you threatening me?" Nick asked incredulously.

"Call it what you want," the doctor replied, "but here it is. I'm giving you one month to resign, retire, whatever it is you have to do."

"Or what?" Nick asked, though he knew full well what was coming.

"Or I call the police surgeon and tell him about your condition."

Nick gave him the same hard stare he'd given countless perps he was about to nail. Dr. Mangone didn't flinch.

"You can't do that," was all Nick could muster.

"I can and I will," returned the doctor. "This is a matter of life or death. If you accidentally shoot the wrong person, their blood is on my hands. I can't live with that."

As Mangone walked away, Nick knew he meant every word. And Nick was at a loss.

Until he realized what he had to do.

The fluorescent lights have a strange corona to them, Nick thought as he walked down the hospital corridor. He tried to retreat into his usual denial about his deteriorating vision, but Dr. Mangone's ultimatum an hour earlier had robbed him of that ability.

Nick turned the corner, promptly bumping into one of two doctors walking together, nearly knocking him over.

"Excuse me," he said hastily. "I wasn't looking."

"Maybe you should slow down," the doctor replied. "This is a hospital."

"Sorry," Nick said, continuing onward. The office he was looking for was just a few yards ahead, which he covered quickly.

But when he got there, he saw that the nameplate had been removed from the door.

He knocked, waited a few seconds for an answer. There was none.

He turned the knob, which gave way. But he wasn't expecting what he saw when the door opened.

The office was empty, except for a clean desk and two chairs. As if no one had ever been there.

As if Claire had been erased from his life.

Even now he wasn't sure what had driven him to see her. But for some reason he knew he had to.

As he gazed into the empty office, the reason dawned on him.

All his life, Nick had been surrounded by friends. Family. His wife, before she sunk into the depths of major depression. His brotherhood of cops.

Dr. Mangone's promise to reveal his condition changed everything. His wife was dead. His friends wouldn't understand. And his fellow cops would curse him for putting their lives in danger because of his failing eyesight. They'd blame him for what happened to his young partner, Wessel, on the subway tracks the previous week.

And they'd be right.

"Can I help you with something?" came a voice from behind Nick. He wheeled around.

"Dr. Curtin," Nick said.

"Detective . . . ?" Curtin queried.

"Lawler, Nick Lawler," Nick answered, extending his hand. Curtin shook it.

"I gather you're looking for Dr. Waters," Curtin replied. "Something about the case?"

"Just closing things out," Nick replied, "and I had a few more questions."

"As you can see, Dr. Waters is no longer with us."

"What happened to her?" Nick demanded.

"You know what happened," Curtin answered without missing a beat. "You were there, weren't you?" he asked, a bit too accusatory for Nick's taste.

"You know I was."

"Then you know what she went through," Curtin replied. "Dr. Waters is taking the rest of the year off. She'll be back again next June."

Nick had no intention of waiting until then. "Can you give me some contact information?" he asked.

"It's against hospital policy to release any information about patients or employees."

Nick thought about this. The guy didn't have to be a prick about it.

"Look, Doctor," Nick started, "I don't know how responsible you hold me for what happened to Dr. Waters, but I was just doing my job, and I'm trying to do it now."

"Todd Quimby is dead, Detective," Curtin said. "What could possibly be left for Dr. Waters to help you with?"

"I need statements from her," Nick replied as nonjudgmentally as possible, "so I can close these cases once and for all."

Whether Curtin saw through his lie was unclear. Or maybe it was pity. Because Curtin's hard expression softened.

Maybe he can see that I need help.

"Come to my office," Curtin said, "and I'll have my assistant give you what you need."

"Thank you, Doctor," Nick said instantly.

"On one condition," Curtin continued. "If anyone asks, you didn't get it from me."

CHAPTER 20

You could tell a thunderstorm was close. The air was thick with humidity, the clouds approaching from Lake Ontario an angry gray.

Just like the day Amy disappeared.

Claire's mind raced as she hurried down Burt Street with the large cup of coffee she'd bought at Clancy's Diner around the corner on Park Avenue. The red banquettes and waitress uniforms hadn't changed since Claire was a child, but that only made her feel uneasy.

Nothing's changed around here, she thought, racing to reach her parents' house before the downpour began. The same house where she and Amy had been playing outside that day her best friend was abducted. There was no easing into a summer storm in Rochester. The first raindrops were always big ones, and they always fell hard.

They were just starting to fall as Claire turned the key in the front door of the stately colonial on Burt Street and scurried through, barely inside when a lightning bolt lit up the sky. A deafening clap of thunder shook the house, and the deluge struck.

It was the middle of the day, and both her parents were at work. Her mother taught high school biology, which is where Claire thought she got her interest in medicine. Her father was a physicist, doing research on fiber optics. But he was religious, too, attending church every Sunday at All Souls Episcopal. He'd told Claire since she was a child that science had made him a believer in God because some questions could only be answered on faith.

Who made the world, Daddy? she'd asked him many times growing up. He always told her he didn't know.

As Claire made her way into the living room, she couldn't help but think that, save for the somehow soothing din of the rain, the house was beautifully quiet.

She let herself fall into the deep, comfortable sofa, sipping her coffee as she watched the rain cascade down the front picture window. The waterfall blurred everything outside, as if nothing existed beyond the walls of this place, her childhood home. She pulled a nearby comforter over her. For the first time in weeks, she felt like she was wrapped in a cocoon, protected from the world.

And more than anything else right now, Claire needed to feel protected. From what she wasn't sure, except for a quiet anxiety that still surfaced, especially at night, when she was alone with her dreams. Something unexplained, a feeling that haunted the edges of her consciousness.

After all, wasn't it her right to feel safe? She'd made it through the emotional upheaval of packing up the apartment she'd shared with Ian, of donating his clothes to charity and putting the rest of their belongings into storage for when she returned to New York and Curtin's fellowship program.

If I ever go back, she thought.

Ian's funeral had been hard on Claire. Curtin and Fairborn were both there, along with all the fellows from the program. Their words were soothing, especially Curtin's, who, in a private moment, reiterated his promise that her place in the program was secure whenever she wanted to come back. But coming back, at the time, was the last thing on Claire's mind. The desire to run as far away from her life as she could nearly overpowered her. Her parents offered to pay for any trip she wanted to take, to do anything that might help erase the horror of the previous few weeks.

In the end, Claire realized there was only one place where she'd feel truly safe. And that's where she was right now.

In the week she'd been home, her parents had done their best. Both had taken a few days off from their busy jobs to dote on her. Now back at work, they were coming home as early for dinner as their schedules would allow so their child wouldn't be alone all the time. Claire's older sister, Diane, who worked in London as an architect, had also offered to come home. But Claire told her not to. Diane was five years older and they had never been close, and Claire wasn't up to repeating to her all the details of the last terrible weeks.

Claire couldn't help but think that her parents were doing more for her now than they'd done when she was growing up. It was ironic, she thought, that it took seven murders and a near breakdown for them to wake up.

Better late than never.

For the first time in her life, Claire wasn't hiding in plain sight. For the first time, she didn't feel invisible.

Boom! Boom! A succession of powerful thunderclaps jolted the house and shook her brain.

In a sudden panic, Claire bolted from the couch and ran to the front door. She fumbled with the quirky dead bolt, yanking it open . . .

. . . just in time to see Mr. Winslow carrying Amy to his car.

"Mommy, Mommy, come out here! Please . . ."

Claire looked back into the house. Her mother wasn't coming. Where was she?

"Mommy! The man took Amy away!"

She ran to the stairs, screaming, getting no answer. She was crying, almost sobbing as she ran back out the door, knowing what awaited her.

Thunder. Claire could see Amy, in tears, peering at her through the window of Mr. Winslow's BMW. Somehow knowing they would never see each other again.

She stood there, as she had all those years ago, letting the pouring rain soak through her clothes, barely keeping up with the tears flowing from her eyes.

Will I ever feel safe again? Anywhere?

Claire turned, leaned against the house, and sobbed like never before. Because this time, she was crying for everything she'd lost.

All her advanced degrees, all the research into neurotransmitters and their effects on human behavior, all the fellowships in the world would never be enough to erase the one emotion she'd felt since that day Amy was taken from her:

Helplessness.

She knew she had to make herself whole. Even if it consumed the rest of her life.

*   *   *

The carton was in the far corner of the attic, behind an old bed frame, right where Claire remembered putting it many years ago.

It hadn't been opened in so long that the packer's tape holding it closed was cracked and powdery. Just before leaving home for her freshman year in college, Claire had consigned the box to what she thought might be its final resting place. At the time, to her parents' chagrin, she'd purged as many of her belongings as she could stand to, emptying even her own bedroom as if she were never coming back.

She'd been tempted to throw out the carton. But something back then had stopped her, an unseen hand holding her back, an unknown voice telling her she'd regret it. Instead, she hid it where she knew no one would see it, far from any of her parents' stored belongings.

Claire dragged the box across the floor of the attic, raising a storm of dust that burned her eyes and triggered a fit of sneezing. Her spasms subsided as she reached the trapdoor and steadied herself on the folding stairs, thinking with some satisfaction that she was making the right decision.

It wasn't until the carton was planted on the dining room table that second thoughts began to creep in. Did she actually have the strength to open this box and unleash the memories stored inside? No more than a few seconds passed before she decided.

I have no choice.

She ripped the lone piece of tape off the top, opened the flaps, and without looking, reached inside and pulled out the first item her hand came to.

It was a large, unmarked photo album. Claire stared down at the white vinyl cover, its inviting, nonthreatening design hardly indicative of what lay within.

If there's any way to face my fears, this is it.

She took a deep breath and opened the cover. Staring her in the face was a clipping from the *Democrat and Chronicle*, Rochester's daily newspaper, dated July 18, 1989, the headline proclaiming the past she had tried so hard to bury:

POLICE SEEK KIDNAPPED GIRL

Accompanying the article was a large, black-and-white photo of Amy, wearing the same T-shirt she had on the day she disappeared.

It's okay, she heard Amy say to her. *Mr. Winslow works with my dad.*

Claire started to read the story she knew so well, the initial pain dissipating as the words soaked into her brain. Maybe it was like removing a Band-Aid, she thought. It hurts less when you rip it off quickly.

She left the scrapbook open as she took the remainder of the contents from the box: two more photo album/scrapbooks, numerous pictures of her and Amy together. Jumping rope. Playing hopscotch. On the carousel at Seabreeze Amusement Park near Lake Ontario. Mugging in front of the elephants at the Seneca Park Zoo. With every photo, the memories Claire had worked her whole life to forget came rushing back into her head. Without knowing it, she started to giggle, remembering how much she loved Amy and what fun they'd had together.

The bang of the brass knocker on the front door brought her out of her near trance. She looked at the mess on the table, knowing her parents would be upset if they saw what she was doing.

She glanced at her watch—1:25 in the afternoon. Way too early for either of them to be home, and she wasn't expecting anyone.

Claire peeked out the front window. The rain had died down, the torrent of water cascading down the glass having given way to just a few drips. There was a Toyota Camry parked at the curb, one she hadn't seen before. So it wasn't a delivery.

Hesitantly, she crept up to the front door. Her parents had never put a peephole in, not wanting to ruin the integrity of the beautiful oak finish.

"Who is it?" Claire asked.

"Police," came the reply, muffled by the pouring rain.

The car parked out front was hardly a police car. Her parents had mentioned a rash of midday burglaries plaguing the neighborhood. Was this someone looking to see if the house was empty?

Though there was no peephole, the door did have a row of glass panes at the top, too high for Claire or anyone else to see over. But Claire thought she could put it to good use. She reached her hand up as if to indicate.

"Put your badge and ID card up against the glass," she shouted.

She heard the light tap of metal against the glass. Claire looked up. And her eyes went wide.

The badge she saw wasn't that of a Rochester police officer. It was the gold shield of a New York City police detective. Claire had seen the number enough times to know whose it was. She unlocked the door and pulled it open.

Nick Lawler stood uncomfortably before her.

"You changed your hair back," he said.

Claire unconsciously twirled a snippet of hair, which she had indeed dyed back to its natural color. "Astute observation, Detective Lawler," Claire replied.

They looked at each other for an awkward moment. Claire wasn't sure whether she was glad to see him or horrified at the prospect of why he might be there.

"You're a little out of your jurisdiction, aren't you?" she asked, breaking the silence.

"I need to talk."

"About the case?"

"The case is over."

"How did you find me?"

"I'm a detective." He brushed a drop of water from his nose. "It's kinda wet out here."

Claire's face flushed with embarrassment. "I'm sorry," she said, stepping aside. "Come in."

Nick entered, closing the door behind him. He took his raincoat off, revealing jeans and a maroon golf shirt underneath.

"That what cops wear when they travel?" Claire asked.

"Not when they travel on official business," Nick replied.

"So this isn't official business."

"Not exactly," he said, squinting to adjust his eyes to the low level of light.

"You drove three hundred fifty miles just to chat."

"I flew."

Claire couldn't help but grin. He reminded her of a nervous high school boy trying to ask her out. Minus the pimples.

"So you were in a hurry to get here," Claire said, automatically turning into shrink mode.

"You're not making this easy, Doctor."

"Are you here for professional help?" Claire nodded toward the living room, and they walked in. Claire sat on the sofa and Nick took the firm leather chair facing her.

"I said I needed to talk to you, didn't I?" Nick replied, annoyed.

"Let me get this straight," Claire said. "You *flew* all the way up here from New York City because you need a shrink."

The expression that crossed Nick's face—one of sheer confusion—told Claire she was right on the money.

"I don't know what to do," he said to her.

"Do about what?" Claire asked.

"This how you ambush all your patients?" Nick asked.

Claire softened. "Why don't you tell me what's going on."

Nick haltingly launched himself into his tale of woe regarding Dr. Mangone's ultimatum. Claire listened intently, empathically, until he was finished.

"So you have some time left until Dr. Mangone makes good on his . . . threat."

"I asked him whether he'd still give me a month to figure out my situation if I took off a couple of weeks."

"In other words," Claire concluded, "you're facing a life sentence and the good doctor agreed to a plea bargain."

Nick grinned at her attempt to make light of it all.

"Something like that," he began. "He said he was okay with it as long as I didn't carry the gun."

"And you're good with that?"

"What the doctor doesn't know won't hurt him. Or me," Nick said, patting his lower leg where he holstered his weapon.

"But it could hurt someone else," Claire said, staring at where she knew the gun rested. "He's right, you know."

"Yeah, I know," Nick admitted. "But I've been a cop my whole adult life. I don't know how to do anything else."

Claire let out a small laugh. Nick looked sharply at her.

"Something funny about that?" he demanded.

"Sorry, I'm not laughing at your misfortune. I'm laughing at myself." Seeing his bewildered look, she explained. "Most shrinks become shrinks because they're so screwed up that dealing with other people's problems is a relief. I've been here a week and you're the first person who was able to take my mind off my own shit."

Nick couldn't help but grin. "Glad to be of service, Doc."

"Where are you staying?" asked Claire.

"Didn't make any plans," answered Nick. "There's a flight home tonight at eight-thirty, and I thought I'd make that."

"Would you like something to drink?" Claire asked. She found something endearing about his hair, matted down from the rain. It made him look vulnerable.

"Water's fine. How do you want to do this?"

"Do what?"

"Well, I don't expect a free ride here," he said, turning uncomfortably in the chair. The living room was spotless, almost unlived in. Nick noticed oil paintings of seascapes and still lifes of flowers, but no pictures of family—as if people had been banned from the room.

"Relax, Detective Lawler," Claire reassured him, taken by his sense of honor. "This one's on the house. You've more than earned it, don't you think?"

She smiled as she got up and headed toward the kitchen, already planning her strategy for their session, but she never made it through the doorway.

"Can I ask you a question?" Nick called to her.

She turned around to face him. "Ask away," she said, giving him a small smile.

"Why were you so obsessed with this case?"

Claire shrugged. "It's my job," she said, trying to throw it away.

"Obsession isn't part of the job. And I'm pretty sure changing one's appearance to get a rise out of a patient isn't in the shrink instruction manual."

A forced smile appeared on Claire's face as she involuntarily glanced at the box on the dining room table containing her darkest secret. "You came to talk about you, not me," she said gently. "I'll be right back."

As soon as she disappeared into the kitchen, Nick crossed to the dining room table, wondering what it was that Claire didn't want him to see. He saw her name written in marker on the side of the carton and noticed the photo album beside it, pretty sure she didn't want him nosing through her life.

But nosing through peoples' lives was what Nick did for a living, and so, without so much as a second thought, he flipped open the cover of the scrapbook. The newspaper headline blaring out like a neon sign shocked him.

"What are you doing?" Claire demanded, horrified, when she came back in.

"Interesting hobby you had," Nick said, never taking his eyes off the article. "Collecting articles about child molesters. No wonder you became a shrink."

Claire slammed the album shut. "It's none of your business."

"At least I answered my own question about why you were so interested in Todd Quimby." He looked down at the closed scrapbook. "You've been obsessed with pervs since you were a little girl."

"Quimby wasn't just a perv. He killed my boyfriend and six other innocent people."

Nick froze. He'd pushed her too far. *Why am I always pushing? Why can't I accept the inevitable?*

"I'm sorry," Nick said. "This was a bad idea. I shouldn't have come here." He grabbed his raincoat and headed for the door.

"Wait," Claire said.

Nick stopped but didn't turn around.

"She was my friend," Claire said, her voice cracking.

"The girl in the article?" Nick asked, turning to face her.

"Her name was Amy. That whole box is about her."

Nick moved back toward Claire. "What happened?"

"We were jumping rope out in front of this house. A guy pulled up, said Amy's father was in an accident and he'd been sent to take her to the hospital."

"You witnessed it," Nick said, coming to the table.

"But I couldn't stop him," Claire answered.

It explains so much, Nick thought. *Of course she's obsessed. About what she lost and can never get back.*

"Did they ever catch him?"

"No."

She looked down. It was the first time she'd spoken about this to anyone since she was eight, and it was making her bottom lip quiver.

"They never found your friend, did they," she heard Nick say, not as a question but as a statement of fact.

Claire shook her head as she turned away. *He's seen enough of my tears,* she thought as her eyes started to well up.

Nick came up behind her, about to put his hands on her shoulders and then thought better of it.

"You were a kid," he said gently. "There was nothing you could have done."

"I . . . I know," Claire stammered, trying to hold herself together. "But Ian—"

"Todd Quimby killed him. Not you."

"But because of me," Claire said.

"Quimby was a monster. You didn't put the knife in his hand."

"All I wanted was to stop people like him from hurting others. And all I got was a bunch of dead bodies with my name on them."

"*His* name. Not yours. This pity party isn't gonna bring any of them back."

Claire wheeled on him. "And you know that because you've never felt sorry for yourself. You don't blame yourself for your wife's death, do you?"

"We're not talking about me—"

"You came here to talk about you. I'm the shrink, remember?" Claire said angrily. "I know you much better than you do. They accused you of murdering her. You may not have pulled the trigger, but something inside you believes you killed her just the same."

"She needed help! But I told her she would be okay! Because I didn't trust you people."

The words were out of his mouth before he could stop himself.

"*You people*?" Claire asked, even though she knew exactly what he meant.

"Shrinks," Nick blurted.

Claire looked at him. "Did your wife seem suicidal?"

"She had weeks when she couldn't get out of bed. And then weeks where she couldn't sleep, couldn't stop doing things."

"Sounds like she was bipolar."

"That's what the police psychologist said after she killed herself."

"Did you go voluntarily? To the police psychologist?"

"No," said Nick, though the answer was much more complicated. A cop who didn't want to drive his career into a brick wall avoided the department shrinks at all cost, for fear that whatever was discussed would wind up in one's personnel file down at One Police Plaza. Any cop who thought he needed mental help saw someone privately, on the outside, someone who could never divulge a word from any session to the NYPD powers-that-be without running afoul of privacy laws and their own oath to preserve patient confidentiality.

"Then someone obviously forced you to see a therapist," Claire said.

"Internal Affairs," Nick answered. "It was that or take a polygraph."

"And what did the doctor say?"

Nick drew a deep breath. "That my wife blew her own brains out."

"A human lie detector," Claire said, "whose testimony is admissible in court, found you innocent. As opposed to polygraph results that can't be entered as evidence."

"You're good," Nick said.

"Not nearly as good as you, though," Claire shot back, her anger growing. "For a few minutes I actually believed you."

Nick didn't understand. "Everything I told you is the God's honest truth," he said sincerely.

"About your wife. Yes. I know you didn't kill her."

"Then what the hell are you talking about?"

"You didn't come here just for my help, did you?"

"It's not that simple."

"Then make it simple," Claire said, "because I'm too tired to play any more games."

"I'm not really sure," Nick said. "We're not finished, you and me. I can't explain it, but it doesn't feel over."

"What?" Claire asked, puzzled.

"It's just a feeling," Nick said. He couldn't find the words to say any more.

Claire had no words, either. But she knew what he meant. She, too, had that feeling of unease. Of not knowing something that was almost within reach.

After a long silence, Nick asked, "Why did you quit?"

Claire could have come up with a dozen questions Nick could have asked her. That one wasn't on the list.

"You know damn well why I quit," was the best she could do.

"I didn't before I came here," Nick retorted, "but you're right. I do now."

He gestured toward the table, realizing he'd found the missing piece of the puzzle that was Claire Waters. "You came back here to find your friend," he said. "You came back here to find Amy."

Claire could feel him looking right through her. "I need to know why."

"I understand. But let me tell you something. *Why* is overrated when it comes to dead people. *Why* sometimes makes it all worse. Because there's no good reason for murder. And sometimes, bad shit just happens even to the best people. Finding Amy isn't gonna bring back your boyfriend."

"At least I know where my boyfriend is."

Nick got it. "If it's closure you want, there'll never be any. Especially for a kid."

"But it'll at least give her parents someone to bury in that empty grave." A look of panic crossed her face. She started to dig through the box.

"What's wrong?" Nick asked.

Claire found what she was looking for and pulled it out of the box. It was a photo of Claire and Amy together, holding a doll.

"What's this?"

"Amy gave it to me. For my eighth birthday. I buried her."

"The doll," he said, clarifying.

Claire nodded, staring at the image.

"Do you remember where?"

"Yes."

The rain had stopped as Claire, shovel in hand, slung mud from an ever-growing hole in the grass of her parents' backyard.

"Why?" Nick asked her.

"I thought you said *why* was overrated," Claire said.

The digging was therapeutic. She pressed the shovel into the moist earth and lifted out a heap of dark soil. "I always imagined he took Amy and buried her body somewhere. I wanted to feel how she must've felt. The dirt on her face. In her eyes. What that bastard felt when he put my friend in the ground."

Nick could see she was crying. Gently, he took the shovel from her. She let him move her aside as he dug until he felt something.

He bent down and grabbed a plastic hand. Pulled the doll from the dirt.

"Stupid, right?" Claire asked.

Nick looked at the doll. Its painted eyes were barely visible. "She was as much a part of you as Amy was."

"We had a funeral for Amy. We buried a casket but it was empty. It shouldn't have been."

"Let me help you," Nick said.

"Help me what?"

"Find Amy. And the man who stole her from you."

"Why do you want to find him?"

"So you can ask him why."

Claire looked at him. She knew the reason was more than what he was willing to say. But she had known all along she couldn't do this on her own. Or was it that she didn't want to?

Maybe it doesn't matter. Maybe we can save each other.

"Okay," she said.

cop, waited by a door. When he saw Nick, his face burst into a huge smile. Nick couldn't help but return the grin.

"I knew that stuff about your wife was bullshit," said the detective, slapping Nick on the shoulder and pulling him into an embrace. "Welcome back."

"You two know each other?" Claire asked, incredulous.

"Detective Allan Hart, Dr. Claire Waters," Nick said, gesturing to Claire.

"I've read all about you," Hart said to Claire as they shook hands. "In the case file, that is. You still look like your picture."

"That picture was taken when I was eight," Claire said, returning his easy smile. "I guess I'll take that as a compliment, Detective."

"My friends call me Al," said Hart, opening the door beside him. "And any friend of Nick's is a friend of mine. Follow me."

Hart led them into the Homicide office, where six detectives (four men and two women) worked individually at standard government-issue metal desks—until they caught sight of Nick, whereupon they rose and gave him a standing ovation.

Claire looked at Nick. "What's up with the hero's welcome?"

"I helped them out with a case a couple of years ago," Nick replied uncomfortably.

"Must've been some case," Claire said, shaking her head as the other detectives came over and greeted Nick, pulling him aside.

"It was," Hart said to her, and proceeded to tell her the story. Two years earlier, three brothers operating a heroin-processing factory in the basement of their home in Rochester's crime-ridden 19th Ward were gunned down by a duo of professional hitters equipped with Uzis. They might've gotten away clean but for an unmarked police cruiser passing the house at exactly the wrong time. The solo rookie cop behind the wheel, Officer Evan Springer, was passing nearby when he heard the automatic weapons fire. A former marine sharpshooter in Iraq, Springer stopped, got out, and positioned himself behind his car as the two shooters burst from the house. He scored head shots on both killers literally before they knew what hit them. They sprayed bullets everywhere as they went down in their death dance. Unfortunately, one of the bullets ricocheted off a light post behind the police cruiser and into the back of Springer's skull, slicing through his brain and killing him.

CHAPTER 21

———❖———

The *click-clack* of heels along the gray-walled hallways Rochester's Public Safety Building reminded Claire of that fir day with Paul Curtin, walking through the cinder-block and concre corridors of Rikers Island. That had been less than a month ago, b to Claire it felt like a decade.

This time, though, was different. Instead of the fear and intimid tion she felt walking behind Curtin that morning, her step was fille with confidence and purpose as she strode beside NYPD detecti Nick Lawler, convinced that with his help, they'd find both her frier Amy Danforth (or her remains) and Mr. Winslow, the man who taken Amy from Claire's driveway so many years ago.

Nick had offered to remain for several days to help Claire, and sh immediately accepted, inviting him to stay in her parents' gue room. Claire thought they should begin with a tour of the places sh and Amy visited together as children, thinking it might trigger memory of a place where she'd seen Winslow. But Nick insisted th only place to start was the case file, which meant contacting th Rochester Police Department's Homicide Unit. Claire's parents we well connected in Rochester's political circles, and she suggeste using her parents' clout to secure the police chief's cooperation wi their investigation. To which Nick replied that he was more co nected in the RPD than her parents could ever be.

Which he proved the moment he and Claire rounded a corner. tall, trim man with a full head of silvering hair, and wearing a tie ar shirtsleeves, the badge and automatic on his belt pegging him as

The last Rochester cop shot to death had been in 1959, when Hart was in diapers, and he wasn't about to let Officer Springer's death go unanswered on his watch. Whoever ordered the hit on the three drug-dealing brothers was as guilty of murdering Officer Springer as the two dead killers-for-hire, and Al Hart vowed to catch the bastard.

A set of keys in one of the dead killers' pockets led to a 2006 Mitsubishi Diamante parked around the corner from the scene of the massacre. The vehicle turned out to have been stolen from an outdoor parking lot on West 47th Street in New York City. Cop brotherhood being what it is, Hart skipped official channels and dialed Manhattan South Homicide on his own, looking for help. When Detective Nick Lawler just happened to pick up the phone, he not only pledged his cooperation, but he also invited Hart to come down to the city to work the case with him.

By the time Hart arrived in Manhattan the next day, Nick had already worked his contacts in Special Narcotics, who'd rousted their snitches and come up with the name Eduardo Pena, the reputed owner of the Juarez Cartel's New York City heroin franchise. Word had it that Pena planned to expand his operations upstate by knocking off the competition—literally.

Heavily armed NYPD emergency service cops burst through Pena's door, followed by Nick Lawler and Al Hart in body armor, and took him down. One of the ESU guys pulled Pena to his feet and held him out to Nick.

"All yours, Detective," the ESU cop said.

Nick turned to Hart. "Your case, your collar."

"Your turf," Hart said, flabbergasted that Nick would hand over such a high-profile arrest to someone from out of town.

"We're still in New York State," replied Nick. "You're a cop here too. Take him home and put him away."

Hart nodded a grateful thanks and cuffed Pena, taking him back to Rochester to face capital murder charges in the death of Officer Springer. And the Rochester police got to announce that one of its own locked up the most dangerous drug-running cop-killing badass scumbag in the country.

For his work, Nick Lawler received an honorary Rochester detective's badge and the assurance that anything he ever needed in the Flower City was his for the asking.

"And in this particular case," Hart said, finishing, "anything you come up with helps us as well. We've been carrying this as an open file for more than twenty years."

"Did you work on it originally?" Claire asked, glancing at a man she pegged as Hart's boss emerging from a glassed-in office and heading their way.

"Sort of," answered Hart. "I was in the academy and they had us out doing grid searches for your friend in Seneca Park."

"You mean, searching for Amy's body," Claire concluded. She looked down to chase away the pain and compose herself. "I can't tell you how much I appreciate all this," she said, managing a smile.

Hart nodded as the man from the office reached them. "Captain Killian," Hart said, gesturing to Claire, "Dr. Claire Waters."

"Your mother taught all my kids how to dissect a frog," the captain said, shaking Claire's hand. "I guess that's a strange way to introduce myself."

"No worries," Claire replied. "I just hope she did a good job."

Nick joined them now, shaking hands with the captain, whom he'd met on the Springer murder case. "We've got you all set up," Killian said, pulling from his pocket two temporary ID cards and handing them to Claire and Nick. "You can come and go as you please, use our computers, whatever you need. Chief's providing us with an extra unmarked car for this investigation and an empty office right down the hall. The files are there, and the three of you can work comfortably."

"Three of us?" Nick asked, shooting Hart a knowing look.

Hart smiled. "You didn't think I was gonna pass up a chance to help you out, did you?"

"Payback's a bitch," Nick said with a smile.

Captain Killian headed back to his office. "Al, just let me know if there's anything else," he said over his shoulder.

"Thank you, Detective," Claire said with relief, as if a heavy burden had been lifted from her shoulders.

"Forget it," Hart replied. "Let's get to work."

It was clear that Nick and Claire had their work cut out for them. Inside their temporary office, more than a dozen boxes, battered from use and yellowed with age, were piled on several metal tables in the windowless room.

"So many?" Claire gasped, filled with trepidation over what she might find inside them.

"There was barely a cop in western New York who didn't help us in some way," Hart told her as he pulled the lid off a box and peeked inside.

"What about the original detectives who ran the case?" Nick asked as he shot Claire a look. "Any value in talking to them?"

"Wish we could," Hart said. "But the captain who ran the investigation died in ninety-eight, the lead guys both passed away last year, and everyone else who was in Homicide back then's retired and living in Florida."

Claire barely heard any of it. Her eyes were focused on one particular box, on which was written "#1" and the date she'd never forget: "July 18, 1989"—the day Amy had been stolen from her.

Nick sensed her discomfort. "You okay?" he asked, moving beside her.

Claire brushed a wisp of hair from her eyes. "I hoped this would be easier," she replied.

"There's no physical evidence to look at," Hart assured her as he stepped over to join them, "because none was found at the scene of the kidnapping. Our CSU techs got a few photos of tire tracks in the dirt on the street but that's about all."

Claire looked up at Nick. "How do you want to do this?"

"From the beginning," Nick answered instantly, pulling the first box from atop the pile and opening the lid. "Best information about any crime comes when the crime is fresh in everyone's mind. We'll each take a box, work through them in chronological order."

He pulled the second and third boxes, keeping the former for himself and handing the latter to Hart, who moved off to one of the three tables. Claire took her cue and began going through the massive amount of paperwork in the first box. Report after report, statement after statement, the sheer volume of what she didn't know about the case made her head spin and, at the same time, cleared up what she'd wondered about for so many years: The police had left few, if any, stones unturned in their search for Amy and her kidnapper. The investigation had been a thorough, professional one, involving numerous cops from surrounding towns and counties, the state police, and even the FBI when a piece of evidence turned up suggesting Amy was abducted to be sold into child slavery. That was ruled out when the ring in question was busted and Amy wasn't found.

Although the file boxes were labeled in chronological order, the paperwork inside was disorganized, presumably from having been gone through numerous times over the past two decades. They worked silently for an hour, leafing through papers, until Claire picked up a manila folder and stared at the label affixed to the tab.

"Someone else needs to read this," she said, the fear in her voice catching both Nick's and Al's attention.

"What is it?" Hart asked, putting down a piece of paper.

"My statement to the police the day Amy disappeared," Claire answered, realizing she'd completely erased or blocked it from her mind. A good part of her didn't want to bring it back in. She dropped the file on the table as if it were burning her hands.

Nick slid his chair beside hers. "We can look at it together," he said, "but you need to read what you told the cops the day it happened."

"Why?" asked Claire, avoiding Nick's eyes.

"Because it may help you remember something," Nick answered. "You're the only one who saw the kidnapper. And you were just a kid. What seemed irrelevant then may have more meaning to you now."

Claire understood. She had seen enough patients unlock childhood memories for the sheer reason that they were now adults who could reason their way through and interpret events in ways a child never could.

She opened the folder and read. The interview she gave to detectives all those years ago appeared in front of her, the words neatly transcribed from a cassette tape she could almost see whirring in a recorder on the table in front of her.

The words themselves didn't ring familiar, for they were the words of a terrified eight-year-old who'd just witnessed a horrible crime.

And then she began to remember. The room at the precinct had stuffed animals on the chairs. She'd sat on a couch beside a psychologist, and the detective sat on a stool facing her. She could tell from the way their questions were worded that they had been gentle, trying not to traumatize her more than she already was. They tried to jog her young memory without crossing the line by asking leading questions. The interview was short, and Claire told them as much as she could remember. Which, she realized, was so much less than she remembered now.

"I barely told them anything," she said to Nick without taking her eyes from the page. "Certainly not enough to help."

"You were eight," Nick said, "and you were scared to death. Give yourself a break."

"They asked me what he looked like," Claire said, pointing to the page in question. "I said he was tall, had brown hair and a big nose, and he was wearing a short-sleeve shirt and khaki shorts. They asked me what kind of car he drove. I told them it was white and had four doors. I never got the license plate."

"That's more than we get from most witnesses," Hart chimed in from across the room without looking up. "Especially the kids."

She kept reading, the scene playing through her head like it had thousands of times over the last twenty years.

He pulled up to the house in the gleaming white car.

He looked nervous.

I blinked. I backed away from him.

Then he told Amy about her father.

"I blinked," Claire said.

"What?" Nick asked, looking up from the file his head was buried in.

"Nothing," Claire answered, though it was far from nothing. Something was bothering her.

Why did I blink?

She tried to rewind the scene in her head and play it back in slow motion. As if it were recorded on videotape. She could clearly see Winslow getting out of the car. Heading toward them. Looking right at Claire.

Looking at me?

She slowed down the tape playing in her head even more, like a film in which she could clearly see each frame.

Eight-year-old Claire looked up.

She made eye contact with Winslow, who was almost directly in front of her.

She felt her nose wrinkle.

His head turned toward Amy.

My nose wrinkled.

An odor permeated her nostrils. Like someone had just taken a picture.

A Polaroid picture.

Claire nearly jumped out of her chair, startling Nick and Hart.

"Are you okay?" Hart asked, alarmed.

But Claire only had eyes for her statement, tears dropping on the pages as she sped through each one. Looking for words, a sentence she knew she wouldn't find.

"It's not here," she said, her worst fears realized.

Nick shot Hart a look as he turned toward her. "What's not there?" he asked, seeing that something had been released deep inside her.

"The smell," Claire uttered. "I never told them about the smell."

"You smelled something?" asked Hart as he closed the folder in his hand.

Claire tried to regain her composure. "My father had this old Polaroid camera," she recalled. "He loved taking pictures of me with it. But then he'd make me sit there as the picture came out of the camera and he'd peel back the paper on it . . . and I hated the smell."

"The smell of the picture," Nick clarified.

"That's why I wrinkled my nose when Winslow came up my driveway. He was looking right at me. He was almost in front of me and I wrinkled my nose and backed away. . . ."

"Because he smelled like a Polaroid picture," Hart deduced. "He stunk like developing fluid."

He tossed Nick a look. Any detective would know this was a huge lead.

"But I never told the police," Claire continued. "I never told them because—" She looked down, trying to catch her breath.

This time, Nick didn't hesitate to put his arm around her shoulder. "Because it was you who Winslow really wanted," he said, just as gently as before. "You smelled him and the look on your face must've repulsed him. You backed away and he turned his attention toward your friend."

"You see?" Claire said, looking up at Nick, her eyes wet. "It was my fault. He wanted me. It was supposed to be me, not Amy." Claire was gulping for air as if she were drowning. "I didn't tell the police because I was ashamed to admit it—"

"No," Nick replied. "That look saved your life. And you didn't tell the police because you were scared someone would blame you. But Winslow taking Amy was never your fault."

Just like that, Claire was that scared eight-year-old girl again. And she did what she remembered doing back then, that day. She began to sob, and buried her head in the cop's shoulder. Only this time, the shoulder was Nick Lawler's.

CHAPTER 22

Fifteen minutes later, Claire, now fully composed, sat in a well-worn leather chair beside Nick and Hart in Captain Killian's office. The room was small, dark, and musty, as if light were the enemy. Claire wondered how many other victims had sat in this chair over the years—and how many ever got answers to their nightmares.

Though the trio had just begun to dig into the myriad of boxes that made up Amy's case file, Nick and Hart pounced on Claire's revelation that Mr. Winslow reeked of developing fluid. That was too big a lead to sit on. Still, the captain shook his head with doubt.

"You grew up here," Killian said to Claire, "so I don't have to tell you what a needle in a haystack this is." He looked at Nick. "You didn't grow up here, so I'll fill you in. Back in eighty-nine, Rochester was still Kodak City. Hell, half the town's named after George Eastman, and until digital cameras came along and decimated the film business, Kodak was Monroe County's biggest employer. I'd hate to guess how many people working in the plants there came home every night stinking of developing fluid."

Hart had anticipated Killian's reaction. "Boss," he said, handing over a folder, "the father of the victim, Amy Danforth, was a sales exec at Kodak. Because the kidnapper said he worked with Amy's father, Kodak cooperated with the investigation." He gestured to Claire. "The composite of the suspect that Dr. Waters gave back then was compared to photos from the ID badges of every Kodak employee. No one matched, and the one employee whose last name was Winslow was a woman who died in 2002."

Nick shifted in his chair. "We're thinking maybe the guy who took Amy was involved in kiddie porn."

Killian's face tightened. "You mean he was looking for another little girl to take pictures of."

"No Internet back then," Nick answered. "Only way for pervs to share their sick pictures with fellow pedophiles was either in person or by U.S. mail. And they could hardly take their film to be developed at some drugstore or photo kiosk, so they had to do it themselves."

Killian closed the folder and put it on his desk. "Did anyone back then look into the possibility that Amy was kidnapped by a kiddie porn ring?"

"Yes," Hart replied. "Her info and photos were sent to the FBI and National Center for Missing and Exploited Children. With no results, obviously."

The captain sat back and crossed his arms. "Okay, Al," he finally relented. "It's a long shot, but I guess the developing fluid is the only fresh lead we've got."

"When I was growing up," Claire offered, both nervous and excited that she may have set them on a new course, "our neighbor down the street was a professional photographer. He was always going to weddings, confirmations, and social events. He belonged to some trade organization—I think it was called the Rochester Photographic Society. Maybe we should start there."

"I have a better idea," Hart said.

A short time later, the trio pulled up to Great Lakes Film Labs, a gray concrete building located in an aging industrial park in the nearby suburb of Henrietta, fifteen minutes south of downtown Rochester. Hart's "better idea" had been to confer with an old-timer in the police department's photo lab who'd assured him in the presence of Nick and Claire that there wasn't a photographer in the area who hadn't gone to the people at Great Lakes for help at one time or another.

They entered the front office, noticing the framed before-and-after prints adorning the walls. Images of brides from the 1920s, once murky and faded, now showed them holding flowing bouquets of tinted pink roses, their cheeks the same blushing color. The brides in the restored photos stared out into the showroom, as if they were looking ahead to a bright, happy future. But no customers were there to see them. The young assistant behind the counter, her arms tattooed with winning poker hands, made Nick and Hart for cops immediately.

"You guys from Rochester PD?" she asked before either detective could open his mouth.

"I'm Detective Hart," he said, displaying his badge. Then, gesturing to Nick and Claire, "They're just along for the ride. We're looking for Douglas Lewis."

"He's expecting you," the girl said, reaching for her purse, "but he's stuck in the back with a customer." She pulled out a cigarette and a lighter. "He'll be out in a second. Do you mind if I—"

"Don't let us stop you," Claire said.

"Thanks," she replied with a smile of relief, obviously tweaking for her nicotine fix as she burst through the front door into the sunlight, lighting up at the same time.

Copies of the company's sales brochure lay on a table near an aging but intact leather sofa. Claire leafed through one and read aloud, " 'We develop and restore disk film, old film, damaged and wet film.' " She looked up, thinking there was a deep sadness to the place, as if it were trying to hold on to a past that was forever gone. "Everything's digital now. I barely remember using film in a camera." Claire walked over to study the restored images on the wall. *They look like phantoms,* she thought.

She was staring at the photographs of people whose lives ended years ago when a door opened. "Film is dead," said a male voice.

Nick and Hart turned to face a sandy-haired, pleasant-looking man in his thirties walking toward them. "I'm Doug Lewis. Which one of you is Detective Hart?"

"I am," Hart replied, offering his hand, which Lewis shook. "Thanks for seeing us on such short notice." He gestured to Nick. "This is Detective Lawler from the New York Police Department, and the young lady over there admiring your work is Dr. Waters."

Lewis looked Nick in the eye as he shook his hand. "What brings the NYPD all the way up here?" he asked in a friendly tone.

"It's actually a local case," Nick answered. "I'm a friend of Dr. Waters and I'm helping her out."

It was Nick's words—and the sudden strong smell of developing fluid—that brought Claire back to the present. She turned from the photographs on the wall and walked over to Lewis. "I've got to tell you, what you do here is fascinating—"

She stopped as she locked eyes with Lewis. She stiffened, unable to turn away because what she saw horrified her.

Oh my God. It's him.

Lewis's smile faded as he read Claire's face.

"Are you okay, Doctor?" he asked.

But Claire was so shocked she couldn't answer.

It's him.

"Where is she?" Claire whispered.

Lewis shot a nervous glance to Nick and Hart, who were as in the dark as he was. He turned back to Claire. "What did you say?" he asked, taking a step back.

"Where is she?" Claire said with a threatening edge in her rising voice that scared the hell out of Lewis.

"Lady, I agreed to see Detective Hart because he said he had some questions. I don't know what you're talking about—"

"What did you do to her?" Claire screamed, rushing toward Lewis and pounding on his face and chest with her fists before Nick and Hart could react. "Tell me, you sick bastard! Tell me where Amy is!"

"Get away from me!" Lewis yelled, terrified by her outburst.

But she kept repeating herself as Nick and Hart pulled her off Lewis.

"Claire, what the hell are you doing?" Nick yelled, clutching her hands in his so she'd stop beating Lewis.

"Can't you see?" Claire screamed at Nick. "It's him!"

"It can't be him," Hart said as calmly as he could. "He's too young."

Hart turned to Lewis. "You were how old in 1989, ten?"

"Eight," Lewis said, the color just returning to his face. "What's going on here?"

"Dr. Waters thinks you're the man who kidnapped her friend," Hart said as Claire caught her breath.

She realized she had made a terrible mistake.

"I'm sorry," she said, the words pouring out. "The man smelled like developing fluid. He took my friend Amy, put her in his white BMW, and I never saw her again. You look so much like him."

The mention of the car made Lewis's face drop.

"Are you okay, sir?" Nick asked him, seeing the fear in Lewis's eyes—the same fear he saw every time he looked at his own face in a mirror.

Lewis caught Nick's sympathetic glance. "This man . . ." Lewis hesitated, then forced himself to ask, "What else can you tell me about him?"

Hart shot a look to Nick as he answered. "Not much. All we have is a composite sketch and the fact that he drove a white BMW."

"And his name," Claire offered, "or at least the name he gave us. Winslow."

"Winslow?" Lewis spat out the name as if it were a curse. "Are you sure?"

"I'll never forget it," Claire said.

Douglas Lewis looked at them with a profound sadness, as if a crushing weight had just landed on his shoulders. They watched as he turned around and walked to a nearby file cabinet. He removed a key from his pocket, unlocked the top drawer, and opened it.

"If your memory is correct," he said as he shuffled through papers in the file drawer, "then I'm the one who should be apologizing to you."

He found what he was looking for, a single piece of paper, and left the drawer open as he walked the few feet back to them.

"Is this the man who kidnapped your friend?" Lewis asked, his voice cracking.

He handed the paper to Claire, who realized by its touch that it was a photograph. Without even looking, she knew what she was about to see.

She brought the picture up. Tears welled in her eyes.

Claire was looking at the man who'd so long ago plunged her entire world into darkness. She glanced over at Nick. All she could manage was to nod yes.

She turned her head back to Lewis, not wanting to ask him the question, already knowing the answer.

"His name is Peter Lewis," he said. "He's my father."

*   *   *

The room in Rochester Police Headquarters was decorated in soft, friendly earth tones, the furniture a step up in appearance and comfort from the usual government-issued crap found in municipal offices everywhere. It was here that Doug Lewis sat with Claire, Nick, and Al. He agreed to tell them what he knew, even consenting to having his statement videotaped on the condition that it never be made public unless needed as evidence in court.

They had piled into Hart's unmarked Ford Crown Victoria for what turned out to be a mostly silent ride downtown. Lewis sat up front beside Hart, directly in front of Claire, who tried not to bore holes into the back of Lewis's head with her eyes. Instead, she forced herself to stare out the window, a jumble of emotions running through her. She wanted to hear everything Lewis had to say and at the same time was petrified to hear a word of it.

But now, at the table, it became clear from the look on Lewis's ashen face that this was going to be as hard for him as it would be for her. He had just learned that his father kidnapped a young girl, who would now be the same age as he was. As Claire was. If Amy were still alive.

We're in this together, Claire thought.

"Are you ready?" Hart asked Lewis, placing the microphone before him.

"As much as I'll ever be," Lewis replied, glancing nervously at Claire.

Hart pressed RECORD on the camera. "Please begin with your full name and date of birth."

Lewis looked at them, took a deep breath.

"My name is Douglas Adam Lewis. I was born April second, 1981, at Highland Hospital in Rochester. I am here of my own free will and am anxious to cooperate with the police on this matter.

"As a child, I lived in Webster, just east of Rochester on Lake Ontario. I am the only child of Marjorie, a secretary, who died of cancer in 1997, and Peter, a chemist who worked for a company called PhotoChem over in Irondequoit, which made developing fluids and emulsifiers for film. He always used to say that he was fascinated with how chemicals could bring an image to life. He passed away from a heart attack in 1999."

Claire was crushed. She'd held out hope that she'd be able to confront the man who took Amy away from her. Lewis caught her disappointment but continued on, staring straight into the camera.

"Dad used to travel a lot. Phoenix, Kansas City, Denver, San Francisco, New Orleans. I used to ask him what those places were like. His answer was always the same. 'Someday we'll go there,' he'd say. 'But if I tell you about it now, it'll spoil the surprise of seeing it for the first time.' I never questioned him. After all, he was my dad. He knew everything. He always seemed to be a happy guy, and he and my mom got along great.

"But when I was eight, everything changed. It was summer and there was a thunderstorm that day. I came home from camp, and my mother was worried out of her mind. When I asked her what was wrong, she said it was nothing. 'It's got to be something because you look so sad,' I remember saying to her. I was just trying to make her feel better, but instead she burst into tears and ran up to her room. I started to cry, too, thinking I had said something terribly wrong. I waited downstairs for my father to come home. I wanted to tell him what happened. My dad always had a way of soothing my mom when she was upset. I just wanted her to feel better.

"So I turned on the TV and lay down on the couch. Dad always got home around seven. When it was eight o'clock, I called his office. Nobody answered. I went upstairs and knocked on my parents' bedroom door. Mom wouldn't open it, and when I tried the knob, I found it was locked.

"I went back downstairs and got on the couch. Next thing I knew, it was morning and Mom was waking me up for camp, something Dad always did.

"When I asked her where Dad was, she said he had to leave for work early. But she was still upset, so I knew he never came home.

"Mom went upstairs and I went into the kitchen, picked up the phone, and dialed Dad's office. His secretary answered and said he wasn't coming back to work there.

"I remember hanging up and wondering what had happened. I thought about it all day at camp. But when I got home, there Dad was, smiling that same old smile. I asked him where he was last night. 'Out with the guys, celebrating,' he said. Mom walked into the room just then, and she was smiling too. 'Your father's taking some time off,' she said cheerily. 'He's going to be spending a lot more time with us now.' I thought it was great. After all, he was my dad. Why wouldn't I want to hang out with him?

"A week later, I was asleep and had a dream that my parents were fighting. At least I thought it was a dream. Until I got up and realized they were yelling at each other. 'We can't afford to live here on just what I make,' I heard her say. 'Can't you ask them for your job back?' My father said he'd never go back there, not for a million dollars. Not after what they did to him.

"So he found another job, working part-time for the water company. I still to this day don't know what he did for them, except that it had something to do with monitoring pollutants. He started going away again, saying other cities wanted him to make sure their water was safe. And he always seemed pretty sad.

"Then, on my tenth birthday, he came home and was very excited. He said PhotoChem had just called, and they needed someone to run a new polymer science division they were starting up, and it was an offer he couldn't refuse.

"He was thrilled. Mom was thrilled. He hadn't been this happy in years. And then he dropped the bomb. We'd have to move to Canada. Mom didn't care. But I had a lot of friends here. I didn't want to leave. But I didn't want to be Dad's buzz kill.

"He left for Canada the next week. He came back almost every weekend. Mom and I waited until the end of the school year and moved with him to a place called Pickering. It was nice there and didn't snow as much. And Toronto was right nearby. Dad worked there, and it was a great place to go. We were there three years, and it was the best three years of our lives.

"And then one night, it all changed forever. I still remember the bang on the door. Police in bulletproof vests with automatic weapons screamed at Dad to show his hands or they'd blow his brains out. I was thirteen then and I was terrified. I ran out of the house just in time to see Dad in handcuffs being put into a police car. He kept yelling that everything would be all right. As the car pulled away, he had his hand over his heart, looking at me. I could see him mouth the words 'I love you.'

"I didn't know it would be the last time I'd ever see him.

"An officer said Mom and I had to go to the police station, too, but we'd be taken in separate cars and not allowed to see each other. When we got there, a very nice female detective came into the room and talked to me. She wouldn't tell me why Dad was in so much trouble. But she asked me all kinds of questions about where he'd been, the places he traveled to. I told them whatever I could remember. I had no idea what was going on. But of all the things my father told me over the years, the one I always remembered was that your word was your bond so you should always tell the truth. So that's what I did.

"And then I asked her to do the same thing, to tell me the truth. She told me my father was in a lot of trouble, that he'd been arrested for kidnapping and murdering a nine-year-old girl from the town next to ours. She didn't tell me that he'd also raped her. I only found out later when I read it in the newspaper. I told the detective, 'My father would never hurt anyone. You've made an awful mistake.' I'll never forget this. The detective looked at me sadly and said that if Dad were innocent, he'd have the chance to prove it in court. That's when the door opened and a man I'd never seen before, a lawyer whose name I don't remember, came in and told the detective that I had nothing more to say. And he took me out of there.

"The lawyer was going to drive my mother and me home. But we never made it. When we turned onto our street, there were TV cameras and reporters in front of our house. Someone had spray-painted the word *killer* under the living room picture window. Mom told me to put my head down and ordered the lawyer to keep on driving. We got away from there and never went back.

"We stayed in a cheap motel that night so nobody would know where we were. The next day, the lawyer came back and got Mom. All she wanted to do was see my father. They left me in the room, by myself, all day. When my mother got back, she had her car and a couple of suitcases full of our clothes. I found out later that the lawyer and his staff had gone back to our house and packed the stuff up for us.

"I asked her if she'd seen Dad. 'Yes,' she said, 'I saw him. He's going to prison for the rest of his life—' "

Lewis caught himself, his eyes wet. Claire felt terrible for him.

"It's okay to cry," she said, handing him a tissue.

"What kind of doctor are you?" he asked her as he wiped his eyes.

"A psychiatrist."

"I've seen my share of those," said Lewis, a sad smile crossing his lips, trying to make light of it.

"Where did you and your mother go?" Hart asked.

"We drove through Quebec, then into Maine. We found an apartment in Bangor, and Mom got a job working for a CPA."

"And why did your dad call himself Winslow?" Claire asked.

"He lived on Winslow Street as a kid, up in Watertown," Lewis answered. "I only knew about the one girl in Canada he hurt. I never knew there was another one—or maybe others."

"When did you come back here to Rochester?" Nick asked.

"After college," Lewis replied, now composed. "Bangor never felt like home. I got an entry-level job at the film lab and worked my way up. Like father, like son. Dad loved taking pictures and taught me how when I was a kid." Lewis closed his eyes, the past washing over him. When he opened them, he looked at Claire. "We both love photography. That was our connection. I hope it's the only one," he said with an uncomfortable laugh.

Claire heard the fear in Lewis's voice that she'd heard from her other patients whose parents had committed heinous crimes—the fear that they, too, might carry genes that would make them do terrible things.

"You never married," Claire observed, noting the absence of a ring on Lewis's finger.

Lewis smiled sadly. "I'm only thirty," he said, looking down. "There's plenty of time."

Claire's eyes caught his. "When was the last time you went out on a date?"

Nick and Hart exchanged glances. "Excuse me," Nick protested, "but maybe you ought to give the guy a break—"

"No, it's okay," Lewis interjected. "I want to answer that."

He turned to Claire. "Do you have any idea what it's like to know that your father violated and murdered a little girl? Can you even imagine what that kind of shame feels like?"

"Have you ever touched a little girl?" Claire asked him pointedly.

"Of course not!" Lewis shot back angrily.

"Do you ever have urges to?" Claire asked, leaning toward him.

Hart shut off the videotape. "Doctor, with all due respect, I think you're crossing the line here with Mr. Lewis, who has cracked your case—our case—wide open and bears absolutely no responsibility for his father's deranged actions. "

"That's exactly my point," Claire said, turning to Lewis. "You are not your father. You'll never be like him. You don't have to be afraid that you are. You can live your life without worrying that you're going to hurt someone. And Detective Hart is right. The sins of the father don't automatically pass down to the son. Whatever guilt you're carrying, you need to let go of for your own sake."

Lewis softened. "Thank you," he said, "but I can't. Not as long as you're telling me that you saw my father kidnap your friend. When was that?"

"In July of 1989," answered Claire, "probably on that same stormy day he didn't come home."

"Do you have any evidence proving my father kidnapped and murdered this little girl Amy?" Lewis asked Hart.

"Only what Dr. Waters told us when she was a kid," Hart replied. "The color and make of the car are the same as the one your father drove, and she's now identified him from your photograph, which matches the description she gave to the police."

"Not to mention the name he used—Winslow," Nick added. "It's not a coincidence."

Lewis looked down. Made his decision.

"Then let's ask him," he said.

Claire looked at him incredulously. "Ask him? But you said he died of a heart attack."

"I had to be sure," Lewis said. Then, for the first time, he leaned toward Claire. "Do you want closure, Doctor?"

"Yes. For me and for Amy's parents."

"My father is in prison in Ontario. If you want, I'll get you in to see him."

It took Claire only a second to answer.

"Please," she said.

CHAPTER 23

Kingston Penitentiary rises like a monolithic stone fortress on the northern shore of Lake Ontario, as if guarding the city whose name it bears. In fact, it's known as Canada's Alcatraz, the country's toughest maximum-security prison, housing its most dangerous convicts, nearly half of whom are serving out life sentences. As Claire approached the dual Doric columns at the doors to the visitor's entrance, she glanced at the guard towers on either corner of the stone wall enclosing the prison.

At least the bastard is where he belongs, she thought.

The bastard, of course, was Peter Lewis, the man who called himself "Mr. Winslow" when he kidnapped Amy instead of her more than two decades earlier.

Claire glanced to her right at the bastard's son, Doug Lewis, grateful he volunteered to take her to the father he hadn't seen for nearly twenty years. They had traveled together to Kingston from Rochester, a three-and-a-half-hour drive. As their journey began, Doug shut down any attempts Claire made at small talk, and she understood why, perhaps better than anyone. He had successfully buried his past and was now being forced (or forcing himself) to confront it once more. It was an unspoken bond between them. Carrying the burden of his father's horrible crimes was a hell like the one she had experienced.

As she and Doug crossed King Street, the two-lane thoroughfare fronting the prison entrance, a sense of foreboding washed over her. She wished Nick had come with them. But she knew there was a purpose to his absence.

The purpose was expediency. A request from the Rochester Police to interview Peter Lewis in a Canadian prison would have to be channeled through the U.S. Department of State, a process fraught with the real possibility of ending in failure if the Canadians refused to cooperate or if Lewis lawyered up.

But how could Lewis refuse—or the Canadian authorities refuse him—the chance to see his only child after so many years? Especially when that child was a citizen of Canada as well as of the United States?

So Claire and Nick made a decision: This would be a stealth mission. After secret meetings involving the police chief and district attorney, Detective Hart took a few personal days off from work so he wouldn't be officially on duty should some part of the plan go south. He and Nick would drive up to Kingston in Hart's beat-up old Subaru Outback so they wouldn't be pegged as cops. Claire and Doug would drive up separately in Doug's Ford SUV, all to avoid the red flags that three men and a woman in the same car crossing the international border might raise. Nick and Hart would check into a hotel on the waterfront in downtown Kingston, where Claire and Doug would meet them immediately after their encounter with Lewis for a full debriefing.

As she and Doug proceeded through the prison's metal detectors and underwent pat-downs for contraband, Claire was relieved she hadn't tried to smuggle in her miniature flash recorder, because it undoubtedly would have been discovered and resulted in their expulsion from the facility.

Though Lewis was assigned to the segregation unit, whose inmates lived in solitary confinement and were allowed out of their cells only one hour a day for exercise, his good behavior had convinced a review board that his first visitors in twenty years need not be cloistered with him in closed, closely guarded quarters. And so Claire and Doug were escorted into the visiting room, a large space with several dozen metal tables at which inmates sat with their various family members. Prison guards peppered the room's perimeter, waiting to pounce on any convict who tried to stick his hand up a girlfriend's shirt or down her pants or, as had happened, attempted to have sex in front of the other visitors.

Claire and Doug were brought to a table near one of the room's walls and sat beside each other, two guards in close proximity. Claire was strangely calm now. She looked over at Doug, who was doing a poor job of hiding the fact that he was a nervous wreck.

"You sure you're ready for this?" she asked him, touching his shoulder.

"No," Doug answered, "but I'll be okay."

"Thank you," Claire said, brushing the hair from his forehead with her fingers. The physical contact was part of the plan to convince Lewis that they were engaged, but she could tell her touch calmed him down. *When was the last time anyone touched you?*

He was about to say something when a door opened at the far end of the room, and two prison guards escorted in a thin, gray-haired man. Claire felt a wave of nausea, for though "Mr. Winslow" had aged, she recognized him instantly. He was shackled at the feet and cuffed at the waist, the two restraints attached by chains that allowed him to merely shuffle across the brown linoleum-tiled floor. He saw his son and a smile broke on one side of his face, lasting only as long as it took him to realize his boy was sitting with a woman.

A woman who now grabbed his son's hand, their fingers intertwined. Like lovers.

Claire and Doug rose as Lewis found his way to the opposite side of the table. A guard pulled out a chair for him.

"Douglas," Lewis said, almost emotionless, as he sat down.

"Peter," Doug returned, never letting go of Claire's hand.

"You used to call me Dad," said Lewis.

"You haven't been my father in a long time," Doug replied flatly.

An uneasy silence followed. Then Lewis looked at Claire. "Are you going to introduce me to your friend?" he asked, turning back to Doug.

"This is Claire," Doug said. "Claire, this is Peter."

"My pleasure," Lewis said, sticking out a shackled hand as far as he could.

"The pleasure is mine," Claire said, only now unclasping her left hand from Doug's and grasping Lewis's outstretched hand with both of hers. The sensation sent a chill up her spine, which she somehow managed to hide.

But what she made no effort to hide was the diamond ring she wore on her left hand. Which Lewis saw immediately, causing him to pull back.

"That's the ring I gave your mother," he said to Doug, never taking his eyes off Claire.

"Yes," his son said plainly, putting his arm around Claire's waist. "Claire's my fiancée. We're getting married."

Lewis showed no emotion. He just sat there, staring at the two of them. "I guess I should know something about you," Lewis said, turning to Claire. "Are you from Pickering as well?"

"No, I'm American," Claire answered as respectfully as she could muster. "I grew up in Rochester."

"What a coincidence," Lewis said, squinting his eyes as if remembering his days there long ago. "I'm sure Douglas told you we lived in Rochester before we moved to Canada."

"Claire and I met in Rochester," said Doug. "I moved back there after college."

Once again, the corner of Lewis's mouth tilted upward in that sadistic half smile. "Oh," he said. "And I thought you didn't come to visit me all these years because you hated me."

"I don't hate you anymore," Doug said. "Hating you took too much energy. It almost destroyed me." He looked lovingly at Claire. "Once I stopped hating you, I got my life back."

"You mean, it was easier just to cut me out of your life. To pretend I never existed," Lewis sneered.

"That's right," Doug replied, ignoring his father's emotion. "And it's all because of Claire."

Lewis turned to Claire. He stared into her eyes. "So this is your doing."

Claire feigned embarrassment. "All I said was that once he let go of the past, he'd be free to move on with his future. *Our* future."

"And I suppose part of that process was to come here and throw it in my face," Lewis shot back.

"No, sir," Claire replied deferentially. "Doug agreed to come up here because I wanted to see you." *At least that's not a lie,* she thought. Though she had no compunction about lying to this monster.

Whether it was the feigned respect or Claire's response, something about Claire seemed to disarm Lewis. "I'm surprised Douglas even admitted he had a father," he said.

"He didn't at first," Claire replied, once again clasping Doug's hand. "He told me you died of a heart attack years ago."

"But you didn't believe him."

"She asked to see your grave," Doug said. "Obviously I couldn't show it to her. I didn't want to have a relationship built on lies. Like the lies you told me when I was a kid."

"And what lies were those?" asked Lewis, leaning forward.

"You know, all those 'business trips' you said you went on. How you didn't want to tell me about the places you'd been to so I'd be surprised when you finally took me to see them."

Lewis smiled. "Obviously I never got to take you because I—"

"Cut the crap, *Dad*," Doug said, spitting out the words loud enough for the guards to take notice. "You couldn't tell me about those places because you never saw any of them."

Something about this struck a note in Lewis, as if he actually felt guilty. "I never once lied to you or your mother about where I'd been—"

"But you sure as hell lied about what you were doing," Doug said.

"And what do you think I was doing?"

"Raping and murdering little girls."

If this fazed Lewis, he didn't show it. "What makes you think that?" he asked.

"Because Claire says a *pedophile* like you would never be satisfied with just one."

"I am not a pedophile. And Claire is hardly an expert on these things."

Doug grinned. "As a matter of fact," he said with great satisfaction, "she is. Claire is a forensic psychiatrist."

For the first time, Lewis eyed Claire with contempt. "Now I get it. You wanted to meet me because I'm some sort of science experiment. Something you can pick apart and then write a paper about."

"No. I've wanted to meet you for years."

Lewis caught his breath. "You're not engaged to my son, are you."

Claire leaned forward, inches away from his gray skin and yellowed teeth. "No. I just met your son yesterday, *Mr. Winslow*."

Lewis looked into her eyes and he knew.

"My God," he whispered. "Claire . . ."

He turned back to his son. "She's trying to manipulate you, Douglas. Shrinks bend and twist the truth. That's why I'm in here—"

"You're here because you murdered an innocent child," Doug replied, raising his voice.

"I'm a sick man!" Lewis exclaimed. "I should be in an institution. I hurt only one little girl! I swear on my life I couldn't help it!"

"You're a lying bastard," Doug said, tears welling in his eyes.

"No, son, no. I don't know what made me do it. Something bad inside me, like an urge that wouldn't let me go. I'm sick, but that shrink convinced the judge I wasn't mentally ill. That's why I'm going to spend the rest of my life in this hellhole."

"You're pathetic. You actually want me to feel sorry for you," Doug said as he stood up. "You disgust me."

Lewis looked at Claire with malignant contempt. "She used you, Douglas. She used you to get to me. You know it's true."

Doug left the room, never turning to look back at his father.

Claire stared at Lewis, who only smirked. Finally, Claire let out the words she'd dreamed of saying all these years. "Where is she? Where's Amy?"

"I don't know who you're talking about, Claire," he said in a friendly tone. "Claire. Claire." Her name rolled off his tongue as if he could taste it. "What a pretty name for a pretty little girl."

Claire didn't flinch. She continued to look straight into his eyes. "I have a deal to offer you."

"I'm in here for life, darlin'. What kind of deal could you possibly offer me?"

"One that comes straight from the Monroe County district attorney. I've positively identified you as the man who kidnapped and probably murdered Amy Danforth. As I'm sure you know, there is no statute of limitations on either of those crimes. The DA has the option of indicting you and filing for extradition, which he will do if you don't cooperate."

Lewis let out a chuckle and shook his head.

"Is there something funny about what I just said?" Claire demanded.

He moistened his lips before he spoke. "When I was arrested, and that shrink said I was fit to stand trial, my first thought was to spare my family the shame of having a husband, a father, on trial for such a horrible crime. So I made my own deal. I told the authorities I would plead guilty and agree to life in prison without parole if they would agree to seal the records, make no public comment, and never extra dite me to the United States."

Now it was Claire's turn to smile. "And you think the Canadian government will honor that deal? When they find out how many innocent children you murdered on those 'business trips' of yours?"

"If anyone had any evidence against me, I suppose I would've found out by now," Lewis replied.

"They didn't, but they will soon," Claire said. "Your son gave a sample of his DNA."

Lewis's face dropped. "He did *w-what?*" he stammered.

"He gave the police and the FBI permission to compare his DNA to any unsolved murder of a little girl. And since half his DNA comes from you, they'll be able to use it to prove you're the murdering bastard we all know you are."

"You bitch!" Lewis yelled.

Then he found a sudden burst of energy and, shackles and all, sprang across the table and tackled Claire to the ground.

"I'll kill you with my bare hands!" he screamed.

Claire dug her fingernails into his face, being sure to draw blood. Lewis screamed as three guards pulled them apart, every head in the visiting room now turned in their direction.

One of the guards hustled Claire out of harm's way. "Stand back against the wall!" he ordered Lewis.

Lewis was struggling against the other two guards restraining him. "Get her out of here!" he bellowed, his eyes shooting daggers at Claire.

Claire showed the first chink in her emotional armor. "Please!" she shouted to Lewis. "Tell me where you buried Amy!"

"You denied me," Lewis snarled, "so now I'm denying you. I'll never tell you! Never!"

A second later, he was pulled through the door by the guards. And gone with him, Claire feared, was any chance of ever finding Amy's remains.

CHAPTER 24

———◦———

"I'm sorry," Claire said quietly. "I screwed up."

It was six hours later and she was sitting with Nick, Al Hart, and Doug Lewis back in Rochester Police Headquarters. The plan to meet at the hotel in downtown Kingston had been scuttled as soon as Nick and Hart heard of Lewis's outburst at the prison. Though Claire was allowed to leave Kingston Pen with little more than an apology from the prison authorities, the two cops didn't want to hang around in case Lewis told his attorney or, worse, the Canadian police about the "deal" Claire had offered him.

So the foursome headed immediately in their two separate cars for the nearby border, crossing back into the United States before the Canadians had time to react. Together now, in the cramped room they'd been assigned, Nick tried to relieve Claire's guilt.

"You stuck to the plan," he said, pulling out a metal chair for her. "You didn't know he would go loony tunes on you."

"And you couldn't have known about his agreement with the Canadians," Doug added. "Hell, I'm his son and I didn't even know."

"All I know," Claire said with sadness, sitting down, "is that we'll never find Amy's remains."

"Then we regroup," Hart offered, a strangely confident tone in his voice.

Claire looked up at him. "You're not giving up?" she asked.

"Give up? This case was cold for more than two decades until you came along, and in just a couple of days we found the perp. Now we've just got to work backward."

He shot a glance toward Doug. "Are you still game to help us out?"

Doug, for his part, was undeterred, as if seeing the monster his father had become gave him new strength of conviction. "In any way I can," he replied.

"Okay, then," said Nick, reenergized. "We need to go back to when you were a kid, to see what you remember."

"I'll do my best," he promised.

Nick, Hart, and Doug pulled out the other metal chairs, and they sat around one of the small metal tables, Nick and Hart facing Doug and Claire.

"The day after the thunderstorm, back in eighty-nine," Nick began. "Your dad said he was out celebrating with the guys. Any idea where he might've gone?"

Doug put his palm to his forehead and thought for a moment, trying to picture the past. "Actually, I remember thinking how weird it was for him to say that. I don't recall my father having a lot of friends."

"Did you ever meet any of the people he worked with at the chemical company here in town?" asked Hart.

"Sure," Doug answered, "but if you asked me their names, I wouldn't be able to tell you. The company still exists, though. We could probably get some names through their human resources department."

"Normally that's exactly what we'd do," Nick offered. "But if someone leaks it to the press, the Canadian authorities will know we conned them."

"Wait a minute," Claire interjected. "Let's take this step by step." She looked at Doug. "The day of the thunderstorm. You told us what happened when you got home from camp. But was your father there before you left the house that morning?"

Doug bit his bottom lip, thinking. "Yeah, he was. I'm pretty sure he woke me up like usual and made me breakfast."

"And he came to my house in the middle of the afternoon," Claire recalled. "The reason he kidnapped Amy that day is beginning to make sense."

Nick caught on. "Because he was fired from his job," he offered.

"Why would that push him to do something so horrible?" asked Doug.

"The same reason people drink, smoke, use drugs, or act promiscuously. Your father was under enormous stress and had always been attracted to young girls. He was probably able to fight the urge, but losing his job put him into a tailspin. He needed a fix to make himself feel better."

"And that fix was you," Doug concluded, shaking his head at the horror of it all. "So, what? Did he just drive around until he saw two girls your age?"

"I don't think so," said Claire. She thought for moment, reviewing her encounter with Lewis. "You were there when I called your father 'Mr. Winslow.' Did you see how he responded?"

"Oh my God," exclaimed Doug. "He called you 'Claire.' He said it as if he remembered you. But how did he know who you were back then?"

"He stalked you," Nick said to Claire. "He saw you somewhere, followed you home, and then waited for his chance."

"But where?" Claire asked, trying to remember if she'd seen Lewis before that July day in her front yard. She looked at Doug. "You didn't live in the city proper, did you?"

"Brighton," said Doug, referring to the affluent suburb adjacent to the southeast part of Rochester. "Off Elmwood, right near Twelve Corners."

"And you grew up off Park Avenue," added Hart, looking up at Claire, "which is only a couple miles away at most. There's a hundred places you and Lewis could've crossed paths. You were eight years old, and unless you had eyes in the back of your head, this guy could've been staring you down and you'd never have known it."

Claire knew Hart had a point. Still, she wasn't about to give up. She turned to Doug. "Were there any special places your father liked to take you back then?"

"Jeez," Doug replied, "we used to go to parks, the zoo, beaches. Anywhere around here you'd go to have fun as a kid is where we went."

"Claire," Nick said, "I know where you're going with this. But we've got to narrow it down. We can't dig up all of Rochester."

Claire flashed Nick a look. "Let me ask you this," she said to Doug. "After your father went to prison, when you left Pickering and moved to Maine. What happened to all of his belongings?"

"I thought about that," Doug said. "But the lawyers took care of selling the house and packing up. Mom instructed them to get rid of everything that belonged to my father. She never wanted to see any of it ever again. . . ."

He stopped, as if he remembered something.

"What is it?" Claire asked hopefully.

Doug looked at her. "I almost forgot. I have the transcripts of my father's court proceedings. From before he went to prison."

"Your mother kept *those?*" Hart asked incredulously.

"No," Doug answered. "I requested them from the Canadians about ten years ago. I thought I wanted to read about what happened. But after they arrived at my house, I could barely bring myself to look at them. I only got through a few pages before I put them in the basement."

"And you're sure they're still there?" asked Nick.

"Yes," Doug replied. "I haven't touched them since."

"Can we see them?" asked Claire, standing up.

"Of course," offered Doug. "Any time you want."

"Now," Claire said.

"Please excuse the house," Doug apologized as he unlocked the front door of his nondescript, single-story white ranch house. "I haven't exactly had time to clean up."

It had been a short drive from downtown Rochester to Doug's home, just east of the city in the quiet suburb of Penfield. As Claire entered with Nick and Hart behind her, she realized Doug's idea of a mess was apparently an empty bag from a local restaurant on the kitchen counter and two dishes in the sink. To her, the place appeared perfectly neat.

And nearly barren. A few random prints hung on the walls. An old blue sofa and love seat occupied the living room, in front of a huge RCA console television that outdated both Claire and Doug. She couldn't help but think that he'd been so busy trying to outrun his past he barely built a present, let alone a future. She pegged him as a guy who went to work every day, came home, and fell asleep watching that ancient TV.

He wasn't kidding when he said he didn't have much of a life, Claire thought. *He's been hiding from his past—like me.*

"Can I get you guys anything to eat or drink?" Doug offered, though Claire could hardly imagine there was anything in the refrig-erator.

Hart and Nick both shook their heads in the negative. "Why don't we get the transcripts and then we'll grab a bite," Claire suggested.

Doug opened the door to the basement. "I can bring everything up," he said, "because it's a little messy down there."

"Nah," Nick replied, "we'll give you a hand."

"Enter at your own risk," Doug said, flipping on a light switch and heading down the wooden stairs.

As Claire followed him, it became apparent that this time Doug wasn't exaggerating. The unfinished room was filled with file boxes, covered furniture, and who knew what else under tarps and old blan-kets.

Everything's neat on the surface, but behind closed doors and inside drawers, it's all a mess. The place reminded her of Tammy Sorenson's apartment—sunny and calm on the outside covering up a storm on the inside.

Doug seemed to sense what they were thinking. "Bought the place a few years ago because I needed a tax deduction," he said. "Organized everything but never really had a chance to go through all the boxes."

Indeed, Claire could see that every carton was clearly labeled with its contents.

"You sure you know where to look?" Hart asked dubiously.

Doug answered by pulling two aging bankers' boxes off the top of a pile. "Right here," he answered, handing one each to Hart and Nick.

"This is all of it?" Nick asked.

"The whole court proceeding lasted only two days," Doug an-swered. "From the little I read, my father pleaded insanity. Most of the testimony is the prosecution's shrink arguing that Dad might've been a sicko, but he knew what he did to that girl was wrong."

Hart headed for the stairs. "Let's get this stuff downtown—"

"Hold on," Nick interrupted. "Where's Claire?"

"Over here," said Claire from across the room, with a shakiness that prompted Hart and Nick to put their boxes down and hurry in the direction of her voice.

Doug reached her first, in a corner of the basement barely visible from where they found the boxes. "What is it?" Doug asked. Even in the shadows he could see that her face was ashen.

Claire pointed, her hand shaking. "Where did you get that?" she asked in a breaking voice.

Nick and Hart joined them just as Doug began to explain. "It's a kite. From when I was a kid."

The two detectives took in the kite. It looked like one of those long Chinese-dragon kites, though this one was red and blue with squiggly lines painted across like fish scales. It flared out to display a single, huge bloodshot eye atop a large mouth open in a wicked smile with pointy, threatening teeth, flanked by short wings. Or fins.

Claire looked like she was scared to death.

"Where did you get it?"

"I don't know. I think my father got it for me."

"Are you okay?" Nick asked her.

But all Claire could hear was the sound of her own voice as a little girl.

"Daddy, I don't like that monster."

"It's okay, sweetie. It won't hurt you. It's not real."

She looked up. The eye hung over her against the clear blue sky, an evil force, watching her every move.

"I can pull it down if you want," came another voice—from a man behind her.

Little Claire turned around and looked up. The man was smiling, but just from the corner of his mouth.

Oh, God.

"You're very pretty, you know," the man said as he reeled in the scary kite.

She backed away as the eye came closer and closer. Until the man grabbed the kite and folded it up.

"I promise, it will never hurt you," the man said.

"I'm sorry," said Claire's father. "I don't know what got into her."

"Please don't worry," the man replied. "I don't want to scare your daughter. Have a nice day."

But Little Claire couldn't help but think there was something about the man she didn't like.

And then the man turned back to her and flashed that same,

*strange smile again. Little Claire turned away. And she saw the
reservoir right across the road—*

The reservoir.

Then it hit Claire. She looked right at Doug.

"You said your father worked for the water company after Photo-
Chem fired him?" she asked, her voice unsteady.

"Yes," Doug answered. "Why?"

"Do you know if he worked at their main office?" Claire asked.

"You mean, over by Cobbs Hill? Yeah, I think so," Doug said. "I remember Mom dropping me off there that summer, after camp was
over. Dad and I would go up by the reservoir and fly this . . . ," he
said, pointing to the kite as his voice trailed off.

Nick put his hand on her shoulder. "What is it, Claire? What do
you remember?"

"My father took me up there too," she said, looking only at the
kite. "That's where I saw this. That's where I saw *him*."

"Lewis?"

She turned to Doug. "Did he take you up there a lot?" she asked,
almost afraid to hear the answer. "To the top of the hill?"

"Not just there," answered Doug, "but all over the park. We'd go
for picnics next to Lake Riley, hike through Washington Grove to the
old water towers. He loved that place. . . ."

He stopped, as if he realized what he was saying. What it *meant*.

Claire clamped her hand onto a nearby box, steadying herself.

"I think I know where he buried Amy."

Just west of the Monroe County Water Authority's headquarters in
Cobbs Hill Park, accessible only through the Authority's parking lot
and a dirt road behind the main building, is a large clearing surrounded on three sides by trees. In late August, when the foliage is at
its thickest, the clearing is invisible from anywhere but that dirt road
leading in.

It was here, the following morning, that Claire sat beside Doug
Lewis in the backseat of Al Hart's unmarked Crown Victoria, watching dozens of police cars, trucks, and buses loaded with cops pour in
one by one. The sun was just coming up, but they'd arrived hours
earlier, at three in the morning, before the city—and especially the

media—woke up to witness one of the area's busiest parks being overrun by a small army of police.

"You think they can pull it off?" Doug asked Claire.

Claire shrugged, though she was awed by what was unfolding before her, mostly because it was her doing. As soon as daylight broke, dozens of cops, some from as far west as Buffalo and as far east as Syracuse, would begin a grid search of the entire park—all hundred and ten acres of it—to find the remains of her friend Amy Danforth. For the next several hours, Claire sat in the sedan, staring out into the darkness, remembering fragments of time spent with Amy. Jumping rope. Hugging each other and laughing wildly at some joke she could no longer remember. Coloring together. Amy's face as Lewis's car pulled away . . .

She stirred. The sun was just peeking over the horizon. *I must've dozed off,* she thought as she sat up, just in time to see Hart and Nick crossing over to the car. Hart opened Claire's door. "It's time," he said.

As she and Doug exited the sedan, a flurry of activity was under way. Platoons of cops were forming as Captain Killian and his boss, the commander of Rochester detectives, assigned each platoon to comb a section of the park.

"We're searching the wooded areas only," Hart told them, turning to Doug. "Your father may have known this place inside and out, but I'm guessing he wasn't so arrogant that he'd bury a body in the open areas around the reservoir or on one of the softball fields."

His statement made Claire and Nick think of another killer—Todd Quimby—who *had* been arrogant enough to drop a body on a softball field. *That was only weeks ago,* Claire mused, *but it seems like years.*

"Are they checking around the water tanks?" Claire asked.

Hart chuckled. "Believe it or not, they've become a big attraction."

"But they were abandoned years ago," she remembered.

"Not by the graffiti artists," Hart explained, "and the photographers who shoot their work. C'mon, I'll show you."

He led them south through the woods. Claire enjoyed the walk. The air was still cool, before the sun would claim the day. The smell of the dewy grass took her back to those wonderful days as a child hiking with her parents. As they emerged from the trees, the two sky-blue water tanks loomed ahead, and she saw Hart had been serious. They were covered in graffiti.

"People come up here to see this?" Claire asked Hart.

"And to add to the mess," Hart answered, shaking his head. "The graffiti artists gather up here admiring one anothers' work. And nobody stops them. State-sponsored vandalism, I call it."

"Nothing a couple hundred gallons of paint won't cure," Nick observed, joining them.

"Which'll be paid for by your tax dollars and mine," Hart added.

Claire had walked away from the men by then, circling the larger of the two tanks. Most of the graffiti was of the usual unimaginative variety, what looked like gang tags and messages. *I'm surprised the police don't crack down on that,* she thought.

But then she came around to a side closer to the tree line, where she saw some work that surprised her. Bart Simpson on a skateboard. A more colorful work in red and orange hues that looked like a spider that had morphed into a symbol of some kind. An Eye of Providence in a pyramid, resembling the one on the back of the dollar bill. Beside it, a badly drawn Eye of Horus, which Claire knew was the Egyptian symbol of protection.

And then she stopped short. She backtracked several steps to the Eye of Providence, thinking she'd seen something that bothered her. Sure enough, she was right. Something about it was amiss.

It was bloodshot.

Just like the eye on the kite in Doug's house. The one Lewis had flown so many years ago.

Claire took a closer look. The Eye of Providence, along with the Eye of Horus, were more faded than the other drawings on the tank, as if they had been painted years before the other graffiti.

Was it possible? Was he that arrogant?

Excited and terrified, Claire looked at the ground in front of the tank. The grass was green, the earth flat. Even if she'd found the spot where Lewis had buried Amy's body more than two decades ago, any evidence of a hole would have long since been erased by the elements.

And then her eyes caught the tree line a few yards away. Walking in a straight line from the all-seeing pyramid, she approached the grove, walked a few feet in, and looked back.

The eye was staring directly at her.

The snap of a twig made her wheel around. Nick pushed a tree branch out of his way and was crossing toward her.

"You've got to stop disappearing like that," he said as he approached. "What are you doing now?"

"Take a look," she said as Nick joined her. She pointed to the Eye of Providence.

Nick stared. Then he stared at her, getting it.

"It can't be that easy," he said.

Just then, Doug and Hart came into view, rounding the larger tower. "Where are you guys?" Hart shouted.

"Over here," Nick yelled back, emerging from the trees. "Think we may have something." He crossed toward them. "Take a look at the art," he said, gesturing to the graffiti-covered tower. "Anything up there look familiar?"

"Sure," he said. "That eye."

"I knew it," Claire said, pointing to the Eye of Providence. "It's just like the eye on your father's kite."

"I wasn't talking about that one," Doug said, pointing up at the other eye. "That one's on an album cover from the eighties."

"An album cover?" Hart scoffed.

"Yeah. My father used to sing me to sleep with one of the songs. That drawing's been up there since I was a kid."

"What was the song about?" Claire asked.

"A guy who was lost and had a dream and didn't know where to go, even though the answers were right there," Doug answered, staring at the eye.

Claire gave Nick and Hart a sharp look. This was too much to ignore. "I think your dad is telling us something," Claire said.

"I'll get a tech up here," Hart replied, and he headed off.

"Over here!" yelled the technician. The search had gone on for two hours with no results except for the discovery of some small animal bones. Until now.

Hart and Nick ran over to where the tech was stopped with his ground-penetrating radar unit, about ten feet in from the tree line—directly in view of the graffiti eyes.

"What is it?" Nick said as they reached the tech, who pointed to the monitor on his unit.

"Call me crazy, but that sure looks like bones to me," he said.

They looked at the screen. The outlines of a human skull and several long bones were unmistakable.

"How far down?" asked Nick.

"About four feet," replied the tech.

Hart looked around, quickly found what he was looking for. He picked up a long stick and rammed it into the ground, marking the spot.

"Get the crime scene guys up here," he shouted to anyone who would listen. "And tell them to bring shovels."

Claire and Doug had gone back to the staging area, where a portable canteen truck was set up to feed the cops helping with the search. They were about to sit down with sandwiches at one of a dozen hastily set up folding tables when a dark blue van whizzed by them, turning up the small dirt road in the direction of the water tanks.

"What the hell's going on?" Doug asked, trying not to breathe in the cloud of dust raised by the vehicle.

Claire looked up from her food just long enough to catch the lettering on the back of the van.

"That's the medical examiner," she said, moving away from the table. "They wouldn't have been called unless—"

She didn't finish her thought. She began running, Doug keeping pace with her as they disappeared into the thicket.

It took only a few minutes before Claire and Doug, breathless, their clothes soaked through with sweat from the summer humidity, reached the water tanks. Claire made sure to look at the time on her phone. It was just before ten in the morning.

"There," said Doug, pointing.

Through the trees, Claire could see the area was already cordoned off by yellow police tape. Inside the perimeter, three crime scene techs with shovels carefully dug at the spot marked earlier by Hart, who stood aside, waiting for what he was sure he'd see.

"Here we go," said one of the crime scene techs. "We're ready for the camera."

A tech with a Nikon strapped around his neck began snapping photos.

"Okay, folks," the first tech said to the group. "We clear the dirt from here by hand."

"Why didn't you call me?" Claire asked Nick as she and Doug reached the taped perimeter.

"I wasn't sure you'd want to see this," he said.

He's looking out for me, Claire thought, her anger evaporating.

"Thanks," she said. "But I'm okay."

"They found remnants of what looks like a plastic trash can liner," Nick informed them. "One of those big, thick leaf bags."

"Bones!" shouted the lead crime scene tech. "We've got bones."

Hart turned to a nearby uniformed Rochester cop. "Let's get the medical examiner in here."

He caught Claire's eye before turning back to the task at hand.

"How long before we'll know?" asked Claire.

"Homeland Security's helping out on this," Nick replied. "They have some new technique where they can get preliminary DNA results in about an hour. It's still in the testing phase, but one of the biotech labs here in town has it and got permission to use it on this case. The DNA from the bones will also be processed the traditional way. But it has to be her, Claire. It has to be Amy."

The reality of it was too much for Doug. He turned and walked away. Claire looked at Nick, then went after her new friend.

"What is it?" she asked him when she caught up.

When he turned to face her, there were tears in his eyes.

"I'm sorry. I'm so sorry—"

He turned away, not wanting her to see him crying.

"We wouldn't be here now if it wasn't for you," she said. "You have nothing to be ashamed of. And nobody has to know he's your father."

Doug tried to hold back his tears. Out of nowhere, Nick appeared, putting his arm around him. "C'mon, pal," he said, meaning it. "I'll get you out of here if you want. Before the news vans show up."

The son of the serial killer shook his head.

"No," he said, with a sudden burst of determination. "I have to face this. Before what he did kills me too."

Nick looked at him with new respect. "Why don't you get in the shade and sit down for a few minutes," he said.

"Yeah," Doug replied. "I think I will."

He looked at Nick and Claire with gratitude. Then he turned and headed for the tree line.

As they watched him sit under a towering oak, Nick said, "I was wrong about you shrinks." Claire managed a small smile, moved by how far they had come since their first meeting. "You know they're calling you a hero, don't you?"

"I don't want to be a hero," she said, turning her eyes back to the crime scene. Between the figures of two techs, she could see the medical examiner, a woman, lifting with a gloved hand a dirty object from the ground.

Claire realized it was a skull.

Amy's skull.

And all at once it hit her. Tears began to fall from her eyes. But, somehow, they were tears of satisfaction.

"I don't want to be a hero," she said to Nick again, her voice breaking. "I just want her to have a decent burial. I wanted to bring her home to her parents."

"You wanted closure," Nick said, putting his arm around her. "And you got it."

"Are you ready?" Claire shouted. "We have to go or you'll be late."

She was sitting at the dining room table in her parents' home, car keys in her hand, waiting for Nick to come downstairs so she could drive him to the airport. As she waited, Claire thumbed through the transcripts of Peter Lewis's court proceedings that Doug had given her.

"Be down in a second," came Nick's muffled voice from the second floor.

It had been five days since Amy's body was discovered and positively identified by DNA. Claire felt a relief she had never known. The small, burning pain in the pit of her stomach she had woken up with every morning was gone.

The remainder of the week had been a whirlwind of official debriefings and interviews with the media. As far as the cops were concerned, she had brought them the solution to one of the longest, most frustrating child disappearance cases in Rochester's history.

Immediately after the DNA results were confirmed, Claire accompanied Hart to notify Amy's parents. As soon as they saw Claire on their doorstep, they knew they would finally have peace. Amy's mother pulled her into a tender embrace and stroked her hair as if she'd been reunited with the child she lost. Claire told them that Amy's remains had been found and that the man responsible was serving a life term in prison. And, at their request, Claire spoke at Amy's funeral. For her, the closure was complete.

But with all this came sobering news. The DNA sample given by Doug Lewis, along with the sample taken from under Claire's fingernails after she scratched Peter Lewis's face, had turned up hits in several unsolved homicides of young girls around the country: Phoenix, San Francisco, and New Orleans. And the list was sure to grow. Arrest warrants for Peter Lewis were issued, and the governors of Arizona, California, and Louisiana were demanding that the Justice Department extradite the elder Lewis back to the United States to stand trial.

Canada was refusing to cooperate. But it wasn't because of the deal Lewis had bragged about to Claire. Instead, it was because Canadian law forbade extradition to any jurisdiction for crimes in which the accused could face the death penalty. Arizona, California, and Louisiana all had active capital punishment statutes.

Knowing that Lewis would likely never face justice in the United States, Claire thought the least she could do was try to find more of his victims. She went over the hundreds of pages of court transcripts from Doug Lewis's basement, looking for any clue that might lead to the recovery of another body.

As she heard Nick bound down the stairs, however, she was coming to the conclusion that the court proceedings were little more than a formality.

"Any luck?" asked Nick, dropping his small suitcase as he entered the living room.

"I wish," Claire answered, never taking her eyes off the page. "Just a lot of legal gobbledygook. Motion to plead insanity—or whatever it's called in Canada—and they're about to call in the prosecution's . . ."

"The prosecution's what?" Nick asked.

But there was no answer. He looked up at Claire, who was staring at the paper in front of her. In shock.

"What? What's wrong?" Nick asked, alarmed.

"Take a look at this," Claire said, "and tell me I'm not hallucinating."

Nick hurried across the room, donning his reading glasses as he reached Claire at the table. She pointed. He read.

His eyes grew wide. "Oh my God," was all he could manage.

Nick had just read the name of the psychiatrist who was hired by the prosecution to testify that Peter Lewis was fit to stand trial in the Canadian murder case.

Dr. Paul Curtin.

CHAPTER 25

Claire sat beside the window of the Airbus A320, staring out at the wispy strands of clouds just below. *They look like a spiderweb,* she thought. Much like the spiderweb that the story of her best friend, Amy Danforth, had become. And in the middle of the web was her mentor, Dr. Paul Curtin.

Claire now knew that Curtin's testimony had put Peter Lewis in a Canadian prison for life. Peter Lewis, who pled guilty to raping and murdering a young girl in 1994. Peter Lewis, aka Mr. Winslow, who killed Amy back in 1989. It was why she was with Nick on the short flight back to New York, to ask Curtin about this strange turn of events. A phone call would have been insufficient. She had to see the look on Curtin's face when she confronted him with this bizarre coincidence.

After all, that's what it is, right? A bizarre coincidence?

Claire's mind played a tug-of-war, looking for an explanation: How was Curtin involved in all this? She noticed that the clouds below her had taken on the shapes of faces. Amy with her pigtails. Lewis with his crooked smile. Ian, his disarming eyes making her ache for him. Quimby. In a rage.

The clouds disappeared, revealing the endless, clear blue sky. "Hey there . . . Claire. Claire," Nick said, trying to get her attention.

Claire turned to him. "What is it?" she said, her face blank.

"You've been staring out that window since we took off."

She let out a deep, quiet sigh. "It's a coincidence, right, Nick?" she asked, her tone unsure.

"It's got to be," Nick answered. "If you were prosecuting a monster like Peter Lewis, wouldn't you bring in the best shrink in the business?"

"I guess you're right," Claire said, sounding relieved but feeling far from it. "He's testified at hundreds of murder cases."

Nick gave her a knowing look. Over the weeks they'd worked together, he knew the signs that Claire's mind was at odds with her words. Her cheeks would turn red and her eyes would narrow.

"Think about it for a second," Nick said, trying to reassure her. "How could Curtin possibly know about you through Lewis? Your name never appeared in those court transcripts."

Claire smiled at him. *He knows me too well.*

"Look, if it makes you feel any better, I'll go with you to see him," Nick offered.

"That'd make it seem too official, like we suspected him of something."

"You do suspect him of something," Nick said, leaning toward her. Their faces were almost touching.

"Not necessarily. I just want to see his reaction."

Nick smiled. "So you're going to call him and set up an appointment?"

"No," Claire said. "I think I'll surprise him."

"And then you'll call me right after," Nick said in way that made her know she had no choice.

Claire nodded. *We're in this together,* she thought.

Claire walked through the entry to Manhattan City Hospital, still wearing the jeans and light blue top she'd worn on the plane. She hadn't taken the time to change in her rush to get to Curtin's office and had left Rochester in such haste that she hadn't yet thought about where she'd stay while she was in town.

She headed for the Psych Unit and checked her watch. It was 4:27 in the afternoon. She looked up and saw one of the fellows down the hallway, writing in a chart. *He must be finishing rounds,* Claire thought. Which meant that Curtin would soon be heading back to his office.

Claire dodged another fellow by turning down a hallway. She knew the news of her role in tying Peter Lewis to Amy's death had gotten play in the New York media, and she wasn't up to facing her colleagues or the questions with which they'd undoubtedly ply her for hours. She could hardly blame them, though. One of their own had now nailed not just one, but *two* serial killers in just a few weeks. If she'd become a minor celebrity over ending Todd Quimby's spree of murder, the Lewis case surely made her a rock star in the eyes of her peers.

She imagined what they would ask her: *What was it like, interrogating the man who almost murdered you? Were you scared? Did you feel like a victim? Or were you able to maintain professional distance?*

Claire found herself walking down the corridor to Curtin's office. She'd been lost in her thoughts, and yet somehow she'd been pulled to the right place as if by some powerful magnet. She turned the knob slowly as she wondered why she felt compelled to do this. *What am I really looking for here?*

Curtin's assistant, Bonnie, was sitting at her computer, staring at the screen, perplexed as always when she heard the door open. She looked up to see Claire walk in and did a double take.

"*You?* You're back already?" Bonnie asked in her thick Bronx accent, her ever-demanding tone always making Claire feel tense.

"Yes, but just for today. Is Doctor Curtin available?"

"Sorry, hon," Bonnie replied, letting up on the attitude. "He's been out with the flu since last Tuesday and his schedule's a mess," she added, pointing to the computer screen. "I'm canceling all his appointments for the rest of the week."

Claire was shocked. Among one of Curtin's more annoying traits was his bragging that he'd never missed a day of work because of illness, which was more than most of his fellows could say. The guy was a triathlete and in great shape. The possibility he'd be out sick had never even occurred to her.

"Oh," was all Claire could say.

Bonnie shot her a look of pity. "You didn't come all the way down here from upstate just to surprise him, I hope."

"No," Claire lied. "I just happened to be in town and thought I'd stop by."

"You know," Bonnie said, a sly smile appearing on her face, "we all heard about what you did up there. With that other killer and all. Don't tell him I told you this, but Doctor C was really impressed when he heard about it."

Her words took Claire by surprise. Maybe there was a side to Curtin that she hadn't seen—or that he had purposely kept hidden from his students.

"Too bad he's not here to tell you himself," Bonnie continued. "Timing is everything."

Claire couldn't help but smile. "Don't I know it," she said. "So do you think there's any chance he'll be in at all this week?"

"I just spoke to him an hour ago, and he still sounds like death on a cracker," Bonnie said. "But I'll pencil you in for next week if you can come back."

"I'll see if I can hang around for the weekend. Thanks, Bonnie," Claire said, turning to head out.

"Whoa, not so fast," Bonnie called after her, prompting her to turn back. "You never left me a forwarding address." She wobbled as she stood up like someone who spent too much of their life sitting, and grabbed some mail and a large manila package from atop the file cabinet. "I got stuff for you that came in since you've been . . . on leave."

She handed the pile to Claire, who looked at the manila package. The return address immediately caught her eye—a post office box in Bedford, New York.

Bedford. Tammy Sorensen's parents lived in Bedford.

And then she realized.

Tammy's medical records. From her doctor.

She was excited again, but her face gave away nothing.

"Okay," Claire said. "I think I will stay in the city so I can see him. How about next Monday?"

"Well, today's Wednesday, so I can't imagine he'll still be out," Bonnie said, back at her computer, typing away. "Monday at ten it is."

"See you then," Claire said as Bonnie looked up. "Thanks. For the mail too."

The mini-suite at the New Amsterdam Hotel had a kitchenette and a pleasant, small living room, and most importantly it was clean. Claire had given up the apartment she'd shared with Ian when she left town, knowing she could never enter it again after the horror she'd witnessed. She'd found the hotel room on the fly after leaving the hospital and had settled in. Now, as she looked through her mail, she ate a piece of buttered toast and thought of Ian. He'd made her toast every morning. It was her favorite food; she loved the flavor and the crunchiness. Savoring it brought back good memories of their time together.

The mail wasn't interesting, just announcements of events that had already passed and the usual mass mailings from drug companies hawking their newest pills. Claire threw out the numerous envelopes and cards she'd ripped in half, having gotten them out of the way before she opened what she really wanted to look at—Tammy Sorenson's medical file.

She almost wanted to laugh at herself. In the trauma of the attempt on her life, Ian's murder, Quimby's death, and then the stress of finding Amy, she'd forgotten that she'd asked Tammy's mother to get the file from her daughter's internist. Even now, she was still intrigued by this medical mystery. How had this woman carried on an active—perhaps overactive—sex life when she was dying of lymphoma?

But if she was hoping the answers to her questions were in the file, she was not only sorely disappointed, but also shocked—not by what was in the paperwork, but by what *wasn't*. Tammy's medical records revealed nothing out of the ordinary, only regular checkups with no major illnesses. Claire flipped to the end of the chart and found that Tammy's last visit to her doctor had been for hay fever, three months before she died. There was no mention of her lymphoma. And the physician who performed her insurance physical two months before her death had found nothing as well, giving her a clean bill of health.

She couldn't believe it. Any physical examination of someone that close to dying from lymphoma would have revealed enlarged, hardened lymph nodes. How could Tammy's doctor not detect such a serious illness, or if he had, not mention it? The only reason could be that he never knew about it.

And that could only mean someone else must have been treating her. But why wouldn't they have reported her unusually virulent tumor to the Tumor Registry?

She flipped through the file again, looking to make sure she hadn't missed anything. Frustrated, she closed it—a little too hard—and some papers fell out. Angry at herself, she bent over to pick them up, and only then saw what she hadn't seen before: a phone message, paper-clipped to the bottom of another piece of paper, dated two weeks before Tammy died. All it said was *Call Dr. Charles Sedgwick*, with a number written beneath it.

Claire picked up her cell phone and punched in the number.

"You have reached Biopharix," came the automated voice at the other end of the phone. "Our offices are now closed. Please call during our normal business hours of—"

Claire hung up, stunned. *Biopharix. That's where Tammy worked,* she thought. *That's hardly a coincidence.*

She pulled out her iPad and Googled *Biopharix* and *Charles Sedgwick*. Up on the screen came a long list of citations.

She opened the first one, Sedgwick's official biography on his company's Web site. *His credentials are stellar,* thought Claire as she read through. Sedgwick was a noted researcher in molecular genetics, who received both his MD and PhD from Yale. He'd presented an impressive list of papers all over the world on oncogenes—the genes in human cells which, when mutated, can cause cancer—all in addition to being the CEO of Biopharix.

He has the expertise, Claire thought. *He must've been treating Tammy. Maybe with an experimental drug.*

She knew it wasn't unusual for desperately ill patients to turn to researchers for any last ray of hope. And if the patients met certain qualifications, they could receive an experimental drug for free. These phase II drug trials provided researchers with data they needed to assess the efficacy of their new drug, along with any side effects, and gave many terminally ill patients extra months, sometimes even years of life.

Tammy Sorenson would have been a natural candidate to enroll in a phase II study at Biopharix. She worked there and had access to the newest and most promising drug treatments.

Claire picked up her phone and punched in the numbers she'd come to know by heart.

"Hello," Nick said, answering on seeing Claire's name come up. "What the hell took you so long to call?"

"I didn't see Curtin," Claire said, without even saying hello. "He's got the flu. But I found something really interesting, and I need your help."

The modern glass box that was Biopharix sat sparkling in the morning sunlight on the north end of a promontory jutting off the eastern bank of the Hudson River in Cold Spring, New York, about fifty-five miles north of Manhattan. Over the objections of pretty much everyone, the out-of-place structure had been built on what was once open parkland with the blessing of local politicians, who could hardly refuse the opportunity of such a high-tech, high-tax-paying industry.

Nick and Claire were escorted through the glassed-in entry corridor, giving them a magnificent view of the glorious Hudson Valley and the army's vaunted West Point Academy just across the river and slightly to the south. Below them, through the transparent floor, flowed a stream that emptied into the river itself. Cobalt-blue trusses held the walkway above ground, giving Claire and Nick the sensation that they were walking on air.

As they neared Sedgwick's office, which was located at the center of the facility, Claire noticed an array of similar glassed-in tubes emanating from the laboratories, also at the center of the complex, making her feel as if she were inside the tentacle of a huge octopus.

They reached the office complex, where Sedgwick waited outside his door. He was trim, of average height and with thinning hair, which he'd tried to correct with obvious hair plugs in the front that turned out to be spaced too far apart. *For someone so rich and vain,* Claire thought, *he really should have gotten himself a better hair transplant.*

Sedgwick reached out and shook both their hands with a powerful grip. "What's New York's finest doing all the way up here?" he asked Nick with a friendly smile.

"We're interested in one of your employees," Nick answered with the same friendly smile.

Sedgwick's smile melted. "You mean Tammy Sorenson. Terrible tragedy."

"Are you referring to her murder or to her illness?" Claire asked wryly.

"What illness?" Sedgwick replied, a look of confusion crossing his face. "I thought you caught her killer. Was she sick too?"

"Mortally," Claire replied. "If she hadn't been murdered, she would have died anyway."

Claire and Nick studied Sedgwick's reaction. He took a step back, as if trying to get away from some bad news.

"I never knew," he said. "Why didn't she tell me?"

"So you had no idea that Tammy was dying of Hodgkin's lymphoma?" Claire asked, pressing him.

"No. If I had, I would've made sure she got the best treatment. But it does explain a few things."

"Like what?" Nick asked.

"Why she stopped showing up for work one day without telling anyone. I tried to reach her—she worked in my lab and we were close."

"How close?" Nick asked, insinuating the worst. "I believe she had a number of boyfriends."

"Our relationship was strictly professional," Sedgwick said bluntly. "I was worried about her. When I called her parents, they said she was on vacation. But she'd used up all her vacation time, so it didn't make sense."

"Why didn't you call the police?" Claire asked, trying to trap him.

"I did. They said she wasn't missing if her parents confirmed she was on vacation. So I got her internist's name and number from her employee file, just to make sure she wasn't sick in some hospital."

That explains the phone message in Tammy's medical record, Claire thought.

"Did he ever call you back?" Nick asked.

"No. We didn't know what happened to her until someone from your office called our human resources department. Now, is there something else you need?" Sedgwick asked them. "I've got a crazy day ahead of me."

"Yes," Nick replied. "One last thing. Do you still do research?"

"I oversee *all* the research here," Sedgwick responded impatiently. "But if you mean do I still do bench science, no, I don't have the time." He opened the door to his office. "If you'll excuse me, I've got to go. Please don't hesitate to call if you need anything else."

"Thanks for your time, Doctor," Claire said as Sedgwick darted through the door, leaving Nick and Claire alone in the spacious glassed-in hallway.

"He's lying," Nick said.

"What are you talking about?" Claire asked, confused.

"The bastard smelled like bitter almonds. Just like the women Quimby killed."

"Oh God," Claire said. "What the hell have we stepped into?"

CHAPTER 26

Tony Savarese looked up from his desk as Nick barreled into the squad room he hadn't seen for two weeks. "Hey, man," Savarese bellowed, "good to see you back."

"You too," Nick barely replied as he headed for his desk, which was still cluttered with the detritus of the Quimby investigation. It was exactly as he'd left it: seven thick, multicolored files awaited him, each representing a homicide Quimby committed.

Or so he'd thought. Until this morning.

Quickly but carefully, he sat down and began returning papers to the files in which they belonged. He would then gather up the files and put them in the trunk of his police Impala. If anyone asked him, he'd say he was taking them to the NYPD's huge evidence storage facility out in Queens. After all, that's where they belonged, right? The cases were closed, weren't they?

Hell, no. Not anymore.

Nick had no intention of taking the files to Queens. They were headed straight for Claire Waters's hotel room. Technically he'd be committing a crime—stealing official police documents and evidence.

He mused at the irony of it all. For nearly a year, he had been suspected of murdering his wife, a crime he never committed. Now, in service of the truth, he was knowingly violating the law and, because what he was doing was a felony, risking his career—which would be over soon anyway if Dr. Mangone followed through on his threat.

Nick stared at the seven files of lives snuffed out early and added the eighth file to the pile for Quimby. He was so wrapped up in his thoughts he didn't see or hear the figure approaching until he was almost at Nick's desk.

"Nice of you to show up," said Lieutenant Wilkes.

Nick looked up to see his boss standing before him. *In full dress uniform—a sharp blue suit with brass buttons, gold braiding, and medallions across his chest announcing all of Wilkes's citations.*

"Big meeting with the boss at One PP?" asked Nick.

"Don't you check your voice mail?" asked Wilkes, more irritated than usual.

Nick looked at his cell. Four messages waiting. "Sorry," he replied.

"I tried you at home too," said the lieutenant. "You know what your mother said? That you were out of town, working on some case. That's what you were doing on your vacation?"

Dammit, thought Nick. He'd been honest with his mother, telling her he was going to help a friend upstate.

"Just helping a friend, Lou," Nick said, making light of it. "I kept my name out of it so nobody would ask questions."

Indeed, he had managed to circumvent any media mention of his involvement in the search for Amy Danforth, making sure all the credit went to Claire. Al Hart had been his partner in this effort, knowing the last thing Nick needed right now was any notoriety for something he technically shouldn't have been doing even on his own time.

"As long as it doesn't come back to bite me in the ass," Wilkes said. "Now go change so we can get downtown."

"Downtown?"

Wilkes gave him The Look. He obviously didn't have a clue.

"Let me fill you in. We—*you*—just closed the biggest case of the decade, if not the millennium. One of those messages you blew off was Headquarters ordering *you* down to One PP this afternoon at two, in full uniform. Same call I got last night."

Nick knew full well what that meant, as did every cop on the job.

He looked up at Wilkes, whose face broke into a huge smile. "I'm getting captain's bars, Nicky, and you're getting first grade." He stuck out his hand. "Congratulations."

Nick shook his boss's hand, stunned. To make first grade was the dream of every NYPD detective. The designation would put him among the elite of the city's elite. First-grade detectives not only worked the choicest assignments, but they also were often given command responsibility. And pay equal to that of a lieutenant. And yet he couldn't make himself even grin.

"What the hell's the matter with you?" Wilkes demanded playfully. "You're the effin' prince of the city. Chief of D's would knight you if he had the power. I took a flyer on you and you paid me back in spades. All of us, everyone in the squad, are getting bumped up a notch. For Christ's sake, Nicky, enjoy it. You earned this."

Nick could only look down at the eight files on his desk. *You won't be saying all that when I tell you Todd Quimby may not be the killer. Or that I'm going blind.*

How could he not be truthful with Wilkes? How could he not trust this man who'd literally given him his career back? His very life?

He looked up at the lieutenant. And Wilkes, sharp in his dress blues, wilted slightly. For he'd seen that look on Nick's face before.

"What is it, Nicky?" he asked.

"Boss," Nick said seriously, "let's go into your office. There's something you should know."

Fifteen minutes later, Wilkes looked up from his desk at Nick, like a man who'd just been hit with a two-by-four.

"Are you sure about this?" he asked.

Nick had told him everything (except for his impending blindness), including that Dr. Charles Sedgwick might somehow be connected to the death of Tammy Sorenson.

"How?" Wilkes asked, becoming more alarmed.

"I smelled bitter almonds on him. The same odor that was on most of Quimby's victims."

"Is it possible Quimby had an accomplice?" Wilkes asked, incredulous.

"Yes," Nick said. "I don't know how to connect all the dots, but I swear to God I'm going to find out."

"Nicky. Do you know how crazy this sounds?" the lieutenant asked.

Nick knew what his boss was really worried about. Wilkes was a political animal, which was necessary in order to survive as a commander in the NYPD. The truth Nick had just laid on him would make everyone look incompetent or, even worse, like blundering fools. Which is why Nick knew exactly what he had to say next.

"Look. You said it yourself. You took a chance on me. Just say the word and this dies right here, right now, in this room. And life goes on."

Wilkes returned his look, considering the offer. "What about Claire Waters?" he asked.

"Claire Waters owes me. The caper I was on upstate was helping her find her friend's killer and where he buried the body. And we did. She'll do anything I ask."

There. He'd given his boss an out. Wilkes took but a second to make his decision.

"Here's what we'll do," the lieutenant began. "Go home, put on your uniform, and get your ass down to the Puzzle Palace so they can promote us." He paused, deciding what to say next. "And then you're going to take those files on your desk, and that shrink, and disappear."

It was exactly what Nick thought he'd say. Brian Wilkes was a lot of things, but a coward wasn't one of them.

"How long can you give me?" Nick asked.

"Three days, on the q.t. I'll cover you with the guys, tell them you took some more vacation time. Bring me something I can use to convince the chief that if Quimby's not the only killer, he's the tip of the iceberg. Otherwise, Nicky, we'll have to do what you said before. We'll have to let the case die."

"We're not letting this die," Claire said as she sat down at a desktop computer and turned it on.

"Calm down," Nick urged. "We've got three days."

They were in Claire's hotel room, both knowing that three days was precious little time to put together what had become a confusing puzzle. Nick hadn't even bothered to change out of his dress blues from the promotion ceremony.

"You look pretty handsome in that monkey suit," Claire said, giving him a smile.

"Never thought I'd make it to first grade. I better enjoy it while I can," Nick answered.

Claire knew he was referring to his impending blindness. "If you want to stop now, Nick, I'll understand," she said, knowing he'd never stop.

"Where do we start?" Nick responded, not even going there.

"The bitter almonds," she began. "That connects Sedgwick to Quimby. You smelled it on Sedgwick and several of the victims."

"And I'm the only one who did," Nick reminded her.

"Because the amount that was transferred was so minuiscule that only someone with a highly developed sense of smell would be able to detect it."

"You mean, like someone who's going blind."

Claire didn't want to come out and say it, but that's exactly what she meant.

Nick read the look on her face. "It's okay," he reassured her. "It's not like I don't know it's going to happen."

"Sorry," she said.

"So," Nick continued, "the question is, why does Sedgwick smell like bitter almonds in the first place?"

Claire had already entered Sedgwick's name into a search engine. "I'm looking for anything about his current research, for something that emits the odor of bitter almonds."

"What about cyanide?" Nick asked.

"The ME looked for cyanide during the autopsies and didn't find any," Claire said. "It must be some other lab reagent or chemical he uses in his research."

Nick peeked over her shoulder at the screen. "He's on the faculty at Yale School of Medicine?" he asked.

Claire opened the link. "No, he attended Yale and just gave a talk there," she corrected.

"What about?"

"Apoptosis," Claire said, trying to skim.

"What the hell's that?"

"Programmed cell death," she explained, looking up at him. "The average adult loses between fifty and seventy billion cells every day."

"Billion?"

"They're replenished. It's a normal process by which the body eliminates stressed or damaged cells. When it's not working properly, mutated cells can become cancerous."

"Okay, but what does this have to do with this mess we're in?"

Claire turned back to the computer. "Sedgwick's talk was about a breakthrough in cancer pharmacology. For years we've been killing tumors with chemotherapy, which is basically a poison that also kills healthy cells. If a way could be found to stimulate apoptosis to kill cancerous cells . . ." She looked up at Nick. "My God, that's it."

"Please, Claire," Nick begged. "Remember, I'm not a doctor."

"I think Sedgwick's looking for a drug that will turn on apoptosis in cancer cells to make tumors literally kill themselves."

"I hope this has something to do with the bitter almonds."

Claire scanned the citations and found the article she was looking for.

"It does. He uses a chemical called *dithiothreitol* to separate and isolate the proteins in the cancer cells," she said with excitement growing in her voice. "Dithiothreitol has a bitter almond smell."

Nick thought he had the answer. "Maybe Quimby worked alone after all," he suggested. "Follow me here. Tammy Sorenson worked with Sedgwick in the lab. So it makes sense she'd smell of something bitter, too, right?"

"Go on," Claire urged.

"And it would make sense that in manipulating and dressing her corpse, the bitter odor could transfer to Quimby."

"Yes," Claire said, eager to hear more.

"Okay. Tammy was the fourth victim we found, but according to her autopsy, she was the third woman murdered. The medical examiner said Quimby probably kept Tammy on ice or refrigerated her for two days before he dumped her on the ball field."

"I'm with you," Claire said.

"What if Ross was off by a day?" Nick asked, referring to the medical examiner, "and Tammy was actually the *first* woman Quimby murdered?"

Claire considered this. "It would explain how Quimby transferred the bitter smell to the other women because he would've still been in contact with Tammy and her clothing."

"And it sure as hell wouldn't be the first time Ross screwed up," Nick observed.

They looked at each other. There was a piece missing. And they both knew what it was.

"Quimby lived with his grandmother," Claire said. "I doubt he kept Tammy's body there for three minutes, let alone three days."

"We never looked for where he might've stashed her because we thought we broke the case," Nick replied. "We'll have to look now."

But the whole scenario was beginning to bother Claire. "I thought I knew Todd Quimby inside and out. I always believed he murdered these women because he couldn't control his impulses. Hiding a dead body for three days doesn't fit his profile."

"Maybe your profile is wrong," Nick suggested halfheartedly.

"It's more like our theory of the crime is wrong," Claire answered. "Maybe Quimby was hired to kill these women."

"Hired?" Nick asked, flabbergasted. "For what reason?"

"To cover up what they were really doing to Tammy Sorenson."

"By 'they,' I assume you mean Sedgwick. And what do you think they were doing?"

Claire pointed to the computer screen and highlighted the word *apoptosis*. "Tammy had a virulent form of lymphoma. We know that Sedgwick is doing research on how to turn off cancer cells—but what if he somehow found a way to turn them *on*?"

Nick stared at her, blinking. "Are you saying he used Tammy as a human guinea pig?"

"I don't know," Claire answered. "Maybe Tammy went to him when she discovered she was sick—he's a cancer expert—and his new treatment went awry, making her lymphoma so aggressive it couldn't be stopped."

Nick turned to Claire, his pulse racing. "If Sedgwick somehow made Tammy sicker, he'd want to cover it up, right?"

Claire nodded. "He'd lose everything—all of Biopharix—if any of this came out."

"So what if he hired someone to murder four other women so we'd think a serial killer got her?"

"Are you saying *he* hired Quimby?" Claire asked, astonished. "Do you have any idea how crazy that sounds?"

"It would explain the connection between Quimby and Sedgwick, and why they both had the smell from that chemical."

"If Sedgwick hired Quimby . . ." Claire didn't finish as she riffled through Tammy's case file. She pulled out two DVDs, labeled *Surveillance video from Red*. "These are from the nightclub the evening Tammy was killed, right?" she asked.

"It's presumably of Quimby using Tammy's credit cards," Nick answered.

"Have you watched it yet?"

"No. Quimby was dead before I even got it."

Claire looked around the room. "There's a TV but no DVD player."

"You want to look at it now?"

"If Quimby's on here, I need to see him," she insisted.

Nick sighed. "I'm going home to change. I'll pick you up in an hour," he said, pulling out his cell phone.

One Police Plaza, the NYPD's headquarters in Lower Manhattan, was built in the early 1970s in the architectural style of brutalism, which several generations of cops had derisively joked was exactly what one usually endured simply by entering the building.

It was also the last place Nick wanted to be seen, since he was officially on vacation and had already been there once today to receive his promotion. But the department's Technical Assistance Response Unit (TARU) maintained a state-of-the-art video lab there, and so a friend of Nick's had agreed to meet him and Claire a block away and spirit them in through the building's subterranean garage.

"So nobody knows we were there," Nick had told Claire.

The friend was Detective Tom Mahoney. He'd worked with Nick on numerous cases, and Nick had gone the extra mile for him once when Mahoney's teenaged daughter had disappeared into the clutches of a religious fringe cult. Nick had done the extraction and intervention himself, and the daughter was now grown up and married to an investment banker with whom she had two young children and an enormous house in Westchester County. Tom Mahoney would've parted the Red Sea if Nick Lawler asked him to.

"That's all you want?" Mahoney asked, almost disappointed as he fired up the equipment in the video lab. "To play a friggin' DVD?"

"We may need you to work some of your magic, depending on what we see," Nick assured him. "Hit it."

Mahoney clicked the mouse on the computer-driven apparatus. On a large monitor appeared the view from four separate cameras covering the club. One of those cameras pointed out from the bar, and Nick now gestured to that video.

"Any way to isolate the bar patrons?" he asked.

"Easy," Mahoney said, maneuvering the mouse like a maestro until the bar video filled the entire screen.

"Great," said Nick. "Now run it at double speed."

Mahoney obeyed. It took just a few seconds until—

"There!" Claire shouted, pointing to the screen. "There he is."

"Play it normally and blow it up if you can," Nick said.

"You got it," Mahoney said, enhancing the image until Quimby became visible.

"What the hell's wrong with him?" Nick asked.

He was referring to Quimby's gait. He was walking unsteadily toward the bar.

"Looks like he's drunk," Mahoney offered.

"He hasn't even ordered a drink yet," Nick replied.

"Hold on," Claire said. "Can you freeze the video once he reaches the bar?"

"Sure," said Mahoney, doing so.

"How closely can you zoom in on his eyes?" asked Claire.

Mahoney maneuvered the mouse. The image was grainy. A few more mouse clicks and the picture began to clear up. Finally, it revealed what she suspected.

"His pupils are dilated."

"You think he did some drugs before he went over there?" Nick asked.

"Or someone drugged him to make him go."

Mahoney looked up at Nick. "What the hell's she talking about?" he asked.

"You didn't hear anything we said," Nick said to him.

"I never knew you were here," Mahoney answered.

Nick turned to Claire, to make sure he heard her right. "You're suggesting that Quimby was forcibly drugged and made to go to this club just to use Tammy Sorenson's credit card? Why?"

"To establish him as her killer."

"It that even possible? To make someone do something against his will by drugging him?"

"Who knows what someone as talented as Sedgwick can whip up in a pharmacology lab?" Claire said.

Nick shook his head, pulled out his cell.

"Who are you calling?" Claire asked.

"The medical examiner," answered Nick as he dialed. "We're going to settle this once and for all."

An hour later, Nick and Claire walked into the morgue. ME Ross was waiting for them at the door. "Well?" Nick asked.

Ross gestured them down the hallway, and they walked beside him. "You were right, Lawler. Guess I goofed again."

"Quimby had some kind of strange drug in his system?" Nick asked.

"Oh, I won't know that for another two days," answered Ross as he escorted them into the spacious laboratory. "But when I filleted Quimby on the table, something bothered me."

"Why didn't you call me?" Nick asked.

"Because I wasn't sure," Ross replied, sounding apologetic for the first time. "I wanted to get the lab results back first."

"Hold on," Nick said. "What lab results?"

"From the water Quimby drowned in," Ross said. "They came back last week, but my assistant forgot to tell me—and I forgot to check."

"What did you find?" Claire asked. "That was such a goof."

"I'm a scientist. I shouldn't be assuming a goddamned thing. But I assumed Todd Quimby drowned in the East River where his car went in."

Claire looked at him like he'd lost his mind. "You were there with us when they pulled him out of the East River. You can't be saying he didn't drown there."

"That's exactly what I'm saying. There's no way he drowned in that river," Ross maintained.

"How is that even possible?" Claire asked.

"Because Quimby's lungs were filled with *fresh* water."

"Rivers are by definition bodies of fresh water," Claire replied.

"Not the East River," Ross informed her. "It's a tidal strait that connects the Long Island Sound to New York Harbor. Which means the water that runs through it—"

"Is *salt* water," Claire realized, shocked. "Quimby's lungs should've been filled with salt water."

"And salt water in the lungs pulls water *out* of cells by osmosis. Quimby's lungs should have had shrunken blood cells, but instead, they, had burst," Ross said. "That's why I sent water samples to the lab. I knew something was off."

"Which means," Nick concluded, "he was drowned somewhere else. The guy had to have been dead when he was put in the car."

"Exactly," Ross said. "I'm changing his manner of death to homicide."

"Do you have any idea where Quimby might've drowned?" Nick asked, shocked by what he'd just heard.

"Off the top of my head? The organisms in the water from his lungs look like those we find in floaters we pull out of the Hudson River. How far upstream he went in will take me longer, like a week."

"Thanks, Doctor," Claire said. "We'll be waiting for your results."

"I'll get them to you as soon as I have them," Ross returned, still embarrassed. "And this time I won't forget to call."

"C'mon," said Claire, pulling Nick, who was too stunned to move, toward the double doors. "We've got work to do."

Nick followed Claire out to the corridor.

"What the hell was that about?" he demanded.

"We don't need his results," Claire said. "Biopharix's headquarters is right on the Hudson River. Quimby was drowned there and put in his grandmother's car—"

"If that's true," Nick argued, "who killed Maggie Stolls? Who tried to kill you in the safe house? And who drove the goddamned car?"

"Sedgwick."

Nick stopped. This was more than he could handle.

"So let me get this straight. Sedgwick, the nerdy doc, murders a cop, tries to take you out, drives Quimby's grandmother's piece-of-crap Buick like Steve McQueen down the FDR Drive, and sends it into the East River. And then, only when the car is in the drink, does he put Quimby behind the wheel and make his escape. Alive."

"It's just a hypothesis," conceded Claire. "I admit, it's out there."

"Are you serious?" exclaimed Nick. "I try to sell that to my boss and he'll ship us off to the funny farm."

"Wait a minute," Claire realized. "How the hell does a high roller like Charles Sedgwick find a nobody like Todd Quimby in the first place?"

"That's the best question yet," Nick said. "And I know just the high roller to ask."

CHAPTER 27

It was just before eight p.m. when Claire and Nick climbed the few steps of a magnificent, pre–World War II apartment building on Central Park West in the Seventies. The summer sun was beginning to set, casting a golden glaze that backlit the edges of the cut stone exterior. The address was one of the most sought after in Manhattan, with a grand marble lobby that made Claire wonder how Curtin managed to parlay a career studying the criminal mind into a life of such wealth and luxury.

She knew that her mentor, unlike many medical academicians, served on no boards of pharmaceutical companies that manufactured psychotropic drugs, despite having been invited numerous times. He always avoided even a whiff of a conflict of interest. "I can't take the chance some 'paragon of justice' will throw that in my face when I'm testifying for the prosecution," was the answer he always gave potential suitors.

They walked up to the front desk where the doorman, a trim black man in his thirties, eyed them. "Can I help you?" he asked.

"Claire Waters and Nick Lawler. We're here to see Mr. Larciano," she said, using the pseudonym Curtin always gave his visitors. "You never know when a patient might make a surprise house call," he would warn his students, conceding their profession wasn't for the faint of heart and carried with it an element of risk and even danger, and urging them to protect their privacy and families at all costs. Claire's predecessors in the fellowship told her this warning came near the end of the program, when Curtin usually became more the father figure and less the tormentor to his flock.

Too bad he didn't warn us at the beginning, she thought. *Maybe Quimby wouldn't have phoned me that night or known where I lived.*

"He's expecting you," the doorman said, not even looking at his list. "Apartment Five A. Down the right hallway, elevator's on your left."

Claire followed Nick down the hall. He pushed the elevator call button, causing the doors to open. They rode silently in the tiny car to the fifth floor and stepped out onto a spacious landing, flanked on either side with the doors of two apartments.

"Wow, being a shrink buys him a place like this?" Nick asked.

Claire pushed the doorbell. "He also sold a lot of books," she said, as if that explained it. "Believe me, we don't all live high on the hog."

She heard the door unlock. It opened, revealing Curtin in a blue silk bathrobe that seemed at least two sizes too large. She tried her best to maintain a poker face, even smiling at him, though she was shocked.

The Paul Curtin standing before her was a shell of the man she had left behind a few weeks ago. "Thanks for seeing us, Doctor," she managed.

"Claire. Detective Lawler. Please, come in," he invited, his voice raspy.

They entered the spacious apartment, and Claire took stock of her mentor. The once-fit triathlete walked stiffly, as if suddenly stricken with a horrible bout of arthritis. His usually neat, wavy silver hair was unkempt and had lost its sheen, and his face was a forest of stubble. Clearly the flu had overwhelmed him.

"Are you feeling any better?" Nick asked him.

"Yes, thank you, despite how I look—and I appreciate your being so polite," he said, ushering them into the maple-paneled living room. He looked at Claire. "I do feel better. But unfortunately, it turns out I have mononucleosis." He sat down on a dark blue couch, facing two upholstered foam green chairs. Claire realized then that the room was decorated in colors of the ocean. "Imagine," said Curtin, "a guy my age getting a disease we typically see only in teenagers."

"You must have kissed the wrong girl," Nick said, managing a smile.

"I wish," Curtin responded. "But it's not just 'the kissing disease.' You can also get mono casually—from a water fountain or, in my case, probably some fork or spoon in our cafeteria that wasn't washed properly."

"I'll try to remember that," Nick said.

"You should get plenty of rest," Claire said to Curtin. "We won't stay long."

"Thank you, Doctor," Curtin said. "I appreciate the advice." He sat back on the couch, the pain evident on his face. "Now, then," he said, recovering quickly, "what's so important that you had to see me?"

Claire drew a breath. "I want to come back. I'm ready to return to the program."

"Are you sure you're ready?" asked Curtin, with no trace of surprise on his face. "I didn't expect you to recover so quickly. You suffered severe emotional trauma."

"Nick helped me deal with it," Claire said.

"Really?" Curtin mused, turning to Nick. "Maybe you should join my program. I could use a cop who's also a shrink. You could teach us how you lay traps in your interrogations."

"I can teach that to you anytime," Nick said with the slightest edge in his voice, "whether I'm in your program or not."

"It's a deal, then. After I recover," Curtin said. "And tell me, Claire, how did Detective Lawler help you 'deal' with your trauma? I ask so that I can be sure you're ready to return."

"He helped me overcome my past," Claire said without a noticeable reaction from Curtin. "I blamed myself for something over which I had no control."

"Peter Lewis," Curtin said simply.

"Bonnie told me you knew I found him," Claire said, referring to Curtin's secretary. She was surprised Curtin hadn't brought it up.

"Bonnie talks a bit too much for her own good. She probably also told you how impressed I was. And how proud I am," he added, correcting himself. "I've had some prodigies in my program, but never anyone who's accomplished what you have. I must say, Claire, you simply amaze me."

"Then why didn't you say anything?" Claire asked, confused. "When we first came in."

"I'm a therapist, after all. I wanted you to bring it up so I could see how this all has affected you."

Claire's mind was racing. All the threads she thought she had woven together were coming undone. *Is Curtin connected to any of this? Or is it a coincidence that he interviewed Lewis?*

She turned to Nick, who looked puzzled too. *Is he thinking what I'm thinking? Is he wondering what the hell is going on?*

Claire decided the only way to find out was to face him head-on.

"You testified against Peter Lewis for the prosecution back in ninety-four when he confessed to kidnapping and murdering a little girl outside Toronto."

"Yes, that's right. Her name was Meredith Palmer."

"Did you know about Amy too?"

"The one on the news?" Curtin responded without blinking. He sat forward and looked Claire straight in the eye. "You must be referring to your best friend. What an incredible coincidence that I testified against the man who murdered her."

"And Lewis never mentioned her?" Nick asked. "When you did your psychiatric evaluation of him."

"I wish to God he had. I know I would have researched the case."

Then Curtin reached out and took Claire's hand. All Claire could think was that his fingers and palm felt cold and waxy, like those of a corpse.

"I could have spared you all those years of grief."

Claire wanted to pull away from him, but he held her hand tight.

"I'm sorry, Claire, for everything. For pushing you so hard, for assigning Quimby to you, for not helping you."

"Helping me?" Claire asked, not knowing what he meant.

"With Quimby. You've obviously been suffering from PTSD all these years. Quimby only compounded it."

He let go of her hand and sat back. "You are blessed, Claire. With resilience. That is a gift." Then he nodded, as if having convinced himself of something. "I do think you're ready to come back."

Claire didn't know what to make of any of this. Yes, she had come through this terrible ordeal, losing the man she loved and finding the man who had made such a gaping hole in her heart all those years ago. Maybe Curtin was right. She had more strength than she was ever aware of. She could go on with her life now. She was no longer a prisoner of her past. She could even accept that it was sheer coincidence that Curtin had testified against the man who had raped and murdered her best friend. After all, Paul Curtin was a world authority on what made psychopaths like Lewis tick.

But what about Quimby? Was that another coincidence? Claire wondered. He murdered six women. At least, she and Nick had *thought* he'd murdered them. Alone. Until they'd discovered the link that led from Tammy Sorensen to Charles Sedgwick.

Claire needed to find out what Curtin knew. Or didn't.

"You look like you have something on your mind," Curtin said to her.

"Doctor," Nick began, "I need to ask you a question."

"Go right ahead, Detective," said Curtin.

"When you accepted Todd Quimby into the early release program, did you know anything about him that may not have been in the file you gave Claire?"

Curtin replied instantly. "That's not how it works."

"Can you take me through it?" Nick asked.

"Sure. At the end of their year of study, my fellows evaluate the next group of prisoners from Rikers Island who are up for parole. The fellows are the ones who choose the parolees. I hear their cases and sign off on who they decide makes the cut and who doesn't— and why. Most importantly, the cases are presented to me without names. And then the parolees are randomly assigned to the new crop of fellows who enter the program in July."

Nick seemed mollified, and then Curtin sat back in his chair and looked him straight in the eye. "Do you mind telling me why you asked?"

"We're just trying to figure out how Quimby might have come into contact with a Dr. Charles Sedgwick," Claire said.

If the name meant anything to Curtin, his face gave nothing away. "I don't remember seeing that name in his file," he answered, "and I don't know him. Is he another psychiatrist?"

"No, he's a molecular biologist and pharmacologist," Claire informed him. "He runs a company called Biopharix up in Putnam County. He worked with one of Quimby's victims, Tammy Sorenson."

"I've heard of Biopharix, of course," Curtin responded. "Unfortunately, Sedgwick doesn't ring a bell. But I'd be glad to check him out for you if you'd like."

"That would be a great help to us, Doctor," Nick said.

"I'm happy to help you in any way I can," Curtin assured them.

Claire stood up to leave. Nick followed her lead.

"Thank you," she said to Curtin. "For everything. For letting me come back so quickly."

Curtin stood up slowly, painfully. Claire wondered why mono would be so debilitating, and then recalled from medical school that it's not uncommon for mono to cause severe muscle aches and weakness.

"I'm a man of my word, Claire," he said as he led them to the door, referring to the promise he'd made her when she left the program. "I said you could come back when you were ready. I'm just glad to see you came through all of this whole." He opened the door and turned to Claire. "I know you gave up your apartment. But I'd be glad to have Bonnie send your reinstatement papers to wherever you're staying."

Before Claire could say anything, Nick jumped in. "She's staying at my place. Until she gets settled."

"Then I needn't worry, because you're in good hands," Curtin said. "Take care."

"Feel better," Claire said to Curtin as he closed the door. She headed with Nick toward the elevator, about ready to burst, but she knew she had to hold off talking until they were out of Curtin's earshot. The moment they were in the elevator and the doors closed, Claire let loose. "Why did you tell him I was staying at your place?" she demanded.

"Because you are now," Nick said, and Claire knew from his tone that she didn't have a choice. "I'm not leaving you alone until we put all the pieces of this puzzle together."

CHAPTER 28

"The question is," Claire asked Nick, putting down her coffee cup, "do you believe Curtin?"

"I'm not sure I know what to believe anymore," Nick said, taking a bite of the stale apple pie that had lost its taste at least an hour earlier.

They'd stopped at the diner on Broadway at 56th after leaving Curtin's apartment, talking for hours, sometimes heatedly, about what they knew, thought they might know, or didn't know about the link between Sedgwick and Quimby, and whether Curtin was in some way involved.

"You know the guy better than me," Nick said. "Did it sound to you like he was lying when he said he didn't know Sedgwick?"

"I couldn't get a read on him," Claire said. "Maybe I was too busy concentrating on how sick he is."

"Here's the thing," Nick said, taking another bite of pie. "For Sedgwick to know about Quimby would be one coincidence too many. I'm telling you, Curtin's in this up to his pointy little head."

"The man has gone after killers his whole career," Claire argued. "Why would he become one? It doesn't make sense."

"Along with all the other evidence in this case that doesn't track," Nick added. He was frustrated and tired and running out of the time Lt. Wilkes had given him to come up with something fresh.

The waitress put the check on the table and said, "You can pay at the register up front."

"What do you want to do?" Claire asked Nick.

Nick eyed the check, then looked at his watch. "It's after midnight," he said, the fatigue beginning to show in his voice. "And we've been going around in circles for hours. Whatever Curtin's involvement, we're not going to prove it tonight. I vote we head home and get some sleep."

Claire's eyelids were starting to feel heavy, despite the three cups of coffee she'd had. "Agreed," she said.

It was past one a.m. when they emerged from the subway station around the corner from Nick's apartment. He was technically off duty and didn't have use of the Impala, and the cab fares they had spent getting around the city were starting to add up. Claire had always been careful about her money, never spending what she didn't have and refusing to borrow from anyone, so taking the subway and staying at Nick's was a welcome way for her to both save some cash and feel safe.

But now, heading back there in the middle of the night, when the city was starting to quiet down, she was having second thoughts. Part of it was that she valued her privacy. But she also didn't want him to feel obligated.

"Are you sure about this?" she asked as they walked down Lexington Avenue.

"What's bugging you?" Nick replied.

"I feel like you're bringing your work home with you."

Nick couldn't help but smile. "If I felt that way, I wouldn't have offered."

"I just don't want to be an intrusion."

"You're not. It won't be the first time I've been banished to the couch," Nick said.

"You really know how to charm a girl."

"I live with my mother and two daughters. Unfortunately, I'm not in a position to charm anyone."

They turned the corner onto Nick's block, just in time to see a man pop open the hood of his ancient Dodge minivan, which he'd double-parked a few yards in front of them. *Must've broken down,* Nick thought.

They walked along Nick's street, coming upon the van, and Nick took a look at the driver, whose head was buried under the hood. *That's odd,* Nick thought. *He's not working on the engine.*

Instinctively, Nick looked down and saw the man's boots. They were black, tapered to the toe, and expensive. Nick didn't think they fit with the piece of crap the guy was driving.

Just then, he heard a grinding sound down the street and looked up and away from the guy and his car. On the corner, brightly lit by the overhead streetlamp, was the profile of a city sanitation truck, backing up to empty the public trash can on the corner.

"Look at that," Nick said, annoyed. "Idiot's blocking the whole damn street."

And then he realized. The truck wasn't beeping as it backed up.

Nick took a breath. Claire could feel him tense up.

She looked at him and asked, "Are you okay?"

"Yeah, fine," he said without affect. "We're almost home."

They were only about fifty yards from Nick's building. His eyes darted between the front door and the garbage truck across the street. The driver was just climbing down from the cab and moving slowly toward the rear. Alone.

They never ride alone. And they never pick up garbage this late.

The driver appeared, passing the truck's rear opening, grabbing a garbage can, and wheeling it toward the compactor. For a split second, he lifted his head, his eyes on them, confirming Nick's fears.

He's looking at us. And he's not wearing gloves.

Nick's right hand found his gun. His left hand tightly latched on to Claire's arm.

"What's wrong?" she whispered.

"Just keep walking," he said.

"You're scaring me," Claire replied.

As if on cue, the unmistakable sound of a car's hood slammed shut behind them. Nick looked back just as he heard the engine turn over.

The minivan.

His head whipped around, just in time to see the sanitation worker leave the trash can behind and reach inside the truck's hopper.

Not to put something in but to take something out.

Nick picked up the pace, pulling Claire with him.

"What's going on?" Claire asked, now terrified.

"Just do exactly as I say."

As he said it, the minivan's engine gunned behind them. Nick turned just in time to see the headlights, blinding him.

The door to the building was still a dozen yards in front of them. The man from the garbage truck walked toward them, and Nick considered running for it.

He's got something in his hand. . . .

He realized they'd never make it.

Nick made his move when the minivan screeched to a stop behind them.

"Get down!" he screamed, pulling Claire to the ground between two parked cars.

"What's happening?" Claire said with hysteria in her voice.

"Stay down!" Nick yelled.

Pop! Pop! Pop! Pop! Pop!

A spray of bullets tore up the cars in front of and behind them. But there was no sound of gunfire. Only metal piercing metal.

They have silencers, Nick realized. *They're professionals. Hired assassins.*

For a second, the fusillade of bullets stopped. Nick knew they were reloading. He raised his head above the trunk of the car in front of him. Both killers stood in the shadows.

I can't see a damn thing.

He handed the gun to Claire.

"What the hell are you doing?" she asked.

"Shoot them!" Nick ordered. "I can't see them!"

Claire looked down at the gun, scared to death. "I don't know how!"

"Just point and shoot! Now, dammit!"

Only a few seconds had elapsed. Claire stood up. The garbageman, surprised to see a woman facing him ten yards away, let his guard down for a second too long. Claire raised the gun and pulled the trigger.

And then she heard a groan of pain.

Nick looked up. Claire had hit the garbageman in the right leg. He dropped his gun and fell to the ground.

"Cover me!" he whispered to Claire.

"How?" she asked, scared out of her mind.

"Just keep pulling the trigger!"

Claire pointed the gun and fired. Nick maneuvered around the sidewalk side of the cars, moving fast but keeping low, covering the distance between them and the corner in no more than five seconds, grateful for the city's bright streetlamps. He ran around the blind side of the garbage truck where he could see the legs of the hired gun, trying to drag himself back over to where he'd dropped his weapon.

Nick reached the assassin before he could get to his gun and grabbed him under his arms, flipping him headfirst into the hopper so that Nick could snatch the weapon he knew was hidden there.

It was an Uzi with a huge, custom-made silencer on the barrel.

Nick saw the wound; somehow Claire's shots had found the man's femur and had shattered it. He was contorted in pain when Nick hit the lever that started the compactor. Then he reached in and closed his hand around the assassin's throat, pulling him up and bending his head backward out of the hopper as the compactor's blade rose above the man's waist, ready to pulverize him. "Talk now or that thing'll cut you in half," Nick threatened. "Who else besides you and the guy in the minivan?"

The killer only struggled against him. Even his agony didn't make him talk. Nick tightened his grip on the man's throat. "How many?" Nick screamed at him. "Who the hell sent you?"

"Screw you!" the killer said.

Nick released the man's neck just as the compactor's blade descended. Nick backed away from the hopper's opening, watching the man scream and blood spray from the rear of the truck.

An engine gunned. The minivan roared up the block, then screeched to a stop.

Right where Claire's hiding.

Nick ran toward the headlights and could see the man in the boots bolt from the vehicle with something in his hand. Nick knew it was a gun, probably an automatic weapon like the Uzi he had taken from the other guy. He wanted to shoot the bastard down, but he couldn't see Claire and was afraid to fire.

He did the only thing he could.

"Police!" Nick screamed, advancing on the guy. "Drop the gun or I'll blow your head off!"

Assassin number two stopped and spun around to face Nick, who pointed the Uzi and pulled the trigger.

Click, click, click.

It's jammed. Shit.

The assassin smiled at Nick. Raised his weapon.

Boom.

All Nick saw was the man's forehead explode from an exit wound. His gun clattered to the ground as he went down, revealing Claire standing behind him, Nick's gun still in her trembling hand, pointed at where the assassin's head had been. Nick bent over the dead man, still holding his Uzi, and ripped the gun away.

And then he smelled it. Again. That bitter, rotten odor he'd smelled before, coming from the dead man's body.

Nick ran to Claire and grabbed his Glock from her hand. She was shaking and crying. He put his arm around her.

"It's okay. You're okay," Nick said.

"We have to call the police!"

"We've got to get out of here!" he yelled. "They smell like bitter almonds. Sedgwick sent them. When he finds out they missed, he'll send others."

"Where are we going?"

"To get my mother and the girls." He took her face between his hands. "I need you with me. Every second counts. You understand?"

This snapped Claire out of her fear and into action. "Yes," she said, looking into his eyes. "I'm with you."

They ran the short distance down the street and into Nick's building, up the stairwell to the third floor and down the hall to the apartment. Nick unlocked the door and they went in, moving as fast as they could.

"My girls are asleep in their room. Second door on the left down the hall."

Claire raced down the dark hall, when the first door opened. She tensed, thinking it was another killer. Until she heard a female voice.

"What's going on?" asked Nick's mother, Helen, pulling on her bathrobe. "Sounds like someone was using a jackhammer outside."

"We've got to get the girls and leave," Nick said to his mother.

"Leave?" Helen asked, her face pale with fear. She switched on a light. "It's the middle of the night. They're sleeping."

And then she saw the blood on her son's clothes. And the two Uzis in his hands.

"Oh my God! What happened?"

"Never mind that now," Nick said. "Just hurry!"

They could now hear sirens approaching.

"Shouldn't we wait for the police?"

"No! Help me grab the girls! Now!"

He handed the Uzis to Claire and headed toward his daughters' room. Helen eyed her.

"Who are you?" Helen asked.

"A friend," said Claire.

"You'll cover us," Nick said, turning back to her.

The sirens were getting louder. Claire, Uzis in her hands, stuck her head out the front door of Nick's apartment building. "It seems clear," she managed to say.

"Then let's go," replied Nick, carrying his older daughter, Jill, who clung to his neck, terrified. His mother carried Katie, the younger one.

"In what?" Claire asked.

Nick pointed to the minivan, right where they left it, its lights on and engine running. "It's all we've got," he said.

Taking one more look, she ran outside toward the minivan, aiming the guns in either direction, Nick and his mother behind her.

Nick boarded the van first through the right side door, buckling his older daughter into a seat before his mother handed him the younger girl.

"You don't think you're driving at night, do you?" Helen asked her son.

Nick hopped into the passenger seat and gestured to Claire to get behind the wheel.

Helen looked at Claire, then back at her son. "Are you going to tell me who she is?" she asked.

"A psychiatrist," Nick shot back.

"Jesus, Mary, and Joseph, it's about time," his mother replied.

"Claire Waters. Nice to meet you, ma'am," Claire said, throwing the minivan into gear and stomping on the pedal.

She maneuvered around the garbage truck and sped around the corner onto Third Avenue, avoiding the first police cars that entered the block from the opposite end.

As it turned out, luck was with them; the traffic lights were all green. Claire hit the gas, her eyes locked straight ahead.

"Where are we going?" Claire asked Nick without looking at him.

"North," he instructed.

They drove for what seemed like hours, Nick directing Claire to stay only on interstate highways that were both well traveled and well patrolled by state police in case they spotted a pair of headlights behind them making the same moves as they did. Nick knew this was a double-edged sword. If trouble came up from behind them, he wanted to be on a road where there was at least a chance a police cruiser would show up. On the other hand, the last thing they needed was to be pulled over by some bored graveyard-shift cop and have to explain their way out of why they were driving what was technically a stolen car. Just in case, Nick also told Claire to drive no more than five miles an hour over the speed limit.

For Claire, the journey seemed not only endless, but also aimless. The adrenaline rush she experienced earlier from the terror was wearing off. The long drive and the effort it took to shut down emotionally were wearing on her, and she felt that if she were to survive whatever would come next, she had to force herself not to think about anything that had happened. Just keep going. Don't stop.

I killed a human being.

She could hear those words turn around in her brain, over and over again. Though she knew what she'd done was by definition self-defense, the act of killing another person was so shocking that she couldn't process it.

Out of the corner of her eye, she saw Nick beside her, literally riding shotgun, holding one of the Uzis between his seat and the door. His face was flat, devoid of emotion, and Claire wondered what he was feeling. Or whether he was trying *not* to feel. Just like she was.

Claire watched him turn his head again for what seemed like the hundredth time, making sure there was no one on their tail, though she could see clearly in her rear- and side-view mirrors that theirs was the only car on the road. And she also knew that in the inky night he wouldn't be able to see much anyway.

"Relax," she assured him. "There's nobody back there."

Nick turned back toward the front, nodding. "How're you doing?" he asked.

Claire couldn't suppress a yawn. "I'm not sure I'm going to be able to drive much longer."

"Hang in there. Just a few more miles."

"You know where we're going? Why didn't you tell me?" Claire was so exhausted that she couldn't hide the anger in her voice.

"You didn't need to know," Nick answered, seeing the sign for the Interstate 84 exit that he'd been waiting for. "Get off here," he said, almost too late for her to make the off-ramp.

Claire swerved just in time—exactly what Nick wanted her to do. He looked behind them again to check if they were being followed. There was only darkness.

"You want to clue me in?" Claire asked, now too tired to be annoyed. "Where the hell are you taking us?"

"Just make a left at the bottom of the ramp and go straight into town."

The town was Beacon, nearly sixty miles north of Manhattan and directly across the Hudson River from the larger city of Newburgh. Their destination was the Beacon Inn, a bed-and-breakfast set in a large colonial on the outskirts of town. The place had been owned for years by Tim Donnelly, a former NYPD detective who'd retired just after 9/11. Tim's generosity was well known to any city cop who had to speak to an inmate at one of the two state prisons nearby and needed a place to crash for the night, whether it be because it was too late to go home, the weather wouldn't allow it, they had too many at the local bar, or home wasn't the most welcome place. Donnelly's B & B was always there for them.

During a gas stop earlier, Nick had called Donnelly and told him what was going on, and in usual fashion, Donnelly assured him there would be three rooms waiting for them at no charge, for as long as they needed.

Tall and trim with a full head of graying hair, Donnelly was waiting outside when Claire pulled up in front of the inn. He was holding a sawed-off, double-barrel shotgun by his side. Nick was out of the car before it even came to a stop and ran to give his friend a bear hug while Claire opened her door, got out, and stretched.

"Timmy, this is Claire Waters. Timmy's a buddy and he knows the drill."

"Welcome," Donnelly said, shaking her hand.

"Thank you," she said.

"My home is yours for as long as you need it," Donnelly said in a comforting tone. "Let's get the kiddos settled in." He took one of Nick's sleeping daughters from the back and gestured to Helen and the other daughter. "And then we'll get this thing out of sight," Donnelly said, tapping his hand on the roof of the old Dodge.

"I'll need to rent a car," Nick said.

"Like hell," Donnelly said with a wave of his hand. "My son just started college and left his car here, so it's all yours."

"Where are we?" Helen moaned, trying to wake up and stretch in the back of the van.

"Somewhere safe, Mom," Nick said, introducing her and his now-awake daughters to Donnelly, who took them into the house and to their rooms.

Nick headed for the driver's seat of the van to move the car. Claire instinctively headed toward him. "I'll drive," she said.

"We're just pulling into the back," Nick said, not without some defensiveness.

"We don't need you running into a tree on the way," Claire chided, almost laughing after this gruesome night.

Reluctantly, he moved over to the passenger's seat and Claire got behind the wheel.

"How long are we staying here?" she asked.

Nick looked at his watch. It was three-fifteen in the morning. "Until tomorrow night," he said, "when you and I go on a field trip."

CHAPTER 29

---

*T*he narrow hallway was dimly lit by naked lightbulbs hanging from electrical cords. Claire walked through the concrete space, confused. It was too dark to see clearly. Where was she?

The lights became brighter and she realized she was back in the jail at Rikers Island. The same cell block she'd been in with Curtin. But this time Curtin wasn't with her.

She picked up her pace, rushing past prisoners who leered at her from the shadows of their cells. She could see their eyes, all a familiar green, aglow.

Frightened, she walked faster, faster, looking up at the lightbulbs, one after the next after the next. Why did they look so strange?

Then she realized. The bulbs were hanging from cords shaped like nooses. Just then, the prisoners in the cells stepped forward to the bars and she saw their faces.

Quimby. Each one was Quimby.

The first one was grinning at her; the second one was laughing; the third screaming, though his words were silent. And the last one terrified her. He was dead. Putrefying. Rotting. His skin dripping like wax from his face.

Claire turned away in horror and saw two men, barely lit, at the end of the hallway. As she approached them, she could see they were dressed alike, both wearing a polo shirt and shorts.

"There's been a terrible accident," one of them said, though she couldn't see his face. "Come with us. Don't be afraid."

The men both reached out toward Claire. "You're a very pretty little girl," said the second man. "I bet you're very smart too."

"Too smart for her own good," the first man said, and the two of them started laughing, which began to echo and build into an ear-splitting roar.

She moved toward them and could see their faces now. It was Curtin and Sedgwick. Laughing so loud that the room began to shake and the floor started to give way as the walls crumbled around her and she ran for her life.

Claire woke up, sweating. She sat up in bed, the sheets soaked through and twisted around her body. The room was dark, though she could see sunlight through a sliver between the closed curtains. She had no idea where she was—the overstuffed chair and armoire were unfamiliar—until she remembered she was hiding out with Nick at his friend's bed-and-breakfast.

She looked at the clock radio. It was 3:08 p.m. Even though she had been asleep since dawn, she still felt a deep exhaustion, the kind no amount of sleep helps. It was that bone tiredness that comes from anxiety and fear, and for the first time Claire didn't question it. She didn't think about a chemical explanation for what she was feeling. She knew the cause. She was in mourning. She burst into tears, letting the grief for Amy and Ian wash over her, crying hard and silently for the two people she'd loved and lost.

After a few minutes, the storm inside her seemed to blow away. Her outburst had released some of the pain, unraveling the tangle of emotions she'd held for decades inside of her.

Claire wiped her face and thought, *I'm calm now,* and pulled on her jeans and blouse. When she turned around, she caught a glimpse of herself in the mirror. The beam of sunlight streaming through the crack between the curtains lit her face in a gauzy glow, like a phantom. Other phantom faces appeared in the mirror. First Amy, then Ian and Detective Maggie Stolls, followed by Tammy Sorenson and the other dead women. And then, Todd Quimby. They pleaded with their eyes for Claire to help them find solace, to free their souls from being trapped for eternity.

She knew what to do.

She flipped on the light switch and the faces disappeared. She grabbed her shoes and the rest of her things and ran out of the room.

*   *   *

Claire found Nick sitting on the sun porch drinking a cup of coffee. He'd just taken a long shower, and his hair was wet and combed, his face clean shaven. The light from the afternoon sun enhanced his handsome, sharp features.

He can help them, Claire thought. *He can help me end this nightmare.*

"How'd you sleep?" Nick asked her, knowing the answer.

"Like a baby," she replied, without smiling.

"You ready?" Nick asked, pulling out a chair for Claire to sit beside him.

"As I'll ever be," she said, sitting down.

They looked at each other for a long moment. *He's got beautiful eyes,* she thought. *You'd never know he was going blind.*

"We'll leave at nine," Nick said, "after sunset."

"To Biopharix. On our 'field trip,' " Claire replied.

"Whatever's going on, whatever this is all about, the answers are in that building. In Sedgwick's office."

Claire looked at him. "And you think they're going to just let us look around?"

"I don't intend to ask their permission." Nick turned to her. "You don't have to come with me," he said, meaning it.

"Of course I do," Claire said. "You can't see."

But her tone told him she'd have gone no matter what.

They sat there silently, looking at the fields, dotted with orange and purple and red wildflowers in full bloom.

It was only a seven-mile drive from Beacon south to Cold Spring, and Claire covered the distance in Donnelly's son's aging Honda Accord in just over fifteen minutes. Driving down Main Street, its stores closed for the night, she and Nick noticed the town's police cruiser parked in front of the police station. Claire hoped it would be there throughout their field trip, which she knew carried life-and-death consequences.

They crossed over the railroad tracks, making their way down West Street before they saw the sign: WELCOME TO BIOPHARIX. WHERE YOUR HEALTH ALWAYS MATTERS. She signaled a turn up the tree-lined driveway when Nick grabbed the steering wheel, keeping her on the street.

"What are you doing?" Claire asked.

"We can't just drive up to the front entrance and tell the guards we're breaking into their offices."

"You sure you know how to do this?" Claire asked, second-guessing what now seemed like a crazy plan.

"I've had twenty years of on-the-job training from some of the best burglars in the business," Nick said. Then he unzipped a black leather kit and pulled out a long silver file that tapered to a series of small ovals. "This tool can pick most any lock."

Nick then pointed down a side street. "Kill the lights and pull into the woods about fifty yards past that house on the left. We'll hike over from there."

Claire drove down the road and turned where Nick had instructed her. She parked the car behind an old oak and got out, careful not to slam the door. The night was warm, but not too humid, lit only by the stars and blinking fireflies.

"You're my eyes tonight," Nick said, taking Claire by the arm. "There's a side entrance near Sedgwick's office on the northwest corner of the building. It's about half a mile to Biopharix, so use the compass on your iPhone and head north by northeast."

"You were here today," Claire realized. "While I was sleeping."

Nick nodded. "Had to come while I could see," he said.

Claire took out her phone and found the compass app. She smiled to herself, thinking that until she met Nick, she never in a million years would have used it. But everything had changed since she moved to New York and entered Curtin's fellowship. She found herself wondering what her life would have been like if she'd turned him down and stayed in Washington, DC, doing research. *Ian would still be alive,* she thought.

They moved slowly, over brush and rocks, Claire guiding Nick around trees that blended into the blackness that Nick saw. They squeezed through a thicket of trees and vines and found themselves down a hill from Biopharix, its glassed-in floors shimmering against the night sky.

"It looks like the Emerald City," Claire said.

"And we're off to see the wizard," Nick replied.

They headed up the hill, and Nick let go of Claire's arm.

"I'm good now," he said, grateful that the building was so brightly lit. "Follow my lead."

Nick pinballed from tree to tree, careful to stay in the shadows, waiting each time for Claire to catch up. They moved this way until they were at the door Nick had targeted. He pulled out his pick, slipped it into the lock, and massaged the tumbler.

Click.

Nick pulled the door open just wide enough for them to slip in. He held the door so it would close quietly. They were in a stairwell.

"Third floor," Nick whispered.

They climbed the stairs as silently as they could until they reached a door that Nick pushed open. He pointed to a security camera on the ceiling, then to the oak door that Claire remembered was Sedgwick's office suite.

"We're going to that door over there," Nick whispered. "Follow me."

Nick got down, crawling on his belly. Claire followed his moves, pulling herself along the floor until they reached Sedgwick's door. Fortunately, the area was underlit, and Nick hoped his arm wouldn't be caught on camera when he reached up to the knob, inserted his burglar's tool, and turned it.

Click.

Nick pushed the door open a crack, and he and Claire squeezed in, still on the floor. They faced a long hallway that was lit by the dim security lighting. Long, narrow cylinders labeled OXYGEN and NITROGEN lined the walls.

Footsteps broke the silence. Claire turned to Nick, her heart starting to pound. He pointed to a door marked SUPPLY ROOM and they entered, closing it just before a security guard passed. They waited until his clicking heels faded away. Then they heard the lock engage and the door they had come through close behind them.

Claire stopped holding her breath in relief. "We've got to find his lab," she whispered. "My guess is it's at the end of the hallway. Prick like Sedgwick would want everyone to have to walk the distance to see him."

They opened the door and Claire checked that the hallway was clear. She saw no one, so they exited the supply room and moved quickly toward the door at the end of the long corridor.

Claire was right. The office belonged to Sedgwick, whose name was stenciled in small red letters on the glass door. Nick tried it and it was open. *That's strange,* he thought. *Unless someone's still working.*

Nick put his finger to his lips, cautioning Claire, stepping silently over the thickly carpeted floor of Sedgwick's outer office. They reached another door and opened it a sliver. And what Nick saw stunned him.

He was looking at a large, brightly lit hospital room where three men lay asleep on gurneys, their arms attached to IVs.

"What in God's name is going on here?" Nick whispered.

He opened the door wider, allowing Claire to take in the scene. Her eyes turned to the IV bags, and she read the names on the labels: Adriamycin, bleomycin, and vinblastine. She turned to Nick and said, "Those are cancer drugs. They're getting chemo."

"Exactly right, Doctor," a voice rang out. Then a hand pulled the door open.

"Welcome to my lab."

It was Sedgwick, in his long white lab coat, wearing a red and white polka-dotted bow tie. Nick reached for his gun.

"Don't, Detective, please," Sedgwick said, aiming a 9-millimeter Beretta at Nick. "Both of you, indulge me and put your hands above your heads."

Sedgwick pulled Nick's Glock from its holster. Then he patted down Claire, finding nothing.

"That's better," Sedgwick said. "Now we can chat."

He gestured with his gun to two wooden chairs. Nick and Claire sat down.

"I had no choice, you understand," Sedgwick said.

"How can you say that?" Claire asked incredulously. "No choice but to kill Todd Quimby and all those women?"

"It was the only way," Sedgwick said.

Claire's eyes moved from him to the emaciated men on the gurneys.

"Your patients are cachectic, Doctor Sedgwick," she said, and turned to Nick. "At the end-stage of their cancer," she explained. "Adriamycin, bleomycin, and vinblastine are all chemotherapies for

Hodgkin's lymphoma—the same cancer that Tammy Sorenson had when she died."

"Impressive for a psychiatrist," Sedgwick said.

"Were you experimenting on Tammy?" Claire asked, looking Sedgwick straight on. "Was it a new drug you gave her that didn't work?"

"It's far more complicated than that," Sedgwick said, narrowing his eyes.

And all at once she realized what he had done.

"My God," she said. "*You* gave Tammy cancer."

Sedgwick blinked as if caught in a lie. "My crime against humanity," he said. "Yes, you're right. I did give Tammy Sorenson and these poor souls cancer. But not on purpose."

Claire and Nick heard the unmistakable sorrow in Sedgwick's voice.

"If you didn't do it on purpose," Nick said, "then how did this happen?"

"Tammy worked with me to find ways to train the immune system to fight cancer. A month ago, she developed a virulent form of lymphoma, and I realized that our experiments had gone awry."

"That's an understatement," Claire said.

"I never intended it to happen," Sedgwick said. "One of the Epstein-Barr viruses we were using mutated, causing Tammy's lymph cells to lose their ability to fight cancer. Believe me, I tried everything I could to save her."

"But the cancer was too aggressive," Claire said, realizing how all the pieces fit together. "So when you couldn't treat her disease, you killed her to cover up your experiment. You made it look like Todd Quimby was killing women with short blond hair he picked up at clubs or on the street. You even drugged him so that he'd be seen at the nightclub where Tammy disappeared."

"But that wasn't enough," Nick added. "You knew if it was *just* Tammy who was found dead, she would've led us straight to you."

Sedgwick looked smug.

"That was very clever," Nick said. "You made it look like Tammy was just another random victim of a serial killer. You murdered eight innocent people."

"You're wrong," Sedgwick argued. "They were *sacrificed* to keep a terrible secret—an *accident*—out of the hands of terrorists or any government bent on destroying humanity."

"You tried to kill *me!*" Claire said, her voice echoing in the room.

"It had to be done."

"But not by you," accused Nick. "You needed a fall guy. So you set up Todd Quimby. You made it look like he murdered those women. You knew he'd been in the Merchant Marines, so you tied knots like he would have. Then you drugged him so he'd be seen at the nightclub where Tammy disappeared."

"You don't understand—"

"And when you were done with him, you drowned him outside this building and put his body in the front seat of his grandmother's car," Nick said. "You must be an excellent swimmer. When you drove into the East River, you swam to safety and he was the one we found."

"He was *expendable*. He was a scumbag sex offender."

"He was mentally ill!" Claire exclaimed. "And he was *innocent!*"

"He was *insignificant!*" Sedgwick screamed. "And they were whores. I had to do what I did for the sake of humanity."

"Yeah, you're a real humanitarian," Nick sneered, pointing to the three unconscious men on gurneys. "What are you going to do with *them?*"

"They're all dying," said Sedgwick. "There's nothing I can do. Fortunately, they're all young, single men without wives and children, so no one's dependent on them."

"So, what, that makes them expendable too?" Nick asked, his voice rising. "Are you going to let them die painlessly? Or are you going to strangle them and drop a few more innocent bodies around to make it look like another serial killer's on the loose? When does it end, Doctor? How many more dead people are we going to find with your name on them?"

"Believe me when I tell you," Sedgwick pleaded, "that I didn't want to hurt anybody."

Claire glared at him with contempt. "You killed a cop. And you butchered my boyfriend."

"Detective Stolls walked in on me searching your apartment," Sedgwick said, somehow trying to justify it all. "And Ian knew too much. He would have pushed the tumor board to investigate

Tammy's lymphoma, and then everyone would have known." He took several steps toward her. "You're a *scientist*, Doctor. You know that science, and the search for cures, comes with risk. I accidentally opened Pandora's box, and all I did was try to put back the terrible knowledge I let escape. I sacrificed eight people to save millions. You would have done the same thing."

"Not in a million years would I have taken a life in the name of science."

"People must be sacrificed to save others," said Sedgwick.

He's sick, Claire thought. *He really believes this.*

And then she looked at the three men on the gurneys.

"You experimented on them!" Claire yelled, standing up to face Sedgwick. "You claim you want to help humanity, but you're no better than the Nazis, experimenting on human beings. You're Josef Mengele. You're a monster."

"You're wrong, Claire," Sedgwick said, defending himself. "Those men contracted lymphoma from Tammy Sorenson."

Claire stared at Sedgwick in shock.

"You found a way to block apoptosis in the human cell," Claire said, her voice shaking. "You shut down the body's defense to stop cancer."

Sedgwick let out a long, mournful sigh. "I was searching for a way to *activate* the immune system. I put an agent on a virus hoping it would boost immune cells to fight cancer."

"And instead you turned off the immune system and gave Tammy cancer."

"It was all a horrible mistake," Sedgwick said.

Now it was all clear. Claire finally understood how this "horrible mistake," this terrible scientific discovery, had led to the deaths of innocent people.

"Tammy kissed those men," Claire said, pointing to the comatose patients lying on the gurneys. "She gave them the Epstein-Barr virus that triggered their lymphoma."

"That's why I had to cover this up. This cancer can be spread with a kiss. Just imagine how many people could become infected."

"It's like getting mono. . . ." Claire stopped short. "Doctor Curtin has mono. Did Tammy infect him, too, you son of a bitch? Is that how he's involved in all this?"

Sedgwick didn't answer. Instead he raised his gun and aimed it at the three men.

"No!" Claire screamed.

Sedgwick shot each man once in the head. "I put them out of their misery."

"You executed them!" Claire yelled.

Sedgwick pointed his gun at her.

Nick jumped up and moved in front of Claire. "So we're expendable too," he said. "Anyone who could blow the lid off this garbage can is expendable. Everyone's expendable, right? Everyone but *you*."

Tears were in Sedgwick's eyes as he aimed straight at Nick's forehead.

"I'm sorry."

"You don't have to do this, Doctor," said Nick.

"Yes, I do," Sedgwick said, squeezing the trigger.

The gun fired, but the bullet hit the ceiling.

Sedgwick had a stunned look on his face as his mouth opened and blood streamed out, splashing a crimson stream down his white lab coat.

Claire grabbed Nick's arm as Sedgwick fell forward onto the floor, revealing the entry hole of the bullet that had just pierced his neck. Behind a drape stood Paul Curtin, holding a .38 revolver.

"It's almost over," Curtin said in a raspy voice. He looked more ashen than he had the night before. Thinner too.

"Almost?" Claire asked, not understanding what Curtin was trying to say.

"The end of the story. You deserve to know."

Curtin placed his gun on a nearby table and moved toward Claire. Slowly, with his hand shaking, he reached for hers and grasped it. *His hand is like ice,* Claire thought. Then he placed her hand on the right side of his belly, just below his chest.

"Feel that," Curtain said to her.

Claire felt his ribs pressing through his blue silk shirt and then a massive lump, the size of an egg.

"You've got lymphoma," she said.

"I'm riddled with it," Curtin replied without emotion. "I've only got days."

"How did this happen?" Claire asked.

"I met Tammy six weeks ago at the club Red. She was utterly beautiful. She came home with me, we slept together, and she infected me with her sweet kisses."

Then Claire remembered. *Red*. Kisses. All the men Tammy had slept with. "We read Tammy's diary," she said. "Her last entry was 'EB.' "

Curtin smiled. "Epstein-Barr," he said. "Tammy was a very clever woman."

"She was giving us a clue?" Nick asked, incredulous.

"Yes, Detective. Sedgwick cleaned her apartment but left the diary to mislead you. He forced Tammy to write Quimby's name into the diary to make you think she knew him." Curtin lowered himself into one of the wooden chairs. "You don't mind if I sit, do you?"

"No," Nick said, watching the once-virile man painfully adjust his thin limbs in the chair. "How did Sedgwick pull you into this?"

"He contacted me after Tammy got sick—she gave him my name and told him she'd kissed me," Curtin said; then he closed his eyes, remembering the night with Tammy that had led him to this. Finally, he opened his eyes again. "Sedgwick said he needed to see me. He told me about his research and how he couldn't afford to let this terrible secret get out."

Curtin stopped speaking, needing to catch his breath. Claire pitied him, the man who was going to train her to be a brilliant therapist. The man who was going to help her see into the criminal mind.

"Sedgwick quarantined Tammy here, made her call her parents and say she was on vacation in Hawaii, and came up with a plan to make it look like Tammy was murdered," Curtin said. "He asked me to find a patient to pin it on, and yes, I gave him Todd Quimby. He promised me that he'd kill only Tammy—a mercy killing, really—because no matter what, she was going to die a terrible, painful death."

"And you gave him me," Claire said. "You thought I wouldn't be able to handle the case. That's why you assigned Quimby to me."

"I knew all about you, Claire," Curtin said, his voice now barely above a whisper. "When you applied to the program, your name seemed familiar. I searched it on the Internet and found the connection. You were with Amy Danforth the day she was kidnapped. And I realized then that you were the little girl Peter Lewis kept talking about. He went on and on about Claire—the child who got away."

"But why me?" Claire asked. "Why did you assign Quimby to me?"

"Because I knew how emotionally fragile you were—your past with Amy still haunted you. I thought you would quit the program and blame yourself for Quimby. I'm a hell of a good shrink, Claire. But you surprised me. I never thought you'd have the strength to investigate Tammy's murder."

"You put murderers away for years," Claire said, sitting down beside him. "How could a man like you let Sedgwick kill all those people?"

"He lied to me. He promised he'd kill only Tammy and Quimby. I could live with that," Curtin said, laughing at the irony of what he'd just said. "I never knew he'd kill the other women to make it look like a string of serial murders. I never dreamed he'd harm Ian to cover up what he'd done to Tammy Sorenson."

"Why didn't you come forward?" Nick asked.

When Curtin answered, his voice was barely a whisper. "For the same reason he killed all those poor people. His secret had to be kept. And I couldn't be the one to let it out."

And then Curtin's eyes filled with tears. Claire turned to Nick, stunned. The man she'd feared, admired, and respected more than anyone else was weeping.

Footsteps came from the hallway, heading in their direction. Nick retrieved his Glock from Sedgwick's belt and moved toward the sound.

"Security," he said. "Do they carry weapons?" he asked Curtin.

"No," Curtin replied.

"Then it'll be easy to cuff them and get them out of the way." Nick bolted from the room as Claire turned back to Curtin.

"You're coming with us," she said to him. "Can you walk?"

Curtin stood up and walked with agony to Sedgwick's laboratory bench several feet away.

"There's one thing left to do," he said, pulling a large wine bottle out of a brown paper bag.

"My God, no!" she yelled as Curtin lit a liquid-soaked rag stuffed into the bottle's opening.

Claire ran to Curtin, but it was too late. He picked up the flaming torch and with all the strength he could muster, he tossed it toward the hood covering a laboratory bench.

The bottle shot across the room like a Roman candle, bursting into bright orange flames as it hit Sedgwick's research.

Pop! Pop! Pop! Pop! Pop!

Bottles of flammable liquids exploded in an array of blues, greens, reds, and yellows, shooting sparks across the room.

"That's the end," Curtin said, staring at the flames as they spread around Sedgwick's body. "The virus is gone."

Claire headed toward the men on the gurneys, but before she could reach them, their IV bags exploded into shards of fire. Curtin grabbed her arm and pulled her back as gray, putrid smoke billowed through the room. Claire was coughing, her throat burning.

"They're dead, Claire," he said. "Leave me here and let me die too."

"No," she said. "Not like this." She pulled Curtin away, his body so light that she felt like it was floating. She reached the door and turned back for one last look.

The laboratory erupted in a gush of flames.

CHAPTER 30

———◆◆◆———

Claire looked out the large plate-glass window of the diner on 11th Avenue. A cool autumn breeze was blowing red and yellow leaves down the dark, nearly empty street. She watched as they swirled upward, catching a glint of light from the streetlamp, then floated back to the ground.

Fall had always been her favorite season; she had fond memories of driving with her parents to view the vibrant, fiery autumn foliage at Letchworth, the state park south of Rochester; of rolling with Amy in the piles of leaves her father would rake up in their backyard; of starting a new grade at school, which she loved. For Claire, autumn marked both an end and a new beginning, and never had she needed both more than now.

A sip of her freshly poured decaf quickly brought her back to the present. She returned the cup to its saucer with a grimace; it was her third refill in the half hour she'd been waiting for Nick, and the coffee had long since lost its taste. She remembered sitting in the same booth, at this same diner, the night Charles Sedgwick murdered Maggie Stolls and tried to kill her. She tried to shake the thought out of her head as she glanced impatiently at her watch. Ten-thirty p.m. *Where the hell is he?*

It had been a little more than a month since they'd discovered Sedgwick's deadly secret at Biopharix, a month Claire wished she could forget. She had thought Paul Curtin's funeral, just two days earlier at a beautiful, secluded cemetery in Connecticut, would bring her closure. Until she realized there was one more loose end to tie up, a wrong she felt had to be righted for a victim who, like herself and Nick and Curtin, had been sucked into the vortex of this horror over which none of them had any control.

A sudden burst of cold air blowing her way made her look toward the open door of the diner. She noticed he moved more slowly, tentatively, despite the ample light.

His sight is getting worse, she thought.

Just then, he spotted her. His face lit up in a grin. Claire couldn't help but smile back as he slid onto the seat opposite her in the booth.

"Nice to see you," Nick said, looking into her eyes.

"You too," Claire replied, unable to hold his gaze for more than just a moment.

Nick knew why. He knew a sad smile when he saw one. "Don't worry about me. It just takes me a couple of extra seconds to adjust from the darkness to the light. I won't have to worry about that much longer."

His truth was said not with self-pity, but with an acceptance Claire hadn't heard from him before. She looked up, meeting his eyes again, unable to find the words.

"It's okay. Amazing what a little head shrinking can do," Nick said.

"You're seeing a therapist?" Claire asked.

A mischievous grin appeared. "Someone once told me people who don't like shrinks are the ones who need them the most," he said. "Good advice, if you ask me."

Claire nodded, more than pleased. "What are you doing about your job?"

"It's amazing, actually," Nick began. "Two months ago they were trying to find a way to get rid of me and put me in prison. Now they're bending over backward so I can stay."

Claire looked at him, amazed. "How can they let you—"

"I had to turn in my guns," he interrupted. "But my promotion to detective first grade won't happen until February, and if I stick around, that makes my pension worth a lot more. So they're putting me on permanent desk duty until I can put in my papers. Said it was the least they could do. Seeing that you and I are heroes and all."

Claire smiled. "Good thing nobody'll ever know," she said.

The irony was inescapable. In the aftermath of Biopharix, they had been placed in protective custody and debriefed by the FBI, who eventually credited them with preventing the deaths of tens of millions of people, a biological holocaust that no doubt would have occurred had Scdgwick's virus escaped the confines of his lab. They'd been secretly whisked into the White House for a meeting with the president himself, who thanked them profusely, bestowed them with "top secret" security clearances, and impressed upon them that in the interests of national security they could never tell a soul what had happened, lest there be widespread panic.

"The guys on my protective detail told me you were with Curtin when he died," Nick said.

"I didn't want him to be alone. In his last words he asked me to thank you for everything. And apologize to you for what he did."

Nick thought for a moment. "Whatever else he did, the guy saved our lives and probably a couple hundred million others. Guess I should be the one thanking *him*."

Just then, a waitress appeared. "What can I get you?" she asked Nick.

"I'll take a cup of coffee and a buttered roll," he answered.

She looked at Claire. "More coffee, hon?"

"No, but can I have a scoop of vanilla ice cream?" Claire asked.

"Be right back," the waitress said, hurrying off.

Nick looked at her, amused. "Vanilla, huh?"

"I was never one to take risks," Claire admitted. "Before all this, I mean."

"Well, you asked for this powwow. What's on your mind?"

"Todd Quimby," she said matter-of-factly, looking into his eyes.

Nick nodded. "I was wondering when he would come up."

"He was never a killer. He's a victim," said Claire.

"I know," Nick replied, wondering what Claire thought he could do.

"Quimby shouldn't be held responsible for what happened. The man was mentally ill."

Nick leaned across the table, speaking softly and evenly. "And if we tell anyone any of this, they'll lock us up and throw away the key. That's why we were given security clearances. So the feds have legal leverage on us to keep our mouths shut."

"I understand we can't do anything publically," Claire assured him. "But I wish there was a way to take the label of 'serial killer' off his name."

Nick considered this for a moment, an idea popping into his head. "It doesn't have to be something that can be found out right away, does it?" he asked.

"What do you have in mind?" Claire asked, hopeful.

"I'm still closing out the files on all seven homicides Quimby was accused of," he said. "The Justice Department wants them sealed but without a paper trail leading back to them. So they got the Manhattan DA to do their dirty work."

"How long do they want the files sealed for?"

"Twenty years, I think," Nick replied.

"How does that help us?" asked Claire.

"Before I deliver the files, I can bury a DD5—that's internal Detective Bureau paperwork—in each one, naming Sedgwick as the killer."

"Will you get in trouble?"

"Probably not," Nick said. "Nobody's going to read the files before they're sealed, and it'll be twenty years before they're opened again."

He seemed okay with all of it. Claire looked at him.

"It's not perfect," Claire said. "But I can live with that." She paused, took a sip of the coffee she didn't want. "Thanks."

"You're welcome."

"What will you do now?" asked Claire. "After you leave the police department?"

"I'll find something fit for a blind ex-cop," Nick answered. "Maybe a consulting gig. We'll see. So to speak," he added, smiling.

Claire couldn't help but respect his acceptance of the future that awaited him. "I just want to tell you . . . ," she said, suddenly hesitating.

But Nick read her mind. "I know. It's not going to be as easy as I'm making it sound. But if I need help, I know who to call," he said, that mischievous grin reappearing.

Claire smiled. "Call anytime."

The staccato *click-clack* of Claire's heels on the mottled concrete floor of Rikers Island reverberated against the muddy-brown cinder-block walls. It reminded her of that first day here with Paul Curtin, and she remembered very well how she'd felt—naked, intimidated, each step reminding her that there was nowhere to hide. Today, however, couldn't have been more different.

"You're sure you're okay?" asked Dr. Fairborn, walking in step beside her.

"Absolutely," said Claire.

She shot a glance at her new mentor, who was dressed surprisingly nonvampirish in a tasteful blue suit, muted lipstick, and eye shadow that made her look like she was actually from *this* world. Claire knew the reason for her transformation was to prevent distracting patients—or, worse, attracting undue attention from some random inmate.

"I'm glad you're back," Fairborn said as they reached the door to the inmate interview room.

"Me too," Claire said, knowing that she was now exactly where she belonged.

"Are you ready, Doctor?" Fairborn asked.

"Yes," Claire answered without hesitation.

"Go get 'em."

Acknowledgments

We are deeply grateful to Alfred Goldberg, Professor of Cell Biology at Harvard Medical School, for his guidance in explaining to us *apoptosis* and *programmed cell death*. Any errors are our own.

For eleven years, retired NYPD Crime Scene Detective Hal Sherman served as our technical adviser on *Law & Order: Special Victims Unit*. His willingness to share his expertise in forensics was invaluable.

Our thanks to Dr. James Rosenberg for explaining to us what it takes to become a forensic psychiatrist.

Michaela Hamilton, our editor, gracefully shepherded us from outline to completed manuscript. Her patience and astute editorial suggestions have made this a better novel. We also wish to thank the wonderful Kensington sales force and rights department for the passion they've shown for *Kill Switch*.

We would not be writers today without the passionate, indefatigable support of our literary agents at Paradigm, Debbee Klein and Valarie Phillips. We are better writers because of their honesty and we value their friendship more than we can say.

Lydia Wills, our book agent, asked us one day if we had any medical thriller movie outlines that we might want to write as a novel. Fortunately, we did—and that outline became *Kill Switch*. Lydia has prodded us, listened to us, made deft suggestions, and supported us throughout the novel-writing process. There would be no book without her.